The

QUINTLAND
SISTERS

The
QUINTLAND SISTERS

A Novel

SHELLEY WOOD

WILLIAM MORROW

An Imprint of HarperCollinsPublishers

P.S.™ is a trademark of HarperCollins Publishers.

HarperCollins books may be purchased for educational, business, or sales promotional use. For information, please email the Special Markets Department at SPsales@harpercollins.com.

FIRST EDITION

Designed by Diahann Sturge

Library of Congress Cataloging-in-Publication Data has been applied for.

ISBN 978-0-06-283909-1

19 20 21 22 23   LSC   10 9 8 7 6 5 4 3 2 1

For Mum

By the light of the moon
One could barely see.
The pen was looked for,
The light was looked for.
With all that looking
I don't know what was found,
But I do know that the door
Shut itself on them.

—"Au Clair de la Lune,"
eighteenth-century French folksong

Fonds consists of 72 cm of textual records including correspondence, diaries, drawings, and scrapbooks of newspaper clippings from the estate of Emma Grace Trimpany (1916–2008), artist, Member of the Order of Canada, 1981, relating to her involvement with the Dionne quintuplets between 1934 and 1954.

Language of material: English and French

Restrictions on access: None

Accruals: Further accruals are not expected.

Custodial history: Documents submitted to the Library and Archives Canada, April 5, 2008, by Ms. Trimpany's sole heir, David L. Trimpany (b. 1955), son.

1934

May 28, 1934

If I don't write this down this very minute, or as much of it as possible, I will forget half of it, or something will happen—one of them will die—and everything I might have written will be changed by that, instead of the way it feels now.

The doctor has just left and everyone else seems to have more or less forgotten about me. Marie-Jeanne asked him if he'd drop me off back in Callander, but before he could answer, I asked if I could stay and the doctor nodded curtly, then headed out to his car. Now Marie-Jeanne and Mme. Legros are busying themselves heating chicken broth on the stove for Mme. Dionne, who is finally starting to stir again. M. Dionne has gone to find the parish priest. He tore off in his own truck, the door slapping closed behind him as if the house itself had done something wrong. Poor M. Dionne. He had been pacing the front porch, back and forth, back and forth, until the doctor finally asked him to step back inside and told him about the babies. His expression made him look like a face from the funnies, stretched wide and delirious with disbelief.

While the midwives were looking after Mme. Dionne, I fetched my pencil and scribble book from my bag and took my seat again beside the chairs at the open stove. I've tried to draw the babies entwined in their box surrounded by all the bricks and flatirons we heated on the fire, then wrapped in rough blankets. I know I haven't quite captured them, but it doesn't matter. I just want something to remember this night, no matter what happens.

IT WAS MOTHER'S idea that Marie-Jeanne Lebel, the local midwife, should come to fetch me, no matter the hour, the next time she was called out. Of course that ended up being in the middle of the night. And naturally it was Mother, not me, who had already decided midwifery might be a reasonable career for me to consider—always in demand, a respectable job for a woman, particularly a bilingual one like me. Mme. Lebel worked mostly with the French families.

"Even those who can't pay with money will find some other way to keep you clothed and fed," Mother liked to remind me. "Scribbles, drawings, and books won't put food on the table."

Mme. Lebel stopped by our place on her way home from church yesterday and asked if I was truly up for attending a birth with her. Mother answered yes on my behalf. The truth is, I really had very little idea what was in store, and if I'd known I would never in a million years have agreed to this. Mme. Lebel said there was a lady a few blocks away whose baby was likely to come at any minute, and that she'd stop by for me later that day or night. I should be showered and dressed in clean clothes. Not my best clothes, mind, but something clean.

So I was ready, reluctantly, when the midwife rapped at the door sometime past midnight. A small man I didn't know was waiting in a battered farm truck at the curb and looked rigid with anxiety. Mme. Lebel said tersely that the lady in our neighborhood had delivered that evening—it had happened too fast

for her to call me—but that a Frenchwoman in the nearby hamlet of Corbeil had gone into labor two months early and there
would likely be complications.

"Two months is too premature," she clucked. "The baby may
not survive."

Mme. Lebel has a deep voice that sounds like an engine running in low gear and she smells like peppermints. "Call me
Marie-Jeanne," she growled, after I mumbled something about
hoping I could be of use. The man in the truck was gripping the
steering wheel like a life ring, his face in darkness, the street-
light illuminating his hands, brown and callused from the fields,
the nails black and jagged. Marie-Jeanne waited until we were
seated in the truck before introducing him as M. Oliva Dionne,
and he mumbled a terse *bonsoir* as he steered out of town, his
foot heavy on the pedal.

"M. Dionne and his wife, Elzire, already have five children,"
Marie-Jeanne murmured, her voice flat. "The youngest is just
under a year."

Fifteen minutes later, M. Dionne pulled up in front of a
small farmhouse tucked in the rocky pasture that runs along
the Corbeil-Callander road. A feeble light glowed softly from
the windows, but the moon was high and bright, revealing a
sagging porch and a short flight of steps leading up to the door.
Faces, those of the other children, I presumed, were pressed
against the glass of a window on the upper floor. One gave a
cautious wave as we hurried into the house.

Elzire Dionne was on her back, clutching the frame of a thin
wooden bed in a ground-floor room off the kitchen when we arrived, bellowing in pain. Two oil lamps flickered weakly, the flames
seeming to shudder with each cry from the bed. M. Dionne hurried to her side, his eyes wild, and his wife clamped a plump hand

around his rough fingers. Marie-Jeanne bustled in and shooed him away, ordering him to head upstairs and to keep the other children from worrying about their mother. Little waifs, all of them—they'd crept down the narrow stairs when we arrived looking like a pack of scarecrows, their mismatched nightclothes swaying off their bones.

Another lady was in the room, seated beside Mme. Dionne, rosary beads clicking through her fingers. Marie-Jeanne spoke with her in French and introduced her to me as Mme. Legros, related in some way to the woman giving birth. Mme. Legros didn't look up or acknowledge me, just continued murmuring in rapid French to Mme. Dionne.

"You can get more water on to boil," Marie-Jeanne told me, joining Mme. Legros. I ducked back into the kitchen, grateful to be away from the sounds Mme. Dionne was making, her face furrowed. "And get the clean towels from my bag," the midwife barked after me.

After a minute or two, Marie-Jeanne came into the kitchen, where I was trying to fill a cast-iron pot with a pump at the sink. "Call M. Dionne back downstairs," she told me gravely. "He must go for the doctor."

Inside the farmhouse, the air was chill and dark. There were no electric lights and the moon was no help, having slipped behind the tall barn. The only warmth came from the kitchen stove, but it was scarcely enough to reach the adjoining room. Spring comes slowly to our corner of Ontario, especially out on these farms, the homesteads little more than blunt boxes surrounded by sprawling fields, marsh, and forest. Here, even in May, the wind racing over Lake Nipissing can still have ice on its breath and leave frost on the windows.

M. Dionne roared off in his truck, wheels spinning in the gravel. The groaning from Mme. Dionne grew even louder, her breath coming in grunts and pants. I poked my head into the room off the kitchen to see what more I could do. One oil lamp glowed sadly on a wooden dresser beside the bed. The other had been set on a spindly chair at the foot of the bed, where Marie-Jeanne now hovered, planting her big hands on the flailing shins of Mme. Dionne and talking to her sternly about breathing and pushing.

I could scarcely look at Mme. Dionne. Her lids were crimped shut as if her eyeballs might have already popped out and rolled away, and her brown hair was plastered to her skull like she'd come in from a storm. I stepped forward to try to wipe her brow, but her head was whipping back and forth so violently she looked like something possessed, hardly human—just mounds of oily flesh, juddering in pain. Mme. Legros was now kneeling by Mme. Dionne's pillow, her head bowed, pulling the string of beads through her fingers and reciting the Lord's Prayer. It seemed to me at that moment that Mme. Dionne probably needed something a little stronger than the word of God, but this was not the place to say it.

"Push, push, push," Marie-Jeanne was commanding Mme. Dionne, who let loose with a bone-chilling howl as the baby arrived, the room filling with an animal smell. I'd always liked babies, or thought I did, so sweet in their prams or cooing in their mothers' arms. But this baby was like nothing I'd ever seen—no bigger than the rats our cat Moriarty used to catch and leave on the kitchen mat to terrorize Mother.

Its eyes were closed and swollen, giving it a reptilian look but with incongruous, long lashes. Its head was enormous, almost equal in size to the rest of its body, which was slick with what looked like kerosene in the dim light. Marie-Jeanne called for me to bring her a towel, and I scurried over.

"A little girl, Mme. Dionne," murmured Marie-Jeanne. Then she bid me crouch close beside her and set the little creature into the towel in my hands, hardly big enough to fill them, then pulled her scissors from a tray and snipped the cord. My sloshing stomach felt like its contents might lurch at any minute into my throat, but the panic of the moment kept my hands steady. The tiny thing was kicking feebly but made no sound. You could see that its face, even in the long, dancing shadows, was turning a deep, mottled blue. I feel worse than terrible for thinking it, let alone writing it down here, but I did not at that moment think of this scrap of life as precious or miraculous: it was grotesque and frightening and I wanted nothing more than to set it down and run.

Marie-Jeanne stood and took the baby from me and walked swiftly to the kitchen, throwing open the door to the woodstove and thrusting the tiny body toward the heat. For a moment, I feared her intention was to hurl the little thing into the flames, which is horrifying and serves only to explain my state of shock. But holding it facedown in the hot breath of the stove, she gently massaged its back, then turned it over, put her mouth over its lips, and blew. Just then Mme. Dionne starting lowing again, a deep, sorrowing sound I could feel, physically, like a blow. Marie-Jeanne thrust the baby into my arms and went back to Mme. Dionne. The little creature was so tiny it seemed I could have cupped it in my palms, like a butterfly. Cupped *her*. Then she moved and started mewing in my hands, and I couldn't help but think of her as a hairless kitten, not a human child. Mme. Legros hurried over and took the baby from me gently and settled it into an apple crate that she set before the open door of the oven.

Back at the foot of Mme. Dionne's bed, Marie-Jeanne ducked her head between the splayed legs and cried out, "Twins, Mme. Dionne! Push-push-push!"

Mme. Dionne's scream would have curdled the milk for miles around, but push she did and a second baby slid from her, this one even smaller than the first. Mme. Legros hustled back to the bedside and took Mme. Dionne's hands in hers, dipped her head, and started in on a fresh round of prayers.

Marie-Jeanne beckoned me over the same way she had before, and together we gently patted down the tiny thing, snipped the cord, and massaged its back just as we had the first, then she told me to settle the second beside her sister in front of the oven.

Suddenly the kitchen door yawned open again. It was M. Dionne returning with Dr. Allan Dafoe, the same doctor who brought me into the world seventeen years ago. He is as stout as ever, his round wire glasses nestled into the eye sockets of his large, round head and his toothbrush mustache tightly groomed, as if his nose were growing a slim beard of its own.

He strode swiftly to the bed in the adjoining room to examine Mme. Dionne, then returned briskly to the kitchen to wash his hands with water I'd set to cool beside the stove. Compared with his oversize head, the doctor's hands looked like those of a child, small and delicate—well suited to this work, I presumed. I hovered in the doorway, uncertain where I could be useful.

"Another is coming," he said brusquely. He spoke in English, but the two women clearly took his meaning because a look passed between them: alarm, tinged with horror. Sure enough, Mme. Dionne gave another piercing cry, and before Dr. Dafoe could relieve Marie-Jeanne of her position at the foot of the bed, a third baby arrived. This one was no more than a scrap of skin stretched tight over bones so tiny you'd think it was a chick just hatched and still slick. When we lived in Ottawa, I knew twin boys several grades below me in school, but I'm not sure it had ever occurred to me that three was possible, or spent a moment thinking about what it would be like for a woman to push out one child after another. By now Mme. Dionne looked like she was ready to give up altogether, she was so weak after the third little baby emerged. Her face and lips were bloodless, and her fingers reaching weakly for Mme. Legros were turning black at the tips.

I retreated as much as I could after the doctor arrived. I busied myself in the kitchen, closing my ears to the wails from the bed and trying not to peep constantly at the little things under the blanket. I boiled pot after pot of water and washed up what I could, even as there were more exclamations of astonishment and prayer from the room next door. Because the night was far from over.

There were five frail babies settled in the apple crate by the time dawn started creeping across the fields. *Five.* Mme. Dionne, by the end of it, was barely clinging to life, collapsing into a troubled sleep after the last little snippet arrived. Mme. Legros stayed by her side while Dr. Dafoe stepped away to speak with M. Dionne. He opened the door that led to the porch and bid M. Dionne enter, explaining in slow, simple English, as if to a child, the events of the past few hours. Neither man paid any attention to me working at the sink.

"*Cinq?*" M. Dionne said. "*Five?*" He is a small, reedy man, and the news seemed to shrink him still further. He looked fearfully at the apple crate but didn't step closer. "I have five already," he breathed. "What will people say?"

Dr. Dafoe put a hand on his shoulder. "The babies will not live—it's too soon for them. They're too weak. And Mrs. Dionne is in grave danger." He spoke so softly I couldn't catch his next words. M. Dionne looked up, aghast. "I will go for the priest," he said, then added, "Can I first please see my wife?"

Dr. Dafoe stood aside and beckoned Marie-Jeanne and Mme. Legros to step into the kitchen as I slipped back into my seat by the stove.

"Your first priority must be attending to Mrs. Dionne," he said gravely. "There is no chance the babies will survive more than a few hours. Make them as comfortable as you can, and if one is thriving more than another, you must focus on the one that is strong. We cannot save them all. I will go now for supplies and nursing assistance for the mother. Remember, your first obligation must be saving the life of Mrs. Dionne for the sake of the five children she has already." He paused and glanced around the dim room. "Indeed, any more would be too much of a burden."

Then he turned to the apple crate on the wooden chair by the stove and seemed to notice me for the first time. I saw his eyes dart over the left side of my face, where, in the flickering shadows, my birthmark would have made my face look even more lopsided and distorted than in daylight.

"Emma Trimpany," the doctor said, and he closed his eyes as if to keep from staring, pushing at his eyelids with his stubby fingers, exhausted. When he looked up again, he was careful to fix his gaze over my right shoulder. "What on earth are you doing here, Emma?"

Marie-Jeanne answered for me, taking a moment to sort out the English words. "She was joining me with M. Dionne when he picked me up in Callander earlier. Emma is considering to become a midwife." She gave me a weak smile. "Possibly she is having a second thought."

Dr. Dafoe took a step closer to the crate, sinking onto one knee so that he could peer beneath the blanket we'd tented over the basket and the open door of the stove. He shook his head as if he was only now processing the events of the long night. "My word," he breathed, finally. "My word. Five babies. Five girls, born alive. It's unprecedented."

He stood and took several glass droppers from his black bag and set them by the kettles on the stove. "If they wake, give them a drop or two of warm water." He was addressing Marie-Jeanne, who nodded, but he turned his stern gaze my way, as if it fell to me to make sure she understood. "Warm, mind, not scalding. Keep the irons and stones hot, but well wrapped, and replace this blanket regularly, with a hot one, draped over the back of the chair, to try to keep the heat contained. We shall do what we can, but—" He shrugged. "I'll go straight to the Red Cross outpost and be back as soon as I can." He left, closing the door quietly behind him.

The frogs have finally finished croaking in the fields behind the farmhouse, as if they know it's time they settled down and let the birds take over. I should be tired, too, but I'm not. I have stayed by the stove, sitting beside those tiny bodies, thinking, perhaps, that I'd see my first life leave the world within hours of seeing a first life arrive. An alarming thought, but also, I think, a suitable punishment. How I recoiled from these little things at first! I feel I've let myself down in some important way, or let down the person my mother is hoping I might one day become. Sitting here through the night, watching them sleep, bidding them goodbye if it comes to that—this is the only way I can think of to make it up to them.

I ducked my head to peer under the blanket just now. They are sleeping and still, so it's possible to see the five of them as humans in miniature. Their similarity to one another is eerie, even with nothing but their tiny heads poking out of their blankets. All of them have black hair and long, dark eyelashes, too thick, it seems, for their sunken cheeks. The longer I watched them, the more I could see that each one of them has something distinct, something to tell her apart from her sisters. I took out my scribble book in the hopes of capturing them. The one that came first has one eyelid bigger than the other. The second has a tiny crinkle in the upper cusp of her right ear. The third has the smallest nose, and the fourth has the most hair, which seems to curl in the opposite direction from that of her sisters. The fifth and last—she has nothing that looks markedly different, but she is the only one with any wriggle in her.

No one has bothered to give them names. Mme. Dionne has managed to swallow a few sips of broth, and M. Dionne has not yet returned. I set down my sketch and lowered my chin to the edge of the crate, close enough that I could hear, faintly, the feeble breaths of these tiny girls. I wrapped my arms around the sides of the box and dangled my fingers over the edges, hoping the babies might sense my hands and face hovering above them. *I'm here,* I whispered under my breath. *At this very moment, I'm here. And so are you.*

May 28, 1934 (*UPI Archives*)

FIVE BABY GIRLS BORN TO CANADA FARMER'S WIFE

NORTH BAY, Ontario—In a rude farm house five miles from here a country doctor fought tonight to keep the spark of life in five tiny baby girls. The quintuplets were born today to Mrs. Oliva Dionne, 25 years of age, who has five other living children.

Neighbor women, acting as midwives, helped the family physician, Dr. Dafoe, at the accouchement.

The doctor confirmed birth of the quintuplets tonight. He had little hope all of them will live.

Total weight of the quintuplets was thirteen pounds six ounces. The first baby girl born weighed three pounds four ounces. The combined weight of the last two was only two pounds four ounces. Dr. Dafoe said so far as he knows the quintuplets are a Canadian record. He had heard of quadruplets, but never of quintuplets until today.

Used with permission.

May 28, 1934

Did my parents worry when they woke this morning to find me gone? I didn't ask. I assume the news must have scurried its way to every lane, porch, and scullery before Mother even had the opportunity to overcook Father's breakfast. I expect they've pieced two and two together. There's no telephone here or I would have tried to reach Father at the post office, but the day has galloped by and there's been no time. I'm only now getting a moment to jot some of it down.

The Red Cross nurse from the outpost in Bonfield, Marie Clouthier, had arrived by the time Dr. Dafoe returned mid-morning. Marie-Jeanne was still with Mme. Dionne, and I was doing everything in my power not to nod off. Dr. Dafoe was, I think, astonished to see all the babies alive.

"Have they cried much?" he asked Nurse Clouthier, who blinked at him blankly, then murmured in French to Marie-Jeanne. The midwife merely shrugged and gestured at me with her chin.

"Surprisingly, they are noisy quite a lot," Marie-Jeanne growled in her low voice, her accent thick. "But it is this young lady who has watched over them all the night." She said it kindly. "Emma, they have been crying, all of them? Or just some?"

I had stayed most of the night beside their box, one hand still draped over the edge. Nurse Clouthier, when she'd arrived, had taken over the dispensing of water to the babies and had gingerly rubbed each of them down with oil and placed them back in the basket. She scarcely acknowledged me in my chair, which I shuffled aside while she was tending to the babies, and after a while it was almost as if she didn't know I was there. This is something I've managed to pull off my whole life, to make myself invisible and unremarkable—no mean task with a crimson stain covering half my face. People meeting me for the first time tend to let their eyes glance off me the instant they process what they're seeing, and this has always worked to my advantage. Even Dr. Dafoe, who'd been the one to console my mother at the time of my delivery, so distressed was she by my appearance, seemed to do a double take when he registered my position by the stove this morning. As if he'd forgotten he'd noticed me there the night before.

"Emma," he murmured. "It was very good of you to help out. How are they?"

"All of them have wriggled from time to time," I said. "They're all breathing and making sounds. Not so much crying as whimpering."

Nurse Clouthier had other calls to make in the French homes of East Ferris Township, but she promised to be back. Dr. Dafoe left soon after, saying he was going to return with a nurse—a bilingual one this time—from the new nursing school at St. Joseph's Hospital in North Bay.

Marie-Jeanne and I remained at the farmhouse all day, as did Mme. Legros. By midafternoon, Mme. Dionne was improving somewhat, enough to take in some more broth and a cup of tea, but the babies were growing more and more quiet. There must have been too many women in the farmhouse for M. Dionne. He stayed outside, tending to the farm or conferring with his brothers and father on the porch, running his bony hand through hair made wild from the habit and rubbing at his eyes as if trying to wake from a dream.

Other family members, several with the other Dionne children in tow, kept coming by and rapping at the door, and we'd redirect them back outside. All day long we watched people pulling up to the farmhouse in their cars and carriages, sending eddies of dust and flies into the kitchen. I managed to doze off in my chair by the fire while Nurse Clouthier and Mme. Legros were bustling about the kitchen and shooing visitors away.

At some point late in the day, M. Dionne burst in with a photographer from the *North Bay Nugget*. The man's eyes bulged out of his head when he saw the tiny girls in the crate by the oven, but he swiftly got to work and convinced Mme. Legros to lift the tiny things from their warm cocoon onto the pillow beside Mme. Dionne. Maybe it was wrong to do it, but Mme. Dionne rallied somewhat when she had her little girls around her, their heads the size of early summer apples. Had Dr. Dafoe been there, I don't think those babies would have been moved, but I suppose M. Dionne was thinking, as we all were, that this might be the only record of his wife with five live babies, all at once. How sad. Even putting those words down in print makes me feel sick with dread.

It was dusk when Nurse Yvonne Leroux—or Ivy, as she's insisting I call her—arrived. I'll never forget the moment she stepped through the front door carrying a black bag and wearing her white uniform. The farmhouse has low ceilings, and the shadows licking up the whitewashed walls must have made the kitchen and the adjoining parlor look that much shabbier.

Even in that light, Ivy shone. Her dark hair, parted in the center, was styled in a twist at the top of her neck, a crisp white nurse's cap perched on the crown of her head. I put her at three, maybe four years older than me, in her early twenties at most, but she has the poise and comportment of a grown woman, whereas I, a good half foot smaller, still feel like I'll never fill out the frame I've been given. She has high cheekbones, a creamy complexion, large brown eyes, and a long nose, which seems to twitch to the right whenever she is trying to hold back a smile, which wasn't very often today. She told me that the message she'd received from Sister Felicitas at St. Joseph's was that a Frenchwoman from a farming family had had a difficult birth and was fighting to survive. No one had bothered to mention anything about five babies. Perhaps Dr. Dafoe assumed they'd be dead by the time the nurse could reach us. She's a brand-new nurse, Ivy. Her class is the first to graduate from the new school at St. Joe's, and this is her first assignment.

The babies were back in the box by the fire when she arrived. I'd been given the task of reheating the bricks and stones for the basket. I'd rigged up some twine across the stove so I could drape the other blankets over top, creating a snug, warm cocoon around the basket and the stove together.

Ivy went first to the room next door and spent several minutes with Mme. Dionne, who was sleeping peacefully after the excitement of the photograph. I heard her exchange a few words with Mme. Legros, then exclaim, *"Cinq!"* before she hurried back into the kitchen.

She came forward and extended a firm hand, introducing herself as Ivy, first in French, then in English. It was the first time someone other than Marie-Jeanne and Dr. Dafoe had actually spoken to me directly, let alone looked at me without faltering.

"Pleased to meet you," I mumbled and told her my name. I was trying to think how to explain what I was doing at the farmhouse, but Ivy was already gesturing at the covered basket. "May I?"

I nodded and lifted off the blanket. Ivy's eyes widened ever so slightly.

"Gosh," she breathed and bent down to peer at them more closely, her hands rising instinctively as if to reach inside, then dropping again to her sides. All the babies were sleeping. The bigger girls were snuggled tightly together in the upper right corner of the box. The third had been placed in the bottom right corner and was curled at the feet of her big sister. The tiniest ones were back to back, their chins tucked toward their scrawny chests. I'd been watching them through the night and most of the day. I still found them astonishing, but less grotesque than they'd seemed last night.

Finally Ivy straightened up and indicated that I could place the blanket back over top. She must have seen the anxiety in my eyes as I lifted them to meet her gaze.

"You're doing an excellent job," she said. "You must be exhausted."

Then she did something unexpected—she lifted her hand and placed it on my right cheek, the good one, and gently turned my face to the light of the oil lamp, studying my left side intently but not unkindly.

"*Nevus flammeus,*" she murmured in the manner of a student dredging up something memorized. "Port-wine stain." Then she must have noticed my face blushing on the right side to match the left, because she stroked the cheek she was touching and said: "Makes you special, doesn't it." Then she grinned so that I saw for the first time that while her front teeth were perfectly straight, the teeth farther back were small and slightly crooked, making her look like she might know a thing or two about mischief. I couldn't help but return her smile.

She turned back to the basket and its blankets, her eyes roving over my cords and sheets. It must have looked, I realized, like a child's play fort. She nodded, appraisingly, then set about making a few adjustments.

"What we're aiming for is as little change in temperature as possible," she explained. "The front door to the kitchen must remain closed, when we can see to it, and we'll put this to use right away," she added, taking a ceramic hot-water crock from her bag.

"I'm sure you're tired," she said, turning to give me her full attention, "but can you stay a bit longer?"

Marie-Jeanne caught a lift home with Dr. Dafoe after his last visit of the day and promised she'd stop in on my parents and let them know my whereabouts. Ivy and I took turns dozing fitfully while the other watched the babies and checked in on Mme. Dionne. M. Dionne had come inside after dusk, the day's work done, but seemed to still be buzzing in bursts of nervous energy. Sometimes he stood absolutely still, only to dart off in a blur for another corner of the little house like a lizard, or a ghost. We wouldn't see him for a while, then he'd slip down the stairs and we'd find him at Mme. Dionne's bedside muttering softly to her in French while both Ivy and I were with the babies in the kitchen. The rest of his brood, it seems, have been dispatched to stay with aunts and uncles elsewhere in the hamlet.

At one point, long after night had fallen, he asked permission to see the babies, which struck me as strange, because they were his children, after all. I watched his face as he stood over them—he looks older than his years, a workingman's face, heavy-lidded, weathered by seasons of hard labor out-of-doors.

Even his earlobes seemed to be sagging away from his skull. As he gazed at his daughters, his twitching features didn't so much soften as grow still. I could tell, these tiny creatures were provoking in him something closer to amazement than affection. And it's true, they are so tiny and strange. The largest, according to a set of scales Ivy had brought, now weighed just 3 pounds, while the smallest weighed just 1.8.

"Will they live?" he asked Ivy. It was impossible to read his expression. She looked at him steadily and said in a firm voice that it was too soon to say.

Ivy is fast asleep now with her head cradled in her arms on the kitchen table, her knot of hair loose on her white throat. Mme. Dionne is snoring, deep in sleep at last. And so, too, are the babies—asleep and alive. I will put away my pen now, but I will let Ivy rest and keep watch a little longer on my own.

May 29, 1934

NEITHER IVY NOR I managed more than a few hours' sleep, straining to listen to the faint cries from the babies over the thrumming of toads in the fields and the surprised warbles of whip-poor-wills hunting in the high grass. M. Dionne swept silently downstairs at dawn, nodded at us through the doorway, then turned to sit with the mountain of rumpled sheets and nightgown that was Mme. Dionne. After a few minutes, he stood from his wife's bed and clumped into the kitchen, his boots leaving a trail of dried mud on the pine-plank floor.

"I'm going to bring Father Routhier again," he said in French. Ivy was stooped over the pump at the sink, filling the kettle, and I looked up to see M. Dionne watching her. His eyes drifted wearily upward as she straightened to standing. He's a funny-looking man: compact and wiry with protruding eyes and large, irregular ears that look to have been an afterthought, inexpertly attached to his head. "The babies will be christened today, just in case," he said, and he headed out to his truck.

"He didn't even stop to look at them," I whispered. Ivy made a face and put the kettle on the stove.

If anything, the babies seemed even smaller that morning. Dr. Dafoe arrived bearing blankets, clothes, and diapers that were far too large and once again shook his round head at the sight of the tiny things.

"I've organized for breast milk to be shipped from Chicago and Toronto on the evening train. In the meantime we will make do with a mix of boiled water, cow's milk, and corn syrup."

Ivy and Dr. Dafoe mixed these ingredients according to a formula the doctor had devised. The air in the kitchen was thick and warm from the fire we'd been steadily feeding with wood through the night. By midmorning, you could already feel that the day had plenty more heat in store, but we couldn't open the windows and door for any length of time without inviting in the flies, mosquitoes, dust, and curious faces of neighbors and children.

Once the milk had cooled, Ivy lifted the babies out of their nest one by one, holding each in the crook of her arm while Dr. Dafoe filled the dropper from the pot on the stove. Tired to the point of collapse, I took out my scribble book and tried to capture Ivy giving this mixture to one of the little ones, but either because I was too weary or because the proportions, in life, were so out of scale with normal, my drawing was terrible. We laughed over it afterward, Ivy and I: she brandishing a dropper the size of a sword, the tin of syrup as big as a grain silo, the babies, by contrast, small blossoms on a bend in a branch.

Midmorning, all the babies were asleep again and we were sweltering with them, the heat making me dozy. To keep ourselves from drifting off, Ivy and I told each other about ourselves. She is of French stock, her family having lived in the area for generations, and the youngest of five, with two brothers and two sisters. Her mother has passed on now, and Ivy had been living in the hospital dormitory at St. Joe's for the past three years while she completed her nursing degree in North Bay. Her father, who works at the only mill left in town, moved to Callander after her mother died. All the other millworkers, like almost everyone else in these parts, are on government relief, particularly after the Payette Mill burned down in '32. The J. B. Smith Mill was supposed to reopen next month, but it, too, went up in a blaze just last week, the flames leaping so high we could see them from our front lawn.

"I'm very lucky to have been given this assignment directly out of school," Ivy said earnestly. She says she plans to work as long as she can and is in no rush to get married. "Married couples can't qualify for relief, if they need it," she said. I didn't know that.

I myself have no intention of marrying. Boys have never shown much of an interest in me—my horrible birthmark—so I've never imagined my future might include a husband and children, a white clapboard house plunked alongside a stretch of pasture, cows that need milking, chickens to be plucked. That's why Mother worries. And it's no doubt why she spoke with Marie-Jeanne Lebel about taking me on as an apprentice. But I didn't say that to Ivy.

"What does your father do?" she asked.

"He's the Callander postmaster now. He worked for many years as a classics professor at Carleton University, which is where he met my mother. She's French, from Hull. Father lost his position at the university a few years ago and, through some family connections, managed to secure the position in Callander when the post office was rebuilt after the fire of 'thirty-two."

Ivy nodded. I can imagine what she was thinking. A government job is a rarity in these hard times. She would know that we're getting along better than most.

"No brothers or sisters?" she asked.

I shook my head. "I think they made a point of being careful after they had me," I said, pointing at my cheek. I've never said anything like that before, but Ivy had made a point of commenting on my birthmark. She had held my face in her hand.

"Nonsense," she said, then set me the task of bleaching and boiling all the cotton diapers Dr. Dafoe had brought that morning.

I didn't hear anyone coming up the porch steps, so I started at the sound of a loud rap at the door.

Ivy pulled it ajar, the back of her hand already abutted against her hip so as to give these latest lookie-loos a piece of her tongue for barging all the way up onto the porch. But they weren't locals—they were two city men who'd arrived in a fancy car. They were carrying big cameras on stilts and said they'd driven all the way from Sault Sainte Marie and Montreal to film the babies for the newsreels.

Ivy was firm. "M. Dionne is not presently at home," she said.

The men started in with a long list of protests and explanations, and one slid his toe past the doorjamb. Ivy lifted a finger to her lips and crunched her eyebrows together at them, nudging the man's polished leather shoe back over the threshold with a tap of her own foot.

"Shhhhh!" she hushed. "You will wake Mme. Dionne, and you'll rouse the babies. They are very, very frail."

The men retreated to the yard, and we watched them through the window to see what they'd do. They leaned on the hood of their four-seater and struck up conversations with the steady stream of curious folks stopping by. After a few minutes, Dr. Dafoe pulled up in his sleek green car, and both men got busy behind their big cameras and started asking him questions.

Ivy had drawn the muslin over the kitchen window to keep people from peering in, but she'd cracked the sash in the hope of getting a bit of a breeze. Now she stood with her ear to the gap to hear what Dr. Dafoe was saying.

No need, as it turned out. Seconds later the door was swinging open again, and Dr. Dafoe was leading the men into the kitchen.

"Of course, of course," he was saying. "A true miracle of creation, all identical. They are unlikely to all be alive tomorrow, so it's important to have a record."

If that was all true, it was a bold move waltzing in with the motion picture men without checking first with Ivy. What if one of the babies had died while Dr. Dafoe was out? What if the newsreels showed just four babies or three?

Ivy was angry, I could tell, but she waited for the men to set up their cameras, then lifted the blankets off the box.

Just then, M. Dionne burst through the front door and all hell broke loose.

"Get out, get out!" he started screaming in English, then in French for good measure. One of the cameramen swung his huge contraption around and tried to film M. Dionne grabbing his colleague by the collar of his shirt. I thought M. Dionne was going to kick the camera right over.

Dr. Dafoe cleared his throat and urged all three men back outside with a sweep of his arm, shutting the door behind him. I could hear him attempting to say something to one of the newsreel men, but they were busy trying to film M. Dionne, who had shouted a stream of obscenities and dashed back into his truck, saying he was going for the police. He spun out onto the road in a cloud of dust, and the cameramen, incredibly, hopped in their big car and started after him, one of the men trying to maneuver his big camera out the passenger-side window!

Dr. Dafoe stood on the porch watching, taking out a little bag of tobacco, packing his pipe, then lighting it. The kerfuffle had woken the babies, first the little ones, then the bigger ones, which is a funny way to describe them when they are *all* so small. Their cries were so soft, like robin chicks piping for their mother to return with a worm. Dr. Dafoe must have heard it all the same, because after a few puffs he tapped the bowl on the rail, pocketed his pipe, and came back indoors.

I lasted until just after two or three in the afternoon, when the Red Cross nurse, Marie Clouthier, returned, bringing with her another nurse and an orderly, both English, plus two ounces of breast milk that Sister Felicitas had managed to drum up at St. Joseph's Hospital. There was not enough to go around, so Dr. Dafoe insisted it be given to the three smallest. By then the priest had returned with M. Dionne and they were praying with Mme. Dionne in the next room, deciding on names for the babies.

At one point M. Dionne drifted into the kitchen and told Ivy he'd be happy to run her home in his truck if she needed some rest. She demurred, saying she wasn't feeling tired, which couldn't have been true. She'd been on her feet most of the night.

I'd been at the Dionne farmhouse nearly twenty-four hours longer than Ivy, of course, and I was exhausted. But I didn't say so, and M. Dionne did not turn my way to repeat his offer. I certainly wasn't looking to go anywhere with M. Dionne. He was a different man now than he'd seemed the night he and Marie-Jeanne had picked me up after midnight. Less than two days ago, I realized. It seemed a lifetime. He appeared calmer now that his wife showed signs of recovery, gliding quietly through the house, fixing Dr. Dafoe and the nurses with long, glowering looks and muttering in French under his breath.

Dr. Dafoe, it seemed, spoke no French or at least had chosen not to speak a word of it since his arrival on the night of the birth. Even M. and Mme. Dionne he addressed in English, which M. Dionne clearly understood. Ivy and I slipped easily between French and English, and stuck with English when Dr. Dafoe appeared. Now, with more personnel from the hospital crowded into the main floor of the farmhouse, the balance had tipped to English.

M. Dionne went back to his wife's bedside, and Dr. Dafoe started packing his black bag at the kitchen table. I touched his sleeve. "Can you drop me at my home?" I asked, and he blinked his small eyes behind his glasses and bobbed his head by way of assent. As I was following Dr. Dafoe out the door, Ivy called my name. The other women didn't look up. "Emma—you'll come back, won't you?" She smiled her crooked smile. "Come back and rescue me as soon as you can."

May 30, 1934

I RODE MY bicycle back out to the Dionne farmhouse this morning, unprepared for the mob of people milling around the edges of the yard like so many clucking chickens—a steady stream of bicycles, cars, and trucks coming and going. The *North Bay Nugget* had run the picture taken yesterday on page one. Now, hemming the Dionne property were at least three dozen men, women, and children, and not a single person I knew from Callander.

An older man I recognized as M. Dionne senior, the babies' grandfather, was pacing the yard, spiking the air with a pitchfork and looking every bit like a bandy-legged devil roused from bed, his cottony hair standing up in a thick clump at the back. He was thundering at people to move on, but everyone was staying put, hectoring him with questions. Newspapermen clearly made up at least half of the crowd, bowler hats pushed back on their heads, some with pencils behind their ears and notebooks in their breast pockets. Others had cameras hanging heavy around their necks, their shirtsleeves rolled up in the heat. After a short while, the door to the farmhouse opened and Ivy stepped out onto the porch.

"Emma," she called. She had one hand pulling the door closed behind her as heads craned to see inside, but she beckoned with her free hand. "Come on in," she said.

The air in the farmhouse was even closer than yesterday. There was a heavyset girl I didn't know working at the sink and another woman at the bedside of Mme. Dionne, who was sitting up somewhat, a bit of color returning to her plump cheeks. Ivy looked tired, but still lovely, I thought, wisps of hair curling out of her bun in the thick, damp warmth of the room.

On the floor of the kitchen, pushed against the far wall, sat a stout wooden box with two round knobs on the lid. It looked like a deep crib or coffin—roughly three feet high and two feet deep with glass set into its top. When I peeped under the blanket of the crate by the fire and saw only two babies inside, I gasped, my fingers flying to my lips. I swung around to face Ivy, but she shook her head and smiled wearily.

She gestured at the big wooden box.

"It came from Chicago early this morning," she said, pulling me toward it and pointing to the thermometer set into its side. "It's an incubator to keep them warm and safe from germs. It's ancient—runs on kerosene instead of electricity." Through the square pane of glass I could see the three little ones, curled around one another like puppies, sleeping soundly.

"They are doing okay now, but you missed the excitement earlier."

She told me the littlest ones had turned blue and their hearts had stopped, but Dr. Dafoe, luckily, had been there when it happened and prescribed some drops of rum, retrieved from a cabinet in the adjoining room. Now Ivy and the other nurses were resorting to rum every time the fragile breathing of one of the babies showed signs of slowing to a standstill. You could see the strain in the faces of the women. The girl at the sink, Claudette, had been brought in from a nearby farm to help with the washing, and the young woman with Mme. Dionne was another sister or cousin, tasked with plumping pillows, spooning the patient her *potage,* joining in prayers, and doing whatever else was needed to ensure the patient remained in bed.

"She's christened the babies," Ivy whispered, smiling her sideways smile. "Do you want to meet them properly? You'll like this."

We went back to the box by the stove, and Ivy slowly lifted the blanket aside. "Madame named this one Yvonne for me," she said, pointing to one of the largest, her face lighting up as she said it. "And the other bigger one here is Annette."

She then walked over to the incubator and pressed a finger against the glass lid. "This here is Cécile and next to her, Marie, supposedly for Nurse Clouthier, but my guess is more likely the Holy Mother. The smallest—" Ivy looked up to watch my face. "The smallest I believe she named for you. This is Émilie. That could be a variation of Emma, don't you think?"

I looked up at Ivy, then leaned closer to peer again through the warped glass. Émilie! They were still little more than wrinkled wads of skin, but after I'd spent so many hours watching them struggle for life, they'd filled my dreams the previous night.

"They are little fighters, they are," Ivy murmured. She'd drifted back to the box and was swiftly removing one of the blanketed hot-water crocks and replacing it with a new one from the stove. "Keep it up, girls," she whispered and adjusted their makeshift tents to cover them again.

EVERY FEW HOURS, we lift them out one by one and rub them gently with oil as if they're clad in the finest tissue, our touch as light as air, and give them a few drops of breast milk from an eyedropper.

M. Dionne had vanished to the stables at the back of the property, but Ivy told me he'd spent almost an hour with Mme. Dionne and the priest that morning, arguing about all of the people in the house and what the medical bills would be. She'd eventually been forced to tell him that Madame needed to rest, and he had gone off in a huff.

Sometime in the afternoon there was a soft knock at the door, and it was a relief to open it and admit a sip of fresh air into our sweltering cave. Ivy had little Cécile in the crook of her elbow and was giving her some milk, and Nurse Clouthier had gone back to Bonfield, so I was the one to greet the visitors, opening the door by a slim crack and slipping into the breeze on the porch.

On the doorstep was possibly the most striking man I'd seen outside of a magazine or film. In his midthirties, I'd wager, perhaps older, he wore a white shirt that looked crisp and starched, despite the strength of the sun. He had thick black hair and a smooth complexion, tanned as if he'd spent the spring somewhere sunnier than Northern Ontario. His eyes were a warm brown, and when he spoke it was in a soft, measured tone. Everyone else who'd been disturbing us all day and yesterday had rapped too loudly or spoken in booming voices that were unsettling for the babies. This man knew better.

But he, too, I noticed next, had a camera slung over his shoulder, tucked almost out of sight behind his elbow.

"No photographers," I said and was about to step back inside.

"Fred Davis," he said quickly. "Please, miss. I'm a photographer from the *Star*. We've driven all the way here today with the equipment ordered by the specialist, in Toronto."

I could feel his soft eyes taking in my birthmark, and, to his credit, he didn't glance away.

"We have the tub, feeding tubes, the clothes, blankets, and I don't know what else." He stopped, waiting for me to find my voice. "Everything we've brought is for the quintuplets."

Quintuplets! I had never heard the word. It sounded like something from Greek mythology, but I realized he was talking about the babies.

At the bottom of the rickety steps that led up to the porch stood two other men, both in their telltale bowler hats, and with them a woman, petite and pretty, in the white dress and cap of a nurse. At that very moment, Dr. Dafoe emerged from the curious crowd on the edge of the yard, his black bag in hand, pipe pursed in his lips.

He removed it as he approached the steps. "Davis?" he asked and looked from one man to another. The men at the foot of the stairs thrust out their hands, and Davis, quicker than you could blink, swung his camera to his face, pointed it at the doctor with the reporters, and started to click and wind, click and wind. The petite nurse smiled and bobbed her blond head, extending a graceful gloved hand of her own.

The men, after conferring with the doctor, headed back to their car. Dr. Dafoe gestured toward the senior M. Dionne, who was hovering nearby, and spoke with him briefly, apparently clarifying that these city men should be permitted access to the house. The junior M. Dionne, the babies' father, was nowhere to be seen. I ducked indoors again, intending to tell Ivy about the handsome photographer from the *Toronto Star,* but to my surprise, Mr. Davis swiftly slipped in after me, shutting the door gently behind him.

Ivy had Cécile back in the wooden incubator again, so none of the babies were in sight. I watched Fred Davis blink as he took in the drab kitchen, his eyes adjusting to the dim room, roving over the sheeting we'd rigged around the stove, the clutter of equipment we'd tried our best to organize on the tables and shelving. Then his gaze came to rest on Ivy. She had turned away from the incubator, her cheeks flushed, her forehead creased with worry. She started when she saw the man behind me.

"Oh," she said. "Hello."

"Ma'am," said Fred Davis. His eyes, which a moment earlier had been bobbing like a brook over everything in our makeshift nursery, now came to a halt on Ivy, as if snagged. He, too, was at a loss for words, finally managing, "It's my great pleasure."

Just then Dr. Dafoe stepped into the kitchen and beckoned Mr. Davis back outside with a wave of his undersize hands. Mr. Davis along with the younger reporter from the *Star* managed to wrestle their crates up onto the porch under the supervision of the older man, Mr. Keith Munro, also related to the newspaper in some way, who stood in the dusty yard barking out commands from behind a bushy, white mustache. The little blond nurse, named Jean Blewett, turned out to be a proper nurse who'd graduated from a college in Toronto. She busied herself ferrying smaller packets and boxes from the crates to the kitchen. Only when the men were done did she step primly into the next room to introduce herself to Mme. Dionne, Mr. Davis right at her heels. I hadn't even noticed him taking up his camera again, but he managed to pop off a few photos of Nurse Blewett and Mme. Dionne, using a flashbulb because the light was so dull. This greatly upset Mme. Dionne, who I presume had never seen a flashbulb before—nor had I—and she started fussing and speaking in rapid French to the new nurse, whose blue eyes blinked. She couldn't understand a word.

Claudette, the hired girl, must have gone to the stables for M. Dionne, because he burst into the farmhouse and started hollering at the photographer and reporters to hightail it off his property. Ivy told me he had been angry that morning with how the newspapers had written about him yesterday. This was the first time we'd seen him truly livid, spluttering with rage in a mix of languages, those strange, long earlobes of his—indecent somehow—quivering in indignation. Maybe I should have more sympathy for M. Dionne. His house is overrun with strangers, his other children dispersed among the homes of family and friends. No one in that part of the world has money to feed an extra mouth, let alone five—he must be looking at all this equipment and the nurses and be worried sick about what the bill will come to, let alone how he'll support a family now doubled in size. But he really scared me then, shouting like a madman in front of the babies and his wife, now sobbing in her bed. Dr. Dafoe was angry too. I could see it. The doctor isn't an easy man to read, but he, too, is likely feeling the growing interest in the little babies and the burden of keeping them alive.

"Mr. Dionne," he said tartly. "A word." And the two men stepped out into the evening.

I waited until all our city guests were gone before pressing Ivy about Mr. Davis. "But had you *met* him before?" I was watching her face. "Mr. Davis seemed like he already knew you, and you him."

Ivy was busy sorting through the parcels and boxes, a seemingly endless number of cotton diapers, tiny bonnets, blankets, petticoats, shirts, safety pins, nursing bottles, tubes, and more. The idea of our minuscule charges ever being hale enough to need shirts and petticoats seemed laughable, but it gave us hope just fingering the tiny things, so clean and white in the gloom of the farmhouse.

"Ah, no, but I think I'd *like* to know him already, if you know what I mean," she said, her impish smile tucking neatly into her left cheek. "It's high time this job came with a few perks, wouldn't you say, Em?"

June 1, 1934 (*North Bay Nugget*)

OLIVA DIONNE SIGNS HANDSOME CONTRACT TO EXHIBIT FAMILY AT CHICAGO

"They are improving steadily. That doesn't guarantee anything. Two of the babies nearly passed last night, but this morning I felt more optimistic than at any time since their birth."

In this way Dr. A. R. Dafoe expressed the condition of the quintuplets born last Monday morning to Mr. and Mrs. Oliva Dionne, Corbeil.

The babies are now being fed on nothing but human milk and this morning 18 ounces arrived from the Sick Children's Hospital, Toronto.

Rev. D. Routhier, Corbeil parish priest, announced this morning that a contract with the Tour Bureau, Chicago, at a meeting in Orillia yesterday, to exhibit the family at the World's Fair, had been signed by Oliva Dionne, the father of the quintuplets. Father Routhier accompanied Dionne to Orillia.

The contract stipulates that the attending physician must first declare the mother and children ready to travel. It specifies that if nothing happens to the children and it is not too late for the fair, the Tour Bureau will provide special transportations for the entire family, including the grandfather, doctor, nurse, and assume all cost of the trip to Chicago, including salaries of the attendants. The contract will provide $250 weekly during the time of the exhibit, including expenses, and 20% of all receipts. Father Routhier of Corbeil Parish will be entitled to 7% of the earnings.

Until such time as the family can be moved, Dionne is to receive $100 weekly.

GOVERNMENT TAKE HAND

A true Canadian atmosphere was thrown on the situation today when the Ontario government stepped in and offered to make arrangements for all services, working with the Children's Aid Society.

Told of the contract Dionne had signed, Dr. Dafoe was glad to hear that the family would get some much-needed money, but said it would be unwise to move the babies within three months, adding "their condition and progress govern the entire matter."

"I was delighted," stated Dr. Dafoe, "when I read the interest the Ontario Government were taking and they are helping in every way possible."

Used with permission.

June 1, 1934

I was dressed for school and seated at the table when Father read the news in the *Nugget* about M. Dionne signing the deal to display the babies at the Chicago World's Fair. We'd already bickered over Father's insistence that I go to school today, the last day before exams. I've spent every day this week at the Dionne farmhouse and wanted to go straight back out there today, but he put his foot down. I truly don't see the point of it. I have no real friends or teachers I want to say goodbye to and I've never been a good student. All I've ever wanted to do is read and draw. Perhaps if we'd stayed in Ottawa and I still had art class on my report card, I'd have at least one decent grade to please my parents. I have no head for maths, history, or geography, and I will do miserably on those exams—another disappointment for Father. But he long ago gave up on me doing anything further with my schooling, so it's ridiculous he insisted on me going back for these last few days.

However, the news about the Dionnes in the paper startled us all into talking again. Father read it out loud and I gasped. Everyone who comes into the post office still grouses to Father about paying two cents instead of one for a postage stamp, so an income of $250 a week is unimaginable. And M. Dionne is already doing better than many farmers in our area. He grows food for his table and owns his own truck, something almost no one else in Corbeil could boast, or Callander for that matter. But I knew he'd also been frantic about all of the supplies and medical people filling his home. This offer must have seemed like a windfall.

"The Catholic priest appears to be in on the deal." Father snorted, snapping the paper. Father has little time for religion of any stripe. "'Father Routhier of Corbeil Parish will be entitled to seven percent of the earnings,'" he read from the paper.

Mother was shocked. "But, Emma, surely those tiny babies won't survive a trip to Chicago, will they?"

The story in the *Nugget* also said two of the babies had nearly died in the night and had stabilized only after oxygen tanks arrived from Toronto. It was almost unbearable going to school, knowing two of the babies were in danger, but I knew I'd catch it from Father if I didn't.

As soon as the final bell rang, I pedaled straight out to the farmhouse. The crowds have tripled in size, with at least forty cars and trucks lining the road that runs between Callander and Corbeil. Several men and women along a makeshift fence were waving newspapers and shouting at M. Dionne senior, who was still pacing the front of the property, now in the company of a local constable. I wriggled my way to the gate with difficulty and managed to attract the attention of Grandpapa Dionne, who let me through.

"There you are, thank goodness," Ivy said, opening the door a mere gap, grasping my arm, and pulling me in. Her eyes were heavy, her expression pinched, and her uniform smudged and wilted. The kitchen smelled of woodsmoke, kerosene, and the sour tang of hot work.

"Have you even gone home?" I asked.

She shrugged and shook her head. "I'm going later today. Dr. Dafoe has organized for full-time help from the Red Cross. They should be here tonight."

I went first to the babies in the canopied box by the fire, Yvonne and Annette. They were tiny as ever, their little fists stirring the air like sewing bobbins, toes like raisins. I crossed the room to the incubator and peered through the glass. Cécile, Marie, and Émilie were no better off, wriggling weakly against one another in their wooden den. A tall cylindrical tank, which I guessed to be the new oxygen supply, stood by the box, a hose snaking into a fixture on its side.

"We almost lost Marie last night." Ivy sighed. "She stops breathing within three minutes when she's out of the incubator. We're giving her rum in her milk every two hours to stimulate her heart, but she is hanging by a thread. Cécile is not much better off."

I started washing the kettles, pots, and a growing mound of soiled cottons. Claudette, the local girl who'd been hired to help, had not yet come in. "She's terrified of M. Dionne, I've noticed," Ivy said glumly. "God knows what he said to her. I sent her to fetch him from the stables last night when Mme. Dionne was asking for him, but he took forever to come in, and said he'd sent Claudette home."

Not too much later, Dr. Dafoe arrived, bobbing up the steps like a cork in water. He had with him a handsome, imposing woman he introduced as Nurse Louise de Kiriline—Scandinavian, I gather, although her French is impeccable. She has large, pronounced teeth, unruly dark hair, and eyes that are such a deep shade of brown it's difficult to discern her pupils, giving her a very tense and hungry look. Her eyebrows, thick and pointy, are set quite high up her forehead, as if they, too, are irked and a little bewildered by the intensity of her expression.

Dr. Dafoe gathered Nurse Clouthier, Ivy, me, and the orderly, Mrs. Nells, and said in no uncertain terms that the quintuplets had no chance of surviving if we did not create some new rules.

"I am Boss Number One," he said in a booming voice, loud enough for Mme. Dionne to hear it, along with anyone else who might have been upstairs at the time. "Nurse de Kiriline is Boss Number Two. Her rules are my rules and must be followed."

With Nurse de Kiriline at his side, Dr. Dafoe examined the babies one by one, making little clucking sounds.

"Completely identical," he told her, and showed her the ribbons tied around the right ankle of each baby, labeled with the first letter of her name. "To avoid any possible confusion," he said.

This made me smile. They all looked similar, of course, but there was no way I could have confused any one of them for another. To me they were so easily distinguishable, not only by their tiny quirks—Annette's eyes, Marie's hair—but even their little cries. If you listened properly, you could hear it.

Dr. Dafoe departed shortly thereafter, and Nurse de Kiriline swept into action.

"These"—she pointed at the heavy drapes in the sitting room off the kitchen—"these must go."

Mme. Dionne is still poorly, but at her insistence had been moved upstairs to her own bed the previous evening. Now the bed used for her confinement was taken apart and rebuilt into additional shelving in the kitchen to hold the medical supplies, baby clothes, and linens that had been steadily arriving from various cities in Ontario, Quebec, and south of the border. A sideboard, a couch, and an upholstered chair were all pushed against a far wall, and the wide-plank pine table that had clearly been put to considerable use by the large Dionne family was re-purposed as a changing table in the middle of the kitchen, now dubbed the nursery. The heavy curtains gone, Nurse de Kiriline had us pin muslin netting tightly against the open windows to supply a steady breeze and keep out the clouds of blackflies and mosquitoes. We hung another white sheet in the open doorway between the kitchen and the sitting room, which Nurse de Kiri-line declared a charting space for the nursing staff. Any vases, trivets, crucifixes, and figurines—anything not appropriate or usable for either an office or a nursery—were sent upstairs or out to the dusty porch.

When the heavy work was done, we took hot water and Lysol and scrubbed the floors, walls, and ceilings. By the time Dr. Dafoe returned, later in the day, his breast puffed out like a robin's, to inform us that another incubator was on its way from Toronto, the Dionne farmhouse had been transformed. M. Dionne, presumably skulking around with a hundred-dollar check burning a hole in his pocket, was nowhere to be seen.

"You." Nurse de Kiriline pointed at me as I helped Ivy oil the babies. In the long hours we'd been reorganizing the farmhouse, she had yet to say a word to me. "You are not a nurse, I gather. An orderly?"

"No," I told her, blushing. "Dr. Dafoe has asked me to help out because I speak French and English."

In fact, it was Ivy who had repeatedly asked me to stay and help, although I was mostly there of my own accord.

"I was here at the birth," I added.

Nurse de Kiriline nodded, almost imperceptibly. "I'm happy to have your help," she said briskly, then turned away.

Sometime late in the afternoon, Grandpapa Dionne knocked

at the nursery door to say that the incubator had arrived, brought by several reporters from the *Toronto Star*. I'd been scrubbing the walls of the sitting room, but I drifted into the kitchen to see the contraption.

Ivy, I realized, had little interest in what was being wrestled from the back of a cream-and-maroon-colored Buick. Sure enough, one of the men was the newspaper photographer Fred Davis.

The men had to partly dismantle the incubator to fit it through the door. Since we had no electricity, engineers at the University of Toronto had rigged it to run off of a noisy diesel-powered generator behind the house, with long cords coiling through the window and across the kitchen floor.

Once it was reconstructed, we settled Annette, Yvonne, and Cécile into the new device, leaving Marie and Émilie in their own sealed nest. Ivy, meanwhile, took a jug of water to the Toronto newspapermen outside. The two reporters were badgering Grandpapa Dionne, asking him to track down Oliva Dionne so they could ask him some questions about the Chicago deal. Fred Davis, however, was leaning against a post on the porch grinning broadly at something Ivy was saying. She was smiling, too, the lopsided smile she'd use when she was trying to hide her crooked teeth, although at one point I saw her tip her head back and have a proper laugh. When I peeked out again, Ivy was leaning against one of the wooden struts, her arms akimbo, and Mr. Davis, having stepped down into the yard, was taking photos of her, one after another. I couldn't see her face.

After a short while, Ivy came back inside, Fred Davis with her, and Dr. Dafoe agreed that Mr. Davis could take a picture of Ivy and Nurse de Kiriline holding two of the babies. Just then, M. Dionne burst through the front doors, fetched by his father, no doubt, from wherever he'd been lurking. The younger Dionne was holding a rolled document in one hand, batting it through the air like a truncheon, and shouting in French that photographs were prohibited. Dr. Dafoe drew himself up, his stout chest swelling manfully.

"Where is your gratitude, sir? These gentlemen have brought a new incubator for the quintuplets," he said in English, looking sternly at the angry farmer. "This is your best chance of keeping the babies alive." Fred Davis had his camera in both hands, raised to his chest, looking like he might at any minute start snapping shots of this altercation. I saw Ivy lay a hand on his forearm, and a look passed between them. He rolled his eyes but lowered the camera again and replaced the cap on the lens.

M. Dionne clearly understood what he'd just heard but barreled on, opening the papers he was carrying and thrusting the document toward our Toronto visitors.

"My babies!" he continued in French. "My rights." Spittle flew from his lips. "All photographic rights now belong to Chicago, to Mr. Spears."

Could he hear how he sounded? The idea that the *Star* photographers couldn't take a single picture of the babies after driving all the way up here with what looked to be a very expensive piece of equipment—it seemed ludicrous. And Dr. Dafoe himself was working around the clock to save the babies while their own father was preoccupied with their profitability! Now, through clenched teeth, M. Dionne was growling at the *Star* men to leave the premises, "or else." They retreated down the steps, and M. Dionne, still bristling like a hedgehog, sat himself on the porch to make sure they didn't return.

Close to nightfall, the crickets chirring, Ivy and I set out to walk back to Callander. It felt like the first spring evening to truly carry the promise of summer. You could smell the lilacs in the breeze and hear the birds quibbling with their young to get them settled for the night.

Ivy was nearly falling asleep on her own feet but insisted she needed the walk and the fresh air. As we made our way along, she told me about why she'd wanted to be a nurse and how her father had managed to save up the money for her to attend the new nursing school in North Bay.

She was curious about what I was planning to do after graduating from high school in a few weeks' time. Even the bulrushes lining the road seemed to lean in to hear my answer.

"No firm plans," I admitted. "Mother wants me to become a midwife, but I don't think that's for me. A teacher, maybe. I'd love to teach art or literature. I love books." In fact, I didn't have the grades to train as a teacher, but I needed to say something.

"Well, I'm going to marry a Hollywood film star that I'll meet after nursing him back to health after a film stunt and we'll have five babies and live in California," Ivy said.

"Oh?" I said. I'm not used to jokes and banter, so it took me a moment to realize she wasn't delirious with fatigue. "Why not settle for a famous newspaper photographer and abscond with these quintuplets?" Ivy pretended to look shocked at the suggestion, but she couldn't keep from smiling.

We were just a half mile outside of Callander when we heard the cough and chug of a vehicle making its way up the road behind us. With the price of gasoline where it is, trucks are relative rarities in our part of the world, and you can often catch a ride if the driver doesn't have a load. Ivy and I took a moment to recognize the man at the wheel. M. Dionne slowed to pass us but didn't stop, merely touching his fingers to his cap and carrying on by.

June 2, 1934 (*Toronto Star*)

FEAR ONE OF QUINTUPLETS IS NEAR DEATH

Father Strives to Break Contract to Show Tots in Chicago

CORBEIL, Ontario—Marie, the most delicate of the Dionne quintuplets, had a bad night. Her heart action was weak and about 4am today it seemed as though it might stop altogether. Fears are felt for her life.

"I was afraid for a little while something was going to happen to her," Marie Clouthier, the nurse in charge, told the *Star*. "She got so blue we had to give her a little rum as a stimulant."

Today Dr. Dafoe emerged from the home after his early visit minus the smile that was so evident yesterday. "They are still all alive," he said. "That's about all I can say. They are so awfully small. Every time I see them they seem even smaller. They are the tiniest babies I have ever seen live."

All children were fed throughout the night, at two-hour intervals, human milk obtained by the Canadian Red Cross Society.

Dr. Dafoe will charge the Dionne family just $15 for delivering the quintuplets. This fee will include the ever-watchful care and the many calls at the three-roomed farmhouse made by the tireless country doctor in his so-far successful fight to keep life in the five infants.

Meantime Oliva Dionne, the father, is making strenuous efforts to break the contract which may eventually put his wife and babes on public view in the main lane of Chicago's world fair midway. On Thursday, Dionne travelled 133 miles to Orillia and signed his first contract. Today he sent his first telegram. It implored Ivan Spears, sideshow maestro, to relieve him of the option taken on his babes. The answer was quick to flash back: "Nothing doing: you are signed to a legal document."

Offers continue to pour in on the bewildered father and his padre manager. No sooner had they signed the Spear's [*sic*] option than telegrams of astonished protest came from near and far. At the same time, a Chicago night club operator wired an offer guaranteeing a minimum of $500 a week with all expenses and offering to post a $10,000 cash bond with any bank named if mother and babes could be persuaded to bed down in his joy cave for 20 weeks. They were not persuaded.

June 29, 1934

Nothing is happening by halves these days, not the birth of the quintuplets, not summer, which rushed headlong to meet spring so fast the smelly swarms of shad flies have already come and gone. There was scarcely time for the bees to buzz about the blossoms before the strawberries were out and not a single quiet moment for me to write things down. I feel like I blinked and the wind turned the page on my own life and now I'm in a completely different chapter.

All through my exams I kept going out to the farmhouse whenever I could, hardly making any effort to do well on my tests. The babies have filled out considerably this month but are still tiny and frail. Dr. Dafoe has appreciated my help, I think, and the other nurses, for the most part, are treating me as if I've come with the territory, which indeed I did.

Last week Ivy, who could coax a whisker from a cat, convinced Nurse de Kiriline to pay me two dollars a week as a part-time "nurse's assistant," and Dr. Dafoe has agreed. He's said that there must be two staff on duty at all times, around the clock, so there's plenty need for me when one of the nurses, orderlies, or housekeepers requires a few hours off.

The Dionne farmhouse is almost unrecognizable now. Nurse

de Kiriline has had a second door cut into the back of the building so that the Dionne family can come and go from the upstairs room without tramping through the kitchen. Dr. Dafoe has declared the kitchen must remain off-limits to the other children because of the risk of germs.

Outside, a rough shack has been thrown together next to the farmhouse as a dormitory for the nurses, and the fence around the property has been extended two feet higher to keep out nosy visitors. We still have no electricity—M. Dionne has flatly refused, even when the government offered to pay for it, calling it a fire hazard. Instead we must put up with the steady drumming of the generator, chugging away as if with a heartbeat of its own. The privy is still out back, but Nurse de Kiriline has insisted on having a water line brought to the kitchen to provide a steady supply for our kettles. Every single scrap of cotton, cloth, bib, or diaper that so much as touches one of the babies gets washed and boiled after the lightest use.

Boss Number Two has brought to the nursery an almost military precision. Ivy and I have taken to calling her the Captain—although not to her face, of course. Ivy nearly got caught saluting her behind her back yesterday. She can put me in stitches with some of her funny faces and horseplay, but she wouldn't dare do it in front of Nurse de Kiriline. The Captain has an accent and a clipped manner of speaking that make you feel as if she's snipped off the second half of whatever it was she'd been about to say. She'll tell you to do such and such a task, but she'll say it so abruptly, with so little intonation, that you'll linger for a moment expecting her to say more. Then you realize she *is* finished, and there you are, standing around like a half-wit rather than snapping to the job at hand.

Ever since the uproar over the contract he signed with the Chicago promoters, Papa Dionne never pokes his head into our side of the farmhouse unless something is specifically needed of him. The entire country is furious with him, or that's what you'd think if you read the papers or listened to all the people who keep arriving every day along this quiet stretch of road. Even Mme. Dionne, who was still on bed rest when she learned about the Chicago deal, went into such a fit we were worried she might not recover.

When I'm not out at the farmhouse, I go into the post office to help Father, who is busier than ever because of all the mail arriving related to the Dionne babies. Many for M. Dionne simply say "To the Father of the Baby Girls," but even more are addressed to Dr. Dafoe or "The Doctor of the Quintuplets." I've seen postmarks from all over the continent. Father will punish me if he catches me peeping at any of the postcards, but truly, some of them are written in such large block letters, it's impossible not to read them.

"One read: 'Dear Mr. Dionne: Time to get yourself sterilized. Enough is enough!'" I whispered to Ivy while we were hanging the endless sets of minuscule nighties and bonnets on the clotheslines, whole rows of diapers the size of handkerchiefs. "Another to Dr. Dafoe said: 'Don't you think it would be a good idea to castrate the father and sew up the mother so she cannot have more children?'" Ivy's eyes bugged out of her head.

"Gruesome!" She grinned. "But effective."

Others sent to Dr. Dafoe are urging him to seek the aid of authorities to help keep Mme. Dionne and her children "away from that brute of a man" and to protect the children—all of them. Because of course there are ten children in total—our five babies clinging to life in the makeshift nursery, plus the five other Dionne children crammed into the top floor of the farmhouse or sprinkled around the parish.

As far as the Captain is concerned, the other Dionne children are a heavy cross to bear, screeching at top volume outside the windows, tearing through the charting quarters, or clattering around in the room above. It's impossible for everyone. This evening there were seventeen people, including the children and babies, crowded into that creaky, sweltering farmhouse in the middle of a scorching Ontario summer, plus a crowd of strangers craning their necks outside. It would have been a laughable situation if the lives of those little girls weren't on the line.

Meanwhile, every hour of every day someone is trying to deliver something we haven't ordered and rarely need: forty-eight rolls of Scotch cello tape, twenty tins of corn syrup, cases of soap and toilet tissue, Jake's potato chips and Royal Crown soda—all donations or gifts from people who've seen the newsreels or read about the babies in the paper. Yesterday a man on a bicycle pedaled up to the front gate with, of all things, ten copies of the new Nancy Drew—as if any of us have time to read!

No one can access the property without first getting past Grandpapa Dionne, and no one can enter the farmhouse kitchen—our nursery—without first being granted permission from Dr. Dafoe himself. He or she must then proceed directly to the washing station and don a special smock that we've bleached, boiled, and ironed before taking a single step in the nursery.

M. and Mme. Dionne are the exceptions, of course: they are still required to wear the smocks, but they don't need explicit permission to enter so long as they do so during the strict "visiting hours" set by the Captain. And the clincher: Dr. Dafoe has now informed the parents they are not allowed to actually touch the babies. Fearing fireworks, Ivy and I slipped out onto the porch when the doctor summoned the Dionnes to explain this new rule. The flimsy screen door filtered out none of Oliva Dionne's outrage.

"*Non,*" he bellowed. "*Non!* This, *this,* I will not allow."

Mme. Dionne murmured something in French that I couldn't catch, likely a plea for translation from her husband—I could hear the arc of confusion in her tone. Sure enough, he launched into a blistering rendition, in French, of the doctor's latest decree, padded with complaints about "*les anglophones*" who put more stock in expensive medicines and machines than they do in God's will and a mother's love. His words were loud enough that the reporters and photographers slouched against the fence line all straightened themselves up and craned their heads closer, like antennae. Inside the kitchen, I heard the floorboards creak and imagined the broad, round shape of Madame, inching away from her husband's spluttering.

But perhaps it was Mme. Dionne herself stepping forward to Dr. Dafoe, because she raised her trembling voice and spoke in a tone I hadn't heard from her before, pleading, but resolute. "*Docteur, docteur, je vous prie. Mes bébés. Mes trésors . . .*"

I was watching Ivy and saw a look cross her face: a flash of feeling for Mme. Dionne. Elzire Dionne is a simple woman, finally on her feet again and baffled by the swirl of her own life these past few weeks, by the commotion in her home, by the efforts being expended to save these five girls. The papers say she had had only a few years of schooling and married M. Dionne when she was just sixteen—younger than I am now. Also, that she had already lost a baby boy, Léo, to pneumonia, four years ago. I can't imagine changing places with her, but nor, I'm sure, can she understand why all of the young women bustling about her farmhouse aren't back in their own kitchens, fussing over their own babies.

The doctor cleared his throat. "Mrs. Dionne, Mr. Dionne. Please understand. This is temporary, but compulsory." He paused, and, after a moment, M. Dionne spat out the words in French for his wife one at a time, his voice calmer now, but seething. The doctor continued. "As soon as it is safe, as soon as the babies show any sign of thriving, I assure you, they will be yours to have and hold."

The screen door flew open then and M. Dionne burst out, slicing across the porch and down the steps in three long strides, his scrawny arms swinging through the air like cleavers.

July 15, 1934

M. DIONNE, SHOWING uncharacteristic concern, has rigged up a much bigger fuel tank for the generator and moved the whole clanking contraption closer to the road, all by himself. He's phenomenally strong, for such a small man. Now Shell Oil Company's bright yellow bowser comes along every morning and tops it up for free. The Red Cross has provided separate incubators for all of the babies and organized for a steady supply of breast milk from hospitals in Toronto and Montreal. The little ones are putting on weight, ounce by precious ounce, Annette and Yvonne especially. But just as we start to get our hopes up, one or the other of them falls sick and scares the dickens out of all of us.

Ivy and the Red Cross nurses, Marie Clouthier, Nancy Ellis, and Nurse de Kiriline, are all living in the cabin built for them on the Dionne property, rotating shifts around the clock. Every one of them is tired to the bone, and they seem to keep a kind of competitive distance, as if they are all vying for the approval of Dr. Dafoe.

Only with me, I think, is Ivy able to simply be herself. She is always absolutely professional and would never think of goofing around with Annette or Marie in her arms. But if, for a moment, we have them all stowed away safely in their berths, fed and oiled, in fresh cottons, with a pause before the next one needs milk or changing, she will ask me to tell her a story or show her my scribble book, and we'll be lifted out of our worries.

The fact is, we *are* worried. Ivy is keeping a journal where she dutifully records the daily weights and heights, feeds and bowel movements for each of the girls. If Marie is a half ounce lighter, or Cécile's diaper is clean when it shouldn't be, we are all scared rigid. Also looming in our minds, Ivy's especially, is just how long the nurses will be allowed to look after the babies. Not a day goes by without Mme. Dionne lumbering into the nursery outside of the strict visiting hours—typically when the Captain is getting some rest—and bedeviling us with questions. "They are stronger, yes? Today? I can hold them?"

The doctor has explained to her again and again that the babies cannot yet be handled by anyone other than his staff. She simply doesn't understand, her face crumpling, then twisting sour when she sees them in the arms of Ivy or the Captain. She contents herself by shuffling between the boxes that hold her daughters, muttering her prayers, and, when the Captain isn't looking, sprinkling holy water on the glass tops of the incubators. We've also seen her knitting five darling little cardigans and bonnets in the softest pink: I shudder to think how she'll react when she's finished all five and is forbidden from dressing the girls.

Ivy says M. Dionne has sent the hundred dollars back to the Chicago businessmen, but it's not clear whether the contract is still in place. Twice today, Dr. Dafoe huffed down the steps from the kitchen and stood in the yard surrounded by newspapermen with an air of studied chagrin, his thumbs hooked into the armholes of his waistcoat, elbows jutting, looking every bit like an owl swaying gloomily on his perch. He's telling anyone who asks—and many who don't—that any contract involving the girls requires his sign-off and that's something he'll never give. It still has us worried.

My world has shrunk, I realize that. I have no interest in anything happening outside the sweltering farmhouse, despite the snorts and exclamations from Father at the breakfast table, his newspaper rustling over his oatmeal. He says there's a madman politician in Germany, blithely murdering his political opponents, and Babe Ruth has hit seven hundred home runs. I couldn't care less.

July 27, 1934 (*The Globe*)

ROEBUCK BREAKS QUINTUPLETS CHICAGO CONTRACT: ORDER OBTAINED FOR GUARDIANS OF DIONNE BABIES

Grandfather, Doctor Are Named Among Those Looking After Infants

NORTH BAY, Ontario—Acting in his function as "parens patriae"—father of the people—Ontario Attorney General Mr. Arthur Roebuck has obtained, through a North Bay solicitor, a judicial order appointing guardians for the quintuplets and so has defeated the "perfidious contract" which the father, Oliva Dionne of Corbeil, was induced to sign when the babies were four days old.

The order effectively removes the quintuplets from the custody of their parents and into government care.

Under the contract, the whole Dionne family was to be placed on exhibition at the fair, with Mr. Dionne receiving 23 per cent of the takings. Seventy per cent was to go to the Chicago tour bureau and 7 per cent to Rev. Father Daniel Routhier of Corbeil, as "personal manager" of the family. Mr. and Mrs. Dionne already have five other children.

Efforts to defeat the contract have been under way up North, but with no success until now. The Children's Aid Society found itself unable to step in, since there was no evidence of neglect, and finally W. H. Anderson, Red Cross chief in the North, personally brought the problem to the Attorney General. Lightning action brought appointment of the guardians who consist of Mr. Anderson, Dr. Allan Roy Dafoe of Callander, who has been in charge of the babies since birth, Kenneth Morrison, Callander Merchant, and Oliver Dionne, grandfather of the quintuplets. They now have charge of the babies and can and will manage their well-being going forward, starting with the prevention of their removal to Chicago.

"If exploiters from American cities come to Canada to pull off this sort of racket, they need not expect the Attorney-General's office or the courts to stand idly by," Roebuck said. "Lives of children are of bigger concern in Canada than the profits of a vaudeville troupe who are playing with the lives of defenceless infants in the name of money."

Used with permission.

July 28, 1934

The babies are two months old today—it's impossible to imagine them reaching the age of two, which according to the newspapers is the age they must reach before the Ontario government transfers their care back to their parents. Any pretense of civility between M. Dionne and Dr. Dafoe has now evaporated. To the nursing staff, M. Dionne's manner has been more unpredictable than ever, at times wheedling and, at others, menacing. It's a hopeless situation. The babies can't be moved—their health is so precarious—but the Dionnes are making it abundantly clear: we are not welcome in their home.

July 31, 1934

Dr. Dafoe told us yesterday that the government has at last approved the construction of a special hospital and nursery for the quintuplets right across the street. Not a day later, an army of young men descended on this quiet street, taking measurements and breaking ground on a stretch of land on the other side of the road. Ivy has been watching them from time to time, teasing me, saying I might find myself a beau if I took a moment to stand on the porch and watch them toiling in the sun. I won't be drawn. All I care about is that the new hospital be clean and fresh, so that the nurses won't have to feel like they are squatters on the Dionne homestead. The biggest problems here are the noise and the dirt, the horseflies and deerflies, the prying crowds, and the wind, hot and wicked, whistling through every crack and seam of this rickety house as if it, too, was trying to run off with a good story. The girls are so frail, they take a turn for the worse with the slightest disturbance.

"But if they are building a special hospital, this must mean that Dr. Dafoe believes the babies will survive," I said to Ivy. She merely chewed her lower lip and looked worried. "It's too soon to know," she said quietly. "No one can know if they'll make it or not."

August 4, 1934

OUT OF NOWHERE, a gift for Ivy.

The girls' guardians have decided they need to secure a steady income for the babies while limiting some of the hoo-ha caused by the dogged press photographers who surround the farmhouse from dawn to dusk. They've hired an official photographer for the quintuplets. Under the deal, the *Star* newspaper will have exclusive Canadian rights to photograph the quintuplets and to sell the photos in the United States via the Newspaper Enterprise of America.

The Captain gathered the nurses, the two hired girls, the orderly, and me on the porch to deliver the news and explain the implications. It was clear from her tone that she disapproved.

"A more unusual situation you are unlikely to encounter again," she began, blinking at us reproachfully. "Effective immediately, the only person permitted to photograph the quintuplets is Mr. Fred Davis."

I heard Ivy exhale softly, as if she'd been holding her breath. Out of the corner of my eye I could see her ducking her head, smiling.

The Captain was straining to purse her lips together, looking at each of us in turn. The shrill chirring of the cicadas seemed to swell in the silence until she spoke again. "This rule extends to any other photographer rapping at the door and telling us he is from the *Star* newspaper, and it extends equally to the parents and other family members. No one is permitted to take photographs of the babies, with the exception of Mr. Davis.

"To be clear," she continued, her voice rising. "The health of the babies at all times supersedes any requests of the photographer. He cannot ask for one of the girls to be taken from her bed in order to be photographed. But during feedings and the routine course of care, Mr. Davis may take his pictures." She sniffed. "Mr. Davis, I'm told, will be moving from Toronto to North Bay, later this month."

I raised an eyebrow in Ivy's direction, but she either ignored me or didn't see it. When we all realized, three seconds too late, that the Captain had finished her speech, we trooped back indoors and there was no chance for me to talk to Ivy. Later, when we had a moment to ourselves, she couldn't be drawn. We have joked about the film-star looks of the big-city photographer for most of the summer, and I'd teased her (harmlessly I thought) about the photographs he'd taken of her on the porch. But now, it seemed, he was stepping out of the pages of a magazine and into our day-to-day lives.

August 10, 1934

DR. DAFOE, AT Ivy's urging, has arranged for me to be accepted into the nursing program at North Bay, all of my tuition paid by a new scholarship in Dr. Dafoe's name. I can't quite believe it. *Me*, a nurse! I am wishing I'd paid more attention in my science classes. It is a one-year program, not the three years of training that the Red Cross nurses were required to obtain, but there is more and more demand these days for practical nurses, Ivy says. Plus, Dr. Dafoe has arranged for me to continue to help out with the quintuplets as part of my training requirements. I'm pinching myself.

All the same, it was a little upsetting to see the relief and pride on the faces of Mother and Father. They've spent more years than I care to imagine wondering what would become of their disfigured daughter.

Ivy would be angry with me for writing that. She keeps saying that my birthmark is a distinction, not a blemish, but it is easy for her to say. She is so naturally beautiful, even more so now that Fred Davis is stopping by most days. I think he is quite as struck by her as she is by him.

"It's not just my birthmark," I told Ivy today, holding up a clump of my thin hair hanging lank and limp, the color of wet straw. "And what of this?" I asked her when I knew the Captain wasn't watching. I put one hand on my hip, striking a pose and running my other hand the length of my torso. "I have the physique of a twelve-year-old boy. It's not even a question of being unattractive. I'm simply invisible." Ivy shook her head and laughed.

But I'm right, I know I am. I come and go from the farmhouse, and I honestly believe, if you asked anyone other than

Ivy or Dr. Dafoe whether they'd seen me, or what my name was, they'd be at a loss to provide an answer.

"And it doesn't bother me," I said to Ivy. "I don't *want* to be noticed."

She just kept shaking her head. Even in the stifling humidity of midday, she doesn't look rumpled and sticky like the rest of us. She glows. "You'll see, Emma Trimpany," she said. "One day, you'll see."

August 18, 1934

THE NEWSPAPERS SAY the quintuplets are not suitably protected from kidnappers during these desperate times. The Lindbergh baby snatchers are still on the lam more than two years after they found that poor boy's body. Now the papers are saying it likely wasn't Italian mobsters who nabbed him, but someone acting alone who might easily have slipped across the border into Canada. Nurse Ellis, a Newfoundlander whose lilting English gives her simple predictions the ring of fabled prophecies, observed that, even if the kidnapper isn't headed our way, the whole terrible tale is just "giving nasty people an awfully good idea." She's right: these babies are the most famous babies in the world and there's no telling what ransom they'd fetch.

Tonight Ivy and I were on duty together for the predawn shift. I was heating milk on the stove in the nursery when we heard strange sounds coming from the adjoining room. Fearing it was M. Dionne, snooping around in what is now the nurses' office, Ivy ducked under the sheet separating the two rooms without taking a lamp. The room was empty. She was about to turn back when she spied shadows moving on the porch outside, and, as she watched, one of the shapes took the form of a man, and the window creaked open.

Ivy screamed. I rushed into the room, and, within seconds, it seemed, M. Dionne was hurtling down the stairs in his night-clothes, Mme. Dionne, despite her still substantial girth, only a few steps behind him. The man at the window vanished. M. Dionne dashed barefoot out the door in hot pursuit. There is still no telephone at the farmhouse, no way to summon help, so we lit all the lamps and invited Mme. Dionne to join us in the nursery. I roused everyone from the nurses' cabin, and the six of us sat nervously awaiting M. Dionne's return. Sometime later he burst back into the farmhouse saying he was taking the truck to fetch the Mounties, but Mme. Dionne was hysterical, begging him to stay and protect us all until morning. I can't sleep, none of us can, although the Dionnes have retreated upstairs.

August 20, 1934

Two RCMP CONSTABLES have been assigned to watch over the Dionne farmhouse, night and day. We are all hugely relieved, although it is two more mouths to feed and two more people tied up in the lives of our five little girls. I was still rattled and spent yesterday and today back at Mother and Father's and will spend the night tonight. Father isn't remotely interested in what could have happened out at the farmhouse. He's rant-ing and raving about the new president of Germany. I can't understand why he cares about things so many thousands of miles away when there are real dangers right here, in our own backyard.

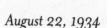

August 22, 1934

NURSE ELLIS, THE Anglophone Red Cross nurse, has quit. The tension here is simply too much. I walked into the kitchen earlier in the day when she was having a set-to with Mme. Dionne, having caught Madame lifting Cécile out of the incubator with her bare hands. Nurse Ellis's French, however, wasn't up to the task of negotiating.

"No, Madame! *Non-non-non. Vous ne* . . . You mustn't!"

I opened my mouth, but before I could say anything Nurse Ellis had lunged toward Mme. Dionne, whose wide face, shiny with perspiration, now flared beet red. She swiveled on her sturdy haunch and snarled, curling her shoulder over the startled Cécile and looking every bit like a bear protecting her cub. Mme. Dionne's dress, I couldn't help but notice, was the same one she'd worn yesterday to milk the cows, the skirt dusty from kneeling in the garden plot most of the morning.

Undeterred, Nurse Ellis swooped around the other side of the incubator, grasping Cécile, whose precious face pinched closed as she began bleating like a lamb. This might have turned into a true tug-o'-war, but perhaps Mme. Dionne had been bracing for the challenge, had been seeking it, because she relinquished her little bundle without a struggle and instead burst into a high-pitched defense of her rights. Her French patter, lightning quick, was utterly lost on Nancy Ellis, who countered with a flood of Newfie brogue that even I had trouble understanding, save for the parts that parroted the doctor's rules and regulations. I slipped quietly out the kitchen door and darted to the nurses' shack to summon the Captain before Cécile or anyone else got caught in the cross fire. M. Dionne must have gotten wind of the hullaballoo as well, because within minutes he was charging across the back pasture like a bull to a flag.

Nurse Ellis went off shift not long after. I forgot about the exchange, not even thinking to mention it to Ivy when she came back out to the nursery that evening and we got busy settling the girls for the night and catching up on the day's washing and charts. But sometime after dusk, Nurse Ellis came flapping back to the farmhouse from the nurses' cabin in her nightdress, very upset, saying she'd woken to the sound of someone trying to jimmy the window. "A man's arm," she kept whimpering. "It was a man's hairy arm." The policemen were summoned and did a full search of the property but found nothing amiss. We stayed up half the night trying to calm her down, to no avail.

I don't know what words passed between her and the Captain, who returned to the nursery this morning having missed all the drama last night. All I saw was Nurse Ellis clomping off to pack her few things, hollering like an auctioneer that she wouldn't stay another minute. I was quite fond of Nurse Ellis. She liked to regale Ivy and me with tall tales about growing up with four brothers in St. John's and had a colorful repertoire of sea chanteys, riddled with unsuitable English, that she'd sing as lullabies to the babies. But her leaving is good news for me: more shifts out at the nursery, at least until my classes begin.

August 25, 1934

A MILESTONE TODAY—ALL the babies are now sleeping in cots, not incubators! We have much more space, and the air is so much fresher without the kerosene smell. I did a sketch of all five of them lying side by side in their tiny berths, and I gave it to Dr. Dafoe, who looked surprised and pleased, tucking his several chins into his collar and making a purring sound.

"You do have real skills, Emma," he said. "You must keep this up."

I've shown him some of the other drawings in my scribble book but took great care that he couldn't read any of these jottings. If he read anything I'd said about him or Nurse de Kiriline or Fred Davis, I'd want to melt into the floor.

The truth is, with so little time for doodling, I suppose I'm starting to let go of my dream of being an artist. In town the lines at the relief office are growing longer and longer, and you see more people sleeping in the streets. Father told me that a brawl broke out at the mill in North Bay after more workers were laid off. There is always a chance that they will close the post office in Callander and move Father's work to North Bay, and, if they do that, they likely won't need Father. I'm proud that I've been able to earn even a modest wage helping at the Dionne farmhouse, and I suppose it's showed me how important it is to be able to make my own way in the world.

The girls are all filling out. Yvonne is still the biggest and now weighs a little under eight pounds—Ivy calls her the "little mountain." My Émilie is just five pounds, seven ounces, and Marie is even smaller. I still have no trouble telling them apart. Cécile is the quietest and the most obedient, while Émilie is the sunniest. We all agree Marie will grow up to be the mischief maker. They had their first proper baths with soap and water today. Despite their gains, they are still so woefully tiny—funny little toads splashing in their basins.

August 28, 1934

LAST NIGHT NURSE de Kiriline overturned a lamp in the nursery while trying to pierce holes in the feeding nipples, which started a terrible fire, flames pouring across the kitchen like they'd been sluiced from a bucket. With the oxygen tanks stacked against the wall and the kerosene lamps, the whole place could have gone up with a mighty bang; I can't even bear to think about it. I was sorry we'd ever spoken ill of the Captain or mocked her behind her back. She is truly a hero, throwing herself on the flames as they dashed toward the babies' cots and smothering the fire with her own body. I can't spend a moment thinking about what might have happened—to her, to the babies, to Ivy—if she hadn't. Now Nurse de Kiriline has very serious burns. We don't know when she'll be coming back, if at all.

September 1, 1934

EVERYTHING IS IN turmoil. Nurse de Kiriline is still in the hospital, and while that's meant more time for me at the farmhouse, it's still not enough. The girls have been sickly again these past two days—crying and not taking their milk. As soon as one of them starts to seem stronger, another will decline; it's awful. Spending any time away from them is like a punishment. I'm terrified every time I ride my bicycle out along the Corbeil road that I'll be met with bad news. So I pedal as fast as I can, perspiring like a farmer over the final rise, just until the homestead is in sight. Then I slow to a snail's pace because I can't bear to arrive and get bad news. My classes at St. Joe's begin in three weeks, and then I will have to get used to *not* knowing how they are doing every hour of every day. I'm dreading it.

September 14, 1934

RIBBON CUTTING TODAY for the new hospital: a media circus, with photographers and reporters jostling to get closer to the doctor and dignitaries. All this brouhaha while the girls are still so desperately ill they can scarcely be lifted from their beds, let alone be moved across the street. The new hospital is very modern, two stories high, with tall sash windows facing in every direction and fitted with electricity, plumbing, and indoor toilets, central gas heating for wintertime, a proper kitchen, dining room, and two play areas, plus dormitories for the nurses. A gleaming plaque on the door reads: THE DAFOE HOSPITAL AND NURSERY.

Dr. Dafoe himself snipped the ribbon, but even we could see that he was straining to bend his mouth into a smile. The fact is all of the babies are feverish, weak, and vomiting. These last few nights, the doctor has ordered enemas, milk of magnesia, and mustard baths for convulsions, but nothing is doing the trick. He may not say it to the newspapermen clustered around him, but Ivy and I can read what he's thinking from the way his chin dimples and his glasses seem to sink even deeper into his face: the quintuplets might not live to make the move to the new hospital.

September 20, 1934

THE CAPTAIN HAS been cleared to come back to the nursery. Dismissing any pleasantries or questions about her own health with a brusque shake of her head, she began tenderly examining each of the girls in turn, clucking over their fevers and color. Then she inspected the nursery, offices, and nurses' cabin, running a long finger across every sill and ledge, her nose wrinkling. From there she tramped upstairs to see that Mme. Dionne was keeping the living quarters clean and tidy—I can't imagine how M. Dionne will react if he finds out about that. Then, summoning everyone together, she started in on Ivy, Nurse Clouthier, me, and the orderly, about all the things that we'd let slide while she was gone, putting the lives of the babies in mortal peril. Ivy and I stayed mum. Truly, we've done as much as we possibly could, but with Nurse Ellis gone and Nurse de Kiriline herself in the hospital, it's been almost impossible to keep everything to the Captain's standards. Nurse Clouthier, the most senior among us, bowed her head meekly and mumbled an apology.

"We have made the health of the girls our absolute focus," she said, "but we've struggled to keep up with the premises and the laundry."

The Captain said nothing for a moment, her eyes blazing at Nurse Clouthier. Then, as if struck with a premonition, she marched down the steps and past the section of field that we'd commandeered for our laundry lines. That's how she came to make the discovery in the stables.

We were back indoors with the babies when we heard her stomping up to the porch and calling all staff to join her again, tout de suite. We hustled back outside to find her, arms crossed and gnashing her large teeth, dark curls springing indignantly from her head. Her impeccable nurse's apron was missing, and we saw now that she'd used it to bundle up a wad of soiled and reeking cottons that she held at arm's length.

"Who is responsible?" Her dark eyes flashed. "Who has left the babies' things, this *filth,* to pile up in the stables?"

A glance flickered between me and Ivy. Week in, week out since Nurse de Kiriline first set the rules, all of the girls and women in that farmhouse have spent some part of their day soaping, scrubbing, boiling, wringing, and hanging every diaper, blanket, blouse, bib, and bonnet that has passed through this nursery. Some of the neighboring farms, we understood, had been taking in some of the laundry, particularly since the hired girls brought in to help Mme. Dionne have proved so unreliable—here one day and gone the next.

"We had no idea that any of the babies' things had even been taken to the stables," Ivy said finally. "We don't go elsewhere on the farm."

Lauren, the pleasant, fresh-faced orderly who joined us this week, also expressed surprise, saying she herself had taken a load of cottons back to St. Joe's Hospital laundry when she went off shift yesterday morning. Nurse Clouthier, blinking rapidly, also shook her head. I believed her. She's not the kindliest, but she's honest and has worked very hard, all of us have.

"There are more in the stables," the Captain said in her terse French. "See that they are burned. All of them."

This time there was no mistaking whether she might have more to say. She stalked off the porch and across the yard, pausing to cram her bulky load, apron and all, into the big B/A oil drum that M. Dionne uses to burn waste. Then, dusting off her hands, she marched into the rocky fields, presumably in search of Mme. Dionne, a stern word, and a matchbook. Her own burns still raw and smarting, I don't expect a bonfire was something she herself intended to set alight.

Ivy and I went out to the stables, and sure enough, a rank

mound of unwashed diapers and other cottons had been stashed in a corner of the far stable, now crawling with flies and maggots. My stomach heaved at the sight, and Ivy's pretty face was as cross as I've ever seen it.

"And we wonder why the babies are ailing," she said, spluttering. We were using rakes to coax the pile into a burlap sack rather than touch it with our hands. "These are the same flies that come into the house day and night, that alight on our pots and kettles, that crawl on the babies."

She twisted her head sideways, trying to avoid the stench. "Dr. Dafoe will be furious," she said. "Mark my words. Heads will roll."

September 21, 1934

AFTER DR. DAFOE found out about the soiled cottons in the stable, he didn't shout or get angry, but we could see his chin pucker and he grew very quiet, then marched out of the farmhouse and across the dusty street. As usual, he was pestered by the flock of newspapermen twittering along the fence line, but for once he didn't stop and take their questions. All of them want to know if the babies are any better, if their fevers have come down, if they've managed to take in any food. The truth is, little Cécile is hanging by a thread and the others have lost all of their pep, their skin turning ashen gray, their cries so plaintive it is squeezing our hearts of all hope.

Dr. Dafoe did deign to speak with the men in blue coveralls who have been erecting the electrical poles around the new hospital across the street. Mind you, the wires themselves are nowhere to be seen. Nor has any of the furniture and supplies arrived. Ivy and I wandered through the new building just yesterday, and, apart from shelving and cabinetry, everything is gleaming white but completely empty.

Within a few minutes, Dr. Dafoe had beetled back over to the Dionne property, heading first to the fields, where we could see him speaking with Oliva Dionne and his father. What passed between them we couldn't hear, but whatever the doctor said, the Frenchmen seemed to offer little in the way of protest, although I saw the senior M. Dionne rest an arm on his son's shoulder and he didn't shrug it away. Returning to the farmhouse, the doctor gathered us all together in our charting quarters beside the kitchen, the air stale and heavy in our lungs. "We are moving the babies today," he announced, rocking from heel to toe, chest out. "They need clean air, sunshine, and some peace and quiet, away from the dust and germs and crowds. The longer they stay here, the slimmer their chances of survival. I've informed M. Dionne, it is my belief, in fact, that some or all of them will perish today." He paused, and his deep-set eyes roved over each of us in turn, registering our looks of horror. "The hospital is not ready, but it is hygienic and bright. This is the best chance we have to save the quintuplets."

At 2:00 in the afternoon, we bundled the babies in fresh sheets and blankets and readied ourselves to rush them across the street. A steady drizzle was falling, and the wind had whipped up, carrying the first real sting of autumn frost. Oliva Dionne stood with his father in the shadow of the porch, their faces inscrutable. None of the children came to watch, which was a blessing—perhaps they'd been herded upstairs by Mme. Dionne, because she, too, was absent.

Ivy carried Yvonne, of course, and Dr. Dafoe, Marie, still

the smallest and frailest of the five. I was expecting to carry Émilie, whom Ivy always refers to as mine. At the last minute, however, Dr. Dafoe asked me to hand Émilie to Lauren and sent me across to the new hospital to help the police constables keep reporters and well-wishers at bay. Lauren had never even held one of the babies before! Then I thought of the newspapermen and Mr. Davis with his cameras, and how this short journey across the street would be captured for all the world in photos and print. Lauren is quite attractive, in her way.

Dr. Dafoe had me take the blankets back to the Dionne farm: he wants everything from our makeshift nursery—all of the babies' clothes and bibs and diapers and towels, even the new blankets we'd used to ferry the babies across the road—incinerated on the Dionne property. It seems such a terrible waste. Most families could never dream of having all of this for their own babies.

I walked back to the farmhouse and stole quietly up the steps of the covered porch, then set down the blankets, folded, by the kitchen door. Through the mesh screen I took a last glimpse at the kitchen: the wide plank shelving covering two walls; the big ceramic sink with working faucets, wide enough to bathe the babies; the bulky woodstove brooding in the corner; and the five sleeping cots, impossibly small, now earmarked for the bonfire.

In the dim light, made murkier still by the darkening sky outside, I almost failed to spy Mme. Dionne seated at the table, her broad shoulders heaving, her head in her hands.

September 23, 1934

DR. DAFOE HAS worked a miracle once again. I'm sorry I doubted him, even for a second. The babies' fevers are gone and their color is back. On Dr. Dafoe's orders they are spending several hours sleeping on the side porch in the full sun, oblivious to the birds chirping over their good health and the steady traffic pulling up beyond the front gate. A fence is being built that will keep any nosy parkers from slipping around the back. What's more, the Lindbergh baby's kidnapper has been captured in New York City! I'm so relieved I could cry.

My classes start tomorrow. I held Émilie for as long as I possibly could tonight before heading out to St. Joseph's Hospital. For the next eight months the nurses' dormitory will be my home. *I'll be back*, I promised little Émilie. *Wait for me.*

October 5, 1934 (*Ottawa Citizen*)

PUBLIC NOTICE TO THE READERS
OF THE OTTAWA CITIZEN

The St. Lawrence Starch Company takes this occasion to acknowledge publicly the receipt of the above letter and is proud of this expression of confidence in its product. The company is particularly gratified at the part Bee Hive Golden Corn Syrup has played in this world-famous case.

Mr. W. T. Gray, Vice President
St. Lawrence Starch Co. Ltd.

September 17, 1934

Mr. W. T. Gray, Vice President
St. Lawrence Starch Co. Ltd.
Port Credit, Ontario

Dear Mr. Gray:

I have made inquiries, and I find that Bee Hive Golden Corn Syrup was the Corn Syrup used as a carbohydrate milk modifier in the first feedings of the Dionne quintuplets by Dr. Dafoe, and I have pleasure in advising you that full permission is granted to the St. Lawrence Starch Co. Ltd., the manufacturers of this brand of Corn Syrup, to advertise this fact.

It is also understood that should Corn Syrup be included in the diet of the Dionne quintuplets again, that Bee Hive Golden Corn Syrup will be used, by reason of the success attending its use to date.

In view of the above facts, and advertising permission granted, the Guardians of the Dionne Quintuplet Fund agree that no other brand of Corn Syrup will be similarly endorsed, as it is understood that this letter gives to the St. Lawrence Starch Co. Ltd., Port Credit, Ontario, exclusive Corn Syrup advertising rights as pertaining to the use of this food in the first feedings of the Dionne quintuplets and also its future use should the attending physicians so decide.

Yours very truly,
Dr. Allan R. Dafoe
Official Guardian

October 9, 1934

Miss Emma Trimpany
Nurses Dormitory
St. Joseph's Hospital
North Bay, ON

My dear Emma,

What on earth are they teaching you up there? Haven't you told them you'd learn heaps more if you just came and helped us at the Dafoe Hospital? I miss you terribly and I know the babies do too. Émilie has started kicking at me when I try to change her nappy and makes this ominous smacking sound with her lips.

They are all doing *so* well. You would scarcely think they are the same babies as those little blue-green corpses we had to whisk across the street last month. All of them have put on at least seven pounds and are gobbling down their milk as if they've been wandering the desert and this is the first liquid they've encountered. They are smiley and strong, and their hair is really coming in thick again. I can't tell you what a difference it makes to be in this beautiful bright hospital, without Mme. Dionne barging in with her holy water and prayers, or M. Dionne slinking all over the place and scaring the daylights out of us.

Captain de K says you will be coming here for some of your practicum soon, but surely you could come by on the weekends as well. The weekend after next, the newsreels are coming to make a short film about the quintuplets and the Dionne family.

The older Dionne children have taken to standing at the

fence to watch all of the furniture and supplies being loaded into the hospital. We had our first big delivery of groceries for the staff larder, and I can tell you, my eyes were popping out of my head, so you can imagine what those children must have thought. Eggs, cheese, buttermilk, and cream; sacks of flour, oats, beans, coffee, and sugar; sides of pork, mutton, and beef; plus barrels of carrots, potatoes, parsnips, and turnips, and a crate of apples that will keep us in fruit until Christmas, I'd think.

But yes, the tall wire fence is now finished, and we feel so much safer in here than we did in our shack across the street. Cars are driving from heaven knows where each day because the papers have reported that the babies take their afternoon nap in the sun on the south-facing porch and we'll now get hordes of people lining up along that stretch of fence, trying to catch a glimpse. The Captain says we'll have to put a stop to this soon, but they are so very dear in their itty-bitty cots, I understand why they are drawing such a crowd.

There is a superstition going around that will make you laugh. Visitors have started taking pebbles from the road outside the Dionne farmhouse: the myth is that the stones can bring prosperity and fertility—as if anyone else would want to have five babies all at once! I didn't believe Nurse Clouthier when she told me, but I've since seen people hunting for the perfect stone. I'm waiting for M. Dionne to invite people into the scrub that borders his west pasture and tell them to take all the bushes and rocks they want. Not a bad way to get the field cleared.

Last piece of gossip, Mr. Davis tells me that a drugstore company is paying for Dr. Dafoe to travel to New York, where he will give a talk about our quintuplets at Carnegie

Hall! The doctor will go first to New York City, then to Baltimore to speak at the Johns Hopkins Hospital, then to Washington, D.C., where—brace yourself—he is going to meet the president of the United States! It's extraordinary, isn't it? It never occurred to me that President Roosevelt would care so deeply about our girls.

Come and see us, Emma. We miss you, all of us. Come and change Little Em's nappy for me, won't you?

All my love,
Ivy
Dafoe Hospital and Nursery
Callander, ON

November 15, 1934

Strange to be back in my old bedroom, sitting at my old desk, and I'll be sleeping under my old eiderdown again tonight. Even having a spare hour for jotting something in my scribble book is an odd luxury. These days my notebooks are full of anatomical diagrams, but nothing more.

Have they missed me, Mother and Father? I truly can't tell. Father had plenty of questions for me over supper tonight about school and the Sisters and what sorts of things I'm learning about. But as for the quintuplets and the day I spent with them today, he either feigns disinterest or truly doesn't care.

The fact is, nursing school isn't so much different from high school. The other girls are not unkind, but they are not particularly friendly either. And despite everything that's happened to me in the last six months, I'm still on the periphery, someone they see but don't. When word got out that I would be doing all of my practicum hours at the Dafoe Hospital and Nursery, they were positively gobsmacked and, for the first time, pressed me with questions. But it was too late, wasn't it? I simply said it had been arranged with Dr. Dafoe and left it at that.

Today was the first day I've seen Ivy in almost eight weeks, and she looks happy and content, with lovely color in her cheeks again. I can see that she is absolutely smitten with Fred Davis, although she will never admit it and he's at least fifteen years her senior. He comes every morning from 10:00 A.M. until noon and takes photos of the babies sitting in the sun, taking their breakfast, or lying on their mats in the playroom. They are just too sweet right now.

Ivy persuaded Dr. Dafoe to let me come to their christening— their second, technically: this time with a flock of reporters on hand and Fred snapping photographs. The babies themselves looked so plump and healthy, I had to fight back tears. My Émilie is by far the feistiest and kept plucking off her white booties while Mr. Davis was trying to fix her in his viewfinder, which made us all laugh—with the exception of the Dionnes. They are such an unusual couple, I can't help but think of Jack Sprat and his wife. Mme. Dionne looks like a different person from the weak and trembling mound who brought these babies into the world. She really is an imposing woman, not unattractive on the rare occasion that she smiles, but her resting face could snuff out a candle. She was none too pleased to see any levity whatsoever during the christening. She is a pious woman and clearly thought this was an occasion for solemn prayer, not joy. I disagree. I can't remember a day I've felt so happy. It is my eighteenth birthday tomorrow. Mother will make a little fuss, I expect, but I feel as if I got everything I might want today.

December 25, 1934

A HORRENDOUS SET-TO with Father tonight. Not exactly Christ-masy! I should never have agreed to spend the night here in town.

I should have stayed out at the Dafoe Hospital and Nursery with Ivy and the babies, where I'm needed.

It all began after I'd sat down for supper with Mother and Father. I was telling them about Christmas lunch earlier in the day, out at the nursery: "The Dionnes—all of them: Maman and Papa and the five other children—came across the road first thing this morning and the tension was thicker than a plum pudding. They were very rude, insisting on reciting prayer after prayer and being quite rough with the older children. Madame thinks nothing of reaching out and cuffing them for the smallest misdemeanor, which makes her whole brood jittery."

Father's voice was quiet, but his carving knife started sawing the turkey faster and faster, as if it were a piece of timber. "Emma, surely even you can see that this is a preposterous situation for the Dionne family? Today, especially."

Mother frowned at her mashed potatoes.

"But, Father, you of all people should understand. You're always saying religion is too often used for the wrong purpose. The Dionnes are so intractably Catholic, they seem to employ their faith with the sole aim of sucking the fun out of everything."

"Emma!" This from my mother. "Please. It's Christmas."

The problem, I continued, is that gifts have been arriving for the quintuplets from all over the world, for weeks on end. "So many that the Captain—Nurse de Kiriline—arranged for truckloads to be taken to the relief offices in Corbeil and Callander, where they can be distributed to families in need."

Mother nodded at this and passed me the stuffing.

"Of course, Dr. Dafoe can't allow the quintuplets to play with any toys made of cloth that could carry germs, so that meant there were heaps of dolls and soft toys given away. Well. The

Dionnes got wind of this and insisted that all the toys belonged to their family and should have only gone to the other Dionne children. Ivy said you could have filled a freight train with these toys! Plus the eldest boy must be eight or nine years old by now, so he knows full well where these gifts are coming from. These are dolls and clothes for girls, or other toys intended for much younger children."

Father said nothing, just thrusting out his hand for my plate and spearing a piece of breast meat with the serving fork.

"The really funny thing is that everyone already spent a very happy Christmas together last week—the quintuplets, Dr. Dafoe, the nurses, and M. and Mme. Dionne, although not the other children, who have been sick with colds. They had an early Christmas so Mr. Davis could get his photos, and Pathé could get the newsreel, and all the reporters, at least a dozen of them, according to Ivy, could get a Christmas story." I took my plate from Father. "Apparently it was a real hoot: Dr. Dafoe dressed up as Santa Claus, and the girls were so confused at his big white beard they all started jabbering at once."

I looked from Mother to Father, both of them chewing and swallowing, their eyes lowered, saying nothing.

"Ivy said she and the other nurses and staff were laughing so hard they could scarcely pull themselves together for the cameras. And the Dionnes, apparently, looked like they couldn't decide whether to laugh or cry."

Father's throat was reddening above the collar—never a good sign. He set down his knife and fork. *"Ivy said this, Ivy said that."* He had adopted a high, sugary voice that is nothing like mine. "Emma, can you even begin to imagine what it must be like to have to visit your own children for Christmas? To have *two* Christmases: one for the cameras and one for yourselves?"

I should have bit my tongue, I suppose. But he's never even met the Dionnes. In fact, neither Mother nor Father knows anything about the efforts Dr. Dafoe has expended to keep the girls healthy and how cautious he must be, every single day. They never bothered to visit the Dionne farmhouse last summer, and they've never been out to the new hospital to see the work we're doing. If they did, they'd understand right away that we're doing the right thing by the babies. The parents simply can't give the girls the care, or the love, they need.

"It's not like that, Father. The Dionnes are . . ." I was at a loss for the right word. "They're quite *hard* people. They're not gentle folk. You can see it in the faces of the other Dionne children—they startle like rabbits when their father or mother so much as looks at them."

Now Father's whole face was a mottled red, quite like my own really, and his beard was bristling. "Emma Trimpany, you have no right to an opinion on parenting until you have children of your own, do you hear me? That nursing school of yours has given you airs of superiority, and I won't sit here and listen to them."

Now it was my turn to get my hackles up, because I will surely be the last person on earth to develop "airs." Father and Mother know as well as I do the chances of me, with my disfigurement, marrying and settling down—having a family—are vanishingly small. I opened my mouth to say just that, but closed it again when I saw Mother dabbing at her eyes with her napkin.

"Both of you: stop it," she said, her voice strung thin. "You are ruining Christmas. I don't want to hear another word about the Dafoe Hospital and Nursery, or the Dionnes. Not another word."

1935

March 20, 1935

Miss Emma Trimpany
Nurses Dormitory
St. Joseph's Hospital
North Bay, ON

Dear Em,

I don't know whether to tell you to come and don your battle garb or to stay as far away from the Dafoe Nursery as possible. You *are* still coming down this Friday, aren't you? I'm not entirely joking when I say that you should try and lay your hands on some arsenal. Does your father, perhaps, have a rifle?

Let me reassure you, the girls are fine. Annette is so chubby these days you can plunk her down on a blanket and she just sits there gurgling and blinking at you like the presiding cherub. You couldn't tip her sideways if you tried. Even the little ones, Émilie and Marie, are filling out beautifully. Those two are as thick as thieves, always clutching and burbling at one another. Cécile, Yvonne, and Annette all have their upper front teeth coming in and are starting to look like bunny rabbits, and all five of them have hair that is darker and thicker than ever. Their eyelashes are long and lovely, and they will flutter them at you coquettishly if you attempt to deny them a thing.

So why the rifle? It started two days ago. Nurse Garnier and

I had managed to get all of the girls bathed, weighed, measured, dressed, and fed their breakfast and cod-liver oil and were waiting for Dr. Dafoe's daily visit. All at once we heard a door slam followed by loud voices, and an instant later, Mme. Dionne burst into the playroom. As you know, the Captain has extraordinarily strict rules about visitors, and the Dionnes are only permitted to visit between 11:00 A.M. and noon, or 3:00 P.M. and 4:00.

The Captain was hot on her heels, demanding in her stern, clipped French that Mme. Dionne must remove her shoes and follow the hygiene processes. Doctor's orders. Then Constable James stepped in—he's the shorter one, with the big ears—and asked to speak privately to Nurse de Kiriline, which meant it fell to *me* to try and coax Mme. Dionne to go and remove her coat and shoes, wash her hands, put on a gown, and all the rest of it. These days she's as large and stubborn as a tractor and wears this horrible frown. I looked at her yesterday and thought, My goodness, if she frowns any more deeply, the sides of her mouth are actually going to meet up on the underside of her chin.

Mr. James told me later that the Dionnes had arrived with trunks and suitcases. Four of them! They told the Captain that they and the other children were *moving in* to our hospital and nursery. Where did they presume they were going to sleep? With us, in the nurses' dormitory? I said that to Nurse Clouthier, only joking, of course, and she burst into tears.

Happily, before things could get any more wild, Dr. Dafoe arrived and sent one of the constables to fetch Grandpapa Dionne, who of course is one of the official guardians—at least for now. He managed to talk some sense into his son, and they eventually dragged their trunks back to the truck and drove them the hundred yards back to their own home.

I'm not without empathy for the Dionnes. They must feel

completely fed up with the government and doctors telling them what they can and cannot do. But the fact remains, the girls are still very young and we can't know whether their immune systems are hardy. I truly believe we are doing the right thing by the Dionne family, but to hear them shout and curse at us, you'd think we were devils from the darkest corner of hell. In fact, Mme. Dionne may have used precisely those words on Monday.

It doesn't end there, however. That very night, and again yesterday, there've been strange noises at night. Nurse Garnier heard something first, of course, and came to wake me, the poor thing trembling like she'd seen a ghost. But we've all heard it now: knocking and tapping at the doors and windows at two, three, and four in the morning. Nurse Garnier is scared absolutely rigid. Yesterday I spotted a paring knife in the pocket of her uniform when we sat down to breakfast, so I confronted her about it. She can't be having kitchen knives jangling around in her pocket when she's lifting Annette out of her crib or changing Em's diaper. The upshot is, we've learned that a third constable will be coming from Callander tonight so that there will be one man at the front door and another at the back at all times, with the third watchman patrolling the grounds. They are also going to extend the perimeter fence by another two feet. It seems ridiculous, doesn't it? Three burly men to "guard" five babies, four nurses, and two housekeepers. But I do think we will all sleep easier tonight.

Now, on that note, are you excited to be coming out for the week? I hope I haven't frightened you off.

Lots of love,
Ivy
Dafoe Hospital and Nursery
Callander, ON

March 27, 1935 (*North Bay Nugget*)

DR. A. R. DAFOE, OLIVA DIONNE APPOINTED QUINTET GUARDIANS

TORONTO, Ontario—The Dionne Bill received the assent of His Honor the Lieutenant-Governor today, a special visit being made to the Legislature in order to give final enactment to the measure.

David A. Croll, Ontario Minister of Public Welfare, is made a special guardian of the babies and the bill gives him power to appoint active guardians. These, he has announced, will be Oliva Dionne, father of the famous girls, and Dr. A. R. Dafoe, their physician.

Control of the babies' persons and finances is vested in the minister, and he must approve all contracts regarding the babies. Contracts previously not approved are rendered null and void.

The bill makes the quintuplets "special wards of His Majesty the King" until they reach the age of 18.

March 30, 1935

Back at St. Joe's for the last six weeks of my program. I can't wait to be finished. I'll work at the Dafoe Hospital and Nursery for as long as they'll have me! Dr. Dafoe confirmed yesterday that I will have a place on staff as soon as I'm finished, replacing Nurse Clouthier.

What an extraordinary week to have spent at the nursery. The weekend was relatively quiet. We didn't see a whisker of the Dionnes, not even for Mass on Sunday, which is unheard of with Madame, who Ivy says insists on sitting with the babies when Father Routhier comes by the nursery each Sunday morning. This meant we had the girls to ourselves, bright-eyed and full of smiles. And Em started crawling while I was there! She is the last to do so. On Saturday morning in the playroom, with me sitting on the floor a few feet away from her, she pulled herself up onto her hands and knees. After swaying there for a bit, she fixed me with a very serious expression, then started toward me. Her face when she'd made it that short distance broke out into a huge smile, and she crumpled herself headfirst onto my lap. It was the sweetest thing I've ever seen.

Then, Wednesday morning, the news we'd been waiting for. The guardianship of the quintuplets has been formally extended *by seventeen years,* wards of the crown until their eighteenth birthday, with four appointed guardians, including Dr. Dafoe, and M. Dionne, who will be replacing his father. I can't help but think of the senior M. Dionne as a more measured and fair representative, but effective immediately, M. Dionne junior will have a one-quarter say. He has no allies among the others, however. He and the doctor are scarcely speaking these days, despite the fact that the doctor's only concern is the fragile health of the babies. The other two men are the welfare minister Mr. Croll, and Mr. Valin, a francophone judge from North Bay.

"Does this mean the girls will stay living here, at the Dafoe Nursery?" Ivy asked the Captain.

Nurse de Kiriline gave a curt nod. "That is the current plan," she said, "but the act also carries the provision that the quintuplets will be reunited with their family at such a time as their health and well-being are stable enough to allow integration."

I glanced around the cheerful dining room, with its smooth white walls and tall windows. Ivy and the other nurses have hung bright paintings of animals and sea creatures, and the early-morning sun making its way into the room gave everything a warm glow.

As for the rest of the week, everything ticked along so nicely. Mr. Davis came at 10:00 A.M. every day to take his photographs of the babies. He was charming with both me and Ivy equally, which is kind of him, because it's no secret where his interests lie. He and Ivy are very familiar with one another now, after all these months of mornings together. Mr. Davis can be a bit of a tease, or maybe that's what all men are like in the city? I've no idea. He asked me whether I'd found myself a handsome doctor up at St. Joseph's who was going to whisk me away from the Dafoe Nursery before I'd even managed to properly come back.

I blushed so deeply my birthmark must have been pulsing blue-black. Fortunately Ivy came to my rescue.

"Mr. Davis! You should be ashamed of yourself. You can't be talking that way in front of these young ladies." She was referring, of course, to the five babies scrambling around on their hands and knees and getting up to all sorts of mischief if you didn't keep an eye on them, all of them, every minute of the day. She might just as well have been talking about me, however. I don't think I said more than five words to a doctor at the hospital that weren't directly related to our lessons. And I know for a fact not one of them noticed me.

Dr. Dafoe and the Captain are still insisting that the babies nap outdoors, at least when the sun is shining, bundled up against the cold. But under no circumstances is naptime to be disturbed by people rattling at the fence. Instead, the doctor has announced that visitors may tour *through* the Dafoe Nursery, from the front door to the back, in order to catch a glimpse of the babies playing through the two large interior windows separating the corridor from the nursery. I had assumed these were placed in order to allow more light into the corridor. Now I wonder if Dr. Dafoe hadn't anticipated the need to accommodate curious visitors back when the nursery and hospital were in their earliest planning stages.

It is the strangest thing. There must be two or three hundred visitors per day pulling up in cars having driven from heaven knows where to see the quintuplets. And more are arriving by train. George Leroux, Ivy's father, has quit his job at the mill and has started a taxi service charging people fifty cents to drive from the Callander train station out to the nursery and back again, making dozens of trips a day. Visitors now come shuffling through the doors during playtime, peering through the windows at us, pointing and gasping at the slightest thing. The guards on duty tell them in no uncertain terms that they must not tap at the windows, or call out to the girls, or make any funny faces to get their attention, but many do it anyway. It seems it's impossible to get them to stop.

The girls notice, of course, and are distracted from their capers. Today a tall, lumpy woman in a green dress, which made her look like a string bean, had to be pried away from the window by one of the policemen after she locked eyes with Annette and started sobbing, inconsolably.

"Ba-ba-bah," Annette mumbled, pointing at the woman. When her sisters ignored her, she crawled to the chair where I was sitting and tugged at the hem of my skirt, repeating herself more urgently. "Ba-ba-bah!"

We've all commented that the girls play differently when there are no prying eyes. They smile more and are calmer. We, too, no doubt. For my part, I try to find tasks to do outside the playroom during observation hours. I hate the idea of so many strangers seeing my birthmark and commenting on it, wondering how someone who looks like me could be allowed to work with these miraculous babies.

Everyone who visits takes a stone, just as Ivy told me. Dr. Dafoe has arranged for the eldest Dionne child to be paid ten cents to fill a bucket with little stones each morning, and it is positioned at the back door of the nursery along with a sign that says GOOD LUCK STONES. And sure enough, people are helping themselves to the pebbles when they leave. Mother and Father finally came out to the nursery to see the babies. I didn't walk with them through the observation corridor, but Ivy and I popped out to see them when they had passed through. Father was in good humor for a change. He helped himself to a stone and passed it to Mother, saying, "We all could use a bit more luck now, couldn't we?"

Mother was still exclaiming about the nursery and all of its modern conveniences—I think she was more impressed by the kitchen than she was by the babies—but she dropped the stone in her purse.

"You might find those stones bring you more than good luck," Ivy said, her brown eyes twinkling. I elbowed her in the ribs. Father gave her a strange look, but I shooed them toward the front gate, where other townsfolk were climbing back into Mr. Leroux's bus.

Back in my tiny room at the dormitory, I'm still wearing my winter coat in the hope that my room will warm up—a lost cause. I think I'll need to leave off my writing and climb into bed. I'm fed up with winter and ready for spring. It's snowing again outside, fat, heavy flakes that look like they might turn to rain by morning. Or that's the hope.

May 15, 1935

I'M FINISHED! GRADUATION is not till the end of the month, but I've already started on a regular schedule out at the Dafoe Nursery. It is so, so good to be with the girls and working with Ivy again, almost every single day.

All of the babies took ill last month—Marie quite seriously: she needed a mustard plaster—but they are busy as a hive of ants again now, crawling to and fro and causing no end of trouble.

The Captain has put a stop to the visitors tramping through

the nursery to peek at the girls. Ivy says it was getting ridiculous, with hordes of visitors tracking grime and contagion into the building.

This is the strategy the Captain has devised to keep the public happy, without unduly disturbing the babies. Four times a day, before we put them out to nap on the private porch and before we bring them back in, we detour out the front door and hold the babies up, each with a sign bearing her name, one after the other. The times for the showings are posted on a big clock out on the road, and visitors must stay on the other side of the fence. The distance is not so great that people complain, but it is far enough that the babies are not quite so discomfited as they were by the taps and calls on the windows right above their heads in the playroom.

It's a perfect solution. If all of the girls are already getting dozy, or they've all had a good nap, we take each one in turn and display her to the crowds that are inevitably waiting at the scheduled time. The other day I was concerned that Marie's infection was returning, and both Émilie and Cécile, too, seemed very out of sorts—the last thing I wanted to do was send them out to be displayed to the mob out front.

"No matter," said Ivy. She gathered up Annette and all five of the signs and stepped out on the porch five times, always with Annette, but with a different name on the sign each time.

When she came back in the fifth time with Annette blinking in her arms, we both were biting back our laughter in case the Captain had seen what she'd done. But when we glanced at Nurse de Kiriline, we could see that she'd put two and two together and she had a sparkle in her eyes. She's under no small amount of stress, keeping everything running shipshape here. I was pleased to see we'd actually given her something to smile about.

May 17, 1935

THE CAPTAIN REFUSED to allow the Dionnes up on the porch today when the quintuplets were asleep in their prams—their outdoor nap is a medical necessity, as far as the doctor is concerned. The exchange turned very ugly, and one of the constables had to step in and escort the Dionnes off the property. All of the babies woke up and started crying. Marie and Cécile settled back down to sleep, but we had to bring the others indoors.

May 20, 1935

IT'S HARD TO believe that the babies' first birthday is just around the corner! If someone had told me last June that this day would come, and that all five babies would be here to celebrate it, I wouldn't have believed it. Gifts have been arriving for the girls from all over the world. It's astounding. King George and Queen Mary sent five sterling silver rattles emblazoned with the royal coat of arms. President Roosevelt sent a set of five wooden cars with wheels that swivel, all of them in different colors. We nurses have spent hours rolling these around and pretending to crash them into one another, which sends the girls into peals of laughter. Then there were gifts of clothes and candy and toys that have come from people near and far, rich and poor. One little girl drew a birthday card and sent it with a nickel, saying she had nothing else to spare.

How do we know all of this, when the birthday is still a week away? In fact, we've celebrated early. The girls are none the wiser, of course, but the world is so eager to see and read the news of the quintuplets that Dr. Dafoe arranged for Fred Davis, two dozen reporters, and the newsreel people to come early, so that the papers can run the news and photographs on the day itself. So we had cake, presents, and dignitaries last week. The Dionne parents came across, and Mr. Davis took roll after roll of photos. It must be said, the girls looked happier crawling over Dr. Dafoe than they did their own mother and father, who scarcely mustered a smile for the cameras.

Needless to say, tensions remain thick between the Captain and the Dionnes. My guess is the papers will want to run the photos of "the Quints," as they've started calling them, clambering all over the doctor or puzzling over their presents. It's sad, but the frowning Dionne parents likely won't be pictured at all.

May 22, 1935

THE MOST EXTRAORDINARY thing today: I painted the girls. I held a paintbrush, its tip as soft as a lock of hair from Émilie's head. I dipped it in paints and dabbed it on a palette. I mixed thirty shades of skin and forty shades of sky. A year ago, what I wanted most in the world was to leave school and become an artist—a total delusion, I realize now. And yet there I was, not an artist by any stretch, but sitting in a warm, bright room, steps from those I love, dotting my brush at a canvas and thinking that maybe, just maybe, dreams can come true.

I will read this later and roll my eyes until they fall out of my head, but I won't think of that now. Here's what happened.

Today the girls had a much quieter day, although it was all the more thrilling for me. The famous American painter Maud Tousey Fangel visited this morning. She is to be the official artist of the quintuplets, if you can believe it. To be honest, I'd never heard her name before the Captain explained who she was—she is the painter responsible for all of the portraits you see on the covers of *Ladies' Home Journal* and *Woman's Home Companion*. She's also painted the babies for Colgate's talc powder, Squibb cod-liver oil, and Cracker Jack. It never occurred to me that those paintings were done by a woman, but of course, now it's been explained to me, it makes so much sense. How could a man have painted anything quite so sweet?

She brought paints and pastels to the nursery, but ended up using only her pastels during the visit. The quintuplets are so busy, clambering all over one another in pursuit of whatever toy they aren't holding at that moment, or crawling over to Mrs. Fangel and trying to snatch at her supplies. None of us could have gotten them to sit still long enough to be painted.

I should have expected it, but didn't. When Dr. Dafoe was introducing Mrs. Fangel to the nurses, Ivy opened her big mouth and told her that I am also an artist and have been drawing the quintuplets since birth.

"Emma, you should show Mrs. Fangel what they looked like when they were born," Ivy said.

I was mortified. I mumbled something about art being a hobby I don't have much time for and was hoping to leave it at that.

To my surprise, Dr. Dafoe chimed in and suggested that I show my scribble book to Mrs. Fangel in his office when she was taking a break from her sketching, so there was no way for me to wriggle out of it.

Mrs. Fangel was so kind. She took her time leafing through my sketches, particularly the early ones.

"They were so, so tiny, weren't they?" she said, her finger hovering over the page as if tracing the lines I'd drawn. "You've really captured something here," she said later. It was one of my sketches of Émilie and Marie curled around one another in the clunky old incubator. "You've caught their vulnerability and otherworldliness, haven't you? You make us yearn for them, but also sense that we can't quite touch them, they're so frail."

She looked up at me. I was blushing terribly and did so even more deeply when I saw her gaze flicker over my birthmark.

"Did you ever consider art school, Emma?"

I didn't know what to say, because before we'd moved north, I'd longed for little else. Living up here, where prospects are so few, I had at last made peace with letting that dream go. Mrs. Fangel said that she'd attended the Boston School of Fine Arts, then Cooper Union in New York.

"There are many international students, you know," she said while I was trying to untie my tongue. I finally managed to say that I'd just finished a practical nursing diploma in North Bay and was hoping to stay on as a nurse at the Dafoe Nursery.

She nodded and didn't say anything more for a moment, instead opening my scribble book and leafing through it again. When she spoke she said, "Have you ever used pastel or watercolors?"

"Not since school," I replied. "And that was many years ago, when we lived in Ottawa."

She closed my book and stood, handing it back to me.

"Let's go paint the girls, shall we?"

For the next two hours, Mrs. Fangel let me sit at *her* easel and showed me how to mix my colors and choose my brush. She taught me angles and strokes and how to shadow my shapes for depth and light. Then, when it was time for her to leave, she gave me her card and said I should keep in touch.

"I'd love to see how you get on," she said and shook my hand.

But that wasn't all. She gathered up her easel and paints and pastels, then turned to me and said, "I have more supplies than I know what to do with; you won't mind if I donate these to the Dafoe Nursery, will you?" She gave me a wink.

This time my tongue stuck to the roof of my mouth, and it was all I could do to choke out a thank-you. I thought I was going to cry.

Ivy put her arm around my shoulders and gave me a squeeze and said she'd make sure I put them to good use. Even the Captain seemed pleased for me, which is saying something.

It's late now. Past midnight, I'm sure. My eyes are trying to go to sleep on me before I've even finished writing this down. What a day! What a day.

June 1, 1935

THE CAPTAIN HAS quit. *Nurse de Kiriline* has *quit*!

It simply doesn't make sense. We'd celebrated the quintuplets' "real" birthday on Tuesday, this time a quiet and private affair. I remember noticing the Captain's look of peace and contentment. The past year has aged her more than any of us; the lines etched into her lean face are deeper and more numerous, surely, than they were when she first arrived at the farmhouse last year. But there is something softer about her too. I watched her lifting little Cécile out of her chair and holding her high in the air, Cécile gurgling happily. The Captain's expression was the same as I feel on my own face these days. Cracked wide open with joy and pride and wonder. I know she has borne the brunt of the tense interactions with the formidable Mme. Dionne in recent weeks, but she is tough as nails.

The quintuplets' birthday was front-page news in all the papers, I'm told. The Captain has a scrapbook where she has been collecting many of these stories, with friends and colleagues in different cities sending her clippings when they see them. Who will collect all these for us now, I wonder.

Ivy says Nurse de Kiriline and Dr. Dafoe spoke in private after the quiet celebration we had for the girls' birthday—their real birthday. The Dionnes came over for cake and tea, the parents as well as the children, and the atmosphere was better, I thought, than at the big party last week with all the reporters and government bigwigs gathered around for the photos. The Captain has been very strict with the other Dionne children in the past—they are so rough-and-tumble, compared to the quintuplets. But she was very kind to them at the birthday, I thought, serving them their cake and giving them little gifts of their own. Mme. Dionne is pregnant again, having never really lost the weight she gained when she was carrying the quintuplets. She is now as wide as an icebox. After tea, she needed help to rise from her chair. I simply can't imagine bearing a single child, let alone spending my every adult year carrying baby after baby. It gives me shivers.

Mr. Davis has a reporter's nosiness, Ivy says, and he may be able to sniff out the reason the Captain has left us so quickly. In the meantime I've asked Dr. Dafoe for her forwarding address, which he gave me stiffly, with reluctance. I would like to write to her to thank her for taking me on last year, when she could have chosen anyone to help during those difficult days.

The upside of all this is, I've been asked to move into the dormitories at the Dafoe Nursery full-time. I think Father and Mother will be glad to have the house to themselves again—they got used to me being away when I was at St. Joe's, I imagine. Father has little to say to me these days, his nose buried in the news from Europe. And Mother seems a bit low. Allergies, she says, making her feel poorly, but she has dark circles under her eyes and no energy for the garden, which she usually loves this time of year. I can't help but worry. Most mornings she's still in bed when I set off for the nursery on my bicycle. By the time I'm home at night, she has already retired for the evening.

August 18, 1935

THERE ISN'T A single hour in the day when I have time to pick up my paintbrush or jot down a few things here. Ivy has been visiting her sister in Toronto these past two weeks, her first proper holiday since the quintuplets were born, and that's meant more responsibilities for me and little time for myself. I've loved every minute of it.

If I take up my pen these days, it is only to note the daily measurements for the babies. Dr. Dafoe is now working with Dr. Blatz, a scientist from Toronto who visits regularly and who has explained how marvelous it is to be able to monitor the progress of five identical girls. We now follow a strict schedule for toilet, dressing, nourishment, and indoor and outdoor play, and we must make note of their moods, activities, and interactions, their height, weight, bowel movements, and any outbursts. Annette and Yvonne now weigh twenty-two pounds each. Cécile is slightly less, but has six teeth, two more than any of the others. Marie and Émilie were nineteen pounds, eight ounces, at today's weighing, and twenty-eight inches tall. Yvonne, Cécile, and Annette crept past thirty inches today.

"We are making an important, an unprecedented contribution to science, ladies." That's how Dr. Blatz put it to us, with

Dr. Dafoe by his side staring studiously into the distance and swaying forward and back, his hands clasped behind his back. "It is an honor and a privilege to be a part of this historic work."

The babies were highly agitated for the first few days of Ivy's absence, nattering at me in a language they alone can understand. Presumably they want me to explain where Ivy has gone and when she'll be back. They will be overjoyed when they wake tomorrow to find her bustling about their cribs. I know Mr. Davis has also felt the sting. I've noticed he spends scarcely half the time with us to take his photos each morning as he does when he's got Ivy here to tease and impress.

The latest nurse to join us on staff is Nurse Inès Nicolette, who hails from a small town near Quebec City. She is very devout and has made a special point of trying to teach the girls to put their wee hands together for the Lord's Prayer. Cécile is the only one who seems to understand this is not a lowly game of patty-cake, donning a serene and studious expression and moving her mouth in silent imitation of her new minder. The Dionnes approve of Nurse Nicolette greatly, partly, I'm sure, because she speaks not a word of English. They have invited her to Sunday dinner tonight, which is absolutely unheard of.

Last thing: Mother is pregnant! I don't know what to think. This explains why she and Father seemed so out of sorts when I was staying at home in the spring. They are over their surprise and worry now, it seems. I haven't seen them looking so happy in years. It is a tough time to bring a child into the world, but my salary here at the nursery will be a big help, and there is no talk these days of the Callander post office closing—the sheer volume of mail arriving for the quintuplets, the doctor, and the Dionnes alone could keep the doors open.

When I was little I was desperate for a brother or sister but assumed that Mother and Father feared having another child who looked like me. It certainly never occurred to me that my parents might actually have been hoping for another all those years.

I haven't been able to get home to see them in weeks, but Mother and Father came out on the bus last week to share the news. You could have knocked me down with a feather.

"I won't be taking a pebble when I leave this time," Mother said, gesturing at the souvenir stones in the baskets by the gate, winking at Father as she said it. I wanted to slip through the slats of the porch! Even the papers are now reporting that these stones bring good luck and fertility. I'd thought it was harmless nonsense, until now. The stones are wildly popular with all the tourists, however. Dr. Dafoe has hired the Cartwrights, father and son, to bring in new stones from the lakeshore by truck each morning, having cleared the nearby fields of all pocket-size rocks.

Dr. Dafoe was already crouched at his desk when I summoned the nerve to knock, his funny egg-shaped head wobbling over his papers, his glasses sliding down his nose. He has started decorating the walls with framed photographs of himself with the quintuplets as well as some of the glossy advertisements that have aired in the past few months: "Why Colgate Dental Cream is Dr. Allan Roy Dafoe's Choice for the Dionne Quintuplets."

"Yes, Emma?" he said and pushed his glasses back into position with a stumpy finger.

"My birthmark," I blurted out. "Will my brother or sister have it too?"

He simply sat there blinking, his small hands clasped primly in his lap. Then he gave me his most reassuring professional smile—broader even than the one in the dental cream advert.

"Birthmarks are random, my dear, and very rare. It is highly unlikely that your little brother or sister will have one."

I'm relieved, of course. I'm glad this baby likely won't be bullied, or pitied, or passed over as I have been. But I also thought: How nice it would be to have someone else in the world who looks a little bit as strange as me.

August 22, 1935

We had torrential rain today, so Dr. Dafoe suggested I accept a ride with Mr. Cartwright, who brought the stones this morning, rather than walk into Callander for my day off. Father was in the front yard weeding the borders when we turned onto my street, and he straightened up as the truck approached. When he saw Mr. Cartwright at the wheel, Father's face broke into a smile—something we don't see too often in our house. It turns out he and Mr. Cartwright used to be quite friendly when we first moved to Callander. At that time, Mr. Cartwright had an office beside the post office. They stood chatting together long after I'd gone in to see Mother. Father told me later that Mr. Cartwright is an educated man—he used to be a bookkeeper to most of the bigger businesses in the region before they went under. Father thinks he sold what he could when the economy started downward, using the money to buy his truck.

"Neil Cartwright used to tell some very funny stories about some of the richest fools in this part of Ontario," Father said, closing his eyes and pinching the bridge of his nose reflectively. "Quite a change of pace, hauling pebbles for superstitious tourists. These are strange times."

The funny thing is, on the short drive to town, Mr. Cartwright had been telling me about his son Lewis, who was doing some other errands today—they typically work together. He said Lewis studied to be a high school teacher, but there are no jobs for teachers these days, particularly with so many students dropping out before their senior year. It seems almost no one's life ends up taking the shape first imagined for it.

August 30, 1935 (*Toronto Star*)

EXHIBITION NEWS: DIONNE QUINTUPLETS

TORONTO, Ontario—"Aren't they darling." That's the byword around the St. Lawrence Starch Co. booth in the Pure Food building at the Canadian National Exhibition, referring of course to the world-famous Dionne quintuplets. A huge photograph of these babies measuring approximately 8 feet long and 4 feet high is on view showing a close-up of the kiddies that outrivals anything ever shown before.

The St. Lawrence Starch Co. is certainly proud of the fact that Bee Hive Golden Corn Syrup was used in the first feeding of the Dionnes, and rightly so as this product is certainly one of the greatest energy builders that is on the market today. This delicious corn syrup is not only good for babies but for adults and growing children as well.

Used with permission.

September 27, 1935

Miss Emma Trimpany
Dafoe Hospital and Nursery
Callander, ON

Dear Nurse Trimpany,

Thank you for your note. I'm sorry it has taken me some months to reply. I haven't quite felt up to it. Please understand that it pained me to leave as abruptly as I did. At some point in the future I may be in a position to explain myself in full, but that is not the case now. Suffice it to say that I believe my number one priority at the Dafoe Hospital and Nursery was the health and well-being of the quintuplets, but my second, perhaps equally important priority is the health and well-being of my staff. It is my belief that the escalating confrontation between everyone vying for the babies has become so volatile as to be unsustainable. I am greatly concerned by the tactics that M. Dionne appears to be prepared to use in his mission to regain full custody of the quintuplets and by the lengths Dr. Dafoe will go to to stop this. Indeed, my own interactions with Dr. Dafoe have become such that I have taken my concerns to the other guardians. My dearest hope is that they appreciate the gravity of the situation and take steps to safeguard the babies, hospital, and staff.

I'm sorry I am unable to say more. You have an artist's eye

for detail and insight into the people around you. Be sure you put it to good use.

Yours sincerely,
Louise de Kiriline

P.S. I am enclosing the scrapbook I was keeping of the babies' lives. It's time I set aside the habit of wondering what the press is saying about them, and us. I hope you can be convinced to keep it up.

December 10, 1935

The film crews and celebrities have finally packed up and left, but what a month! The film is to be called *The Country Doctor,* with Jean Hersholt starring as "Dr. Luke" and Dorothy Peterson playing the head nurse. If you told me two years ago that I'd be shaking the hands of two Hollywood film stars before my twentieth birthday, I'd have laughed until I was hoarse.

Dr. Dafoe was very strict with all of our Hollywood visitors. Every day the actors and actresses, technicians, cameramen, and any other support staff entering the nursery had to don gowns and masks, then have their noses sprayed by me or Ivy, while the doctor paced the room, his hands clasped behind his back. Me, Emma Trimpany, spraying the hairy nostrils of Mr. Jean Hersholt twice a day. It is simply too funny.

I hope they will use some of the scenes with Ivy holding the babies in the background or leading them out to the yard to play. I was never asked to be in front of the cameras at all, and I'm perfectly fine with that.

December 14, 1935

DR. DAFOE DRESSED up as Santa for our early Christmas with the girls today, Fred snapping photo after photo. This year the girls weren't the slightest bit put out by his costume. Émilie marched over to him laughing and pointing, and when he stooped down to lift her into his arms, she reached up and tugged his beard clean off. Half of Fred's pictures will show all of them gathered around the world's most famous physician inexplicably dressed as an elf. Annette, Yvonne, and Cécile then trundled over, and it was dog pile on *le Docteur* while Marie scrambled to join in. "Doh-Doh," they call him, Yvonne and Annette managing "Le-Doh-Doh." The doctor loves it. He is a different man than he was before the quintuplets were born—less of a fuddy-duddy and more comfortable with being the center of attention, even when he pretends he doesn't like it.

The real stars are the babies. You see them everywhere now, and not just in the newspapers. They are pictured in advertisements for Bee Hive corn syrup, Lysol, Quaker Oats, and Palmolive. Mrs. Fangel did the artwork for many of these adverts, but I think she needs to pay us another visit to see how much the girls have changed. There is one out now for Pears baby powder, and the drawing of the babies does not look much like them at all.

December 24, 1935

BACK IN MY little bedroom in Callander, or what used to be my bedroom. Father and Mother have redone the room completely— new drapes and shelving, a crib and change table, a fresh coat of egg-yellow paint on the walls, and all my silly girlhood things packed away in the attic. They will keep my bed, they've assured me, and I'm welcome to come and visit anytime. But I can see that they feel, as I do, that I've flown the nest and it is now being feathered anew for the little one due any day.

Mother is tired and slow on her feet, but she otherwise looks better than I have seen her in years. Christmas is always a terribly busy time at the post office, but Father, too, seems to be brimming with energy. How strange for them to be repeating this process, so many years later. They don't seem to see it that way at all. I'm hoping the baby will come while I have these few days off from the nursery so I can be of some help to Mother. Otherwise I will have to ask to take additional time off, and I'm loath to do so.

It was the younger Cartwright who drove me back to my mother and father's tonight. Lewis Cartwright has ferried me home or back several times now. He is a good foot taller than his father, well over six feet, with gangly limbs that seem to struggle to stay still, twitching the way a bird on a branch will shift and reshuffle its feathers. It is quite something to watch him fold himself behind the wheel of the truck. He's a very kind young man, I can tell, but it is simply impossible for me to imagine him as a teacher in front of an unruly class. His father, Neil Cartwright, could talk a leg off a donkey, but Lewis needs to be cajoled by his father before he'll utter a word, and, even then, he sometimes has a hint of a stutter and speaks so softly, it's hard to catch what he's saying. When it is just him and me in the truck, there is little in the way of conversation. Our drive to Callander tonight was entirely silent apart from a few pleasantries at the outset. As we drove along, I'm sure I could hear the first snowflakes landing on the cab. How utterly different from my noisy days in the nursery.

Lewis hurried around the side of the truck and opened the door for me after we'd pulled up at my house. "Merry Christmas, Mr. Cartwright, and to your father and family too," I said, stepping to the street. He gave me a warm smile, which really changes the look of his anxious face. "Y-you too, Miss Trimpany," he said, bobbing his head. Then he stooped to gather the bag at my feet and accompanied me up the walk.

December 27, 1935

I HAVE A baby sister. Edith Lorraine Trimpany, born today at 8:00 A.M. She is perfect. At eight pounds, three ounces, she seems huge to me—roughly the same as the combined weight of Émilie, Marie, and Cécile at birth. She has a dusting of flaxen hair and pale blue eyes like mine, but no bright red blotch staining half of her face. She is beautiful.

1936

January 31, 1936

I think we will have to cut down the babies' afternoon nap soon. Half the time Annette and Yvonne don't sleep more than an hour, and Yvonne has learned how to climb out of her crib and will bustle around to visit her sisters, fetching them items requested from the toy box. Yesterday I went in to wake them and Annette, Cécile, Em, and Marie were standing in their cribs in high good humor, taking turns tossing their dolls to the floor while Yvonne trotted around fetching them.

During their naptime today, Dr. Dafoe summoned Ivy and me to his office, ushered both of us into seats, and shut the door behind us.

When he was seated again behind his desk, he folded his neat hands together and fixed us with a serious frown. He cleared his throat. "What I have to tell you, I must ask that you keep confidential."

He paused, looking from Ivy's face to mine until we both nodded to show we understood.

"M. Dionne is using his position on the board of guardians to make certain demands pertaining to the quintuplets, many of which are frankly ridiculous." Dr. Dafoe snorted. "They are insisting that all staff be French. Both of you, of course, are perfectly bilingual and I would ask that you continue to speak to the girls in both French and English, with the caveat that it would be prudent, in my opinion, to speak only French to the girls when their parents are visiting.

"As you know, last year's guardian agreement provides for the babies to move home with their parents at some point in the future." He paused again, his chin dimpling as his lips drooped downward. "In my professional opinion, this is not in the best interests of the children, and I will do everything in my power to ensure this does not happen until such time as we can be assured that it is what the girls themselves want to do. This, however, will put increasing pressure on our funding efforts."

This is something I hadn't spent much time wondering or worrying about—how everything we want or need for the nursery simply materializes, no effort spared, even in these lean times. I had assumed the government was paying for it, but of course this is the same government that has cut back on relief payments and levied stricter rules as to who qualifies for help. I don't know why I hadn't worried about this earlier.

As if he could read my mind, Dr. Dafoe continued: "The government, as you know, paid for the construction of the Dafoe Hospital and Nursery. Operational costs currently are managed by the guardians based on revenue raised through various endorsement and publicity materials."

Dr. Dafoe gave a brisk cough, his small hand curling like a snail shell and hovering briefly in front of his mustache. Such topics pain him. "It is Premier Hepburn's request that some of these funds be spent in the coming months on alterations to the Dafoe Nursery in order to accommodate the mounting numbers of visitors, without unduly influencing the normal development of the children.

"It is my strong belief that the girls are reaching an age where displaying them on the patio may be increasingly confusing and upsetting for them. Upon consultation with Dr. Blatz and the guardians, we are moving forward with the construction of a more private play park, where the nurses and babies can peacefully enjoy the sunshine without the distraction of hundreds of tourists waving from the fence line. We are working on a design that allows visitors to watch them from an observation area, but screened from the babies so they will be unaware of any visitors."

I shot a glance at Ivy, whose expression mirrored mine. The girls would be getting a new playground, but one where the public could watch? I couldn't picture it.

Dr. Dafoe looked sternly from my face to Ivy's, tucking his chin to his chest. "The aim here is for the girls to have a safe and fun outdoor space that they can visit several times per day, safe and secure and free from any germs, and where they can be observed without being disturbed."

He unfolded his fingers and spread his hands wide as if to help us embrace the concept. "You understand, I think, the extent to which the world has fallen in love with our girls, every bit as much as we have? To deny visitors a chance to see them, when there is so little else that brings joy to the common man, is something that the government refuses to consider."

I cast a look at Ivy and could tell she was summoning the right words to phrase the same question I had, with her usual delicacy. I was already blurting it out.

"Will we be charging admission?"

"Absolutely not." Dr. Dafoe managed to look offended at the suggestion. "And every effort will be taken to make sure that the quintuplets remain unaware of the visitors—I think this is an important first step to normalizing their lives."

I thought of my own childhood, no brothers and sisters, no playground, little time, in fact, for such a thing as play. The bright, clean, safe world in which our five girls were so quickly growing up was like nothing I'd ever imagined, and surely it was just as unreal for all the people following their lives in the papers and newsreels. The thing is, I *want* this for them. I want their lives to be special and cherished.

"What do the Dionnes think?" Ivy asked.

Dr. Dafoe gave a long sigh. "M. Dionne is the one who believes visitors should pay a small fee." He grunted. "No doubt with a hefty share of the proceeds paid to the Dionne family." He shrugged. "We would never do that, of course. We will do everything to protect the girls from exploitation, even if it means making nice with Dionne and enduring his bullying."

He glanced up at us and paused, as if he was about to say more, then didn't. After a moment, he stood up to indicate that the discussion was over. We got to our feet and stepped toward the door. Dr. Dafoe got there first and put his hand on the knob, then hesitated.

"I understand Nurse Nicolette has become quite friendly with the Dionnes," he said. "I would remind you that our discussion today is not to be shared with anyone outside this room."

Once again, we nodded mutely and scurried down the hall.

"How can they afford to build this play area if they are not charging admission?" It seemed extraordinary, given the harsh economic times affecting our part of the world. Nearly 70 percent unemployment in North Bay, according to the *Nugget*.

"Don't be ridiculous, Emma!" Ivy laughed. "The quintuplets themselves are paying. Fred says their trust fund will be paid one hundred thousand dollars for their motion picture, *The Country Doctor*—can you imagine? Plus the revenue from all of the products they are supposedly eating or drinking or enjoying daily. These are the richest babies in Canada. Why on earth do you think the Dionnes are fighting so hard to get them back?"

February 17, 1936

SOMETHING EXTRAORDINARY TODAY. First we dressed the girls in their new hockey jerseys—custom-made and very sweet, each one "playing" for a different team with matching miniature hockey sticks. But when Fred was finished with his photos, instead of having me help with the daily measurements, Dr. Dafoe asked me to accompany him back to his office. The doctor rummaged around for a bit in a big pile of mail and papers and finally found what he was looking for. It was a postcard of the quintuplets issued for Valentine's Day that pictured three girls standing and peering through a wreath of red roses, with two others seated below. Not a photograph, but a painting. I recognized the style right away as that of Mrs. Fangel, but the babies really didn't look much like our girls. There was something strange about their noses, and their hair was curling in funny directions, plus none of them had their tiny distinguishing characteristics.

Dr. Dafoe was watching me sternly over his glasses. "What do you think of it?"

I was instantly flustered and could feel my face heating up. I had suggested to him that Mrs. Fangel visit us again, to see how the babies were coming along, but I'd regretted it. It sounded like I was only raising the issue for my own selfish reasons. I'd long ago run out of the paint Mrs. Fangel had left for me, and the pastels, which I admit I find a good deal easier to use, I'd worn down to stubs.

"It's very sweet," I managed to say and lifted the card to my face, pretending to study it closely in the hope he wouldn't see me flushing beet red.

"Do you know," he said, "we sold more than fifty thousand of these cards this month, and those aren't the final numbers."

I couldn't help myself, my mouth fell open. Fifty thousand! Living here, with the babies, and watching them grow day by day, you forget the outside world to some extent, especially in the winter, when the deep drifts keep the visitors at bay. But fifty thousand people bought these cards? It boggles the mind.

"But what do you think?" Dr. Dafoe continued. "Does this look like the babies?" They were hardly babies anymore, but all of us still called them that. "Which one is Yvonne, do you think? Which one is Marie?"

This felt like a trap. I didn't know what to say. Dr. Dafoe watched my face, his own expression giving nothing away.

"I have a proposition for you, Emma. I've discussed it with the other guardians, although Dionne, as usual, was absent. We've agreed to provide you with the supplies you need in order to paint or draw the girls yourself, plus some dedicated time in your workday to do so. Would this be agreeable?"

Dr. Dafoe, for all of his medical wisdom, could be such a stick-in-the-mud about regular human interaction. I laughed about it later with Ivy because I was simply mute in disbelief. Here he was offering me the most wonderful thing, yet his round face was flat as a pancake, as if he truly had no idea how I'd respond.

When I could finally pull myself together, I said that of course I'd be over the moon and would do my very best, but that I could by no means produce portraits as beautiful as Mrs. Fangel's, and that there was so much I didn't know, but that I was ever so grateful and on and on.

Dr. Dafoe dismissed all my bumbling gratitude with a flick of his fingers.

"In fact, it is Mrs. Fangel who suggested we do this," he said. "She has been working off of the photographs of Mr. Davis, but she says it is impossible to capture your subject unless it is living and breathing in front of you. Is that the case?"

He looked at me intently, but I found myself unable to answer, my birthmark pulsing. He shrugged and reached for the postcard. "Going forward, Mrs. Fangel will work off of the portraits you provide, either adapting them as needed or more likely producing her own work with yours as her base subject."

"Will she not visit herself?" I asked, finally finding my voice. This seemed to me to be by far the more sensible solution, although I hated to suggest that I wasn't overjoyed by the plan he'd outlined.

"She may do so, yes, at some point, but not in the foreseeable future. She has offered to provide you some feedback on the work we send her, if you would find that useful."

It was clear from his tone that he had no idea what would be useful to me or not, or to Mrs. Fangel for that matter. I didn't care. This was such an extraordinary offer.

"You will need to provide the guardians with a list of the supplies you require, and then we shall discuss with Nurse Leroux a suitable schedule so that you have several hours in the week to devote to this task."

I was bursting to tell Ivy. She was absolutely delighted for me, standing and giving me such a hug when I told her the news. I had dashed back to the playroom straight from Dr. Dafoe's office and found Ivy in a corner, playing blocks with Annette and Marie. They watched Ivy and me embracing and immediately pulled themselves up and threw their little arms tightly around my legs as well, burying their faces in my skirt.

Later that evening, when the girls were finally down for the night and Ivy and I had a few minutes to ourselves, she asked me what I'd be paid for my work. I hadn't even thought of it. I'm already well paid, as far as I'm concerned. Ivy sat up and thwacked me gently on the arm.

"Fiddlesticks! They are paying you for your talent, that's not the same thing as paying you to change diapers and spoon mashed carrots into little mouths. Look at Fred. He's paid handsomely for his photos."

We hashed this over at some length and agreed that she would speak with Mr. Davis and see what he thinks. I simply can't imagine standing in Dr. Dafoe's office and asking for more money, after everything he's done for me. But I admit I'm curious as to what Mr. Davis will say.

Most of all, I'm over the moon that Dr. Dafoe even thinks my art would be of some use to the babies. And if Mrs. Fangel would actually give me some pointers? Wouldn't that be something!

February 29, 1936 (*Toronto Star*)

DR. DAFOE "VERY PLEASED" WITH THE COUNTRY DOCTOR

Witnesses Private Screening in New York of Movie Starring Famous Dionne Sisters

Dr. Allan Roy Dafoe, O.B.E., is to be a guest of honour at the world premiere of "The Country Doctor" at the Uptown theatre in Toronto Thursday evening next. The occasions on which this distinguished man, who is a legend even in his lifetime, may be seen are few and far between because of the fact that he remains, despite his fame, what he was before fame found him out, a true country doctor.

It will, of course, be Dr. Dafoe's only appearance, and it is his delight with his beautiful quintuplets' first appearance on the screen, as artists, that persuaded the doctor to attend the premiere. It is the first world premiere of a picture Toronto has ever had.

In New York City on business of the quintuplets, Dr. Dafoe last night saw a private screening of the picture and expressed his boundless delight with it.

Although the plot and characters of "The Country Doctor" are wholly fictitious, still there can be no question that Dr. Dafoe's character inspired this romance in honour of country doctors everywhere.

March 6, 1936

A colossal dump of snow this morning and more coming down every minute. We woke to thick pillows of it heaped high as far as the eye could see. The girls, squawking with excitement, were tripping over one another in their haste to get bundled up and into the yard after breakfast. They know the words *bottes* and *tuque* and *mitaines,* but it's a stretch to understand their funny pronunciation, the words laced into the vocabulary that is theirs alone. "Nay!" they squeak, for *neige,* and "fwa" for *froid.*

We got them swaddled in coats and woolens and out the door as fast as we could. In the swirling air, thick with flakes, you could scarcely tell where sky stopped and the downy drifts began. Ivy tried to teach them how to make snow angels, but whether it was the white-on-white or the joy of the morning, they couldn't quite grasp the concept. Instead they would drop themselves backward in the soft heaps, flailing their arms and legs, then dissolving in giggles. Of course Annette and Marie both lost their boots in the deep snow, then stood there jabbering and pointing toward their feet, eyes wide: *Bottes! Fwa!* It was a shame to go back inside, but we have to be so careful that one of them doesn't catch a chill. It is never the case that only one of them gets the sniffles.

I had planned to spend my weekend off in Callander with

baby Edith and my parents, but when we woke to snow, I assumed I'd be staying put. In the end I was able to get a lift with Lewis Cartwright, so made it home just fine.

Lewis has rigged some kind of plow to the front of his father's truck and spent the morning furrowing a path along the road, only to have Dr. Dafoe and Mr. Davis cancel their visit to the nursery. But Lewis came into the kitchen to warm up midafternoon and offered to run any staff into town who needed it. I found him perched by the stove on a stool far too short for him, his bony knees jutting up to his chest, shoulders hunched, and his long fingers curled around a mug of tea. He seemed delighted to hear that someone was taking him up on his offer, bobbing his head and smiling, then taking my bags for me as we slid and slithered through the drifts to get to the truck.

And now I'm home.

I'm glad I came. Little Edith is very funny right now, alert with big blue eyes. Mother looks tired, but blissfully content. And Father is clearly happy as I've ever known him to be, even leaping from the table to help clear the dishes after supper, which I'm sure I've never seen him do before.

March 11, 1936

THE *STAR*, WANTING special St. Patrick's Day photos, sent out five of the sweetest little outfits, dresses, bloomers, and bonnets, all mint green in color and covered in tiny sprigs of emerald clover. Mr. Davis—Fred, as he's insisting I call him—also had tissue-covered shamrocks for the girls to hold for the photos. Annette is always the ringleader, and the rest scrambled to mimic her, putting the shamrocks on their heads like crowns or in front of their faces as if they were peering through the port-holes of a ship, then waving them wildly over their heads like they were going to lasso a steer. They are such clowns.

This was all going on in full force when the Dionnes made their appearance. Nurse Nicolette, despite being fully aware that the Dionnes are to visit only during their allotted hours, allowed the parents into the playroom, thinking, I suppose, that they would also enjoy the fun. Instead, Mme. Dionne's face clouded, dark as a storm. She started shouting in French and stomped over to the girls, snatching away their shamrocks, one by one.

She was angry—we were swiftly made to understand—because St. Patrick's Day is a religious holiday and should be marked more solemnly, not with trinkets and symbols and horseplay. She turned on Fred with a stream of angry French that I knew he would scarcely have understood. Meanwhile, the girls, who had been having such fun, broke into sobs, tottering over to me and Ivy, arms outstretched. This of course infuriated Mme. Dionne even further. She grabbed at Cécile, who has always been her favorite, and clamped her tightly to her breast while Cécile wailed and wailed. I hope Fred got enough of his photos before the Dionnes arrived, because the girls were a blotchy mess when they finally settled down again for lunch.

April 3, 1936

A FUNNY CONVERSATION with Ivy tonight. If we are both work-ing the evening shift together, which we often are, we'll linger for a while in the girls' bedroom until they're all asleep. We started doing this back when Yvonne and Annette first learned to climb in and out of bed like monkeys and would scamper over to one of their sisters to try to get a game going. Some nights we'd pop in to check on them only to find Yvonne in Émilie's bed, or Annette snuggled in with Cécile. I was all for letting them sleep like that, but Dr. Blatz believes it's confusing for the subconscious to not have consistency each night. Whatever that means.

So Ivy and I will get them all tucked in, then we'll seat ourselves on the bench under the windows. If it's been a long day, we often sit in silence, listening to the girls muttering to one another and settling themselves down for the night. Other times we'll talk about pretty much anything, silly or solemn, keeping our voices low and mild. I think the girls find it soothing, hearing us close at hand. This is the time of day when our home, the nursery, seems to pull away from the rest of the world and dips below the horizon so that all the squinting eyes that follow us every hour of every day can't quite make us out. We're left in peace.

Mme. Dionne hasn't set her plump foot on the property since the St. Patrick's Day fiasco. The biggest shadow across our doorstep these days is a bizarre lawsuit between the St. Lawrence Starch Company and the Canada Starch Company. It's front-page news in the local paper and the *Star,* which is extraordinary given everything else going on in the world these days. Supposedly the companies are fighting over which has the right to declare itself the official corn syrup of the Dionne quintuplets. I would laugh about it if I wasn't so worried what it might mean for the girls. Fred heard from a reporter at the *Star* that both companies have paid thousands of dollars into the girls' trust fund. I'm worried that, depending on how things turn out, some of this money may need to be given back.

"That's never going to happen," Ivy said firmly, her voice low.

She is always so confident about this, Ivy. She says the girls will never, ever have to worry about money and that there is no point in me worrying about it either.

"The tricky part will be how they'll ward off all the gold-digging suitors knocking down their door when they're old enough," she said. She liked this image, I could tell. She was smiling in the dim light, wide enough that I glimpsed her snaggle-tooth. I love Ivy's smile.

"I don't think the girls will ever get married, do you?" I said. "I can't even imagine them wanting to be with anyone other than each other. So they will need their trust fund to last a very long time."

Ivy gave me a strange look then. She thinks I should be thinking more about marriage in general and certainly not advocating a life of spinsterhood for our little girls.

"They'll want to live normal lives, Emma. You know that, right? All of this"—she waved her hand around the bedroom, but I knew she was referring to the entire nursery and hospital— "this is just for now, right?"

I didn't say anything; I looked at the dark shapes outside the window. The snow was almost gone and the moon had not yet risen, so the shadows in the yard below seemed all the more absolute and unknowable.

"I guess I just can't picture them having other kinds of lives," I said finally.

What I didn't say is that I can't picture *me* having a different kind of life either. A life without them. I have a purpose here that I didn't have before, and I can't imagine I'll find that again elsewhere.

We sat there for a long while, not saying anything, our ears tuned to the sighs and murmurs of the girls. Sometimes one of them will make a sudden start or a louder cry and I want to go to her, to lift her in my arms and cradle her until she falls asleep again. The doctors don't like us disturbing them, even when they wake crying or upset, but some nights I can't stop myself.

As I was about to rise and leave, Ivy spoke. "I will have my own babies one day, Em. I love our girls, but the point is, they aren't ours, are they? I need to have my own. And so should you. You are so good with them."

Ivy and I have shared so much together—when she talks like this, which she does more and more these days, I can't quite bring myself to say again what I've told her so many times. I don't want children of my own. I don't want marriage and a husband. I don't have dreams like that crowding in on the dream I'm living now.

April 14, 1936

Miss Emma Trimpany
Dafoe Hospital and Nursery
Callander, ON

Dear Miss Trimpany,

I was delighted to receive your sketches—you prefer the pastels to the paints, I gather! I'm of the same mind. Perhaps oils are best suited for fruit bowls, flowers, and dowagers. There is a fluidity to the strokes of pastel or charcoal that a paintbrush certainly matches, but there is simply no time with our young subjects to pause to dip the brush, don't you find?

First things first. You have the eye, my dear. You have the eye. You must keep at this.

I've enclosed a list of specific suggestions related to the five pieces you've sent, which I hope you'll find useful, mostly technical tips and a few ideas regarding lighting. That said, the most important thing I think I can tell you is to trust your heart and trust your instincts. Understand who you can learn from and what you might learn, but don't rely on anyone else too deeply lest you lose what is uniquely yours.

I'm intrigued by your careful comments about the girls and their telltale distinctions. It's an interesting dilemma you pose for me, because of course their adoring public believes the quintuplets to be identical in every way. It is, in part, my duty to paint them to suit expectations. But your letter moved me to think of these little girls somewhat differently than I did when I met them last year. Each, as you say, is one unique part of a unique whole. I will take your suggestions to heart and will do my best to make sure we don't lose sight of that, or that at least you and I don't lose sight of that. I've taken a fresh piece of paper and tacked it on the wall in my studio to remind me, with this line from your letter:

They are in as many ways different as they are alike.

Thank you and best wishes,
Maud Tousey Fangel
145 East 72nd
New York, NY

April 25, 1936

Ivy and Fred are engaged. Fred asked her the moment he got back from Nova Scotia. Now Ivy is floating around the nursery as if a light breeze is circling her feet and keeping her aloft. I've never seen her so happy. Fred didn't stay long this morning—he must be exhausted after the past week—but I saw him when he and Ivy announced their news. He, too, looks like he might burst with gladness. The girls crowded around to see what we were all exclaiming over when Ivy was showing us her ring. Marie and Em were very worried at first, because tears started leaking out of Ivy's eyes, and the two of them conferred, then trotted off to find a handkerchief that they brought for Ivy, who laughed and gathered them in a big hug. It's on her face, plain as day: joy but also a sadness. One way or another, things here will change.

It's been a strange week for us, with Fred gone to cover the mine disaster in Moose River. It's the first time the *Star* has assigned Fred to a story other than the famous Dionne quintuplets, or at least in the time we've known him. His photos from Moose River have been on the front page of the *Star* for days. I like to think my sketches can capture something that a photograph cannot, but I'm not sure I can say that of Fred's haunting photos—the stooped men coming out of the mines, their long faces as they sat in the back of the ambulance waiting to be taken from the dark grave they'd finally escaped.

Last week the Canadian Radio Broadcasting Commission actually had a man stationed at the mine itself, giving hourly updates on the rescue efforts. Ivy and I agreed, we've never heard anything quite like it. We were on tenterhooks—he made us picture the barren plains, the dark mine shaft, the chill of the rocks, and the steady drip of rising water. It gave me goose bumps. Ivy was even more caught up in it, no doubt convincing herself that Fred and all of the newspapermen, photographers, newsreel men, broadcasters, and medics camped out at the site for days were themselves at risk of plunging down a mine shaft the very next instant.

We cried when we heard the men coming out of the mine, on the radio. One man didn't come out, of course, or not on his own two feet. That is the worst thing to think about. Not only were the men trapped in a space the size of a privy but they were trapped with the body of Mr. Magill for days.

I have a hundred questions for Ivy, but she was given the night out to visit her father with Fred. With luck the Dionnes won't show up for Mass tomorrow; we could use a quiet day to settle back into our regular routines. Dr. Dafoe has told us the work crews are coming to break ground for the new playground and gallery starting Monday. I can't imagine what M. Dionne thinks about that.

May 8, 1936

NURSE JACQUELINE NOËL has joined us on staff. She is short and stout, to put it kindly, but surprisingly dainty on her feet. She moves like a barge gliding silently down a river and has twice made me jump by tapping my shoulder as I sat behind my desk, thinking myself alone. The girls have fallen swiftly into line, leaping to obey her commands.

I came here to Mother and Father's house tonight. Mother has been asking me to bring my art supplies home from the nursery so I can sketch Edith, and I've done so. I'm trying to ignore the irony here—Mother spent years discouraging me from "scribbling," as she always called it, only to turn around and ask me now if I'd sketch my baby sister.

I arranged to get a lift with the Cartwrights after they'd delivered the day's stones. I had my overnight bag plus my easel, sketchbook, and the big case that holds my paints, palette, and pastels at the back door when they brought their truck through the inner gates of the nursery after supper. Both Lewis and his father hustled over to help.

Lewis smiled and dipped his head, saying nothing, but Mr. Cartwright had half a dozen questions, asking me if I was running away from the nursery. I laughed and explained that I was going to do some sketches of my baby sister, and they both seemed delighted. I don't suppose they knew about my drawings of the quintuplets, or that I had been helping Mrs. Fangel, which is a good thing, I suppose. I said that I'd been drawing the babies since they were born and that Dr. Dafoe encouraged me, even supplying me with my pastels, charcoal, and paints.

Lewis nodded his head slowly and murmured, "It's r-rare these days that we get the time to do the things we care about."

Mr. Cartwright opened his mouth as if to say something, then snapped it shut again, as astonished as I to hear his son speak up. That's the most I've ever heard Lewis say in a single breath! He carried my supplies to the truck, then put his hands on the sides and swung himself up, settling himself beside my things, his back against the rear of the cab. For someone so tall and gangly, he moves with surprising grace. I suppose he must be very strong, filling all those buckets of stones.

Climbing behind the wheel, Mr. Cartwright launched into a long story about how he used to dabble in writing the odd verse and how he had intended to do more of that in his retirement. "But look at me now!" he said cheerfully, gesturing at the road and laughing. "This doesn't look much like poetry, does it?"

When we pulled up at the house, Lewis hopped out of the back again and helped me lift out my easel and bags. He cleared his throat and said, "My father and I would love to see your sketches, if you'd be willing."

"I'll likely have something to show you Sunday night. Unless Edith's a monkey and won't keep still."

He looked like he was going to say something else, but didn't, doing his default blink and nod. Lewis has quite unusual eyes, wide-set and a bit large in his long face, but a lovely hazel color, like his father's—deep blue at the edge, turning dark amber near the pupil. Tricky to paint, I'd imagine. I must be getting to know him better, because I realized from his silence that he didn't mean Edith.

"You mean, you want to see my sketches of the quintuplets," I corrected myself.

He looked up and flashed the ghost of a smile.

"We would indeed, Miss Trimpany," he said and busied himself brushing the dust off my bag. "It's a bit of a joke Father and I have that we've made more trips to the Dafoe Hospital and Nursery than anyone in the world, yet we almost never get a chance to see the babies."

May 10, 1936

I SHOWED LEWIS and his father some of my sketches of Edith once they'd brought me back to the nursery. Very rough work, but I think I captured her quite nicely—it's enough that I can keep working on something larger back at the nursery, if I get the chance. Lewis was very complimentary, and I promised to show him some of my work of the quintuplets another time. It seems he actually knows something about drawing, which I hadn't expected.

He helped me ferry my things back to the kitchen door, and I asked if he'd taught art when he was a schoolteacher. He blushed almost as red as my birthmark and said he'd taught mathematics and physics, but only as a substitute teacher. I must have looked confused: his father has told me several times that Lewis studied to be a schoolteacher.

He cast a look at the truck, where his father sat waiting. Standing with my bags and cases made him look even more lanky than usual, the cuffs of the shirt beneath his dusty overalls straining to reach his bony wrists. He stooped to set down my things, lowering his soft voice even further, but when he spoke it was clear as a bell, his stammer gone.

"I actually studied engineering at the University of Toronto," he said. "I specialized in aeronautics. My dream was to build airplanes."

I was astonished by this declaration, but knew better than to say anything. He straightened himself up again, his face creased. "Father thinks, if I build airplanes, I will want to fly them, and he saw a lot of what happens to pilots in the war. In the end he convinced me to turn to teaching instead, saying there'd be more work for teachers than engineers."

I looked up, and he managed a smile. Lewis has one of those faces that is entirely changed by smiling—the bones of his long face shift so that his cheekbones bounce upward and out, making wide dimples. "Turns out there's not much work for teachers either," he said.

"Have you been up in an airplane?"

He nodded, smiling wider.

"Wasn't it terrifying?"

He nodded again. "Terrifying and wonderful."

May 29, 1936 (*La Voix*)

BIRTHDAY BROADCAST RINGS OUT AROUND THE WORLD

Babies' Wealth Approaches $500,000

CALLANDER, Ontario—A special radio crew and celebrity commentator, Frazier Hunt, were the only visitors allowed into the Dafoe Nursery for the much-anticipated second birthday of the Dionne Quintuplets. Visitors and dignitaries were turned away and, with the rest of the world, could only listen to how the celebrations played out over the radio. And what did this sound like? Why, that was Émilie blasting on the tinhorn, Yvonne on the drums, and rascally Cécile tugging on the microphone cord while Dr. Dafoe tried to say his piece. It was not until Nurse Yvonne Leroux began to sing a quaint French folksong that the Quints fell into line and did a little dance, raising their plump arms in the air and spinning this way and that, their petticoats flaring.

The Dionne parents were not in attendance although they, too, received a gift today: a cheque to the tune of $1,000, paid them by the guardians. Minister of Welfare, Mr. David Croll, citing a new film contract signed on behalf of the babies, announced today that the coffers of the Dionne Quints have now reached half a million dollars and that this estate belongs to the Dionne family as a whole and not the Quints alone.

"I convey the government's congratulations to Mr. and Mrs. Oliva Dionne. These are their babies—we have never forgotten that fact. The important thing is that the children are here in the nursery specifically designed for their particular needs: that they have never been moved from the safety of Callander, never exploited nor cheapened, available always to their parents, who can—and do—visit them daily. . . . We would like everyone in Canada and the United States to come and visit them this summer."

In the newly signed contract, the Twentieth Century Fox will pay $250,000 for the rights to the next three feature pictures featuring the children, to be completed before the end of 1938. Another $50,000 will be paid in two years, in addition to the 10 per cent royalties the babies will receive from the net receipts from each picture. Thursday's new movie contract brought the quintuplets' cash on hand to $450,000, with more waiting in the wings.

June 5, 1936

Marie-Jeanne Lebel and Mme. Legros, the midwives who allowed me to stay the fateful night the quintuplets were born, have done the most astonishing thing. They have opened a souvenir stand just down the road toward Corbeil on a street-facing corner of the Legros property. Ivy convinced me to go and see it today. It is an enormous two-story structure with an open-air restaurant upstairs and shop on the bottom, topped with a sign that says MIDWIVES' PAVILION: REFRESHMENTS AND SOUVENIRS FROM THE MIDWIVES OF THE DIONNE QUINTUPLETS.

We wandered around the shop and gawked at all of the trinkets you can buy featuring our five babies. Etchings, postcards, spoons, cups, plates, bibs, baby bonnets and booties, tea towels, thimbles, hairbrushes, coasters, and candy bars, all of them adorned with the five faces of Annette, Yvonne, Cécile, Marie, and Émilie. They even had a slim pamphlet that they were selling for fifty cents detailing the night of the birth entitled "Administering Angels to the Dionne Quintuplets."

They both recognized us from that harrowing first week, but neither was particularly warm, although Mme. Lebel asked in her deep, minty voice about my mother and baby Edith. Neither of them is delivering babies anymore, they said. They are busy enough here, clearly, with all of the visitors stampeding through the doors.

Back at the nursery, Dr. Dafoe summoned me to his office to tell me that he has arranged for a special account to be opened in my name and that the stipend I receive for my artwork for Mrs. Fangel is being paid directly into that, rather than being added to my regular pay. I suspect Dr. Dafoe knows that I'm sending my entire salary home to Mother and Father, who need every little bit for baby Edith, so the fact that he is keeping this money separate has given me mixed feelings. Of course, I can do with it as I please, he said. "But if these times have taught us anything, it's that we should all have something set aside for a rainy day."

I can't think what rainy days he envisions in my future. But for now, this is my little secret, perhaps the first real secret I've had from my parents. It makes me feel older than my years.

Perhaps I should see about having Mme. Legros and Mme. Lebel sell some of my paintings in their shop. I bet they'd sell like hotcakes.

July 2, 1936 (*Toronto Star*)

PUBLIC MAY NOW SEE QUINTUPLETS BUT NOT QUINTUPLETS THE PUBLIC

NORTH BAY, Ontario—For the first time yesterday the quintuplets' new playground at Callander with its surrounding circular passageway to enable the public to view the children without the children themselves being aware of the fact was opened for public inspection.

Dr. A. R. Dafoe has been responsible for the construction of this unique children's recreation field.

In order to prevent the children being disturbed by the footsteps of visitors, the floor of the passageway will be covered with felt, over which will be laid cork linoleum. Inside the aluminium-sprayed wire screen will be sheets of glass to prevent the voices of the visitors carrying to the children.

This latter precaution was decided upon by Dr. Dafoe yesterday afternoon after he had carefully observed sound and visibility conditions when the first visitors were admitted. In conjunction with the playground and opening out from the passageway itself will be a private boudoir for the babies where they can be dressed and dried after their activities in the wading pool.

Used with permission.

July 8, 1936

Miss Emma Trimpany
Dafoe Hospital and Nursery
Callander, ON

Dear Miss Trimpany,

My father and I are hoping you might consider raising a delicate issue with Dr. Dafoe on our behalf. We've written to him ourselves, but I appreciate the good doctor receives a bushel of mail every day and our letter may have been lost in the shuffle.

My father and I are now making two, sometimes three trips per day between the nursery and the lakeshore—I fear we are in danger of emptying Lake Nipissing's beaches of stones once and for all. Indeed, we may be soon dredging the lake. It sounds improbable, but let me tell you: finding pebbles to fill the souvenir buckets at the Dafoe Nursery is becoming a considerable challenge. Our suggestion might be a sign reminding tourists to please restrict themselves to a single Quint-stone as a memento of their visit. In the past two years we estimate we have brought one and a half thousand tons of rocks and pebbles to the nursery and they have all disappeared into the pockets and purses of your many visitors, who take them God knows where. If I were Lake Nipissing, I might feel like someone was making off with the walls of my house. If the lake, set free, decides to take off after her stones, this will be a thirsty part of the world indeed.

I'm making light of the matter, but would you consider raising this issue? Joking aside, my father and I feel the public should be urged to exercise some restraint with regard to the fertility stones, if not to spare the world a population spike, then at least to keep us from digging a new quarry. Maybe the hospital would consider charging a small fee per pebble that would help keep some of these stones in our neck of the woods for future generations.

Yours respectfully,
Lewis Cartwright
25 Poplar Road
Callander, ON

July 10, 1936

We are melting. For the third day in a row the heat has soared above one hundred degrees. We've finished choking down a cold supper for which none of us had the slightest appetite. I am too hot to work on my sketches; the pastels slip from my fingers like sticks of butter.

Now that the sun is down, we've got the windows thrown open and fans whirring throughout the nursery to try to stir the soupy air. Nothing seems to help. The girls are cranky and restless and everything is *Non-non-non-non*, accompanied by much foot stamping and head shaking. Today, they peeled their dresses over their heads the minute we got them back inside from their outdoor play, and we resigned ourselves to letting them scamper around naked. We are trying to keep them cool with ice, constant fluids, and plenty of cool baths, but both Cécile and Annette have terrible heat rash and the others will no doubt get it too. Until this heat wave breaks, I think all of us will be crabbier than usual. Dr. Dafoe has wisely canceled the afternoon showing in the new playground until the heat abates: he believes it is simply not safe to have the girls outside. Even in the morning showings, we've had several ladies faint in the observation corridor, where it is hot as a furnace, with not a whisper of a draft. It's got plenty of windows, of course, but they are useless in terms of fresh air, since they all look out onto the girls' playground and can't be opened. Plus they are coated in a dark mesh, which makes them even hotter.

It took twice as long today to get the girls fed and dressed and their hair brushed and curled, only to have them look wilted within minutes. Their new playground is in shade for a few hours in the morning but gets very little in the way of a breeze, being surrounded by the walls of the viewing gallery on three sides and the entrance into the private playground and nursery on the other. Its saving grace is a wading pool, which all of the girls adore.

It's dreadful knowing that our every action there is on display. The babies don't realize a thing, thank goodness, and have been delighted with their new playground. It has a swing set and teeter-totter, a large sandbox with every shape of pail and trowel, the wading pool, a large grassy area, and a track around the perimeter, where they can push and pull their vast collection of wagons and wheeled toys. As for us nurses, we feel like fish in a fishbowl although no one is the slightest bit interested in us; they only have eyes for the little girls. I've spent my whole life with people gaping at my birthmark, and it seemed to be pulsing like a beacon my first few days in the public playground. It has gotten easier, although this heat is making my whole body flush as red as a strawberry; it's hard to know what is self-consciousness and what are the first signs of heatstroke.

The observation gallery is open for only half an hour at a time, but we've started to see long lineups forming hours before the doors open. Both of the entrances to the gallery have been fitted with a turnstile with an automatic counter built in: today's tally was 6,039 visitors over the course of the two showings. Nurse Noël has taken it upon herself to coax the girls to toddle around after a ball or play a game of copycat with her. Nurse Nicolette on the other hand tends to sulk on a bench in the shadows unless one of the girls summons her or needs her help. She is still on civil terms with the Dionnes and visits the farmhouse quite regularly although she's tight-lipped about her visits. What I wouldn't give to be able to take a peek into Elzire Dionne's kitchen and see how it's changed. I know M. Dionne is driving a new car, even though he still uses his truck on the farm. Ivy says M. Dionne receives five hundred dollars a month for being an official guardian for the quintuplets, even though he has never shown up for a single one of their meetings. That means the other guardians never received his approval to move ahead with this new playground.

I can't write another word. I'm too hot and irritable. I hope the heat breaks soon.

July 10, 1936—11:30 P.M.

AN UPDATE—IVY KNOCKED at my door about an hour ago. I wasn't asleep. It's too hot to sleep. She slipped into my room and whispered, "Grab your robe," then ducked back out into the corridor.

We tiptoed through the nursery, out the back door, then kept to the shadow of the fence as we crossed the old playground, or the "private" playground, as we call it now. We know all of the guards quite well, but what on earth would we tell them if one of them came across us sneaking through the property in our nightclothes in the middle of the night?

Ivy produced a key from her housecoat and unlocked the gate

that leads into the public observation playground, then locked it again once we were inside. The moon is merely a crescent tonight, peering down on us with a puckish, sideways smile as if it approved of the giggle fit that overcame us. The stars were as bright as I've ever seen, so many of them closely packed together that they seemed to smudge the black sky with silver, dusting the playground with a milky glow. The air tonight must be twenty degrees cooler than it had been during the day, but you could still feel it pulsing out of the walls of the enclosure and rising out of the earth itself.

I'd pulled my robe over my nightdress when I left my room, but the layers were unbearable. I could feel perspiration prickling on my back. I turned to Ivy to ask what on earth she had up her sleeve, but she had vanished. Squinting, I could just make her out by the wading pool at the other end of the yard, where the observation hall cast a long shadow over the grass. I skirted the yard on the tar track to join her. While I'd been ogling the night sky, she had been unhooking the canvas top from the wading pool and wrestling with the hose to top up the water.

Cranking the faucet closed, she bent over the pool to stir the water with her hand.

"Oh yes," she said. "I've been thinking about this for hours."

Before I could say anything, she was shrugging out of her housecoat and had whisked her nightdress over her head.

"Ivy!" I squeaked, my hand involuntarily slapping against my mouth to dampen the sound, wheeling around to look at the windows circling the yard.

"Shhhhh, Em!"

Ivy was stepping over the edge of the pool and into the black water. I could hear her breath catch as she sank herself down.

With her head below the rim of the pool, all I could spy was a flash of her white breasts beneath the water.

"What if someone sees you?" I asked, keeping my voice as soft as I could.

"Sees *me*? Sees us, you mean! Aren't you coming in?"

I could sense rather than see her limbs undulating in the shallow pool. "This is heaven," she murmured. "Heaven."

All I could think of was the long row of windows. What if people could still get into the observation area? What if the guards patrolled it? What if they could see Ivy, naked as the day she was born?

Ivy read my mind. "No one can see us, Em. Think of it. The doors to the observation area are locked religiously outside of visiting hours, and they've built this place so that you can't see in from anywhere else on the property. It's perfect. Now get in here."

I was slick with sweat in my robe and nightgown, and the sound of the water lapping at the edge of the pool was irresistible. Stepping back toward the wall, where the shadows were darkest, I slipped out of my robe. Then I took a deep breath, tugged my thin nightie over my head, and stepped clumsily into the pool.

The water was warmer than I'd expected, but still cooler than the air. I sank down until my chin was brushing the surface. I'd never done anything this brash in my life, and it felt, quite suddenly, amazing.

I started giggling, and Ivy joined me. I slid even more deeply into the shallow pool, so that any laughter leaking out would be muffled by the water. Then I sat up abruptly, goose pimples springing up on my skin.

"Do you think the girls pee in the water?" I asked. Now it was

Ivy's turn to smother her laugh with her hand. "Thierry changed the water today," she said when she could get the words out. "I saw him do it after Dr. Dafoe canceled the afternoon showing. So as long as *you* don't have a little accident, we're fine."

It was hard not to think about the windows, all those blank eyes staring, but Ivy was right. No one could get in there at this hour.

"Dr. Dafoe would kill us if he found out," I whispered.

"Do you think so?" Ivy mused. "I doubt it. As long as the newspapers didn't get ahold of the story." She snorted. "We're the only ones other than him that have lasted this long in this loony bin. I doubt he could get by without us."

Her words hung there for a moment, until I said quietly: "How much longer will you stay, Ivy?"

She didn't say anything for a long while, just lay back with her face turned toward the stars. She was languidly stirring the water, swishing her hands like the fins of a slow fish so that every now and again I saw her wrist bone, creamy white, nudging above the surface.

"I'm in no rush to go," she said at last. "I've told Fred I don't want to be wed until next summer. I'm needed here still, I think."

I felt relief, like a cool stream, flood through me.

"I'll stay as long as they'll have me," I said. Then, to lighten the mood, I added: "Or as long as I can stand working with crabby Nurse Nicolette." I thought I saw Ivy's crooked teeth flash in the starlight. "So take your time, please. I don't know how long I'd be able to survive here without you."

We stayed for another half an hour or so, stirring the water with our toes, talking from time to time, but mostly lying there quietly, looking up at the blinking stars.

"You know, I think I'm actually cooler," Ivy said finally. "For the first time in weeks!" I nodded my head. Then we both rose and stepped out of the pool.

September 14, 1936

THE NUMBER OF tourists passing through Callander has brought a kind of madness to our little town: half the houses on my old street now have rooms to let for a night or two, and Mother and Father have decided to do the same. They moved the baby's bassinet and change table into Mother's sewing room, which is really little more than a nook under the stairs, and have done over little Edith's room—my old room—to rent out to visitors.

"Just for the summer months, mind," is what Mother told me. I'm pleased for their sake that they are able to get a little extra income, but it does mean I can't spend a night with them anymore, at least not until winter, when things quiet down.

It was Lewis Cartwright who knocked quietly at the back door for me after he'd finished unloading the truck first thing this morning. His tongue seemed to be more tightly knotted than usual, and it took several long moments for him to untangle it and bid me good morning. I finally managed to get out of him that his father was feeling poorly so he, Lewis, would be delivering today's stones on his own, which takes a good deal more time.

I'm fond of chatty Mr. Cartwright and was sorry to hear that he wasn't well. "I hope your father starts to feel better soon," I said to make conversation as we walked to the truck. Lewis nodded earnestly and managed eventually to stammer something to the effect that his father was on the mend already and I needn't worry.

I hadn't spent any time on the Callander road since Ivy and I had gone to see the Midwives' Pavilion before the public playground opened in July. Our lives are so cloistered at the nursery, although I never think of it that way. Ivy will often go into North Bay to see a film with Fred and has encouraged me to join them, but I always beg off. I like to use my spare time to paint or draw. If I'm not working on my portraits of the girls, I will ask the guards to let me out the gate at the back of the property so I can take my sketchbook with me for a ramble through the forest, marsh, and pasture, rather than brave the traffic on the street.

It was not yet 8:00 in the morning by the time Lewis was nosing the truck out onto the road in front of the nursery, yet dozens and dozens of cars were already filling the new parking lot that's been cleared across from the nursery grounds. What I saw properly for the first time now were the structures M. Dionne has built adjacent to his farmhouse on the road to Callander, kitty-corner from the nursery. The larger building is long and squat, but a tall billboard rises at least another two stories out of the façade, capped with two-foot letters that spell OLIVA DIONNE. Beneath his name is a painting of the five girls, which in my opinion bears little resemblance to his daughters, flanked by bright white signs in French and English that read: THE ONLY SOUVENIR AND REFRESHMENT STAND OF THE FATHER OF THE QUINTUPLETS. Dotted on every square inch of the frontage were signs for ICE CREAM, REAL ENGLISH WOOLENS, and POP ON ICE. By comparison, the Dionne farmhouse, tucked behind and to one side, looked even smaller and more dilapidated than ever. To the left of the souvenir shop was a third building, almost as large but set well back from the road, with signage that read

PUBLIC WASHROOMS. Through my open window I could hear lively dance music being piped through loudspeakers somewhere on the Dionne property—a tinny, rasping sound that seemed falsely gay.

Most astonishing of all was the strip of canvas, at least five feet high and perhaps fifty yards long, strung between two towering poles on either side of the road with the words WELCOME TO QUINTLAND! in large block letters.

"My word!" I said, mostly to myself. "Quintland!"

Lewis nodded at me but said nothing.

We drove the few miles into town, and I gaped out the window at the steady stream of cars making their way to the nursery. I hadn't thought so many different makes of automobiles existed, let alone within driving distance of Callander. I spotted plates from as far away as British Columbia, Oregon, Florida, Texas, and California. Last year when I was regularly walking or riding my bicycle between the nursery and town, the road was a rutted track. Now the government has paved it all the way south to Orillia. Tiny cabins that have long sat in disrepair looked to have been spruced up with a coat of paint and bright curtains in the windows, all of them with signs that read ROOM FOR RENT and NO VACANCY. Halfway along the road to Corbeil we passed a filling station on a patch of land I swear was thick forest the last time I'd been by. Now I counted thirteen cars idling in wait for one of the five shiny new gas pumps painted in different colors, each emblazoned with the name of one of the quintuplets: Émilie, Cécile, Annette, Yvonne, and Marie.

"I had no idea," I breathed. Lewis glanced at me and bobbed his head, finally managing to say, "It's quite something, isn't it, Miss Trimpany?"

Closer to Callander, the vehicles were scarcely moving, with more cars and trucks of every shape and size joining the queue that snaked north out of town toward Corbeil.

We must have been thinking the same thing at the same time, because just as I was about to ask Lewis what time the line of cars might be expected to dissipate for the evening, he said softly: "It stays busy heading out of town until the two-thirty showing, then gets a bit jammed in the other direction. If you don't mind, Miss Trimpany, I'll wait until after six to fetch you this evening."

I was looking out the window at the clouds of dust mingling with the puffs of exhaust from the cars, a mix of eagerness and irritability written across the faces of the drivers and passengers.

"Of course," I said, realizing as I said it that even by taking me all the way into town instead of down to the lakeshore, Lewis was no doubt adding an extra hour to his workday.

I thanked him earnestly when we reached Mother and Father's house and again later when he deposited me back out here at the nursery. Our drive in the evening was much quicker and more peaceful, scarcely a car on the road. With my window open to the evening, I could hear the loons calling on the lake, the frogs croaking in the swamp, and the rustle of the birch leaves in the wind—all sounds I hadn't thought to miss that morning amid all the engine noise. I turned to look at Lewis and realized his eyes were on the sky, although they dipped every few seconds to keep an eye out for moose or wild turkeys dashing onto the empty road. I leaned forward and saw a flock of little birds, diving and wheeling in the dusk, but as if in a single formation. Lewis glanced my way and smiled. "Starlings," he said. "There are more and more on Lake Nipissing every year. They call this"—he made a circle in the air with his hand, as if clearing steam from a mirror—"a murmuration." He slowed the truck, and the flock seemed to warm to its audience, the many birds funneling this way and that, as if they were being swirled in a pot.

We sat in silence for a moment. "Extraordinary," I said, straining to watch as the little swarm climbed into the darker sky, then dipped past the truck. And quite abruptly they were gone.

I was bursting to talk about it with Ivy—not just the birds but the daytime crowds, the lines of traffic, M. Dionne's gigantic shop. But Ivy gave a laugh and rolled her eyes at me, saying, "I've been telling you for ages, Em! It's been like this for months."

September 28, 1936 (*Toronto Star*)

QUINTS WORTH MILLION
ANNUALLY TO NORTH BAY

Estimates Indicate 350,000 U.S.
Tourists This Year Spent That Sum

U.S. citizens left over a million dollars in this city and district during the past summer's visits to the Dionne quintuplets, according to estimates. Dr. Allan Roy Dafoe reports that about 500,000 persons made the trek to the Dafoe hospital to see the infants. At least 350,000 were from the United States.

Every night during the summer months all hotels, tourist homes, and cabins were dragging in the welcome mat and hanging out the standing room only sign. Men, women, and children literally went begging for a place to sleep.

Used with permission.

October 25, 1936

Something is troubling Ivy, but she won't tell me what it is. I've pressed her, but she just shakes her head. It's not Fred—if anything, they seem even closer, more openly tender to one another than I've ever seen them. They still have not announced a wedding date, but Ivy insists she is in no rush.

We are all so exhausted. Nurse Nicolette left Saturday for a few weeks' leave to visit her family in Quebec, so I hope, when she is back, Ivy can take a proper holiday. The girls are also running us ragged. We've had to move the bookshelves and rocking chairs out of the playroom because the girls were forever trying to climb on top of them. The other day they took the cushions off the settee and heaped them underneath the windowsills, then one by one were boosting each other up onto the ledge and leaping off. I nearly had a heart attack when I walked in to find my little Émilie readying herself to launch into the air. Cécile and Annette are always very contrite after they've been reprimanded for doing something silly, but Yvonne, Marie, and Émilie will don expressions of utter surprise, as if to say, *I'm terribly sorry, it never occurred to us that this would be a problem for you!*

Dr. Blatz believes they should be given total freedom in their play, so long as they are not putting themselves or others in harm's way. Mme. Dionne clearly disapproves of this and scolds the girls in a loud voice if she sees them doing something she doesn't like. Last week they'd made up a game that saw them twirling one another around and around until they all fell over in a heap, giggling and rolling about. Cécile, who typically does anything she can to please her mother when she visits, unwittingly performed a floppy somersault that left her upside down with her skirt over her head. The others found this immensely funny and immediately started trying to imitate her maneuver. Mme. Dionne was not amused, however. She marched over to Cécile and yanked her upright, tugging her skirt back down over her knees and calling her a naughty girl. I could see Ivy's face flushing, and a minute later she had Cécile in her arms and announced it was time for a snack, which meant the visit was over.

Perhaps it's Mme. Dionne that's causing Ivy to look so piqued.

November 5, 1936

Nurse Nicolette is not coming back. Dr. Dafoe gave us the news this morning after he'd been through the daily charts with Ivy and had his visit with the girls. They can all say "Doh-Doh Dafoe" and will rush to the windows when they hear his car crunching on the gravel outside. He delivered the news about Nurse Nicolette as if he were telling us the day of the week, his expression blank, his voice flat, giving no reason or explanation. I shot a glance at Ivy, and I could tell right away that this wasn't new information for her.

Ivy managed to avoid my questions all morning, sequestering herself with Dr. Dafoe to review applicants for the open position—only Francophones, of course. The Association

Canadienne-Française d'Éducation de l'Ontario has waded into the fray at the request of the Dionnes, demanding assurances that the girls would be raised as French Catholics.

And of course the girls don't actually need nurses anymore. They are all robust and healthy. I can't help but worry that this means they might be returned to their parents sometime sooner than we'd hoped, but, on the other hand, why would the government have spent the time, effort, and money to build the observation area if the children might soon be living with their parents again?

When Ivy finally joined us in the playroom, we were doing "art" with the girls, which means colorful handprints all over their tables, chairs, smocks, and faces. Ivy smiled to see the mess they were making, but I could tell her thoughts were elsewhere.

Only after the girls were all tucked away for the night did I tap on the door of Ivy's room. Fred had given her a windup gramophone for her birthday and it was playing "I'm Putting All My Eggs in One Basket" from a film they'd seen together.

She opened the door, making a face. "I knew you'd come."

She beckoned me in and closed the door behind me, then went to her machine and gently lifted the needle, placing it back at the beginning of the record.

I plunked myself on her bed while she fussed with things, pulling a pair of stockings from the radiator and bundling them into a drawer. Fred Astaire crooned into the silence.

I couldn't keep quiet any longer. "Ivy."

She sighed and pulled the chair away from the desk and sat down.

"It's Inès," she said. "Nurse Nicolette." Ivy's eyes flickered. She looked tired, and sad. "She's pregnant."

I thought I'd misheard.

"Pregnant?"

Ivy watched it sink in.

Nurse Nicolette almost never went anywhere; she certainly had never mentioned having a beau as far as I knew. There are so few men in our sheltered lives, other than the visiting doctors, the handyman, the groundskeeper, and the police constables charged with protecting us. Then there's Fred, who is spoken for, and Dr. Dafoe, of course. But Dr. Dafoe seems ancient— more like an avuncular antique than someone who could sire a child. I realize, writing this, that he's likely not much older than my own father, who now has an infant daughter at home. But Inès Nicolette with a lover? Inès Nicolette, with her lumpy uniform and twitchy face, always starting like a rabbit?

"Who is the father?" I asked finally.

Ivy shrugged and said nothing.

"How far along?"

"I don't know." She sighed. "I bet Dr. Dafoe doesn't know either. She was back in Quebec City, or whatever the name of her village is, over Easter as you'll recall, but who knows." She looked down at her hands.

"My best guess is she has someone back in Quebec or"—Ivy paused—"or it's someone she's met through the Dionnes. They seem to be related to half of Corbeil." I thought back to all the Sundays Nurse Nicolette had spent having dinner across the street.

Ivy was quiet for a moment, then said: "Whatever it is, we're not going to hear it from her."

"My word," I breathed. The song had ended, and the needle was making a swish-bump, swish-bump sound at the center of the player. Ivy stood again and lifted the needle back to the edge of the record. She wanted the music to muffle our conversation, I realized.

"Nurse Noël doesn't know," I said.

Ivy shook her head.

"But Dr. Dafoe does?"

Ivy nodded. "And he's adamant that it stay quiet, that nothing be done." She lifted her hands to her face, covering her eyes and shaking her head. "I told him Inès may need some help, there may be something we should do, especially if someone in Corbeil is the father, not someone out East. A young woman, with child, unmarried—in small-town Quebec, no less. Who knows what will happen to the baby, let alone to her. Her family might take in the child, but—" She didn't finish, didn't need to. We'd both grown up hearing the same wide-eyed tales of unwed mothers—all scandalous plots with no proper endings.

She sat down on the bed beside me. "But Dr. Dafoe says there's nothing we can do, nothing we *should* do. He doesn't want the newspapers to learn of it." She glanced up at my face. "You can't breathe a word of it, Em. He can't know that I told you. It's not my secret to share."

I reached over, took her hand, and gave it a squeeze. "Of course," I said.

"This place is getting to me." Ivy waved her free hand, gesturing at nothing in particular. "The strict schedules, the rules, all the things we can and cannot do, when we can cuddle the girls and when we can't. Everything done for the sake of appearances. For Pete's sake, we curl the girls' hair every morning, yet their hair is perfectly beautiful straight. Why are we curling their hair, Em?"

She closed her eyes and put her head on my shoulder.

"You need a break yourself, Ivy. You've taken on so much here."

What I was thinking was that Ivy now wouldn't be able to take a break, not until we found Nurse Nicolette's replacement.

As if reading my mind, Ivy murmured, "We're starting interviews tomorrow. There are several local women who trained as teachers. French, of course. I hope we can find someone who's a good fit."

"As good a fit as Nurse Nicolette?" I said, then bit my lip.

Ivy's head was still on my shoulder so I couldn't see her smile, but I could feel a muscle moving ever so slightly in her temple.

"It would be hard to find a worse fit than Nurse Nicolette," she agreed, and we both had a quiet laugh.

November 20, 1936

I'D BE FINE if I never heard the words *corn syrup* ever again, let alone tasted the wicked stuff. It is all anyone can talk about. The Dionnes have now come out and said point-blank that they only ever buy Crown brand and that this must have been the corn syrup given to the quintuplets when they were born. Dr. Dafoe, meanwhile, is adamant that the girls were fed Bee Hive brand. Ivy says it's all ludicrous because if anyone should remember what blooming brand of syrup she bloody well gave to the babies, it would be her, and yet she herself can't recall. Fred has told us that it all boils down to money. Doesn't it always? The Crown brand company delivered a crate of corn syrup a few days after the babies were born and paid M. Dionne five hundred dollars in exchange for exclusive advertising rights. The other company, St. Lawrence Starch, sent a hundred-dollar donation to Dr. Dafoe right after the babies were born, then delivered a whole case of Bee Hive brand corn syrup to the farmhouse a week later. It's a wonder we weren't all bathing in it! Later that summer, after the government took custody of the babies, the

Bee Hive company paid one thousand dollars to the guardians for exclusive rights to call themselves the official corn syrup of the Dionne quintuplets, and they've held sway ever since. And I suppose, as a result, M. Dionne lost the chance of making a lot of money, along with the Crown brand syrup people, who are now suing. I really don't understand business or law one bit, but it is plain as day that this lawsuit isn't merely about money and syrup, it's about the Dionnes and Dr. Dafoe. The ridiculous thing is, we don't even feed the babies corn syrup. Dr. Blatz believes sugar in any form is bad for children. I should tell that to the newspapers.

November 30, 1936

IVY HAS CONVINCED me to join the staff outing to North Bay to see *Reunion*. The newspapers say the quintuplets appear in the movie for only a few minutes, which means hours' worth of film must have been cut! A shame given the hassles of shooting in the middle of a hot summer. Everyone from the nursery received a special invitation from the theater, and so we are all going, including Fred, Dr. Dafoe, and the quintuplets' newest minder, Miss Stephanie Beaulieu—everyone is going to go except for the guards and Nurse Noël, who says she doesn't like films anyhow. Miss Beaulieu is fully bilingual, comes recommended by Dr. Blatz, and has trained in his program at St. George's. She strikes me as a very serious woman, her brow constantly furrowed, her close-set eyes blinking behind tiny wire-framed glasses. She has clearly read a book about the importance of smiling, however, because several moments after the girls have done something silly, her cheeks will jolt upward, yanking her thin lips into a smile as if someone has pulled a cord.

Ivy says she wants to talk to me tonight, when we're in the city. We will try to slip away from the others for a cup of tea or something so as to snatch a bit of time to ourselves.

December 2, 1936 (*Toronto Star*)

QUINTUPLETS' NURSE IS OFF FOR HOLIDAY

Miss Yvonne Leroux Is Granted Leave of Absence

NORTH BAY, Ontario—Nurse to the Dionne quintuplets since the day of their birth, Yvonne Leroux is taking a holiday, Dr. A. R. Dafoe announced today. Miss Leroux will take a leave of absence for an indefinite period, Dr. Dafoe confirmed.

Miss Leroux arrived at the Dionne home about five o'clock on the afternoon the world-famous sisters were born, and except for an occasional brief holiday has attended them ever since. The case was her first after graduation from St. Joseph's General Hospital here.

Dr. Dafoe has decided not to see the latest Quints picture, "Reunion," now showing here. The hospital staff were guests of the theatre Monday night, but Dr. Dafoe was taken ill and did not join his hardworking team.

December 4, 1936

Today is Ivy's last day before she heads off on her "holiday," as she persists in calling it. As if she is definitely going to come back. I don't think either of us believes it.

I'm just so desperately sad. I've known this was coming, I suppose, but I didn't expect her to leave until she actually got married. I can't imagine what it will be like here without her any more than I can imagine being in Ivy's shoes and setting off on this great adventure.

The Newspaper Enterprise Association has organized for her to spend six months giving a series of lectures all across the United States about her work as the head nurse at the Dafoe Nursery. Her first stop is New York, where she is going to broadcast a five-part radio serial on the first two years of the babies' lives. I've always thought Ivy had a lovely voice. It's a tremendous opportunity and she will be very well paid, with all her expenses covered, and she'll get to see so much of the world. She and Fred have agreed to postpone their wedding until the following year, at the earliest, but I can't believe that means she will come back to us when her tour is over.

Whatever she and Dr. Dafoe discussed the day of the premiere left her very upset, and the doctor didn't join us at the theater after all. I asked Ivy if he feels she is nabbing some of the spotlight from him, because he has certainly enjoyed many American speaking engagements himself over the past two years. When I said that, she flashed her snaggle-toothed smile and threw an arm around my shoulders, saying, "You don't miss a beat, Emma Trimpany."

The thing is, I simply don't think she would have accepted this offer if it had come a few months ago, before Dr. Blatz arrived with all his rules and measurements, before things got so ridiculous with the Dionnes. M. Dionne is now threatening to sue Dr. Dafoe for speaking English to the girls. We're fed up with all the talk of lawsuits. The corn syrup lawsuit is dragging on and on—there's a good chance Dr. Dafoe is going to be called in to testify. I can't understand why this all matters so much.

Ivy won't discuss it, but I think she is also upset about what happened with Nurse Nicolette. We've never heard another word from her, although even if she'd written there's a chance her letter might have gone astray. Father has told me that the nursery continues to get bulging bags of mail every week, all of it handled by Dr. Dafoe. He has said he is getting a secretary in the New Year to keep up on the volume.

"Did you write to *her*?" I asked Ivy. She was in her room packing up some last things. I could scarcely watch.

She looked upset at my question. "I have asked Dr. Dafoe for her address and he flatly refused to provide it, saying he needs to protect her privacy. I asked Fred if he would help me track it down, but he, too, says that if she wants to get in touch she will."

She paused and let the dress she was folding fall rumpled into her suitcase. "But what happened, Em?" She shook her head.

"Something happened. Something happened here, I think, and Dr. Dafoe has decided it's no one's business."

Then she turned to me and pulled my hands from my lap, holding both of them in hers, looking me straight in the eye. She looked sad and worried.

"You'll be careful, won't you? You keep your eyes open. Keep the girls safe, but keep yourself safe too. Can you do that for me?"

I nodded and stood, giving her a hug. Then, because I thought I might start crying, I left and came back here to scribble down all my silly self-pity. I keep expecting to hear her knock and poke her head around the door to say, "Forget it, I've changed my mind, I don't want to see the world. My world is here, with the girls and with you."

But of course she won't be knocking.

December 10, 1936 (*Montreal Gazette/Canadian Press*)

$150,000 SUIT OVER SYRUP FED QUINTS

Callander Grocer Testifies as to Brand Purchased by Oliva Dionne

TORONTO, Ontario—James McDonald, manager of a Callander grocery store, said in assize court today that Oliva Dionne bought a ten-pound tin of Crown Brand corn syrup from him "two or three days" before the Dionne quintuplets were born.

The brand named is a product of the Canada Starch Company, which is suing the St. Lawrence Starch Company for $150,000, claiming that the defendants falsely advertised their brand of corn syrup was the first to be fed to the Quints.

Canada Starch contends that its Crown Brand has this honour.

Also acting as witness for the plaintiffs, was Miss Alma Dionne, the quintuplets' aunt, who said she was at the Dionne home May 30, 1934, following the birth of the quintuplets. She had helped Nurse Leroux prepare the food in the evening and had assisted in feeding the children and that Crown Brand syrup was used.

Before the suit ends, Dr. Allan Roy Dafoe, physician to the famous sisters, will likely appear as witness, having been subpoenaed to testify for the defence.

Sidelights on the birth of the Dionnes was given the court when Marie-Jeanne Lebel told how she was called as a midwife by Oliva Dionne to his home about 2am on that eventful day. She stayed until 8:30 at night on the Monday following the babes' birth and testified that they only got warm water that day. Mrs. Lebel told the court that when she visited the babies on the Wednesday following their birth on the dining room table was a big tin of Crown Brand syrup.

December 21, 1936

Miss Emma Trimpany
Dafoe Hospital and Nursery
Callander, ON

Dear Em,

Just because I haven't written doesn't mean I'm not thinking
of you and the girls and the nursery a dozen times a day. How
are you all doing? Who else has joined the staff? More impor-
tantly, what is the latest on Maman and Papa Dionne? I can
tell you, the Americans absolutely adore every bit of news they
can get on the quintuplets and Dr. Dafoe, but they are very
hard on the parents. The press characterizes them as ignorant
peasants, which makes me smile when I think of M. Dionne in
his shirt and tie and his fancy hats, selling his signature for 25
cents from his colossal souvenir stand.

Mind you, if I were born and raised in New York, I might
think the same thing. This city is simply extraordinary—you
will have to visit one day. The buildings are so tall you'd think
they might blow over in a strong wind if they weren't made
of stone and steel. And all of the restaurants and theaters and
dance clubs, the crush of people and cars on the streets, it's hard
to describe how busy and noisy it all is. It puts the Callander-
Corbeil traffic in perspective, I can tell you. And the ladies'
fashions here would amaze you. Every day I'm seeing more
women in trousers, often cut so wide that each leg could be a
full-length skirt in and of itself. But wouldn't that be so much
more comfortable than skirts and stockings, particularly this
time of year? What would Fred think of me in trousers, I won-

der. He is coming down to visit after Christmas. Perhaps I'll splurge on a pair and surprise him.

Suffice it to say, this experience has been everything I imagined it would be and more. I am enjoying the preparations for the radio show, and everyone has been wonderfully kind and enthusiastic, saying they expect the ratings for the show will be off the charts. Frankly it's hard for me to understand why anyone would be interested in tuning in for a half hour to hear how many diapers we changed each day, or how we managed bath time for five, but our listeners, I'm told, will be hanging on every word.

I miss them so much. Do write and tell me how they are doing. Funny. Now I'm the one wanting desperately to know about diapers and baths.

All my love,
Ivy

1937

January 6, 1937

Ivy's voice on the radio this afternoon: her program comes on when the girls are having their outdoor nap. The weather was clear today and not too cold, so they were bundled in quilts and mufflers, the winter sun desperately trying to seek them out through the bleached canvas tops of their prams. If it weren't for my girls, I would wish for colder weather and bleak days, something more suited to my gloomy spirits.

Is it better or worse to hear Ivy's voice? It is hard to think of the voice as Ivy's, because for it to be Ivy it means she is, in fact, miles and miles away, in New York City. Yet the voice is hers, absolutely, in every way. Low and rolling, which is how I know she is smiling as she speaks. If the girls had woken today and heard her, they'd have been dumbfounded with joy, twisting this way and that, I'm sure: "Nurse Lewoo? Nurse Lewoo?" They missed her dreadfully those first few weeks, tantrums, tears, and looking up sharply whenever a door opened and a white uniform stepped into the room. The sight of their little faces falling over and over again. It tore my heart in pieces, every time.

The announcer calls her Nurse Yvonne Leroux, Nurse to the Famous Dionne Quintuplets. A mouthful. Today he asked her about the health-giving qualities of fresh-air naps, and that prompted me to pop my head out on the porch and make sure the girls were still sleeping. He asked her about cod-liver oil and pabulum, and when to introduce carrots and peas. "And do the Quints all play together? Or do they tend to keep each to herself? What are their favorite toys?"

Ivy had all the answers on the tip of her tongue. So do I. If we didn't, we could consult the record books, shelves of them, every little detail observed and noted for posterity. But we know them, we know them so well.

January 8, 1937

MOTHER HAS BROKEN her ankle on the ice. They kept her at St. Joe's in North Bay for a few days, but she's now been sent home. Dr. Dafoe was clearly vexed by the news, as if somehow I could be at fault, but agreed with a deep sigh to let me cut back my shifts so I can spend more time helping at home.

Strange to be back in my old room—all done up fresh for paying guests in the summer months—but lovely to have some time with little Edith. She is a chubby, busy bundle these days, all tiny front teeth and smiles, lumbering around the house on sturdy legs.

Dr. Dafoe has arranged for the Cartwrights to pick me up at Mother and Father's and take me out to the nursery before the 8:00 A.M. breakfast, then bring me home straight after the late-day meal. A local girl comes in during the day to help Mother and look after Edith while Father is at the post office, but I'm typically back home to help with supper, bathing, and bed. I'm exhausted, but at least it's kept my mind off missing Ivy.

Most days it's Lewis Cartwright who ferries me to and fro. He is marginally more at ease with me now that we're seeing each other twice a day, his words faltering only if I catch him off guard with a nosy question. When I insisted that he stop calling me Miss Trimpany, he shyly asked that I call him Lewis, which I am doing, although I notice he has yet to call me by my given name. He is a homely man, Lewis, with large, protruding ears and a long, pointy nose that looks as if it was somehow stretched to fit the proportions of his narrow face. But it's a kindly face, I think.

He surprised me tonight by asking after Ivy.

"Is she enjoying her travels down South?"

I feel her absence like a wound that won't knit. Her radio program has ended and she's written only the once. Fred brought news of her from his trip to see her over the holidays. Some newspaper friends of his took them to see jazz music in Harlem, which is a part of New York City that is almost all Negroes. I've never seen a Negro in my life. Fred also told me that Alexander Dolls, which are made in Harlem, have released a Nurse Leroux doll and Ivy got to meet Madame Alexander herself. Maybe I need to order myself a Nurse Leroux doll.

"I miss her so much," I said softly.

I was blinking back tears so turned to look out the window. After several weeks of clear skies, we had fresh snow today, inches of it lining the roofs and fence posts like icing on a cake. Even the trees looked surprised by the weight of it in their branches. The wheels of the truck made a shushing sound in the fresh snow, and the moon was painting the road and fields with a soft blue wash. Warmer lights streamed from the windows of the neighboring farms, smoke curling from their chimneys. Everything looked so calm and quiet, quite the opposite of summer's honk and hubbub.

How strange it must be for all these hardworking folks, tending their sleepy farms for all these years, now having to contend with a crush of cars, buses, and strangers making their way out to see the quintuplets.

"These farmers must be glad in winter, when all the tourists leave these roads," I said. Lewis cocked his head. "That they must," he said. Then, after sorting out his words, he added: "There's n-not a farm on this stretch that hasn't taken to renting rooms in the summer, though, and that—that's been a big help for families. So winter brings both good and bad."

We drove in silence for a minute or two, then Lewis cleared his throat and said:

"You and Nurse Leroux, you are the only ones who've been with the babies since they were born, is that right? You—you are like mothers to them, I'm sure. It must be hard on them too."

I turned to look at him. Everyone knew Ivy had been with the quintuplets since the day they were born, but almost no one tended to remember that I'd been there too. That I'd been there from their first halting cries.

"They miss her very much," I said.

"So much coming and going, it can't be good for them," he said gruffly as he pulled up outside of Mother and Father's. "Don't you up and leave them now."

I opened the door and stepped down. "I'm not going anywhere," I said. "Unless of course you forget to fetch me tomorrow morning."

His lips twitched a fraction, then he tipped his hat, and said, "See you tomorrow, miss."

January 9, 1937

Miss Emma Trimpany
Dafoe Hospital and Nursery
Callander, ON

Dear Emma,

Greetings from frigid New York. I hope you are staying warm and dry.

I think your latest batch of sketches is very good. You are trying something different with the eyes, I see. The big beautiful eyes on those girls! They aren't easily captured with charcoals. Are you using the watercolors at all? Send me some of those if you can. I think being able to nuance the colors more subtly might help you get the effect you are looking for.

I've been following with interest the big corn syrup debacle up there. Would you believe it made the *New York Times*? That's how much Americans love the Quints. One of my first portraits of the girls was purchased by the Bee Hive company, whichever one that is—I can't keep them straight. I'm sure you've seen the ad: the girls gathered around a daisy in the garden. I'm very fond of that series. It did make me think of your earliest drawings of the babies—remember the sketchbook you showed me when I first met you at the nursery? I recall very clearly the pencil drawings you did of the babies in their first few days of life, how you captured their tiny alien forms, yet also somehow conveyed their preciousness, if that's not too trite to say. Surely there was a series of sketches you did with the corn syrup tins and the eyedroppers? Did those drawings, perchance, include the detail on the syrup tins? I mostly remember that everything seemed wildly out of proportion, the babies were so very small and the droppers looked like turkey basters. You've come a long way since then, my dear. None of my business, of course, but I wondered if you'd thought to look back at those drawings. Perhaps they hold the clue!

I look forward to seeing your latest,
Maud Tousey Fangel
145 East 72nd
New York, NY

January 11, 1937

Dr. Dafoe asked me to come to his office this morning while the girls were having their midmorning snack, or "Nourishment" as Miss Beaulieu insists on calling it. I know the doctor is under a good deal of stress these days as the wretched corn syrup suit drags on, and the prospect of being summoned to appear before the court must be weighing on him. Even when he's with the girls, his mind is elsewhere, despite them tugging at his white coat and dragging him this way and that, badgering him with questions in their mix of French, English, and Quintuplese, as Nurse Noël has started calling it, her several chins wobbling in disapproval. Today the doctor twice confused Yvonne and Cécile, which he hasn't done in a long time. We've started dressing them in different colors: Annette in red, Marie in blue, Yvonne in pink, Cécile in green, and Émilie in a creamy white. Even Miss Beaulieu has no trouble telling them apart now, unless they are in the bath.

When I got to the doctor's office, he was frowning over a large ledger, but closed it quickly as I entered. He offered me a brief smile, little more than a crease in his moon-shaped face.

He patted the ledger on his desk.

"You've no doubt been following the newspapers. They are having a field day over this corn syrup lawsuit."

I nodded.

"Of course, it was, without a doubt, Bee Hive brand corn syrup, the brand produced by the St. Lawrence Starch Company, that we used in the first feedings, and I am quite prepared to testify on that point. It occurs to me, however, that no one has likely asked you. In fact"—he paused and looked uncharacteristically sheepish—"I've quite forgotten whether you were there at the farmhouse at that time, before the breast milk arrived, or not."

I cleared my throat. "Yes," I said. "I was there that whole week."

Dr. Dafoe was watching me closely, then said: "You may not be aware that Nurse Leroux has submitted a signed affidavit saying she cannot remember which brand she used. And yet I *know* unequivocally that it was Bee Hive brand."

He paused, his beady eyes unblinking. "If she does happen to recall, even the smallest details, she will almost certainly be called upon to return from her American tour to appear before the court."

I was looking at Dr. Dafoe's mustache, which was wider and longer than it had been when the girls were born. Whiter too. Many men were growing their mustaches differently now, I noticed. No one wanted to look like that madman in Germany. Then I registered what he was saying. *Ivy might come home.*

"I'm afraid I don't remember either," I said. "I would have spoken up sooner if I had, but it's all a blur now."

Dr. Dafoe pursed his lips and tucked his chin, but he was watching me steadily. When he spoke, it was in a low voice, slow and careful.

"I expect you, like me—like all of us here at the nursery—have concerns about the quintuplets' futures. They are likely to lead very special lives. I do see it as a key part of my duties as guardian to help safeguard their futures."

He reached across his desk for his pipe. "St. Lawrence Starch Company has, for some time, been a major benefactor of the quintuplets, in return for advertising rights, of course. Canada Starch Company, on the other hand, has been sour grapes, although I gather they've signed a deal with M. Dionne involving his other children." He patted his pockets, looking for matches. "I hope, for the sake of our girls here, that this case gets thrown out once and for all."

"If there is anything I could do, I would do it," I said earnestly. I meant it.

"Of course, of course," Dr. Dafoe murmured and slipped his pipe in his mouth. "Let's hope Nurse Leroux remembers something. Anything. Anything at all." With his pipe tucked in the corner of his mouth, it was hard to tell if he was smiling or wincing. "And it might be nice if she had to come back for a bit, wouldn't it? If she was called back to testify? Perhaps, when she was finished in court, she could rearrange some of her tour dates and come visit us for a few days. I'm sure the girls would like that."

January 12, 1937

Miss Emma Trimpany
Dafoe Hospital and Nursery
Callander, ON

Dear Em,

I'm sorry to hear about your mother. Can't Dr. Dafoe give
you a bit of time off? I bet there's no time for sketching with
all that to and fro.

Fred and I had a wonderful week—has he told you much
about it? He has so many connections through the newspaper syndicates, we were swept from one party to the
next. We saw some live music, we danced our shoes off,
and had some extraordinary suppers. What a production it
is, dining out in New York. I'm not sure most New York-
ers are aware of just how hard a time people are having in
other places. Mind you, there are long lines of people out
of work here, too, lining up for hot meals at the churches
and sleeping under the bridge not far from my hotel. It
gives you pause.

How are my beautiful girls? Has Marie put on any more
weight? I hope so.

I had a letter from Dr. Dafoe, who remains unimpressed
with my decision to go on this speaking tour. He thinks
I might need to testify in this ridiculous corn syrup case
after all. I've already made a statement to the lawyers that
I have no recollection whatsoever of what blooming syrup
we may or may not have used, and I simply can't take the

time away from my tour to go to some stuffy courtroom in Toronto.

I miss you. Write and tell me that you are sketching again. Better yet, send me a drawing of the girls.

My very best,
Ivy

January 13, 1937

I decided to do something today, something to help the babies. If I'd felt, in my heart, that what I was doing was wrong, my hands would have trembled and my pencil lines would have betrayed me, I'm sure of it. But they didn't. I was steady. I'm not sure this is honest, but I also think there is something even more important than honesty at stake, and that is doing what is right for our girls. I told Dr. Dafoe I would help if I could, and I have. I will bring this to him tomorrow and it will be for him to decide what to do.

It was Mrs. Fangel who made me think of it. I'm grateful to her, even if I can never tell her what I've done. I can't tell anyone what I've done, not even Ivy.

January 20, 1937

THE THING I wanted most was to talk to Ivy, just the two of us, even if that meant ducking out of the courthouse for a cup of tea. How naïve to think such a thing would even be possible. The court was an absolute zoo, inside and out, and I never got within twenty feet of Ivy, let alone close enough to have a private word. After court was adjourned, Mr. McCarthy's assistant whisked me to the train station, and I hoped I might see her there or, better yet, perhaps we'd be taking the train back to Callander together so she could have a visit with the girls. Ridiculous. According to McCarthy's man, St. Lawrence Starch put her up in a hotel in downtown Toronto and she'll be on the first train back to New York tomorrow. Does she truly realize what I did? Is she okay with it? Back when the babies were born, I drew my little sketches for myself and myself alone. They were never intended to be anything more than mementos of those extraordinary days.

Mr. D. L. McCarthy, defense attorney for the St. Lawrence Starch Company, is surely the only person who could have enjoyed himself today. He strutted around the courtroom like a peacock, badgering Ivy with questions and pestering her for irrelevant details, all of which delighted the mob crammed into the public gallery. Ivy sat so tall and poised, meeting his eye and ignoring the whistles and catcalls from the gawking crowd, everyone frantic to get her attention. I was so proud of her I could have burst.

"Miss Leroux, can you please remind the court, in brief, about the state of the health of the five Dionne babies when you arrived at their place of birth?"

For Pete's sake. There wasn't a person in the province of Ontario who didn't know how dire things were those first few harrowing days.

"They were born two months premature and were extremely frail," Ivy said evenly. "They had tiny arms and legs, no thicker than my thumb, and relatively large heads and abdomens. Several were having trouble breathing. Expectations for their survival were very low."

"Tell me . . ." Mr. McCarthy paused for effect, nestling his chin toward his chest. "Is corn syrup generally considered an important component in such cases?"

Ivy, I could tell, was trying not to roll her eyes. "I do not believe so, no."

Mr. McCarthy then took his line of questions along a wide and meandering path: where did Ivy train as a nurse? When did she arrive at the farmhouse that fateful day? How did corn syrup come to be used? How had it been given? How much was used?

Ivy explained that Dr. Dafoe had provided a specific formula of water, cow's milk, and corn syrup, to be given by dropper because no breast milk was to be had. When she explained that a mere ounce or two of corn syrup had been used, the crowd in the courtroom started hooting with laughter again, so that the judge had to bang his gavel. I can well imagine what everyone was thinking: what a tremendous waste of time, money, and newsprint for two lousy ounces of syrup.

The lawyer then asked Ivy whether she had recorded the brand of corn syrup in her nursing notes. This time Ivy gave him a withering look. She was thinking the same thing I was: that we, summoning every ounce of energy to keep the girls alive through the night, would never have dreamed of jotting down the *brand* of corn syrup in the nursery records.

"Let the record note that Miss Leroux says she did not make note of the brand of corn syrup in her nursing report," Mr. McCarthy chirruped. "Now, Miss Leroux, you signed an affidavit December 20, 1936, stating that you had no recollection what brand of corn syrup was used on the day that the mixture was prepared and given to the Dionne quintuplets. Is that the case today? You have no recollection of what brand of corn syrup was used?"

Ivy held his eye. "The brand of corn syrup was Bee Hive."

"Bee Hive brand corn syrup, produced by the St. Lawrence Starch Company of Port Credit, Ontario?"

Ivy glanced down, and I didn't hear her response.

"Can you please repeat your answer more forcefully, Miss Leroux? Do you believe the corn syrup used in the formula fed to the Dionne quintuplets to be Bee Hive brand corn syrup, produced by the St. Lawrence Starch Company of Port Credit, Ontario?"

"Yes."

A loud rumble erupted around the courtroom as if set loose from a cage. The judge again called for order.

Mr. McCarthy now sounded positively jubilant. "Miss Leroux, can you explain why your testimony today contradicts your earlier affidavit of December twentieth? What has jogged your memory?"

Ivy's voice was soft but firm. "I've recently been shown evidence that Bee Hive brand was the brand used."

"Evidence?" Mr. McCarthy raised his eyebrows in mock surprise. "Can you be more specific?"

Ivy was trying not to look at me, I was sure of it. "Another nurse—actually, a nursing assistant—who was helping to care for the quintuplets: she did several sketches of the babies in the first week after their birth. One of the drawings includes the tin of corn syrup."

"A drawing of a tin of corn syrup?" he repeated, and the courtroom roared with laughter.

"A pencil sketch of me, giving one of the babies the formula from an eyedropper, but a tin of corn syrup and a bottle of milk are also pictured in the drawing."

Mr. Payne, the attorney for Canada Starch Company, had

been chewing angrily on his lower lip, his mustache twitching. Now he sprang up from his seat, the words spraying from his mouth. "Objection! Your Honor, this is hearsay evidence. No such drawing has previously been produced or cited in the course of these proceedings."

The judge glowered in the direction of the defense. "Mr. McCarthy, can you produce these drawings?"

"Your Honor, I can."

I sank as low as I could in my seat while Mr. McCarthy approached the bench and, with a flourish, deposited the page I'd torn from my scribble book. The judge pushed his glasses up his nose and gazed at it for a long minute before growling: "Mr. McCarthy, proceed."

"Thank you, Your Honor. Miss Leroux, were you aware that these sketches were being done at the time you were feeding the babies this formula? Do you have any recollection of those sketches at the time?"

Ivy's voice was subdued. "Yes, I do."

"And the artist, your assistant, who was responsible for these sketches, what is her name?"

"Her name is Emma Trimpany."

"And is Miss Trimpany in the courtroom today? Can you identify her?"

The entire courtroom turned as if on a single pivot to follow her pointing finger, hundreds of staring eyes fixed on me like a spotlight. It took every ounce of strength I could summon to look straight forward, unblinking, and give my assent when Mr. McCarthy asked me to confirm that these were indeed my drawings. I forced myself not to glance at Ivy, not for more than an instant. Instead I looked directly at the judge in his long robes at the front of the court. He gazed right back at me, inscrutable, using a thick forefinger to slide his glasses back down his nose. Such a long and terrible look.

Worse still was the look I got from M. Dionne. He was near the front of the courtroom on the other side of the aisle and turned slowly in his seat, fixing me with a glare the likes of which I've never experienced in my life. I felt in that instant as if Oliva Dionne, with all of the compressed tension and malice I'd seen him mete out on others, saw me today for the first time, *truly* saw me. That's despite the fact that I was in and out of his home dozens of times that first summer, that I'd fallen asleep at his kitchen table, that I've held his daughters in my arms count-less times, indeed, more times than they've ever been held by him. And that's the problem, I suppose. But whatever veil I've been wearing that has allowed me to pass unnoticed these last two years—I lost that with M. Dionne today. When he turned and fixed me in his gaze, it was as if his eyes were stripping away my skin, my skull, and reading everything I'd ever written, or said, or even thought about him in the deepest corners of my mind. It makes me shudder now to think of it. His cold, dark stare followed by a slow, pensive blink.

What gave me strength was the look I got from Ivy, her beauti-ful big brown eyes. She didn't nod, or smile, or wink, or anything like that, but I felt in that moment: she knows what I did, and she's okay with it.

Mr. McCarthy had already turned back to Ivy. "Miss Le-roux, can you confirm that you saw Miss Trimpany sketching this exact sketch on the day that you mixed the formula con-taining the corn syrup for the Dionne quintuplets?"

"Yes, I can."

"And your conclusion from the characterization of the corn syrup tin, the label and visible lettering, is that this is indeed Bee Hive brand? That it was seeing this drawing again, after a period of nearly thirty-two months, that has jogged your recollections sufficiently to enable you to claim beyond all reasonable doubt that it was Bee Hive brand that you used in the mixture fed to the quintuplets?"

Ivy nodded. "Yes."

Mr. McCarthy looked to have swelled to twice his previous size.

"Thank you, Miss Leroux. No further questions."

As soon as court was adjourned Ivy was mobbed. Not only by the newspapermen who'd been furiously taking notes throughout the day but by dozens of other people, mostly women, who seemed to have turned up for the proceedings for the sole purpose of getting Ivy's autograph. Photographers were huddled on the steps outside, flashbulbs at the ready, but Fred shepherded her through the crowd and into a waiting taxicab out front. I didn't follow. I was terrified the press and the cameras would turn on me next, and I just couldn't sashay through them, my blotchy head held high. I'm not like Ivy that way. Instead, Mr. McCarthy's assistant helped me exit through a side door and took me straight to Union Station and put me on the train himself.

I'm exhausted. The throb and rattle of the carriage should be enough to put me to sleep, but whenever I close my eyes, the day plays itself like a film in my head. Dr. Dafoe has arranged for the Cartwrights to meet me at the station in Callander, even though I'm arriving in the middle of the night. I only want to get home.

January 21, 1937, 12:30 A.M.

LEWIS WAS WAITING for me on the platform when I stumbled off the train in Callander. There were very few people waiting at that hour, and at first I worried no one had come to meet me, until his height gave him away. He was dressed in a long wool coat and dark trousers, a fedora pulled low against the chill wind, his anxious face softening to see me. It struck me that I've never seen Lewis wearing anything other than his billowing dungarees and wide-brimmed hat.

In typical fashion, he asked me nothing about the day and how it had gone in the courtroom, although he must have known that Ivy was testifying today—the papers speak of little else. He simply said, "Y-you must be very tired," and led me out to the truck, where he tucked a thick wool blanket over my legs and didn't say another word until we pulled up at my old house.

"Here we are," he murmured.

I thanked him then, and he turned to me as if he had something he wanted to say and couldn't quite manage to make the words behave themselves. But the kindness in his eyes was enough to make my own brim with tears, which was mortifying. I simply don't know what came over me. Partly I was wishing so badly to be with Ivy that very second, to be hashing over those horrible courtroom hours with her, late into the night. But partly I was glad to be right where I was, sitting there quietly with Lewis. It had been such a long and awful day—sad and frightening—all those strangers gaping at my birthmark, the frank rebuke in the eyes of the judge, and, worst of all, the icy look from M. Dionne, positively vibrating in contempt. Something shifted today, I could feel it. But sitting beside Lewis in that gentle silence, I was grateful to him, I truly was. He reached over and patted my arm before stepping down from the truck and coming around to open my door.

Father had waited up for me, but he didn't ask me anything either, just showed me to my old room with little Edith. Bless her heart. She is sleeping as sound as a stone, oblivious to my scratching pen.

January 28, 1937

STILL NO WORD from Ivy. She has a woman in Toronto who manages all her mail for her these days. Even my letters go through this secretary now. Or I hope they go through.

February 1937: Daily Routine: Dionne Quintuplets
(Age—2 years, 9 months)

Time	Activity	Secondary Activity	Supervisor #
6:30	Toilet Dressing	Orange juice and cod-liver oil (Play)	XX X
7:00	Washing Dressing	Toilet (Play)	XXX
8:00	Breakfast		XX
8:30	Toilet	(Play)	X
8:45	Prayer	(Play)	XX
9:00	Dressing Drink of water	(Play)	XXX
9:30	Outdoor free play	Washing	X(X)
10:00	Undressing Toilet	(Play)	XX
10:30	Nourishment		X
10:40	Music group		XX
11:00	Constructive play	Washing	X X
11:25	Story group		XX
11:35	Relaxation		XX
11:45	Dinner		XXX
12:15	Toilet	Dressing	X
12:30	Outdoor sleep		(alternate)
2:15	Toilet Dressing	Drink of water	X XXX X
2:30	Outdoor free play		X(X)
3:00	Undressing Toilet	(Play)	XX X
3:30	Nourishment	(Play)	X
4:00	Bath		XX
4:15	Directed play		X
5:15	Toilet		X
5:20	Story group		XX
5:40	Supper		XX
6:00	Toilet	Dressing	XX XX
6:10	Story group Drink of water	Prayer	XX X XX
6:30	In bed	(Night supervision)	XXX (X)

Blatz, W. E., N. Chant, M. W. Charles, et al. *Collected Studies on the Dionne Quintuplets.* University of Toronto Studies: Child Development Series. University of Toronto Press, October 1937 (adapted).

February 21, 1937

Miss Emma Trimpany
Dafoe Hospital and Nursery
Callander, ON

Dear Emma,

I'm sorry! You absolutely deserve to have heard from me sooner, but I came down with a very bad cold after my trip to Toronto last month and am only now on the mend.

I've thought about that day in the courtroom so much and what it must have been like for you—it was nerve-racking for *me* and I'm used to being the center of attention these days. I'm not sure we should ever speak of this again, and this is all I'll say: I'm proud of you. Truly, the whole world has gone gaga and forgotten that at the center of all this are five perfectly normal girls who by some strange stroke of chance happen to have been born the same day, with the same features. Corn syrup? Baby Ruth? Lysol? All these masses of people flocking to see them? Or worse, the prospect of them moving back in with the dreary Dionnes? Keep them safe, Em. No one can do this better than you.

And now my news. I'm coming to Callander for the day, March 3. I can't wait to see my baby girls, and of course I can't wait to see you.

I love you and miss you,
Ivy

February 27, 1937

I am the one the girls turn to now. A stubbed toe, a puzzling toy, a masterpiece of finger painting that requires praise and admiration—it's me they seek out. Nurse Noël is the game master who won't take no for an answer; Miss Beaulieu is the instructor with the strict rules and plastic smile. Nurse Sylvie Dubois is the latest practical nurse they've brought in to help with all the record keeping and measurements—she has not yet earned the girls' trust, let alone their affection, although she is cheery and pretty. Meanwhile Mme. Dionne has been scarce since the autumn, ever since Nurse Nicolette's departure, and I haven't seen M. Dionne since that awful moment in the courtroom. How ridiculous, but also wonderful, that I, who have always insisted I was not cut out for motherhood, have ended up as a de facto mother of five.

My own mother is back up on two feet and I'm out at the nursery full-time again, delighted to be here when the girls wake in the morning and to tuck them in after dusk.

The rules and schedules are more complicated now that we are potty training, according to Dr. Blatz's methods. *Doh-Doh Blah-Blah,* the girls call him now, which makes me want to laugh out loud. I need to remember to put that in a letter to Ivy.

We still have them in diapers, of course, but they don't need changing as much as before—not surprising given how many times per day we plunk them on the toilets and tell them to "go." Cécile has become Miss Beaulieu's favorite because she has the fewest accidents. Me, I love Cécile for her silly pranks, and for the make-believe flowers she picks for me in the nursery "garden." *What a beautiful bouquet!* I'll say, and when she leans in to give them a pretend sniff, I get to kiss her on her soft head.

Miss Beaulieu does not approve of the kisses.

March 3, 1937

IVY CAME TO the nursery today, her first visit since leaving in December and the first time I've seen her since the court case in January. She could stay only a few hours before going back to Toronto, where she is the speaker at a fund-raiser for Havergal College. It wasn't enough, not for any of us. I'd hoped we'd have time for a quiet word, just the two of us, but in the end that didn't happen. She seemed to want to spend every moment with the quintuplets, and I understand that, I do.

The girls recognized her right away and were utterly astounded that she'd materialized again. They turned and looked to the door when they heard someone enter the quiet room, then hesitated only an instant before trundling over to her, shrieking her name, *Nurse Lewoo!* She sat down on the floor to gather them all to her, and they swarmed her, practically wrestling to be the one to climb into prime position on her lap. Ivy had tears in her eyes when she looked up at me, managing to keep her arms around all five of them while they chattered away at her in a mix of French and their own incomprehensible babble, their eyes wide and earnest.

"You missed me," she said, unable to keep the wonder out of her voice. "You missed me! I missed you too."

Soon they were on their feet again and pulling her in five different directions, wanting to show her their new toys or new dresses or latest works of art. Fred was there with his camera, snapping away. I could be mistaken, but I think he looked a bit misty-eyed too. He's seen Ivy several times over the past few months—meeting her at different points of her tour, but he must have loved seeing her back in the place where they'd first gotten to know each other, among the girls that I know mean the world to him too. I had the sense that maybe these pictures wouldn't be for the papers at all; they'll be for Ivy herself, and for Fred.

Ivy glanced back over her shoulder at me, beaming with pleasure, as Yvonne and Cécile dragged her toward the games room. "I missed you too, Emma Trimpany," she called back.

I missed you too, Ivy.

APRIL 10, 1937

AN ACT FOR THE PROTECTION OF THE DIONNE QUINTUPLETS

WHEREAS YVONNE DIONNE, ANNETTE DIONNE, MARIE DIONNE, CÉCILE DIONNE, AND ÉMELIE [SIC] DIONNE, THE QUINTUPLET INFANT DAUGHTERS OF OLIVA DIONNE AND ELZIRE DIONNE, HIS WIFE, RESIDING AT OR NEAR CALLANDER, IN THE PROVINCE OF ONTARIO, AND WHO WERE BORN ON OR ABOUT THE TWENTY-NINTH [SIC] DAY OF MAY, 1934, ARE THE ONLY KNOWN LIVING QUINTUPLETS IN THE WORLD AND AS SUCH ARE THEREFORE OF SPECIAL INTEREST TO THE PEOPLE OF CANADA AND TO PEOPLE OF OTHER COUNTRIES; AND

WHEREAS THE LEGISLATURE OF ONTARIO HAS PASSED AN ACT (1935) FOR THE BETTER PROTECTION OF THE PERSONS AND ESTATES OF THE SAID QUINTUPLETS AND FOR THEIR ADVANCEMENT, EDUCATION AND WELFARE; AND

WHEREAS UNDER THE SAID ACT, A BOARD OF GUARDIANS HAS BEEN APPOINTED AND ARE ENTITLED BY LAW TO POSSESS, HAVE, HOLD, DEMAND, AND RECOVER THE ESTATES OF THE SAID QUINTUPLETS AND THEIR PROPERTIES, MONEYS, FUNDS, ASSETS . . . AND THE BENEFIT AND ADVANTAGE OF ALL CONTRACTS, ARRANGEMENTS, ENGAGEMENTS AND OBLIGATIONS, AND TO PROTECT SAID QUINTUPLETS AGAINST EXPLOITATION.

THEREFORE, NOTWITHSTANDING ANYTHING

CONTAINED IN THE UNFAIR COMPETITION ACT, 1932, THE WORDS "QUINS,"™ "QUINTS,"™ "QUINTUPLETS,"™ AND "CINQ JUMELLES"™ SHALL BE TRADEMARKS AND THE EXCLUSIVE PROPERTY IN AND THE RIGHT TO THE USE OF SUCH TRADEMARKS IS HEREBY DECLARED TO BE VESTED IN THE GUARDIANS.

THE GUARDIANS MAY LICENSE THE USE OR CONCURRENT USE OF THE WORDS "QUINS,"™ "QUINTS,"™ "QUINTUPLETS,"™ AND "CINQ JUMELLES"™ AS APPLIED TO ANY NUMBER OF ARTICLES AND MAY ALSO LIMIT SUCH USE BY THE TERMS OF THEIR LICENCE, AND THE GUARDIANS MAY BRING ACTION IN ANY COURTS OF COMPETENT JURISDICTION TO ENFORCE THEIR RIGHTS UNDER SUCH LICENCES.

ACTS OF THE PARLIAMENT OF CANADA (18TH PARLIAMENT, 2ND SESSION). ASSENTED TO 10TH APRIL, 1937.

April 23, 1937

I met the famous aviatrix Amelia Earhart today. So many dignitaries, film stars, and industrialists have passed through our little nursery and gaped at our girls. Just last week, the brother of the emperor of Japan stopped in to meet the girls on his way to the coronation of King George VI—somewhat out of his way, I would think. Jimmy Stewart and Mae West are rumored to be planning a visit for later this summer. Still, I think my encounter with Miss Earhart may stay with me longer than most. Mrs. Earhart-Putnam, I should say. But isn't it extraordinary that she should still go by Earhart? That's how she introduced herself to Dr. Dafoe, and it didn't seem to annoy Mr. Putnam one bit.

The Putnams missed the public visiting time this morning due to some car trouble in Orillia, but Dr. Dafoe swept them through the door and into the nursery without hesitation. Fred, who had already left for the day, was rustled up from somewhere by telephone and arrived in time to snap a few photos of the doctor with Miss Earhart. The girls were busy with their crayons and books and scarcely looked up at Dr. Dafoe when he ushered the guests into the playroom.

Mr. Putnam trailed right at the doctor's heels, his eyes popping at the sight of the girls, squatting down beside their tables and marveling at their identical little bodies, their soft brown hair and gentle eyes. Miss Earhart hung back, as if she wasn't sure what to make of them. She's like me, I realized, or like I used to be. Unsure around children or not particularly interested in them. We women are supposed to gasp and cluck, yet here it was clearly Mr. Putnam who was entranced, exclaiming at the girls' drawings and glancing up at his wife, hoping to draw her in. But Miss Earhart had crossed the room and was pacing by the windows, looking out at the sun sinking low over the trees. She kept tousling her own short curls, then raking her fingers through them again as if to set them back in place. There was an energy radiating from her unlike anything I'd ever felt before, at least not from a woman, as if she was pent up in some way, a foal in a stable, kicking to be free. Or not like a foal, I suppose, nothing so earthbound as that. Like a bird in a cage, itching to fly away from all her earthly tethers. I wish I could say I'd had the gumption to ask her about her flying, about her plan to try to fly across the Pacific, but I could not even bring myself to interrupt her thoughts and introduce myself.

Imagine what Lewis, lover of all things aeronautical, will say when I tell him I met the famous Miss Amelia Earhart!

May 1, 1937

DR. DAFOE'S NEW secretary arrived today, a dapper young man named George Sinclair, who will work here at the nursery, in Dr. Dafoe's expanded office. The doctor says Mr. Sinclair's primary concerns will be handling correspondence and helping with a number of columns the doctor now contributes to newspapers in Canada and the United States. We are to give him full access to the girls' medical records that we keep for Dr. Blatz, as well as the freedom to observe them at play, indoors and out.

Mr. Sinclair is in his early twenties, I'd say, mild mannered, and clearly awestruck by the quintuplets. *"Bo-jo,"* they greeted him, then cheerfully persuaded him to join their game, which involved him lying facedown on the floor while they piled their toys on top of him, leaving his jacket and trousers—expensive, by the look of it—much rumpled. Nurse Dubois—Sylvie, she insists I call her—remarked several times today that he is "easy on the eye," which may be true, but I'm not going to give her the satisfaction of agreeing with her. Everything going on in Sylvie's head ends up being said aloud, it seems. Somehow she managed to winkle out of Mr. Sinclair that he'd been a competitive swimmer and was good enough that he might have gone to the Olympic Games, had times been different. Surely he was still within earshot when Sylvie started twittering about his broad chest and how nice it will be to have a big, strong man around to help with any heavy lifting. As if we don't have a selection of burly policemen at our beck and call every hour of every day! I blush just listening to her. Besides, Mr. Sinclair isn't particularly tall.

May 9, 1937

DR. DAFOE ASKED me to stop by his office after lunch. He now has a little seating area with a large table and chairs, where he can meet with some of his many guests, as well as a second desk for Mr. Sinclair, situated just inside the door.

The doctor led me to the new table and offered me tea, summoned by the ring of a bell on the wall. Then he laid out my latest sketches and paintings for Mrs. Fangel, the ones I did last month. I had presumed they'd been sent off weeks ago.

"You've really done extraordinarily well with your art, Nurse Trimpany. I know little of these things, but people who do understand art tell me it's unusual for someone to develop her talents so swiftly, with so little tutelage."

He pulled out the two sketches and a small painting that I'd done of the girls playing with their umbrellas. The umbrellas were a gift from the *Star* newspaper, one in each of the girls' colors, and Fred had taken a series of pictures with the girls holding them in the garden on a sunny day last month. Émilie, my little monkey, was the funniest, peeping up at the sky and holding out her hand as if to feel for imaginary raindrops. Fred's pictures wouldn't have done them justice, of course, being in black and white. Same thing with the quick charcoal sketches I'd done at the time. But over the next few weeks, I'd played around with my watercolor paints and, in the end, painted what I think is one of my best works so far. The watercolors give the painting a true spring feel, and the colors are really the thing that everyone associates with the girls now that each has her own official color. Call it a tiny act of rebellion, but I mixed up the colors in my painting, matching green with Annette, cream with Yvonne, and so on. I suppose I wanted to show that each girl is more than a single color; as far as I'm concerned each is a rainbow unto herself. I expect no one else will notice. I knew Maud would like this one, but here it was in Dr. Dafoe's office, presumably having never made it to New York.

"This is really lovely, really lovely," Dr. Dafoe was murmuring, brushing his mustache with his index finger. "I thought of keeping it for myself, you know."

So had I.

"But no, no," he said, waggling his round head. "The other

guardians and I, the minute we saw it, we knew it must be shared with the world."

He eased himself into a chair across from me. "What would you think, Nurse Trimpany—Emma—what would you say if this picture was sold to an advertiser?"

He paused and waited. I opened my mouth and closed it, unsure of what to say. He chuckled at my reticence. "We didn't send this work to Mrs. Fangel because we are of the belief that she could not improve on it, not at all. Instead, we have met with a company man and he has expressed an interest in buying this painting for an advertisement."

I blinked at him for a minute, then managed to say: "An umbrella advertisement?"

Dr. Dafoe chuckled again. "No, no, Emma. A candy bar advertisement. Do you know Baby Ruth chocolate bars? This man was from the Curtiss Candy Company. They would like to use this for Baby Ruth."

I have an entrenched habit of saying the wrong thing at the wrong time.

"But the girls aren't allowed to eat candy."

A shadow crossed Dr. Dafoe's face, I'm sure of it, but he answered kindly enough. "For now, yes, we cannot expose them to too much sugar. Dr. Blatz is in full agreement with me."

He cleared his throat, then said, "But, Emma, we have discussed this before, how important it is that we build up the trust fund for the quintuplets with whatever opportunities come their way. Our poor girls"—here he gave a deep sigh—"people will always be interested in their lives, won't they? They will always need to have sufficient funds to make sure they can live as publicly or as privately as they like."

I didn't know what to think, not about the girls and their trust fund. But what was dawning on me at that very moment was that my art, something I myself had painted with no help from anyone else, was going to be seen by the wider world. Something I had created would help my girls.

"Will it go in magazines, Dr. Dafoe?" I asked.

"Indeed." He nodded. "It is so beautiful in color, is it not? It would be a shame to have it be seen only in black and white."

He must have read my mind, which I am grateful for, because he said: "The Curtiss Candy Company is paying no small sum for the opportunity to have our girls endorse their candy bar, Emma. And a portion of that revenue will be paid to you for your work."

He stood and started collecting the pictures from the table, carefully putting pieces of tissue paper between them and returning behind the wall to wherever it was he was storing them.

"How much will they pay?" I managed to croak out when he returned, his pipe in the corner of his mouth. It was hard for me to imagine what amount of money this painting would be worth. I would like to ask someone, Fred maybe, or perhaps Mrs. Fangel.

"And Mrs. Fangel, what will she say?"

Dr. Dafoe took his pipe out of his mouth. "I expect she'll be pleased for you. She thinks of you as a student."

"So she knows?" I repeated.

"She will soon," he said.

It was only later that I realized he hadn't answered my question about how much money I was to be paid. I will talk to Fred when he's back from New York. And I will write to Ivy to tell her the news.

May 22, 1937 (*Toronto Star*)

THREE YEARS OLD FRIDAY
QUINTS WORTH $861,148

CALLANDER, Ontario—Impish young capitalists with the world at their feet and a future no one can predict, the Dionne quintuplets toddled on today toward their third birthday, the wonder babies of the universe.

They will be three years old next Friday, May 28—these babies who were grudgingly given a million to one chance to live.

It will be just another 24 hours in the lives of the Quints with little to distinguish it from the birthdays they already have celebrated for newspapers and motion picture photographers. They may be urged to chatter into a microphone for an international broadcast and perhaps thousands will visit them, but that won't make up an unusual day for the Quints.

But with the coming of their fourth year serious efforts will be started to educate the children now worth almost $1,000,000. Now they have $573,765 in cash or bonds and money due them under 24 contracts will bring that to $861,148. In the past year their wealth has increased by about $300,000.

Without even trying, Cécile, Marie, Annette, Émilie, and Yvonne (TOP LEFT TO RIGHT) have enriched the whole Callander district, as well as made a fortune for themselves. A screen of trees (SECOND ROW LEFT) has been planted outside the nursery this spring to keep them less conscious of the crowds. Oliva Dionne, the quintuplets' father, has recently replaced the porch roof and put new sides on the humble home that was the quintuplets' birthplace (SECOND ROW RIGHT). Tourists will find a new straight road through the bush from Callander to Dafoe hospital before the summer is out. Pictured here, part of the 100 men working on the new highway are shown either side of the old winding road.

May 23, 1937

Miss Emma Trimpany
Dafoe Hospital and Nursery
Callander, ON

Dear Em,

That's extraordinary news about your painting, I'm so proud of you. You must insist on a reasonable payment, and you must have it paid directly into that account set up for you earlier.

I'm enjoying my time in the southern states; their ways are certainly different from the North, although they seem equally interested in hearing about my time in Quintland. Everyone here calls it that, not the Dafoe nursery or the Dafoe hospital. It makes it seem more exotic, I suppose.

Fred and I have finally set a tentative date for the wedding for next summer. Any longer and I think my father would need to be institutionalized. We are thinking late July, and we will likely have it in Toronto. You must set the last two weeks aside, okay? That's because I'm insisting you be my bridesmaid. Don't try to get out of it with your customary protests about your birthmark; I won't hear of it. I'm coming home for a few days next month and I will tell you about everything then.

All my love, and give a special birthday hug to each of the babies from me.

Ivy

June 5, 1937

Father's fiftieth birthday. Dr. Dafoe continues to be very worried about kidnappers, believing even the nurses may be at risk, so he arranged for the Cartwrights to take me into Callander tonight. Father and son pulled up to the rear door of the nursery a little after five in the evening. Lewis seemed to have lost his tongue again, although he smiled broadly and tipped his hat before hoisting himself up into the flat bed of the truck, leaving the passenger seat for me. Lewis has many of the same mannerisms I do, I realize, that of ducking his head and turning his face from view.

I thanked them for waiting for me as they surely must have finished delivering their second load of Quint-stones shortly after the public viewing ended at 3:30, but Mr. Cartwright senior merely shook his head, all but scolding me for intimating that I might have walked the distance into town.

"You can't be braving all this commotion on foot, Miss Trimpany," he chided. "It wouldn't be safe for a lady on her own, battling the crowds of Quintland."

The public viewing time had ended more than ninety minutes earlier, but the parking lot beside the farmhouse was still teeming with cars of every model and shade. Visitors were milling around the troughs newly refilled with Dionne souvenir pebbles, swatting at the blackflies, and snapping pictures of the farmhouse, the nursery, and everything else in between.

Our truck attracted no small amount of attention when the guard opened the second gate to let us pull out. Mr. Cartwright senior waved gamely at the tourists, but I kept my gaze fixed straight ahead, my birthmark—I hoped—in shadow. For as far as I could see, a line of cars inched in the direction of Callander, the tired faces of children pressed against the rear windows.

I had heard the other staff talking about an Algonquin chief who had pitched his tepee across from the makeshift carpentry that passed for a tourist information hut on a corner of the Dionne property. Sure enough, a regal Indian sat cross-legged on a red blanket set back from the roadside, poker-faced in full regalia, the breeze stirring his headdress. A large sign on the ground beside him read: PROFESSIONAL PHOTOS: 50 CENTS. OWN CAMERA: 25 CENTS. A group of older boys, their shirttails untucked, appeared to be heckling the man, trying to get a smile out of him, while others inspected his tent and queued to get their pictures taken. Next to the man was a long line of wheeled carts, tables, and makeshift stands: local folk selling homemade preserves, candy bars, cigarettes, hard-boiled eggs, folding fans, buttermilk biscuits, harmonicas, postcards, Cracker Jack, ashtrays, sunhats, tea cozies, soda pop, embroidery, candy apples, whirligigs, and lemon meringue pie by the slice. A jowly man in full tails and a top hat was pacing back and forth through the traffic, bellowing at the top of his lungs, "Ladies and gentlemen, just fifteen more minutes until feeding time, fifteen minutes! Step up and see Rupert the Bear tuck into his supper!" On a wooden platform wobbling over a patch of scrub brush was the sorriest-looking brown bear I've ever seen, scrawny and bedraggled, his coat dull, lumbering listlessly at the limit of his short chain. A youngster in a sailor suit dangling a blue balloon on a string stood transfixed, his eyes glued to the bear while his mother tugged vainly at his sleeve. The air smelled of dust and automobiles mixed with fairground smells—hay and horse, popcorn, hot dogs, and cotton candy. Despite the warmth of the evening, I cranked my window closed.

As we pulled past the veranda surrounding one of Oliva Dionne's souvenir shops, I spied Nurse Dubois—Sylvie—leaning out over the railing with a slim man, smartly dressed, his hat pulled low. She was sipping from a pop bottle through a long red straw, and, as we crept closer, she pointed at something on the street and the two of them started laughing, Sylvie letting her head fall back, her bosom rising and falling. The man turned away before I could get a proper look at him, ducking into the shadow of the porch, but it seemed I could hear her booming laugh from inside the cab of the truck, despite the distance and the noise all around us, our windows closed tight. I waited for her companion to step forward again into the light, but he didn't. I've come to like Sylvie, but we don't have the kind of friendship where I could imagine asking her about the man on the porch, the way I might have done with Ivy. Although I'm curious, I admit. I twisted my head to look through the rear window at the busy rooftop refreshment stand at the Midwives' Pavilion, a line of tourists curling limply away from the stairway. They were waiting, I presumed, for a table to open up. Lewis, seated in the back of the truck, was watching them, too, one hand grasping the rail, the other holding his weathered hat to his head, half an inch from my own on the other side of the glass.

"It really is something," I murmured.

"That it is, miss," Mr. Cartwright agreed cheerfully. "That it is."

June 15, 1937

A TELEGRAM FROM Ivy today saying she's canceling her trip home in order to accept an offer to speak at a nursing school in California! She says she will travel by both train and airplane to get there. I can't imagine being so brave. I'm desperately disappointed not to see her, but perhaps she'll have time later in the summer.

June 16, 1937

PUBLIC OBSERVATION HOURS were officially extended, so the quintuplets now play in the observation area for a full hour, twice a day, at 9:30 and 2:30. No one sees me—they only have eyes for the girls. The crowds are astonishing. The lineup for the morning viewing now starts before seven-thirty.

M. and Mme. Dionne came today during the viewing hours and insisted on sitting in the play area with all of us. It's the first time M. Dionne has done this, although Mme. Dionne has been coming off and on for several weeks. My guess is she likes the public to see her with her famous babies, although she never joins the girls in their play. Instead she sits heavily in her chair, fanning herself in the shade, calling out to the girls and trying to get them to come and sit with her, when it's clear they are happy with their various games and projects.

M. Dionne, meanwhile, spent every minute tugging at his ridiculous ears and frowning at the shadows moving behind the screens in the observation corridor. He bristled with anger when one of the girls ignored her mother and continued with whatever she was playing at. He seems to go out of his way to glare at me and snapped angrily at Miss Beaulieu, although whatever set him off, I'd missed. Nurse Dubois stood up from the sandbox, where she'd been watching Marie and Annette, and walked over to him and spoke with him quietly. The next minute, wouldn't you know it—she actually had him smiling.

July 3, 1937

MISS EARHART'S PLANE is missing in the Pacific and with it that strange woman who so recently left such an impression on me. I can't imagine how that would feel, to be adrift in the vast ocean, sharks circling, my radio batteries growing fainter and fainter. Battleships, destroyers, and airplanes have been sent out to search for her, but they can find no trace of the plane. She was here so very recently, perhaps the most *alive* woman I've ever met, so sure of her own mind and her own intentions. How can she no longer be of this world?

Sylvie wouldn't stop nattering about the missing plane in her ringing voice, layering one awful speculation on top of another until I told her I had a booming headache and needed some peace and quiet.

July 15, 1937

ANOTHER HEAT WAVE and tempers are flaring. The girls bicker with one another at all hours of the day. Yesterday Annette tipped a full bucket of water over Émilie's head in the pool, then all of the girls joined in on the water fight. We could hear the people behind the screens in the viewing corridor laughing and clapping. The girls, of course, could hear it, too, and this made them monkey around even more. Dr. Dafoe keeps insisting in the papers that the girls are unaware of the public in the viewing area. *Baloney.* That's what Ivy would say.

More than fifteen thousand visitors came during the weekend showings—that's what Dr. Dafoe told us today. I can't get my mind around this number, but Sylvie prattled on about it as if she herself is part of the draw. Perhaps she is. I've never asked her who she was with when I saw her that day at the souvenir stand. She likely has a number of friends in the area if she grew up nearby, and no shortage of suitors. Nurse Noël has muttered disapprovingly that Simon, one of our policemen, is "too familiar" with Sylvie, but I honestly can't imagine how she's reached this conclusion. Tonight Sylvie was wearing a necklace I've not seen before, something sparkly. I saw it catch the light when she stooped to tuck Marie into bed after supper.

August 6, 1937

EM HAS BEEN sick all week with a sore throat and a fever, so we haven't permitted her to play with her sisters in the "big" playground as they call it. The newspapers are blaring about infantile paralysis, but how could Émilie have come in contact with the polio virus? The girls meet no other children. Even their own siblings have not been over the street to play since the winter—they are too busy on the farm. Maman and Papa, too, I presume, since they've been scarce this last month.

Meanwhile Mr. Sinclair has been snowed under with letters

and telegrams wishing Émilie a speedy recovery, including one from a woman in England. "I would have thought people on the other side of the Atlantic would have more important things on their minds these days than these five children," he said, shaking his head. He has quite a bit to learn, I'd say, about our little girls.

August 7, 1937 (*Toronto Star*)

ÉMILIE'S PLEADING FACE WINS RELEASE, AND WHOOPS FILL YARD

CALLANDER, Ontario—The most noted sore throat in many a day was adjudged better today and Émilie Dionne whooped for joy as she joined in the fun of Quintuplet play hour. Kept apart from her sisters for five days, Émilie pressed her nose against the glass door of her room when Dr. Allan Roy Dafoe called this morning.

"I couldn't resist that pleading look in that little face," Dr. Dafoe smiled. "I opened the door and sent her out to play with the others. She wasn't scheduled to join the forces till Monday."

Joy was unconfined in the yard of the Dafoe nursery when Émilie scampered out and was greeted by Yvonne, Annette, Cécile, and Marie who threw their arms around the middleweight Quint. The babies had never been separated for more than a few hours until Émilie took sick.

A crowd of more than 1,000 tourists watched the reunion and then saw Émilie conducted around the yard by her sisters who helped her locate her playthings.

Used with permission.

August 10, 1937

All of the girls are down with Émilie's flu, complaining of sore throats and kicking their blankets from their hot limbs as they sleep. Not a one of them is ill enough that she wants to rest all day, so we've had lots of subdued playtime indoors. Today, at least, Dr. Dafoe canceled the public showing, which is as much a relief for the staff as it is for the girls. Something is eating at the doctor. When the girls take ill, even with the sniffles, he treats it as both a personal failure and a national calamity.

Today he asked to speak with me in private. I assumed he might have news about my painting of the girls that the candy company purchased—the Baby Ruth ad should be out any day, I'm told, and I've received a very generous payment. Instead the doctor seemed reluctant to meet my eye, asking me a stream of questions. How well was I getting on with Nurse Dubois? And with the other staff? What do we do in our free time? Do we spend it together or alone? Do the nurses tend to stay on the property or leave it, after hours? Did I keep in touch at all with any former staff? His questions went on and on.

I answered as best I could, but I was mystified by the whole exchange. If anything, he should be asking our observer in chief, Miss Beaulieu, and I said as much. He ducked his round head up and down like a ball bobbing in the pool and said yes, yes, he would be speaking with all of us. But he sent me back to the nursery shortly thereafter, and, minutes later, I spied his car leaving through the front gates.

August 18, 1937 (*Toronto Star*)

QUINTS CONTINUE DAILY "SHOWINGS": EVERY SAFEGUARD TAKEN AGAINST PARALYSIS INFECTION

CALLANDER, Ontario—All traces of the "mild upper respiratory infections"—sore throats—which bothered the Dionne quintuplets, individually and collectively, have vanished, word from the Dafoe nursery advised today.

Precautions to guard them against the possibility of infantile paralysis, now prevalent in southern Ontario, have been ordered by Dr. Allan Roy Dafoe.

All visitors have been barred from the nursery, even tradesmen and others who have habitually entered.

Dr. Dafoe said he could not permit even the parents or the six other Dionne children to visit their sisters.

The quintuplets will, however, continue their twice-daily "personal appearances" for the benefit of tourists who've come from far and wide to glimpse the famous five and always leave with a lucky pebble in their pockets.

Used with permission.

August 23, 1937

A nasty altercation with M. Dionne, who came by yesterday with Maman in tow. I hightailed it upstairs to watch from the window. M. Dionne marched right up to the front door and insisted to Miss Beaulieu that plenty of time had passed for the girls to recover from their illness and it was time they saw their family. Dr. Dafoe had already left for the day, but Dr. Blatz is here visiting from Toronto, and he very officiously told the Dionnes that the girls are still ill and susceptible to further illness.

This can't be true, can it? The girls seem fit as fiddles.

But Dr. Blatz stood his ground and sent Miss Beaulieu to summon one of the guards to escort the parents from the property. M. Dionne let fly then with a string of words that I won't record here—indeed, I hardly know how to spell them—blaring that Dr. Dafoe would be hearing from his solicitor. His wrath seems to roll over Mme. Dionne as if she doesn't hear it, or has heard it all before. She'd been hunched behind him on the stoop, her stout frame taking up most of the step and swathed in a pretty flower-print dress, swaying slowly with her head bowed. As the quarrel grew more heated, she drifted back down the steps and over to the tall fence, hooking her fingers through the chain-link and pressing her face close, even though there was no one in the yard and nothing there to see.

August 25, 1937

LEWIS WAS WAITING in the truck by the back door by the time I'd finished breakfast and brought me home to spend a day with Mother, Father, and little Edith. Quintland is swarming with visitors from sunup to sundown, but weekends are especially bad.

The worst is the scrutiny we face passing through the outer gates, people snapping photos and craning to see who is being ferried out of the inner sanctum of the nursery. Lewis typically keeps calm and collected, neither frowning nor smiling, and not distracted in any way by the people who wave or, worse, tap on the sides of the truck. Today before we pulled out, he said, "If I can make a suggestion, miss," then gestured toward my hat, reaching as if to touch it. Then he hesitated, blushed deeply, and retracted his hand.

"It's Miss Beaulieu who put me in mind of it," he managed to say, his eyes dipping. "I've never taken her to or from the station without her pulling her hat down and sideways, just so." He mimed a motion in the air, and I reached up to touch the wide brim of my hat.

"It may not be the fashion, Miss Trimpany, but Miss Beaulieu, she pulls her hat so far to the side and down over her face, I don't think she can see anything until she knows we are out of the traffic again."

I laughed then, because he was plainly amused to be giving me advice as to how I should be wearing my hat, but I rewarded him by unpinning it and angling it so that it was almost completely covering my birthmark, leaving my entire right face exposed to the passenger-side window.

"Like this?" I said.

He cleared his throat. "I meant the other side, miss." I knew what he had intended, of course, and when his face reddened even further, I regretted my little joke.

"I'm sorry, Lewis, I'm teasing and I shouldn't," I said and, surprising myself, gave his arm a light tap where it rested on the wheel. I reached up and swiveled everything around again so that my hat was tilted rakishly toward the side window, my whole horribly blotchy left side perfectly exposed for Lewis and in shadow for anyone else.

Poor Lewis, he didn't say another word for most of the rest of the journey, even after I repositioned my brim when the cars and pedestrians thinned out again. I may be mistaken, but I think I saw a flicker of a smile when I did so. Perhaps I didn't hurt his feelings after all.

It's nice not to be so miserably self-conscious around someone. Afterward I kept thinking: I tapped his arm. I *teased* him. Some days I don't recognize myself.

August 29, 1937 (*New York Times*)

THE QUINTUPLET PROBLEM

(Editorial) If human mothers were in the habit of giving birth to sets of five babies at once, the lives of the Dionne sisters would doubtless have been uneventful. They are distinctive, and indeed unique, not because of any peculiarities they possess but because of the mere accident of their birth.

We may assume that the little Dionnes take it for granted that one is visited from one's earliest infancy by thousands of pilgrims, who gaze at one through the protective glass and are spellbound by one's most casual antic. That, for the Dionnes, is as much a part of life as eating, sleeping and playing. Some years hence they will learn and understand the reason. But by that time what will a quintuplet's eye-view of the world be like? Will they be disposed to lament the day that made them five instead of one or two? Will they be harassed, as royalty must be, by having to live up to a fame they have not earned? Will they be shocked and appalled when they realize that as long as they live they cannot escape notice—that, indeed, the longer they all live, the more remarkable they will seem?

What the Dionne girls would want is normalcy. Normal risks, normal adventures, games with other children, going to school like other children, flirtations in the moonlight, wifehood, motherhood, perhaps, if their imaginations ran that far, some kind of career. But they will not have these things, unless, in time, the great scientific experiment of rearing them under cover is dropped and they are allowed to go their separate ways.

One does not envy Dr. Dafoe—or anyone else connected with the case—his responsibility. The first objective must be to keep them alive, but close to that is the desire to make their lives as happy and normal as possible. If they are made a sideshow to interest and amuse the public something precious is sacrificed. If they are allowed to become five individuals, instead of a mass movement known as the Dionne Quintuplets, there may be hope that other members of the human race, despite dictators and demagogues, may also achieve the right to be their individual selves.

September 1, 1937

Mr. Sinclair spends time with the quintuplets every day, to their delight. And ours, I suppose. He is unfailingly gallant with all of the nurses and staff and a natty dresser, but also has a rather wicked sense of humor that is keeping us all amused. Ivy would like him. He livens the place up like she did. Maybe it is because he is also a city man, from Toronto, but he strikes me as a younger Fred. And, like Fred, he doesn't look right through me. So many physicians, scientists, politicians, artists, film stars, and dignitaries have passed through these halls without registering my existence, my invisibility intact. George—Mr. Sinclair—has never made a comment about my face and I've never caught him looking at my birthmark. He even holds my eye when he speaks with me, something Dr. Dafoe himself has a hard time doing. He has quite nice eyes, actually. Deep brown, with long dark lashes.

George has to write three newspaper columns each week about the daily lives of the quintuplets. These are Dr. Dafoe's columns, but, according to George, the doctor scarcely even looks them over and seldom suggests any changes. We'll be breakfasting with the girls and George will be pacing up and down the corridor outside, his fine shoes clattering. Then, as soon as we're finished, he'll needle us with questions. "How often do the girls eat scrambled eggs? What about hard-boiled eggs? How many?" If he wasn't so polite, he'd get on our nerves, but if anything his questions amuse us.

A few days later, right as rain, "Dr. Dafoe's Column on the Quintuplets and the Care of Your Children" will devote several inches to the health benefits of eggs for toddlers. Today George was hot on the case of potty training. Dr. Blatz believes the toilet schedule has been successful, so starting next week the girls will wear diapers only at night. I'm expecting we'll be doing a lot of laundry. But George is already poring over the past twelve months of the girls' "toilet records" and asking us about bowel movements and hydration. I'm sure most men would find this terribly embarrassing, but not George. Dr. Dafoe also has him reviewing the major Canadian and American dailies for any articles about the quintuplets. Today I got up the nerve to mention that I've been keeping up a scrapbook that started at the girls' birth, and he is kindly providing me with anything he comes across.

In the afternoons, he tends to sequester himself at his desk in Dr. Dafoe's office to tackle the mail, and we might not see him for several hours. But we can usually count on him to reappear later in the afternoon to regale us with stories of the latest lunatic advice to arrive by post—the necessity of goat's milk for healthy toenails or coffee rinses for shinier hair. Not all of the letters are funny, of course. The doctor and the quintuplets receive mail from cities and countries I've never heard of, where people live in quite different circumstances than we do here. It's astonishing that people, no matter how hard their lives, might take the time to write to our little nursery, to tell us how comforted they are knowing that the girls are healthy and safe.

September 10, 1937

Ivy VISITED TODAY. She looked beautiful in a white dress covered in butterflies of every hue, caped sleeves, a full skirt to just below the knee. The girls quickly abandoned their games to dash over and examine this latest princess-visitor, pointing at the fabric and exclaiming at the colors. They were so sunny and friendly, it took both Ivy and me a moment to realize they didn't recognize her. They were simply being welcoming. After their interest in her dress, purse, and hat had abated, they bumbled off again, more or less forgetting that they had a visitor at all.

Tears welled up in Ivy's beautiful big eyes, and she started fumbling through her bag for a handkerchief. I put my arm around her and tried to explain that they get so many glamorous visitors these days and had been quite ill recently so were still a bit under the weather. Ivy couldn't be consoled. Sweet Annette, who is truly the most maternal of the group, noticed Ivy dabbing at her eyes and returned, her own eyes pooling and her arms outstretched, offering a hug. "No ba-ba-bah," the little one said. This was too much for Ivy, who crouched down and permitted Annette to reach around her pretty dress and stroke her gently on her back, as she'd seen us do with her sisters, repeating herself in a soothing burble. "No ba-ba-bah."

I had thought Ivy would stay for lunch, but she said she was too upset. We scarcely had time to visit at all.

September 17, 1937

IT IS NIGHTS like these I would do anything to have Ivy back here so we could sit up late and talk things through. There is no one else who'd understand.

Sometime around five this afternoon I was reading to the girls in the quiet playroom. There was a bit of a commotion at the back door, so I stepped into the hallway to make sure everything was okay. It was Simon, our policeman, speaking with Marguerite, the housekeeper, saying that a visitor was asking for Dr. Dafoe. Of course we are always having visitors seeking Dr. Dafoe, but typically the guards turn them away at the main gate or contact Dr. Dafoe themselves. Somehow this one had made it past the external and internal gates and was, presumably, waiting on the back porch to be admitted.

"She was causing some trouble across the street," Simon was saying in a low voice. "It was M. Dionne who asked that she be escorted off the property, so I brought her here."

Marguerite said something I didn't catch, and Simon said: "I can't send them away like this, ma'am. And she's insisting on speaking with the doctor." I heard the screen door creak open—an anxious sound, it seemed to me—as I hurried into the kitchen.

Imagine my surprise. It was Nurse Nicolette. I almost couldn't recognize her. Her baby face was much thinner now, her hair longer and unkempt, and her eyes were swollen, her gaze flickering all over the room like the nervous flame of a candle waiting to be dowsed. No sooner had I recognized her than I realized what she was carrying: a baby, quite a good-size little chap, or at least I assume it was a boy—the soiled blanket in which he was swaddled was a pale blue.

Simon and Marguerite looked relieved to see me.

"Inès?" I said, unable to keep the surprise out of my voice.

She looked up, but if she recognized me, she didn't show it. Instead she started crying again and saying in French, "I must see Dr. Dafoe, I must see Dr. Dafoe."

"We've put in a call to the doctor in town," Simon said to me in English. "I told him Nurse Nicolette was here for a visit, but he says he is otherwise engaged and we must convince her to go."

I paused, wondering if I should summon Miss Beaulieu, but she had never met Nurse Nicolette and I didn't want her to be angry with the guards for admitting Inès to the premises. Simon turned his head sideways so as to be able to murmur something more quietly, beside my ear. "She was creating quite a scene at the Dionne farmhouse, hammering on the door and scaring the other children. Some of the tourists were taking photos . . ."

I crouched down beside Nurse Nicolette and explained in French that the doctor was away and asked her if she needed medical attention, or whether there was anything I could do to help. She glared at me, then shook her head, wiping at her blotched face with her sleeve, turning her shoulder toward me, and hunching over the child. Truly it was so hard to comprehend the changes in her—she'd been so fastidious about her appearance and her comportment when she left us last year. Now she seemed older and more drawn, but also unraveled, undone. So things had worked out for her just as I'd feared.

"This must be your baby," I murmured, trying to calm her down. I reached toward the baby, meaning only to lay my hand on his little head—he was a boy, I could confirm that now, but with curly, dark brown hair and long dark lashes, so much plumper than the quintuplets had been at this age, which I estimated to be roughly three months old.

Inès wrenched her arms to one side, away from my outstretched hand, letting out a sound that was part cry, part growl. I had a feeling in that moment that she'd already fought to keep her arms around this baby and she wasn't going to let go of him here. She curled her gaunt frame around the boy and started sobbing again, her thin shoulders quaking in her drab and faded dress.

I stood again and said that I was going to go and get Miss Beaulieu, which I did. By the time we returned, however, Inès was gone, and Simon with her.

"She burst out the door when you left," Marguerite said. "Sergeant Blaine went after her, and I've just seen him helping her into the car. He offered to take her back to the train station," she added.

Miss Beaulieu pinched her glasses primly on her nose and gave me a stern look, which suggested I'd interrupted her for no reason, but I hadn't. Why had Inès come back? Why wouldn't she let me hold the baby? Now I have a million questions and no chance of getting answers. I need to write to Ivy.

September 18, 1937

I TRIED TO speak with Dr. Dafoe about Nurse Nicolette's visit, but he brushed aside my questions, telling me it was none of my concern. But surely it should have been his?

He is completely preoccupied with the upcoming publication of Dr. Blatz's research on the quintuplets and has been asked to write the foreword, which of course will simply mean more work for George. In fact, I'd like to talk about Nurse Nicolette with George, or Lewis maybe. But what exactly would I say? This was some private tragedy, surely, some medical secret for which she felt she needed the doctor's help. Had Simon taken her to see Dr. Dafoe in town, or to the station, as Marguerite had suggested? Surely Dr. Dafoe could tell me something to let me set my fears to rest?

October 1, 1937

I STILL HAVEN'T sent my letter to Ivy. I don't have her address and I don't want to send it to her "secretary" in Toronto. Fred is meeting her back in Toronto over Thanksgiving weekend and says he'd be happy to take her a letter himself. I'm not sure what I'll do.

Fred took some very funny photos with the girls today. The *Star* sent us a turkey, of all things, a live one! I was worried about this great fat bird and what he might do to the girls, but this one was very tame and harmless. Indeed, the girls were more afraid of him than he was of the girls. It took considerable urging by Fred before Annette, Émilie, and Marie could be persuaded to stand anywhere close to the turkey—Cécile and Yvonne were having none of it. Émilie was the bravest, reaching out to stroke the funny thing, then shrieking with laughter as he jolted away on her.

"Shoh-shoh!" she proclaimed before he clucked off across the yard, flapping his wings. I'm sure they must have thought they'd received a very strange pet—yet another thing that will be here today and gone tomorrow. I certainly won't be the one to explain to them what they are eating for Thanksgiving supper!

October 24, 1937

DR. BLATZ's *Collected Studies on the Dionne Quintuplets* is finally being published. Dr. Dafoe, Miss Beaulieu, and of course Dr. Blatz, who will arrive this weekend, are crowing from the rooftops about this groundbreaking publication. I'll have to read this great oeuvre to understand all the commotion. We've slavishly stuck to his silly schedules for Nourishment and Toilet Time while the girls have submitted patiently to all the prodding and poking, the countless photographs and measurements, and the endless prints of their hands and feet. My deepest wish is that they could now be allowed to simply be themselves.

Not just yet, however. We've heard that several hundred scientists will be descending on us Sunday. A year ago we could rely on the Dionnes to kick up a fuss about this kind of thing, but Oliva Dionne is no doubt rubbing his hands together in glee at the idea of hundreds of deep-pocketed doctors and university professors visiting his souvenir stand.

The girls are blissfully oblivious, preoccupied today with mastering their tricycles, building their sand castles, and hooting over the costumes they were given for their Halloween photo shoot.

November 1, 1937 (*Toronto Star*)

300 SCIENTISTS ON EDGE ON MEETING QUINTUPLETS; TAKE STORK-STONES

CALLANDER, Ontario—Yvonne is the most motherly of the Dionne quintuplets, Marie is the most sympathetic, Émilie is the most independent, Cécile the most unpredictable, and Annette the most aggressive.

So Dr. William E. Blatz, University of Toronto psychologist, thinks. Dr. Allan Roy Dafoe, their physician, thinks they are "just five smart kids."

The descriptions were given as 300 child specialists, psychologists, and students concluded a two-day meeting in which they studied the Quints on the basis of reports by Dr. Dafoe and his brother, Dr. W. A. Dafoe, of Toronto, and a group of eight U of Toronto psychologists under Dr. Blatz.

The scientific meeting was divided into two stages, discussion of the reports in Toronto Saturday, and a visit to the children here yesterday. The psychologists travelled to Callander by special train and peered through glass and wire mesh at the youngsters singing and playing. The youngsters seemed even more entertaining than usual. But they forgot their toys when their father, Oliva Dionne, entered their yard. The five rushed to him to be kissed.

After watching the quintuplets in action for about two hours, the scientists left muttering much the same adjectives as the average tourist uses: "A rare treat"; "wonderful children"; "Gosh, they're great," and so on.

The Quints, dressed in their Sunday best, took the whole thing in stride, and were less nervous than were the visitors themselves.

Some of the women picked up a few of the famous Callander "maternity pebbles," reputed to have a magical influence on the stork, before they left.

November 17, 1937

Émilie didn't have a single accident in her underwear all morning! She's been the slowest of the girls to make progress with the potty schedule. I'm so proud of her, and I told her so.

November 18, 1937

WINTER HAS COME, with a vengeance, yet the girls are still playing outside in the observation area twice per day. They are enthralled with their new toboggans—our arms are aching from pulling them along through deep snow—and they don't seem to mind the cold. But *I* mind. I'm tired of the public show. The snow has slowed the number of visits, but it hasn't halted them altogether. Lewis has had to plow the road between the train station and Quintland for the last three days.

November 24, 1937 (*Toronto Star*)

TOO MUCH TURKEY TALK!

CALLANDER, Ontario—This garrulous old gobbler survived Thanksgiving all right, but talked so much about his clever escape that people began to think of Christmas. Now he realizes his error, but it's too late, because sturdy Émilie Dionne of the famous quintuplets, pictured here, has a good grip on his tail feathers and her foot in his leash, and all he can do is gobble a warning to his heirs against the dangers of bragging. In the few weeks left before Yuletide he will have time to meditate upon the fruits of his indiscretion.

Used with permission.

December 1, 1937

Another year, another nurse—now it is Nurse Dubois who has packed up her bags and flounced out of our lives and, more to the point, out of the lives of our little girls. They are bereft once again, asking me where she has gone and when she'll be back. They really loved Sylvie—her booming laugh and endless energy for games and capers. She was larger than life, even more so in their strange and shrunken world.

As best as I can tell, she didn't quit—Dr. Dafoe and the other guardians asked her to leave. She was summoned to Dr. Dafoe's office this morning and that was that.

December 5, 1937

THE NEW TEACHER's name is Claire Tremblay—God, I miss Ivy. Miss Tremblay is quite strict and formal, a very devout Catholic, as she managed to inform me within the first thirty seconds of her arrival. The Dionnes no doubt approve. She comes all the way from Trois-Rivières and speaks almost no English. I am frequently acting as translator for George and Dr. Dafoe when they wish to ask her a question, or when she wishes to address one of them. She has taken the girls' French education in hand and is particularly hard on Marie, whose speech is the weakest. Whenever anyone fumbles a verb or an article, or pronounces something incorrectly, Miss Tremblay pinches her shoulders back and thrusts her chin in the air, then takes a deep snort through her beaky nose so that the nostrils collapse inward. She looks like she's trying to turn into an arrow. The girls are all a little afraid of her.

December 17, 1937

MY LAST DAY of work before Christmas—I have the week off and won't return until after Edith's birthday. Dr. Dafoe is visiting New York, which allows George to go on leave until the New Year. Miss Beaulieu will go back to Toronto for the holidays, and Fred is leaving soon to visit Ivy in Florida. It would be nice to stay at the nursery during this quiet time, but I, too, need a bit of a break. I'm sorry to miss Christmas with the girls, but of course we celebrated last week before Dr. Dafoe left on his holiday. He dressed up, as usual, in his red Santa suit and emptied his sack of toys as Fred took photo after photo. The Dionnes did not make an appearance. Perhaps Miss Tremblay will invite them all over for Christmas—she's organized for Father Routhier to give Mass at the nursery. Needless to say, she has settled in quickly.

Lewis is coming to fetch me tomorrow morning after he's plowed the road. I've been working in the evenings on a water-color of Edith—a surprise for my mother and father. I'm not sure how I'll manage to smuggle it into the house without them knowing.

December 18, 1937

EDITH FELL ASLEEP on my lap, a hand clamped to my waist, as I was reading her a bedtime story. I waited until I was sure she was really and truly out for the count before wriggling from underneath her and tucking her in under the covers. It's not so comfortable trying to write in my cot in this dim light, but I don't much feel like going back downstairs and getting caught in a political discussion with Father.

Lewis gave me some news which I can't stop thinking about. He's leaving Callander and starting a job next month at Canadian Car and Foundry in Montreal. I'd never heard of it, of course, but that's no surprise. He says it's a company known for automobiles and trains, but that they are expanding into aeronautics and taking him on as a junior engineer. He's obviously thrilled—I don't think he stumbled over a single word the whole time he was talking, his hazel eyes dancing. I'm happy for him, of course—*of course*—and I said so. But I will miss him. He's been like a brother to me, a sounding board for some of the strange twists and turns at the nursery this past year, with Ivy gone. Now he's leaving too, heeding the call of the big, wide world.

"What does your father think?" I asked.

Lewis's smile dimmed for a minute, but not by much. "He's pleased for me, and proud, I know he is. But he's also worried, particularly because of the tensions in Europe."

"Have you told him you won't be flying any planes? That might reassure him."

I don't know why I said that.

Lewis turned to look at me, a flicker, then turned his eyes back to the road.

"No," he said. "No, I haven't. I can't promise him that."

When we reached Mother and Father's place, I said again that I was very pleased for him and wished him a merry Christmas, his father and mother too.

"You'll have to keep in touch," I added brightly. "Write and tell me all about Montreal. I've never been." *How brash!* I realize now. How presumptuous. I think I made him blush.

"I've never been east of Ottawa," I babbled on, trying to sound light. "Plus I love getting mail and Ivy doesn't have much time for writing anymore."

Now he had trouble finding his tongue again. "In fact, I was going to ask if perhaps you could write to me with news of how the quintuplets are getting along," he said at last. "Could you do that? I want the real story, not just what I can deduce from Fred's photos in the paper."

We laughed about that, which was a good way to part. But Lewis *flying* planes. Such a strange thought. When would that happen, I wondered. How often? I have an inkling now of why Mr. Cartwright would prefer Lewis spend his days stuttering in front of a noisy classroom rather than cutting a swath through the skies.

December 30, 1937 (*Toronto Star*)

WON'T EXHIBIT QUINTS
DESPITE $500,000 OFFER

CALLANDER, Ontario—An intimated payment of $500,000 from directors of the 1939 World's Fair in New York has failed to convince the guardians of the Dionne quintuplets that the five babies should be taken to the exhibition a year from now.

"Nothing doing," Dr. A. R. Dafoe and Judge Valin, two of the Quints' guardians, said today.

It may be a long time before the world sees a group picture of the Dionne family, including the quintuplets. Conflicting contracts over pictures prevent Mr. and Mrs. Dionne from being photographed with their five famous children.

Mr. Dionne is under contract to a New York syndicate with exclusive rights to photograph him. Another syndicate has exclusive picture rights to the quintuplets, which provides a considerable portion of their living expenses of $24,000 a year. Until these contracts expire, it will be impossible to pose Mr. and Mrs. Dionne with their five famous babies.

Would-be amateur photographers of the babies are still causing some concern at the nursery, Dr. Dafoe said today. Despite signs warning that no snapshots of the Quints may be taken, a few tourists attempt to get pictures of the babies through the viewing screen.

"It was necessary to seize film every day last summer," Dr. Dafoe said. "On one occasion Annette noticed a man taking a picture of her and called to her nurse, who immediately asked for the film. It was even necessary to destroy a complete roll of moving picture film which one tourist had taken of the babies. We hung this film over the front door as a warning to others, since taking pictures of the quintuplets is strictly forbidden."

The Hollywood moving picture company which has already made two full-length features of the quintuplets will begin work on a third picture next June. Their $300,000 contract with the quintuplets, providing for four full-length features, has provided the bulk of the babies' fortune.

Used with permission.

1938

January 3, 1938

I'm back at work after what ended up being a longer Christmas break than planned: I came down with bronchitis and Dr. Dafoe asked me to stay with my family in town until I was feeling better rather than put the girls at risk. I was glad to have the extra time at home with little Edith, despite feeling poorly. Mother and Father seemed genuinely pleased to have me back home for such a stretch. They are proud of me, I realize. A new sensation. They loved my painting of Edith with her toy bunny, but, more than that, they are pleased to see me so settled in my "career," as they've started to call it. I don't think of it as a career, myself. It is simply my life.

Dr. Dafoe came by the house Friday to make sure I was cleared of any infection and agreed I was 100 percent recovered, so I'm back at the nursery today. Mr. Cartwright senior picked me up and brought me out first thing. For once he didn't much seem in the mood for talking other than to say that Christmas had been lively. His other son, Bernard, Lewis's brother, was in town with his wife and their little girl, Sheryl, who must be about the same age as Edith.

I let a beat pass before I said, "And how is Lewis making out in Montreal?"

Lewis left for Quebec New Year's Day, Mr. Cartwright replied stiffly, but they hadn't heard from him yet. "I reckon he'll make out just fine." His tone implied he wanted to leave it at that.

The girls absolutely mobbed me when I came in the door at breakfast time, spilling their juice and rattling their spoons. Émilie more than all of them scarcely let me out of her sight all day.

Almost everyone else is also back at work today, or returned before I did: Fred and George came up to Callander from Toronto yesterday, and Dr. Dafoe returned from his vacation last week. Miss Beaulieu will arrive tomorrow, joined by Dr. Blatz, who is expected to visit for several days to discuss plans for the quintuplets' education and care in the coming months. I can't say I'm thrilled to hear he's coming back.

Still, something shifted here while all of us were away, or that's how it feels. Maybe it's these short, dark days, but a certain levity is missing from the nursery. The girls seem more guarded and anxious to please. I can't help thinking that without Sylvie's booming laugh or the goofy antics from George and Fred, there's been a lack of gaiety in the nursery these last few weeks.

Miss Tremblay and Nurse Noël have formed a strong bond, that's clear. Miss Tremblay told me that M. and Mme. Dionne were over most days during the Christmas period, which is astounding given how seldom they visited last autumn. There is much talk of Maman and Papa from the girls, too, which is unusual. But then Miss Tremblay seems to be taking pains to remind them of the kind of girls their Maman wants them to be. I predict a clash with Miss Beaulieu, who tends to rule the roost when it comes to what constitutes good behavior and what doesn't.

January 5, 1938 (*Toronto Star*)

QUINTS LEARNING ENGLISH— "PLEASE" IS FIRST LESSON

Use Only That Language at Lunch

CALLANDER, Ontario—"Please" is the first English word which the Dionne quintuplets are learning.

"They are able to chatter back and forth fluently in French," Dr. A. R. Dafoe says. "Each quint has a vocabulary of between 300 and 400 French words. They began to hear English a month ago, and they know 20 to 25 English words now."

All conversation at the lunch table in the nursery is now carried on in English. "This is bread," "this is butter," say their three nurses and teachers.

Dr. Dafoe, who has been in charge of the babies' health ever since they were born, is called "docteur" or sometimes "Docteur Dafoe" and occasionally "Da-da."

This spring, the public will be barred from viewing the quintuplets the minute they show any signs of strain or fatigue, Dr. Dafoe declared, acknowledging that occasionally the girls can hear their visitors. Half a million tourists visited them in Callander in 1937.

"We are bringing them up to take all this attention in their stride. Their attitude must be like that of princesses in England: they must not notice anything unusual in all of the attention that is bound to be lavished upon them."

January 6, 1938

The New Year is just a few days old and already the mood in the nursery is curdled with tension, the poor girls at the center of it. This would be funny if it wasn't so awful, and if I had someone to laugh about it with.

Mme. Dionne has been sick, I learned, likely with the same cold that triggered my own illness over Christmas. She—or Papa Dionne—must have decided she was well enough to visit today, and visit she did, bringing with her a large cake she'd baked to celebrate the "Solemnity of Mary," whatever that is. Well, I shouldn't say "whatever that is," because I got an earful about it from Miss Tremblay, who clearly knows her Catholic holidays. It's a big feast day, apparently, to celebrate the eighth day of Christmas. The problem is, today's the wrong day. Even Miss Tremblay looked a tad sheepish about this. January 1 was the feast day, but as Papa Dionne explained to the girls, Maman was too ill last Saturday, so they would be celebrating today.

The Dionnes arrived all bundled up against the cold, snow melting on their hats and shoulders. Mme. Dionne was carrying a pedestaled cake platter with a domed tin cover that she set down on the games table, then lifted off the lid with a flourish. The girls' eyes practically bugged out of their heads, and they rushed over to take a better look, squealing, "Legato, legato!" Maman's broad face broke out in a smile—so rare a sight, I was caught off guard. Nurse Noël sailed off to get a knife, forks, and plates while I stood back and tried to keep my mouth shut. The girls are not allowed cake and other sweets—this is one of the strictest rules in the Blatz handbook—but they know *le gâteau* from the few times they've been allowed to have it, usually for a photo shoot for special occasions (the Solemnity of Mary not included). Moreover, Dr. Dafoe was due to arrive at any moment with Dr. Blatz and Miss Beaulieu. Miss Tremblay had pulled a large chair over to the quintuplets' tea table, and Mme. Dionne had managed to lower herself into the seat, her eyes shining as the girls reached out tentative little fingers and poked them into the frosting. I know I should have spoken out, but I was loath to draw attention to myself and something about the sight of the girls crowded around their beaming mother made me keep my distance.

Of course, just as Maman Dionne was cutting the cake, the doctors arrived and fireworks ensued. Miss Beaulieu bustled in, clucking, and tried to take the cake from the table. Mme. Dionne bellowed at her to back off and grabbed at the platter, dislodging the cake, which tumbled facedown onto the linoleum. The girls froze, poor lambs, their eyes wide and darting as their treat plunged through the air. Marie and Cécile started whimpering and groping for each other's hands, while Émilie simply stared from Miss Beaulieu to Mme. Dionne. Yvonne, little rascal, dropped to all fours and thrust her fingers into the side of the cake, bringing a sizable handful swiftly to her mouth before anyone could stop her. Dr. Dafoe actually laughed, but Dr. Blatz was furious, launching into a high-pitched diatribe, in English, about why sugar was not permitted, particularly in the morning. I thought M. Dionne was going to combust, and Mme. Dionne burst into tears, bending awkwardly to try to retrieve the cake, looking every bit like a sofa cushion trying to fold itself in two. I managed to sweep the girls out of the playroom before the fight began in earnest, but they could hear the argument despite my best efforts to get them into their snow gear and out into the private yard. We didn't see the Dionnes leave.

Later, Dr. Dafoe summoned me, Miss Tremblay, Nurse Noël, and Miss Beaulieu to his office, where he and Dr. Blatz had been sequestered for most of the afternoon. They didn't say a word about the incident with the cake, merely presented us with Dr. Blatz's new "quintuplet schedule" as he likes to call it. It is much the same as the old one, with every single minute of the day accounted for, including Toilet Trips, Nourishment, Relaxation, and Directed Play.

"The parents must be reminded of the importance of visiting during Outdoor and Indoor Free Play times, but not during Directed Play or Constructive Play times," Dr. Blatz said sternly. "We have explained this to them today, but we would ask that you help to reinforce this message. This is essential for the equilibrium of the nursery."

I did my best to translate for Miss Tremblay. I could see none of this was sitting well with her, or with Nurse Noël, but they didn't say a word.

January 11, 1938

LAST WEEK'S FIASCO with M. and Mme. Dionne has left a bad taste in everyone's mouth, especially the girls'; they keep asking when the "legato" is coming again. Miss Tremblay and Nurse Noël are clearly fuming over the treatment of the parents and are at pains to make the girls take sides. Yesterday, when the girls heard Dr. Dafoe's car pull up outside the rear playroom, where they like to wave and blow kisses, Miss Tremblay pulled them away from the windows, telling them, "No, no, Docteur is not nice, the doctor is dirty." *Dirty* is a ridiculous word, but it's clearly something the girls picked up over Christmas. I find it very unsettling. Things they don't like are now "dirty" and "naughty"—words we've never used with them in the past. They scrunch their sweet faces when they say it and whip their heads back and forth as if smelling something bad, plainly mimicking their prudish minders.

I took Miss Tremblay to task over this today, and she was cold as ice, blinking at me sideways and twitching her beaky chin up and down like a sparrow, saying I must have misunderstood what she'd been saying.

On the other hand, when M. and Mme. Dionne visited this afternoon—the first time they have done so since the Virgin Mary's rescheduled Feast Day—Miss Tremblay put on a great pantomime of enthusiasm and happiness at their arrival, working the girls up into bewildered excitement. Nurse Noël was actually nudging Em and Marie to go and give their mother and father a hug and a kiss. It is terribly confusing for all of them.

January 23, 1938

Miss Emma Trimpany
Dafoe Hospital and Nursery
Callander, ON

Dear Miss Trimpany,

Happy New Year to you and everyone else at the Dafoe Nursery. I've spent the past month trying to think of something interesting to tell you about Montreal. The plain truth is, I haven't had much spare time to explore the city, although I'm quite taken by what I've seen so far of the architecture. I've never visited Europe, of course—not yet—but I'd say some of the buildings here have the same grace and grandeur as those in Paris.

I do miss home. I miss the bright white of the fields and the fresh sprawl of the open land. We had a foot of snow here yesterday, but it turned to sooty slush in the city streets within a matter of hours. And the cold here is worse than the cold back home. The bitter wind funnels around the city buildings like it's being chased by winter himself. There is a church on the corner that serves a hot supper in the basement every evening, and you can't help but feel for the folks lining up around the block while the wind slices through like a knife.

It's been a real change of pace, sitting at a desk again with paper and instruments. These are skills I feared I'd lost. My current project relates to landing gear—those are the wheels used when a plane takes off and lands again. I dreamt last night of wheels that can retract like the legs of a falcon when he tucks them tight to his stomach, or perhaps trail behind, like those of a stork. Something to make our plane more streamlined and aerodynamic. Can you picture it? I can.

I'd wager this is going to be a lonely city for an Anglophone, although the men at work are a mix of French and English and seem a decent, if serious, group of chaps. I hope you'll write.

Yours truly,
Lewis Cartwright
11 Rue Saint Ida
Montreal, Quebec

January 27, 1938

I love to be in their bedroom before the girls wake, listening to them sleep. Yvonne and Cécile have started snoring sweetly, something Dr. Blatz naturally feels needs to be thoroughly investigated. Émilie is an early riser these days, like me, but she simply lies looking up at the ceiling nattering to herself. I can't understand a word of it, but occasionally one of her sisters will wake and answer her in the same lilting sounds and syllables. It's only when they try their private language on us, the nurses and doctors, that it lets them down, and unless we can swiftly guess their meaning they'll start stamping their feet, incredulous at our stupidity. Dr. Blatz disapproves of their strange language and scolds them when he hears it, insisting that they speak in "proper" French or English. I like it. Whatever they are discussing softly at first light sounds happy and soothing, like a burbling brook. I've even picked up the odd word: *ba-ba-bah* for crying, *shoh-shoh* for soft, *le-lay* for milk.

By 6:30 A.M. I've got them all up and to the toilet. They still soil their diapers at night, but they are getting better and usually produce something for Dr. Blatz's charts during the first morning toilet visit. For months now he's insisted that they no longer wear diapers by day, which has led to a lot more laundry and a few "accidents" on the playroom floor, which fortunately is linoleum. Miss Tremblay disapproves of Dr. Blatz's methods in general, but she is particularly put out by the seven daily scheduled trips to the bathroom. She supervises the 8:15 and 10:30 visits, but does so with much harrumphing and ill will.

From the toilets, they head to the bath. The littlest three go in the one tub and Annette and Yvonne in the other. I usually am finishing up the notes for the morning toilet visit, so Nurse Noël and Miss Tremblay take charge of the bathing and I don't pay too much attention to the screeching and splashing.

Today Marie came scampering out of the bathroom, naked as a jaybird and dripping wet, while I was seated in the charting area. I could hear the other girls calling after her and assumed it was some new game, so I snatched her up and started to carry her back to her towel. Miss Tremblay, as it turns out, was in hot pursuit and took Marie from my arms, none too kindly.

"Naughty girl!" she said, giving Marie a very angry look. "Very naughty. Naked! That's dirty."

It was absolutely preposterous. I followed them back to the bathroom and was met by all the girls grabbing for their towels and trying in vain to cover themselves up in some charade of modesty. "Very naughty!" Annette parroted Miss Tremblay. "Dirty girl!"

"Don't be silly!" I tried to say to Annette, but little Cécile was already hustling over to close the door behind me while the others scurried around the corner to their dressing room.

Nurse Noël turned to me, her chins quavering indignantly. "The girls are learning modesty, Nurse Trimpany. They know it is not right for them to be dashing around unclothed."

I simply didn't know how to respond. They are toddlers, for goodness' sake. Not even four years old. When on earth did indecency become a part of their lesson plans?

I managed to slip away to Dr. Dafoe's office, and George tactfully left his desk to allow us to speak in private. I told the doctor about the bath-time incident and all this talk of dirty and naughty. He didn't say anything, but he nodded his head and made a note on a piece of paper. He said: "It is the religious influence, I fear. Miss Tremblay is particularly pious, which is why the Dionnes recommended her for the position."

This was news to me, which must have registered on my face. "Oh yes," he said, nodding. "M. Dionne is now privy to the staffing decisions, although he does not have final say."

He put his pen down carefully, interlaced his fingers, and looked for a moment like he was going to say more. Then he said, "I appreciate you telling me," and left it at that.

February 8, 1938

DR. BLAH-BLAH HAS fired Miss Tremblay. On the spot! I must say, I'm relieved, but it wasn't a pleasant scene. Worse, the girls never got a chance to say goodbye to her. I think they were rather terrified of Miss Tremblay, but that doesn't make anything less confusing for them. They were peeking around the door of the playroom when she was marshaled from the premises, still hissing in French at anyone who would listen. Now the girls have decamped to the reading corner with their dolls, blankies, and pillows, and are conferring softly among themselves, their little foreheads furrowed. So here we are, another one of us gone. I can already imagine what Lewis will say.

It was Miss Beaulieu who figured it out: Miss Tremblay has been putting diapers on the girls after their second toilet visit, underneath their bloomers! I don't know how long she's been doing it, and it must have been only in the mornings, after Nourishment, when she is the sole nurse watching over them during Constructive Play and they tend to stay seated. It was quite by chance that I popped into the quiet playroom today at precisely the moment Annette unwittingly exposed the secret. Miss Beaulieu was in the room, too, writing the alphabet on the blackboard at the front of the room—I think now that this was likely intentional on her part. In any case, Annette stood up and, pinching her nose in her fingers, marched over to Miss Tremblay and announced in French: "Marie is very, very naughty in her diaper."

I scarcely paid attention, assuming Annette had misspoken, that she'd meant underwear. They often use a word that is not quite the right one.

Miss Tremblay quickly rose to take Marie to get changed. But Miss Beaulieu turned and said in French, "No, stay, Miss Tremblay. Nurse Trimpany, can you please see to Marie?"

"Nonsense," Miss Tremblay said, "Nurse Trimpany is busy." She beckoned for Marie to accompany her. I was already crossing the room, my hand outstretched to take Marie's, smiling to show her that she wasn't naughty, not at all. I hesitated.

"*Merci*, Nurse Trimpany," Miss Beaulieu repeated, and her voice was icy. "Miss Tremblay, please be seated."

I should have guessed, I suppose, from that miniature battle of wills and from the belligerence crimped into Miss Tremblay's face. But I didn't put two and two together until I'd walked little Marie to the bathroom and crouched down to help her to step out of her bloomers. She stood rigid as a pole, her face stricken, the way they look when they're being subjected to every new measurement and test dreamed up by Dr. Blatz. I gave her a kiss on her temple and tried to make light of it.

"It's perfectly fine, my little cabbage. No tears. No ba-ba-bah. Weren't you just concentrating so nicely on your alphabet! Accidents happen. They happen to the best of us."

Then, of course, I found the diaper. The girls haven't worn daytime diapers in months—or so I'd thought—and indeed, we are supposed to stop diapering them at night before the end of March. So says Dr. Blatz's schedule.

Marie started sobbing then, burying her face in my breast as I pulled her legs, one by one, out of the soiled diaper. "Marie dirty," she kept saying, despite all my shushing. "Naughty-naughty Marie."

I got Marie all cleaned up with fresh panties, and then took her to the toilet to spend a few minutes seated on the potty, just in case, all the while reassuring her that she'd done nothing wrong.

I expect Miss Beaulieu already had an inkling of the outcome. She took Marie's hand from mine and asked me to head to the office, where she'd already sent Miss Tremblay. "Dr. Dafoe has asked for you to be there to translate," she murmured.

When I arrived, Dr. Blatz was summoning his best French, but Miss Tremblay was speaking so fast and with such anger, spittle flying from her lips, he clearly couldn't make out a word. Dr. Dafoe, of course, understood not a thing, his head quivering in frustration. She spun around when I arrived and turned her fury on me, saying that Dr. Blatz knew nothing about child rearing, that he was raising the children to be like English children or, worse, like American children, that they were godless and vain. It was poisonous. I turned to Dr. Dafoe, mortified, and he said quietly: "Tell her plainly that she is dismissed. She must pack her things and go."

Miss Tremblay paused, glaring at me, waiting for me to translate. To his credit, Dr. Blatz used this pause to say, in French, that he was sorry Miss Tremblay disagreed so strongly with his methods and that her dismissal was effective immediately.

The Dionnes are going to throw a fit when they learn that Miss Tremblay is gone.

February 10, 1938

THE NEW NURSE has arrived, a graduate of Dr. Blatz's school in Toronto. Her name is Sigrid Ulrichson, a Dane, I believe, although she speaks fluent French, with an accent. She is tall and blond, with wavy curls like honey being drizzled from a spoon—the girls have taken to her right away. She spent her first day mincing around with Dr. Blatz's book tucked to her chest or consulting it like a field guide, her plump lips mouthing the words. I myself haven't had the heart to read the first page despite having been given my own copy, signed by the great man himself.

February 13, 1938

I HEARD THE Dionnes when they arrived at the back door, M. Dionne scraping his heavy boots like a bull about to charge. This is my cue to retreat. Whenever it snows, I notice, they'll come over to visit the girls before Mr. Cartwright has come through with the plow so they know they won't run into Dr. Dafoe.

I've taken to visiting George in the doctor's office when the Dionnes appear. If he's very busy, he'll give me a stack of mail and put me to work slitting envelopes and helping him sort out personal mail from the deluge of commercial offers. Other times I bring my sketchbook and pencil. I've been working on some close-ups of the girls' faces, trying to capture what sets each apart.

Most days George is chatty, often reading me some of the extraordinary advice flooding in from around the world. Today he was subdued. I glanced up from my sketch of Yvonne and saw he was watching me, which made me blush terribly. He smiled and stood, then paused.

"Can I guess who it is?" He made his way around the desk so that he was standing behind me. He put a palm down on the corner of the desk and leaned over me. Not close, mind you, but close enough that I could smell him, a clean, soapy scent. He keeps his hair rather long and parted on the side, but slicked back, which makes it look darker at the temples although it's clearly more of a golden brown, with a bit of a wave in it. When he leaned over my book, his hair swung forward, almost like a woman's, and he reached with his free hand to smooth it back again behind his ear. I felt as if I'd turned to glass, hot and combustible, like a Mazda lamp. I don't even remember what George said, who he thought I was drawing, or how I responded. After a minute he straightened up again and stepped back, stretching his arms toward the ceiling and swiveling his head to stretch his neck. I was tingling as if singed. But in a good way, if that's possible. I waited until I thought I was breathing normally again, then mumbled some excuse that allowed me to go hurrying back to the nursery.

February 17, 1938

NONE OF US were expecting Dr. Dafoe today because of the blizzard. He surprised us all by coming out *with* Mr. Cartwright first thing this morning in the plow-mounted truck, then slipping in the kitchen door, where the path through the yard was the clearest. I had finished off my morning notes and was heading to help Nurse Noël get the girls brushed and clothed. They are wild these days after too much time cooped up inside, and I could hear Nurse Noël scolding Annette over her latest perceived misdemeanor. Then, unexpectedly, Dr. Dafoe's voice in the playroom, booming, "Where are my little monkeys?" A pause, then shrieks of excitement from the girls, *"Le Doh-Doh!"* I could hear their little feet squeaking, shoeless, across the linoleum. By the time I got to the playroom, Nurse Noël was already trying to herd them back to their rooms, Marie and Cécile wearing only their bloomers and the others in various stages of dress. It was as if Nurse Noël was purposefully ignoring Dr. Dafoe or so angry with the girls that she didn't let his presence curb her reaction.

"Girls!" she barked in French. "*Girls!* This is very, very naughty. Jesus is very angry with you. Very angry! Nice girls do not run around showing themselves without their clothes."

Dr. Dafoe had stooped to lift Émilie into his arms, but he seemed to freeze at these words, standing stock-still in his damp socks, staring at Nurse Noël, no doubt laboring to translate her words in his head. After a moment, he tore his gaze away and smiled at Émilie. "It *is* winter," he said to her in English. "You're going to catch cold. Go and put on something warm." He planted a kiss on her brow, then set her down on the floor.

The girls scampered away, quiet as mice. I should have gone

with them, but instead I stayed as if rooted. Neither nurse nor doctor seemed to have seen me slip into the room. The anger surging between them was like an electric current, back and forth, back and forth. I was close enough to Nurse Noël that I could see perspiration moist in the folds of her neck, her bosom heaving. She pursed her lips and jutted her chin out, then strode after the girls.

Dr. Dafoe swiftly followed, speaking in English, softly and slowly, so that I could scarcely catch the words. "I will not have you threatening my girls," he hissed. "I will not have you threatening them with their faith. They will not be taught to think of themselves in this way." She understands enough English, Nurse Noël, I know she does. She would not need me to translate.

Then, once again, the doctor stopped abruptly, this time just inside the doorway to the girls' dressing room and toilet. His round head bobbled briefly atop his squat body, snow melting on his hat and his pipe clutched in his mitten. For an instant I thought of the snowman the girls and I had built last month, now smothered by the thick snow. I had the urge to laugh, but it was nerves that were driving me.

Then, as I watched, Dr. Dafoe's head dipped and he slowly lifted his stocking foot, toes pointing skyward as if in accusation. My heart leapt into my throat, and this time I had to slap my hand over my mouth.

I couldn't see his face, but heard his words clearly, his voice reedy and broken.

"A turd," he croaked. "A *turd* in my nursery!" He lowered his heel gingerly to the floor. "You shame my girls, you threaten them with God's wrath, yet *feces* lies unheeded on the floor of my nursery!"

I backed out of the room and made it to my dormitory before the laughter burst out of me as if from a pierced balloon. I buried my face in my pillow, my breath coming in gasps, until I thought I could safely make my way back to the playroom.

And now she's gone too. Nurse Noël is gone.

February 18, 1938

FORGET ABOUT GERMANY: the real battle lines are shaping up here at the nursery. Scarcely ten minutes after Dr. Dafoe's arrival this morning, M. Dionne was storming through the front door in shiny new shoes accompanied by M. St. Jacques, his solicitor. Dr. Dafoe had driven his own car again, the sun shining for the first time in weeks, bright and winking over the white drifts.

M. Dionne didn't even pause to look in on the girls when he clattered past, his lawyer trailing behind him like a plume of exhaust. Dr. Dafoe ushered them into his office and closed the door.

Now an emergency meeting has been called, and all of the guardians will attend, including Judge Valin and the government man from Toronto.

February 28, 1938

TODAY'S MEETING BETWEEN the guardians started at noon and went all through the rest of the day and into the evening, and is still dragging on now. At 11:00 P.M.! George is locked in there with them this time. I shall have to persuade him to tell me what transpired.

March 1, 1938

NO SIGN OF Dr. Dafoe or the other guardians when I went down this morning. Dr. Dafoe's office was locked, and even George was gone. No one returned to the nursery all day. A rare quiet day for me and the girls and Nurse Ulrichson.

I used the time to crack the spine on *Collected Studies on the Dionne Quintuplets* by W. E. Blatz. I hate it. Worse: I hate the part I've played in its creation. The pictures alone are enough to turn your stomach—page after page of the girls being stretched out and sized, measured, weighed, and calipered, their soft eyes meeting the camera's lens with such a wretched mix of dread and resignation. Dr. Blatz and the other scientists write of them the way you might a troop of monkeys—indeed, two of the scientists we've had in our midst were not "child psychologists," which is what we were led to believe, but zoologists. *For the first time in history five children are growing up in a restricted social atmosphere of multiple contemporary siblings.* The words make me sick to my stomach. I leafed through the rest of the book and learned nothing, not one thing about who these girls truly are and what makes them so special. I refuse to read another word.

March 2, 1938

WE HAVEN'T SEEN Dr. Dafoe since the meeting, but George is back and he's being extraordinarily tight-lipped. He didn't make his usual visit to the girls to gather inspiration for his column, and we didn't see him at lunch. I slipped away again during the 3:00 P.M. free play and popped my head into the kitchen to ask Marguerite to put together a tray of tea and biscuits. She offered to bring it by, of course, but I took it to Dr. Dafoe's office myself.

"Come in," George said, and when I entered with the tea he smiled ruefully. He had his jacket off and his shirtsleeves rolled to the elbow, his hair tousled like a schoolboy's.

"I know what you're up to, Nurse Trimpany." Then he sighed and pointed me to the other chair.

"Is everything okay?" I asked. "What happened?"

George made as if to settle back behind his desk again, then walked to the door and closed it softly. We'd never been alone in the office together with the door closed. I felt my birthmark begin to pulse. George, however, started pacing from one end of the room to the other, his arms clasped across his broad chest so that his shirtsleeves strained over the muscles bulging above his elbows. I busied myself with the teacups.

"Dionne has a long list of grievances," he said finally. "He's incensed about the dismissal of the two French staff, Noël and Tremblay. He's furious about Dr. Blatz and his research, he's angry about the Hollywood movies and the English lessons, he's worried about 'Protestant influences' and the lack of French Catholic values. He's suspicious of the endorsement deals and believes he's not getting his fair share. It goes on and on. Frankly, I missed some of it because he occasionally switched to French and spoke so quickly I couldn't make head or tail out of it."

I took a seat, but didn't say anything, I just watched George striding back and forth, his chin tucked, his cheeks flushed beneath the shadow of a beard. Then he stopped abruptly in front of my chair, inches from my knees.

"The big one," he said, looking down at me. "He wants Dr. Dafoe removed as guardian."

Removed? It made no sense. A heat had flared in me when he

planted himself so close his trousers seemed to be brushing my skirt. Now a chill had chased away the warmth.

"But the girls wouldn't even be here if it wasn't for Dr. Dafoe." I'd spoken with a quaver, which irked me. I tried to steady my words. "He's the one who saved them and he's the one who's managed to keep them safe all along, through all of this." I gestured around the office at the filing cabinets and papers, the framed photos and paintings of the girls with Palmolive soap, Life Savers, and cod-liver oil. The same brands, no doubt, that the Dionnes were selling at the souvenir shop across the street. "Without Dr. Dafoe's protection, who knows what harms could have come to them," I added. Even as I said it my thoughts strayed to Dr. Blatz and his awful book, and my voice faltered so that my last words were almost a whisper. "They belong every bit as much to Dr. Dafoe and this hospital as they do to anyone else, in any place."

"I beg your pardon?"

George was still hovering above me, there was no chance he hadn't heard.

I tried again. "It's just, at this point, after all he's done for them, they think of him as their father."

George gaped at me. "You can't possibly believe that, Emma."

When I didn't answer, he stared at me a moment longer, then shook his shaggy head and stepped away, yanking at his chair. It stuttered backward with a squeak so that his cup, on the desk, trilled in its saucer.

"Thanks for bringing the tea and biscuits," he said, sitting. He pulled out his pocket watch, then looked up at me. "I'm afraid I have some work to get back to."

I opened my mouth to say more, closed it, then opened and shut it a second time. I must have looked like a guppy bubbling mutely in my bowl. Just then, of course, Marguerite barged in, high-bosomed and smelling of onions, fussing with the tea things and warbling about whether George would stay for supper. There was nothing for me to do but take my spinning head and go.

March 3, 1938

MISS NORAH ROUSSELLE arrived today. She's Nurse Noël's replacement, but in fact she's a teacher, not a nurse. Our healthy girls need only two nurses now, it seems. Miss Beaulieu will also be leaving us soon, Dr. Dafoe has told us. I can detect a slight accent when Miss Rousselle speaks French with the girls, but they of course don't notice. They have their own funny accents anyhow.

March 10, 1938

Miss Emma Trimpany
Dafoe Hospital and Nursery
Callander, ON

Dear Emma,

I trust you are surviving the Canadian winter. I myself am relocating to Florida for two months next week so wanted to make sure you got these back before I left.

Enclosed are the last sketches you sent me of the babies. The children, I should say, because they really are shooting up, aren't they? I have very little in the way of feedback. I'm starting to feel you've already surpassed my talents. There is something in these portraits that elevates them above mere drawings, and I struggle to put my finger on it, other than to say that the expressions you've managed to capture are extraordinarily complex. Those of us who only know the quintuplets through their daily photos in the paper assume that they live a blessed life, wanting for nothing. They are plump and shiny little girls, new outfits and new toys in every photo, not a care in the world. Your sketches, if I may say so, particularly the close-up sketches you did in pencil, hint at something far more nuanced: anxiety, uncertainty, or worse. In any case, they are lovely and you should be extremely proud.

Now, my news. I will no longer be painting the girls. My understanding is that the guardians have commissioned another artist now that they are getting a bit older. Indeed, my passion and perhaps my talent are best suited to infants and toddlers. I do hope you will keep at it, whomever they hire. I believe you have a rare talent and would strongly urge you to consider following it as far as it will take you.

Yours truly,
Maud Tousey Fangel
145 East 72nd
New York, NY

March 17, 1938

Ever since I received Mrs. Fangel's letter I've been trying to find a spare minute to speak privately with Dr. Dafoe and ask about the new artist for the girls. The doctor has been under a great deal of stress, written plain as day on his features. Today, however, he called me to his office and asked George to give us some privacy.

The upshot: the guardians have *not* found another artist to paint the girls. They would like to offer me the opportunity. At the moment, the Corn Products Refining Company of New York and Chicago has commissioned a series of advertisements for their Karo brand corn syrup and would prefer paintings to photographs of the girls. And I'd hoped I'd heard the last of corn syrup!

We did not discuss a specific payment, but Dr. Dafoe muttered that the compensation "will be generous." That kind of talk makes me uncomfortable, as Dr. Dafoe could clearly see. He gave a sigh and reached as he always does for his pipe and tobacco.

"Remember, Emma," he said. "As much as we may disagree with the commercial side of things, every little bit benefits the girls. Their trust fund continues to grow, but I fear it is a long ways from reaching the point where we can be sure they will want for nothing, their whole lives long." He jabbed the pipe in his mouth and took several seconds to light it, his eyes crossing as he brought the match to the bowl. "You are aware, of course, of the increased pressure being brought by the Dionnes. Publicly, it is important that we portray unity and shared purpose, but my dearest wish is that we will be able to continue to manage the girls' finances such that they will not be forced to move back into the farmhouse with the rest of the family."

The farmhouse! Was this what George was getting at when we'd had that strange exchange about Dr. Dafoe being removed as guardian?

"Surely that's not a possibility?" I blurted out. I couldn't imagine how the family of six children plus the parents were managing in those cramped quarters, let alone how the five girls could be accommodated among them.

Dr. Dafoe shrugged and puffed on his pipe.

"These are the kinds of things M. Dionne's lawyer is requesting," he said. "I see it as my duty to protect the girls in every way I can." He paused and lifted the pipe momentarily from his lips. "I hope you see things the same way."

I would like to have a word with Fred about what kind of commission I should be paid by the American corn syrup company. He comes in only a few days a week now and rarely stays at the nursery long enough for us to speak. Perhaps George might give me some advice. He might know what Mrs. Fangel was paid, although of course I couldn't be paid at the same rate. Perhaps I'll write to Ivy.

March 25, 1938

FINALLY SOME LAUGHTER again in the nursery. The *Star* newspaper has provided all the props and costumes for a special series of photos of the girls in which they act out scenes from Mother Goose. Today they dressed up for "Sing a Song of Sixpence" and thought it was wonderful fun.

They scarcely stayed in one character long enough for Fred to get his pictures before tearing off their robes and dresses and climbing into something else. Yvonne played the king while Marie had the choice role of queen, managing to devour the bread and corn syrup before Fred could even duck behind his camera. I was tickled at the idea of Émilie as the maid, hanging laundry on the line and not a clue as to what she was supposed to be doing. Nurse Ulrichson has been painstakingly teaching them the rhyme, explaining each English word, and they have been singing it at top volume, although their accents make them almost unintelligible. They love the end the best, piling on Yvonne, captive under her thick robes, and trying to clamp their sticky mouths over her poor nose.

> *Sing a song of sixpence, a pocket full of rye.*
> *Four and twenty blackbirds, baked in a pie.*
> *When the pie was opened, the birds began to sing;*
> *Wasn't that a dainty dish to set before the king!*
> *The king was in his counting house, counting out his money.*
> *The queen was in the parlor, eating bread and honey.*
> *The maid was in the garden, hanging out the clothes,*
> *Down came a blackbird and nipped off her nose!*

March 26, 1938

Miss Emma Trimpany
Dafoe Hospital and Nursery
Callander, ON

Dear ~~Miss Trimpany~~ Emma,

I was sorry to hear of more comings and goings in the nursery. All that flux must be awfully hard on the little girls. How are they faring?

We had a mild weekend here, so I got the harebrained idea to hike to the top of Mont Royal, which is the mountain in the middle of the city. At the top, the Saint-Jean-Baptiste charitable society has erected a cross more than 100 feet tall, lit up at night by dozens of electric bulbs. I can actually see it from the window in my rented room. Up close, by daylight, it is not nearly as impressive, but the views of the city are something. The air at the peak seemed fresher and cleaner than it does down below—more like home. And the sky was cloudless: the kind of blue that makes you feel like it goes on forever and could take you anywhere you wanted to go.

Back in my cold room now, my legs are stiff and I have blisters the size of a silver dollar on both heels. I will regret my little expedition tomorrow.

I have a rock dove who has taken to roosting on my windowsill. He arrived last month and has really settled himself at home, making a terrific mess of the wall. The green and violet iridescence on his throat is quite something to see up close. He seems pleased as a peacock to have me admiring him through the glass, strutting to and fro and sizing me up with his orange eye. I've named him Howard Hughes.

Yours truly,
Lewis
11 Rue Saint Ida
Montreal, Quebec

April 11, 1938

Dr. Dafoe gave me the afternoon off today to work on my first painting for the corn syrup company. I'm trying a different type of oil paint that is much brighter in color. It's taken a bit of practice to understand how to mix and layer it, but I've got the hang of it now, I think. I'm not painting a scene for this one, just the faces of the girls based on the pencil sketches I've been working on. I'm pleased with how it's going. Today I could hear the girls playing outside in the private yard—this was the first warm day we've had—and their happy voices helped me work.

At one point, George tapped lightly, then popped his head around the open door. I love it when he stops by to see my progress. Today he peered at the painting for no more than a second or two, then strolled away.

He did a distracted loop of the room the way he does when he's looking for ideas for his column, then plunked himself on the bench by the windows. When I glanced over, he appeared to be watching the girls outside, a faint smile on his lips.

"Imagine being so carefree," he said.

I scarcely paid attention. I was struggling with Marie's mouth, which is smaller than those of her sisters.

"They're in a bubble. We're all in this bubble, aren't we? It's as if the rest of the world doesn't exist."

He turned to look at me. I kept puttering with my paints, but I could sense his gaze on me and felt myself growing flustered.

Then, out of nowhere he said: "Do you know that more than ninety-nine percent of voters in Austria voted to join Germany in yesterday's plebiscite?"

I blushed even deeper, jabbing my brush into my palette and smudging the colors.

He gave a groan. "Emma, you must follow *some* news, surely? Europe is falling to pieces while a self-proclaimed demi-god marches around, annexing countries for Germany. Europe is sliding again toward war, you know that, right?"

I set my brush down and turned to look at him, the heat still in my face. "Of course, I'm aware," I snapped, wiping my hands on a rag and standing up. I drew back from my easel and pretended to assess my work. "It's not as if Canada will get involved again," I said, although not with the certainty I would have liked.

George stared at me, then stood and was across the room in seconds, laying a hand lightly on my shoulder. I wheeled around, and he lifted his hand away and spread his fingers, a gesture of apology.

"That's not true, Emma. You must realize that. Canada *will* get involved. You're so mired in the lives of the girls, but you can't bury your head in the sand while the rest of the world goes to pot, you see that, don't you?"

I got angry then. I don't like it when George is patronizing like this, when he discounts the work we're doing. He reminds me of my father. "You of all people should know we have our own important battles raging right here!" I said.

I intended to flounce out of the room, but his big brown eyes held me there a moment or two, wearing an expression of disbelief, or worse—disappointment.

"What you have 'here' are five perfectly healthy little girls, who through no fault of their own are worth an awful lot of dough. If this is a battle, Emma, what is the point of the war? And who, tell me, are the good guys and who are the bad?" He scraped at his lower lip with his front teeth, his chin jutting, waiting for me to answer. When I said nothing, he snatched his hat from the window seat and was out of the room before I could imagine what it was he'd been expecting me to say.

April 14, 1938 (*Toronto Star*)

EDUCATION OF QUINTS AROUSES CONTROVERSY OVER ENGLISH TONGUE, CHANGES IN STAFF

Guardians Hope to Give Same Schooling to Entire Family

CALLANDER, Ontario—While the famous Dionne babes were serenely making mud pies and singing childish songs in their nursery playground, controversy over their educational future reached an acute pitch. The *Star* has learned that the education of the Dionne quintuplets, up to now entirely in the hands of the active guardians, will in all likelihood be taken over by the Ontario department of education, under the bilingual section.

This development is the outcome of a controversy over their teaching following changes in the Dafoe hospital staff six weeks ago. Retirement by the active guardians of Nurse Jacqueline Noël and Teacher Claire Tremblay, both French-Canadians, raised a storm of protest from French-Canadian organizations, representatives of the Roman Catholic Church, and from Oliva Dionne, father of the children. These two attendants were replaced by Norah Rousselle, as teacher-in-charge, and Sigrid Ulrichson. Miss Ulrichson, it is said, speaks little or no French, while Miss Rousselle, of French parentage, is more at home in the English language. Mr. Dionne has stated that French should be the language of the Dafoe hospital and nursery for at least the next two years.

Judge Valin, chairman of the board of guardians for the Quintuplets, is himself a French-Canadian and is equally at home in either tongue. "If the girls are to live on the North American continent," asserts Judge Valin, "they must be thoroughly familiar with the

English language. The girls would be miserable if they grew up without a knowledge of English, no matter how well they spoke French, and they would reproach us when they reached maturity if we neglected our duty in that respect. And they would be justified in doing so."

At 81, Judge Valin impresses one as being alert and active, physically and mentally, despite the fact that he limps slightly and walks with a cane. Indeed, the judge's cane is one of the quintuplets' most prized playthings when he visits them. The Quints dig in the sand with it, ride it around as a witch is supposed to do, and don't relinquish it to the judge until he leaves.

Used with permission.

April 15, 1938

Dr. Blatz has been fired! I feel giddy with relief for the sake of my girls, but also nervous about what this means for the nursery. Nurse Ulrichson was very upset by the news, her pretty face looking pinched and tired. Mark my words, she'll be the next to go.

The official word is that the education of the quintuplets will be managed by the provincial education authorities, but according to George, Dr. Blah-Blah's dismissal is the Dionnes' doing. Indeed, M. Dionne was over here this afternoon, strutting about on his skinny legs with his chest puffed out, all but crowing in Dr. Dafoe's office. He stayed an hour, the door closed, then stalked back out to his car to drive the hundred yards to his farm, not once poking his head into the playroom to bid *bonjour* to the babies. They had heard the car pull up, of course, and scurried to the windows to watch him march inside. What must they think when the man they're told to call "Papa" is so busy fighting over their future that he forgets to actually pay them a visit?

I'm in a muddle. I've come to despise the way Dr. Blatz treated the nursery as his own private laboratory, but for M. Dionne to be holding the balance of power? This scares me no end.

April 16, 1938

Miss Emma Trimpany
Dafoe Hospital and Nursery
Callander, ON

My dear Emma,

Before you say anything, I know, I'm a terrible correspon-
dent. I have spent every spare minute working on my book, and
somehow this leaves me with zero energy for any other type
of writing. Why on earth can you not get a proper phone in
the nurses' dormitory? It's ludicrous that the only phone line is
in Dr. Dafoe's office. Judging by the number of products I see
plastered with the faces of the quintuplets, I'd say the Dafoe
nursery could easily afford to install a private line for the nursing and teaching staff. Ridiculous.

Of course I have followed all of the news over Dr. Blatz,
the toothy old toad! I will see Fred next week and he can give
me the full scoop, although I bet you with your quiet step and
sharp eyes could tell me a better story, if you just took the time
to call. Can you not ask Dr. Dafoe for special permission to
take a call from me? I've got heaps to tell you about. Let's say
April 21 at 5:00 P.M.

All my love,
Ivy

April 21, 1938

It was so wonderful to hear Ivy's voice. I think she's picked up a slight American inflection with all the time she's spent down there, but she is still Ivy through and through. Ivy's big news: she and Fred have decided to have a private wedding this July, just the two of them, the priest, and her father. Both of Fred's parents have passed. She says there is simply too much publicity around their romance: *The nurse and the photographer to the Dionne Quints!* So I will not be a bridesmaid after all, and I'm relieved, it's true. It's a credit to Ivy that she asked me in the first place, knowing that someone with a face like mine in her wedding party might be a distraction. So I'll glide along a little bit longer, it seems, keeping myself to myself.

Ivy told me several astonishing things I didn't know about M. Dionne and Dr. Dafoe—much of it happening right under my nose. Fred hears things from Keith Munro, his old colleague from the *Star* who has for some time been in charge of overseeing the bookkeeping for the quintuplets' fund—the butter and egg man, George calls him. I hardly know how to write about this, it's so confusing and sensational. Much of it sounds like it's been lifted from a Hollywood gossip column—too salacious, somehow, for me to want to put it down in print. But the other part of it could very much come home to roost with me.

Apparently Mr. Munro told Fred, who told Ivy, that M. Dionne's lawyer wishes to review *all* of the incoming and outgoing payments for advertising contracts. So far Dr. Dafoe has refused, but Ivy believes M. Dionne will get his way. I already feel, very keenly, that M. Dionne has not forgiven me and my "art" for fouling his lawsuit over the corn syrup. I'm not sure what he'll do when he learns that my paintings are actually now being used to boost the girls' trust fund and, specifically, that I'm being handsomely paid.

Of course Ivy wanted to hear all about the girls, although she went on a bit about their isolation and their public-private life, as she calls it, plus all of the changes on staff. She thinks all this will have lasting ill effects on the girls. I reminded her that, despite my repugnance for what Dr. Blatz and his scientists have done, their work does prove that the girls are happy and healthy.

"If they're happy and healthy, Em, what on earth are they doing still living in that hospital? All the more reason for Quintland to shut its doors and for you to get on with your own life."

Afterward I kept thinking about all the things Ivy had said and all the nurses who have come and gone. How Ivy herself has moved on too. It's hard to get her words out of my mind, and I have no one with whom to discuss this. Perhaps I'll write to Lewis.

April 22, 1938 (*Toronto Star*)

DR. DAFOE CHALLENGES DIONNE AND ATTORNEY PROVE THEIR CHARGES

Papa Has Six Expensive Cars in 18 Months, Doctor Says

CALLANDER, Ontario—Dr. Allan R. Dafoe, physician to the Dionne quintuplets, openly challenged Oliva Dionne and Attorney Henri St. Jacques, of Ottawa, to prove that he is wasting the babies' money and alienating their affections towards their parents.

In a declaration containing separate complaints against Dr. Dafoe, St. Jacques charged the health of the quintuplets had been impaired to satisfy Dr. Dafoe's determination to please tourists, that they had been forced to learn English before mastering French, that Dr. Dafoe had been guilty of wanton waste of the children's money to assure himself of an elaborate headquarters and management staff, and that Dr. Dafoe had alienated the children's affections for their parents. St. Jacques is demanding a government probe of the guardians' activities.

Dr. Dafoe today countered that a former teacher and former nurse at the Dafoe hospital are behind the demands for a probe of his care of the quintuplets and the administration of their affairs. He says the two women, after they were discharged, talked with the girls' father and sowed these latest seeds of discontent. He added that M. Dionne had been invited to attend the meeting where the discharge of the two nurses was discussed, but he did not attend.

Dr. Dafoe revealed that the five babies, now four years old, have $600,000 in the bank in their own names, after payment of all expenses for the hospital and the administration and the care of them.

"Mr. Dionne is doing very well for himself," Dr. Dafoe added.

"We do not charge admission for visitors to see the children. He is the one, the only one, who benefits from the tourists because his shop of trinkets is located right across the street.

"Mr. Dionne has done so well that he has six expensive automobiles in a year and a half. He trades his cars about once every two months. He has a beautiful car now."

Dr. Dafoe revealed that he had personally seen to it that Mr. and Mrs. Dionne's income from contracts signed on behalf of the children had been increased from $100 a month to $300 a month since the birth of the last Dionne baby only three weeks ago.

Mr. St. Jacques, the Dionnes' lawyer, has declared that, through the request to Attorney General Conant, Mr. Dionne hoped to regain custody of his children and control their education. Reinstatement of Miss Jacqueline Noël, nurse, and Miss Claire Tremblay, teacher, recently dismissed from the Dafoe nursery, and a curb on "extravagance" in the management of the Quints' business affairs also will

be sought in the probe, St. Jacques said.

The *Star* has learned from a reliable source that the invested fortune of the quintuplets is insufficient to meet expenses. Upwards of $600,000, carried in Dominion and Ontario bonds at an average of 3.5 per cent interest, is said to yield about $21,000 a year. With $24,000 a year for the hospital, $36,000 annually to the Dionne family, and $2,400 a year salary for Dr. Dafoe, a total of $30,000 in addition to other expenses, current revenues from endorsement contracts are being used to supply the balance of more than $9,000 a year.

"This is just another move by the father to get personal control of the quintuplets and their funds," said Keith Munro, business manager of the Quints. "The appointment of Mr. Percy D. Wilson, guardian of Ontario, to the quintuplets' board of guardians ensures that all expenditures from the Quints' funds are scrutinized and made with his full knowledge and consent."

April 23, 1938

The strain on everyone this week is almost unbearable. Nurse Ulrichson will indeed be leaving us, at the Dionnes' insistence. The girls will be inconsolable.

April 28, 1938 (*Toronto Star*)

ONTARIO CABINET REFUSES DIONNE'S INQUIRY DEMAND

Dr. A. R. Dafoe to Remain in Supreme Charge of Quints' Health, Stays as Guardian

Demands of Oliva Dionne for an investigation into administration of affairs of his quintuplet daughters, and that Dr. A. R. Dafoe be required to relinquish his post as one of three active guardians, have been turned down by the Ontario government.

The government's decision was made known by attorney general Mr. Conant, who issued a statement following the meeting summarizing the government's conclusions. First, the education of the quintuplets will be forthwith placed under the direction of the department of education. Second, that payment for the quintuplets' education should be paid by the girls' fund. Third, that Dr. Dafoe's position as supreme in authority in all matters affecting the health of the quintuplets be maintained.

"Every effort should be made to promote cooperation between the family and guardians and to break down any existing antagonisms," Mr. Conant said. "Moreover, I do not recommend a judicial investigation."

May 19, 1938

Miss Emma Trimpany
Dafoe Hospital and Nursery
Callander, ON

Dear Emma,

Your letter has me very worried. Did you end up raising all this with Dr. Dafoe? I can't see that he would ever allow a situation in which you or anyone else would come to any harm, and I do think you deserve some answers.

I've also been stewing over what you wrote about your privacy. Are you sure our correspondence is confidential? Doesn't Mr. Sinclair handle all those sacks of mail coming in and going out? I'm not so sure I should respond to your many questions here, in print, if you're unsure who might read them. I'd be happy to write to you via your parents' address in future, if that would put you more at ease.

As for being paid for your paintings: my father would say, don't worry your pretty little head. Too often the work of lady artists is seen as nothing but a hobby, and a frivolous one at that. You, on the other hand, are a true talent and deserve to be paid. My guess is, they're not paying you enough as it is.

I have little in the way of news myself. I went with some of the chaps from work to the grand opening of the new Woolworth's building downtown. It is being billed as the grandest art deco structure yet built in Canada. I think it's quite something, but at least in the engineering department here, I'm the minority view.

My feathered Howard Hughes is courting. Or maybe he's

already tied the knot? Bette Davis arrived on the windowsill earlier this month amid much cooing, fluttering, and flapping. They are sweet together.

Yours truly,
Lewis
11 Rue Saint Ida
Montreal, Quebec

May 20, 1938

Another day of meetings between the official guardians, including M. Dionne and his lawyer, plus a half dozen other men in suits traipsing in and out of the nursery looking grim, while throngs of reporters waited outside the gates. The guardians are using the quiet playroom for their meeting, which has produced no end of questions from the girls. Annette asked, "Do *le docteur* and Papa not get any free play today?" She's a smart cookie, that one. The tension is thicker than porridge this week, and the girls can feel it.

I found George during the lunch break, seated on the steps of the back porch with his jacket off and his tie loose, his eyes closed and his face turned up to the sun. He has dark smudges under his eyes, but didn't look to be asleep, just tired. I sat on another step and waited to see if he wanted to speak. He opened one eye to look at me, then smiled crookedly.

"Nosy Nurse Trimpany," he said and winked, tilting his chin back to the sky.

"Can you tell me anything?" I asked in a hushed voice.

George was quiet. For a long moment the only sound was the trembling of the birch leaves, as if they, too, were anxious for an answer.

"Miss Rousselle believes she will be fired," I offered.

Still nothing from George. I said: "I can't help wondering if M. Dionne has set his sights on me too."

George opened one eye and fixed me with it intently, then let his lid drop again. When he spoke, it was almost a murmur. "If you heard half of what's being said, you'd likely quit of your own accord."

I was staring at him, thinking of Ivy's gossip, and I sensed he could feel my fretful gaze darting over his features. He sighed. "There's been no talk of any more staff being fired, and none coming back either. Satisfied?" His face rearranged itself in the sunshine.

When I didn't respond, he opened one eye again to meet my gaze, then sat up to look at me properly, tugging at the knot of his tie again as he did so. My fingers twitched as if they had a mind to reach out and help him put it straight.

"Most of the talk is about the girls' trust fund, how it's being spent, and what sort of time line might be required to build a new house, for the whole family—one that would accommodate the quintuplets and their staff."

"But Dr. Dafoe told me—"

George waved a hand to stop me. "I know what you're going to say. Don't say it. I'm telling you what's being discussed, not what's going to happen. You're a smart girl. The best thing you can do is stay out of the way."

He stood and stooped to pick up his jacket, hooking an index finger under the collar and hanging it over one shoulder, like a man in a magazine. Then he stopped and, for a fleeting instant, rested his warm hand on the top of my head as he stepped to open the door. "Don't worry about the wrong things, Emma," he said. Then he went back inside.

I stayed on the steps for a long while, half my thoughts thrumming alongside my racing heart, the ghost of his touch still tingling on my head. The rest of my brain was digesting George's words. The very idea of the girls moving with the rest of the Dionnes to a bigger house, with all of their nurses and teachers in tow, the doctor making his daily visits—this, I knew, would never happen. I, for one, would never make that move. But Ivy's words have stuck with me: the girls can't stay here forever. And nor can I.

The outside world knows so little of what's really going on behind these walls. They lap up Dr. Dafoe's weekly column and assume that's the merry life we're living. And the funny thing is, these days, I'm not sure I know what life I'm living either.

May 22, 1938 (*King Features Syndicate Inc.*)

DR. DAFOE'S COLUMN ON THE QUINTUPLETS AND THE CARE OF YOUR CHILDREN

By Allan Roy Dafoe, Personal Physician to the Dionne Quintuplets

Watching the five Dionne Quintuplets, especially when they are really going places, is too much of a job for any one nurse. In fact, it often takes our two nurses, backed up by the teacher, to keep track of them all and see that they don't get into any mischief.

Not that the children are given to being naughty or annoying: they are just fell [*sic*] of animal spirits. When I arrive at the nursery in the morning, the whole five charge at me. They weigh over forty pounds apiece, and when they're done I feel as though I had been mauled by the Cornell line and backfield.

A few months ago, Émilie got herself dressed to go out a bit ahead of the others. She stood around for a moment or two, waiting for the others, and then she announced she was tired of waiting and was going out. As she went out the door, the nurse in charge told her to stay in the yard.

Well, Émilie stayed in the yard for a moment or two and then decided that Tony, one of the police dogs, must be lonely. So she opened the gate, left the yard, and went over to Tony's doghouse to pay him a visit. Since she openly disobeyed the nurse's instructions, she was told to go back to the house and stay there for five minutes before she came out again. This is all the punishment the Quints ever get—being put in a room for solitary confinement for a few minutes.

The nurse turned her mind to other things for a minute or two, but when she looked again, Émilie didn't seem to be at all chastened by her solitary. She was at the window and seemed to be having a great time.

So the nurse went in to investigate and as she tiptoed into the room where Émilie was supposed to be doing penance, she found the little girl with enough snowballs to make a fair-sized snowman. She was having a whale of a time, skidding them along the floor and watching them bounce off the baseboards when they hit the wall. When she investigated further, the nurse found that the four Quints outside in the yard had taken pity on Émilie and since she couldn't play with them in the snow, they would bring the snow to her. So they had opened the window and were making snowballs and handing them in to her through the window.

Émilie stayed for the mopping up process and said over and over again that it was too bad that the snow had made all the mess. "But really, Émilie didn't make the mess, did she, Nurse?" she asked again and again, a twinkle in her eye.

May 28, 1938

Happy birthday to my beloved Annette, Yvonne, Cécile, Marie, and Émilie. You are so big and strong and kind and beautiful, you are breaking my heart.

M. and Mme. Dionne and the rest of the brood came over for a birthday party, and Dr. Dafoe stayed away. It felt more like an army occupation than a festive occasion. Maman and Papa Dionne gave the girls a big wooden train with a locomotive, a passenger car, and a caboose. The older Dionne boys swiftly commandeered it and were charging all over the playroom while their sisters watched in awe. Of course, they've never once seen a train in person, let alone been in one themselves. Daniel sent the train careening along the floor to the circle where the girls were sitting quietly, and the locomotive struck Émilie in the knee, not hard, but it caught her by surprise. She sprang up, her eyes flooding with tears.

Her mother was submerged in the settee within arm's length of the girls, but Émilie wheeled around, looking frantic, then darted over to me, her hands out, sobbing. I lifted her up, rubbing her back.

"Oh, pumpkin, you're fine. You just got a little fright. Nothing too terrible."

I glanced over her shoulder as I said it and saw the expressions on the faces of her parents. Maman Dionne's face had puckered in pain at the sight of her daughter running to me in her moment of panic. Most days Mme. Dionne is fearsome, commanding her children this way and that, her thick arms jabbing the air. Other times, times like these, she's like a balloon with a leak, her whole countenance falling and her face slack with longing. M. Dionne I could only glimpse in profile. His eyes were on his wife, but he was clearly seething, his funny red earlobe trembling like the snood of a turkey. Then he abruptly turned and glared at me so ferociously I had to turn my face to the side. I whispered, "Let's go see if Nurse Trimpany can find you a plaster, shall we?" Then I hurried Em from the room.

After that, I made myself scarce. I sent Em back to play with her sisters, and the Dionnes left shortly thereafter. Only later did I get all five girls to myself in the private playground outside. "This is my birthday gift to you," I said and showed them how to make daisy chains, threading the tiny flowers together through tiny splits in the stems. Their little fingers are too clumsy for this kind of work, so I set them picking the flowers and bringing them to me. They all insisted on wearing their daisy necklaces to bed, which I permitted. Imagine what Miss Beaulieu would have said? Or Dr. Blatz? They will wake tomorrow to find them wilted and brown and I'll have to explain that nothing beautiful lasts forever.

June 1, 1938

Miss Rousselle is leaving as soon as they can find a replacement this summer. Score a point for M. Dionne.

June 7, 1938

I'M BACK FROM a day at home with Mother and Edith, but I didn't spend the night. In fact, I managed to miss the paying guests who stayed in the rented room last night by arriving after they'd departed, then slipped away before the next couple arrived. It's hard these days, going home—it feels more and more as if I'm merely a guest myself or, worse, an inconvenience. Back at the nursery, I learned I'd missed a visit by Shirley Temple! On my only day off, of course. She was given a private audience with the girls. (Private, that is, plus photographers.)

"She even took a Quint-stone," George said and winked at me.

"Isn't Shirley Temple a little young to be worried about fertility?"

(I can't quite believe I said that. Honestly, sometimes I wonder who I'm turning into.)

"Ah, *but she will soon be all grown tall*!" he sang in a chirping, childish voice, marching and swinging his arms beside him, bungling all the lyrics. "*She's got to think what she will want when she's not quite as small.*"

He makes me laugh, George. He really does.

June 9, 1938

THE NEW NURSE on staff is Louise Corriveau. She is dark and sallow with the downy beginnings of a true mustache, which I have to keep myself from staring at. She's conscious of it, clearly—her fingers are constantly fluttering above her upper lip. Under her bushy brows, she has a startled, blinking look that makes me worry she may not last any longer here than the others. For now, she and Miss Rousselle (who will be with us for only a few more weeks) are more than happy to take the girls into the public playground without me. The Dionnes, either Maman on her own or Papa as well, are coming over every day, particularly in the afternoons, which are already scorching. We are desperately in need of rain and the dry farms even more so. The girls spend most of the hour in the wading pool, which I suppose is not quite as much fun for the tourists. They'd prefer to see them on the swings or riding their tricycles—something that brings them closer to the windows, I'm sure.

Meanwhile the movie crews have been here once again, this time bringing a litter of cocker spaniel puppies for one of the scenes with Mr. Hersholt. The girls were terrified at first, Cécile the only one bold enough to reach out a cautious hand when "Dr. Luke" first proffered one of the wriggling pups. But they swiftly fell in love with their new pets, lugging them around the lawn, rolling with them in the grass, and trying to "nurse" them with baby bottles.

"If I pick a booger from my nose, the puppy licks it!" cried Annette, elated by the discovery and eagerly teaching her sisters to replicate the experiment.

They will be crushed tomorrow when we have to tell them that the puppies were here only for the cameras and won't be coming back.

June 10, 1938

THE STRESS AND the workload are getting to George, I'd say. He's put on a bit of weight with all the desk work he's been doing, the rest of him growing into that broad swimmer's chest, I suppose. It suits him nicely, softening his face a bit. I'd done a little line drawing of the girls plucking daisies in the private yard, and I'd planned to give it to George, if I could summon the nerve. Nothing special, just a little something he could tack on the wall above his desk to cheer him up or inspire his next column.

Today George was hunched and frowning over a stack of letters. Dr. Dafoe is away in New York again, giving another speech.

"What has you glowering today, George?" I asked as I poked a head around the office door. He looked up and rubbed his face with one hand and waved me inside with the other.

"These letters are so strange, and so—well, sad." He pointed to a stack of thirty or forty envelopes. "We are getting more and more from Europe now, desperate people, all of them writing to Dr. Dafoe to ask for help. I have the sense that Dr. Dafoe and the quintuplets must be the only Canadians many of these people have ever heard of." He shook his head and plucked one from the pile. The envelope was rumpled and soft, as if it had been passed through many hands, or carried in a pocket for many days before making it into the post. Or perhaps George himself had been carrying it with him. It was from an Austrian girl, named Klara. He read it aloud.

When he was finished, he handed me the letter. The penmanship was beautiful, with scarcely a word blotted out or spelled incorrectly. Astonishing, really, since English wasn't her first language.

George was watching me. "I have an aunt on my father's side who has married into a Jewish family in Toronto that immigrated before the Great War, but they still have family in Europe.

You've read of the labor camps in Germany, I'm sure. Now Herr Hitler has opened another camp in Austria."

His eyes were searching my face. "Canada cannot simply stand by, as a member of the Commonwealth. I'd bet my bottom dollar: we cannot and we won't."

Not sure what he was expecting, I made to hand Klara's letter back to him, but he shook his head, muttering, "Keep it. I have three dozen others just the same."

I know George wanted more from me, a political position of some kind, no doubt. It's simply not a topic I fully understand, and this clearly frustrates him. Obviously it's upsetting, unimaginable, really. But what was I to say? I forgot all about the sketch I'd done for him and, not long after, excused myself to go fetch the girls inside for lunch.

May 29, 1938

Dear Dr. Dafoe,

My name is Klara Eisler and I am 13 years old. My father is Dr. Walter Eisler, a renowned physician in my country, Austria.

I write to you because we have studied Canada at school, and also because my father and I have for many years been interested in the Dionne Quintuplets, whose lives you saved.

My mother and father are deciding we must leave Austria because we are Jewish. Therefore I write to you to ask if you could use an assistant. My father received his medical degree from the Sorbonne University in Paris and received his fellowship in internal medicine from the University of Bologna. He has for many years been a professor at the Medical School of Vienna in addition to his clinical practice and has published many medical papers. I am an only child. I play the violin and can read and speak German, French, and English. My favorite subjects at school are literature and mathematics.

I hope you will consider having my father join you as your assistant in Canada at your earliest convenience. Please convey my warmest regards to Annette, Yvonne, Cécile, Marie, and Émilie.

Yours sincerely,
Klara Eisler
No. 7–14 Tuchlaubenstraße,
Vienna, Austria

June 11, 1938

I was sitting on the back steps outside the kitchen writing a letter to Lewis when George tracked me down. He was carrying two glasses of lemonade with ice, a real treat. The perks of being Dr. Dafoe's secretary, presumably, or perhaps the perks of being George. Marguerite is clearly smitten with him and is continually finding excuses to pop by the office when Dr. Dafoe is out.

"Are you writing about me?" he joked, setting one of the glasses down beside me before easing himself onto a lower step.

I didn't say anything because, of course, I *had* been writing about him! I wouldn't give him the satisfaction of knowing that.

He pretended to furrow his eyebrows at me. "Who are you writing to, Miss Trimpany? You have a new pen pal, I see, in our Quint-stone friend, Lewis Cartwright. Is it to him you are writing this evening? Or to Ivy?"

George can be so irritating, truly. It's as if he can see right through to my bones. We'd been relatively cool to each other since our conversation about the letter from the Jewish girl. Now here he was with a peace offering and the first thing he does is start nettling me about whom I'm writing to and what I might be saying!

I blushed beet red, as usual, and my hand went up to my left cheek, the way it always does. In an instant, George's face was smooth again, his mock frown gone. Calm as glass, like a lake the instant the breeze drops.

"I'm sorry, Emma, I shouldn't tease. It's none of my business who you're writing to, obviously. I came out to say I'm sorry for being so moody yesterday morning. I've had a lot of long days and late nights." He flashed a smile: two rows of shiny teeth, white and perfect. It's no wonder Marguerite is happy to squeeze a dozen lemons for him at the end of her workday.

I shook my head, not knowing what to say. I didn't have anything to apologize for, other than being sorry we didn't agree on, well, whatever it was he was hoping we should be agreeing on. And then I lied, I don't know why. I outright lied. "I'm writing to Ivy," I mumbled. Then I blundered on. "Lewis is like a brother to me. We went to the same school in Callander." This *was* true, although we were never actually there at the same time. "I write because I promised him I'd keep him up to date on Mr. Cartwright, his father, who was poorly over Christmas."

George was still watching me with a slight smile, his floppy hair sliding out from behind his ear. Then we chatted casually for a bit, him asking me whether I was taking any time off this summer and saying that he was heading to Ottawa for his sister's wedding. We talked about a few more things while we finished our drinks, then I stood up and gathered the glasses and went back inside. I finished my letter to Lewis in my room. A rather abrupt ending, I realize, but somehow I'd lost the thread of whatever it was I'd been planning to write.

July 1, 1938

MARIE AND EM got their Dominion Day outfits absolutely filthy, filling the moat for the sand castles they'd built with water they hauled over from the pool. They looked very sweet, splattered with muck, but it made for an extra bath, midday, and more work for the housemaids to get the outfits laundered in time for the weekend.

The guards were moving the hordes of people through the viewing corridor so quickly today it sounded like a herd of elephants. At one point, I looked up from where I was seated in the sandbox with Annette and Yvonne to see that Émilie was standing right under the viewing glass frowning at the shapes behind the screen. Even from where I was sitting with her sisters I could hear the exclamations of excitement from the visitors' platform. I've noticed that the women who visit us, no matter what their class or country, make a strange, low purr when they see the girls for the first time, a gasp or a covetous little moan. It doesn't matter whether they are French, English, Canadian, or American, they sound the same when their hearts are being tugged in this special way. I've even heard it from the men, from George, and even from Dr. Dafoe, who is just as likely to be stern and clinical with the girls as he is to coo over their dear antics. The girls are simply that sweet and enthralling. And, of course, little rascals too.

Watching Émilie, her tiny hand reaching up to tug at her earlobe the way she does when she has a particularly tricky puzzle that needs solving, squinting at the shapes crowded behind the one-way glass—I knew she could hear them too.

The Dionnes, of course, arrived smack in the middle of the public playtime and made their usual grand entrance, and it was like a cloud swiping across the face of the sun—our boisterous, clown-about girls falling so suddenly still and silent. It squeezes the heart to see it.

"Bo-jo, Papa," they say quietly, their eyes dipping to the ground, then darting aside. "Bo-jo, Maman."

July 3, 1938

I HAVE FINISHED my commission for the American corn syrup company and handed it in to Dr. Dafoe, who will share it with the other guardians tomorrow. I'm very pleased with it. I've painted Annette and Yvonne in the foreground and the other three grouped behind. The painting shows only their heads and collars, which I've painted in white and turquoise, although in real life these collars are in the official color for each child. But I think I've achieved what Mrs. Fangel never quite cottoned on to—and how could she?—and that is the essential differences between the girls.

I dodged the public playtime this morning by saying I had to put some finishing touches on the piece, which wasn't true. But it got me out of a sweltering hour with the Dionnes, who arrived as Nurse Corriveau and Miss Rousselle were leading the girls into the playground. I guess I was distracted by the thrill of showing Dr. Dafoe the finished product, because I left my easel, drawings, and this notebook in the quiet play area when I went to visit George. Then I lost track of time.

When I returned, Mme. Dionne was in the playroom, planted stoutly over my things. What was she doing inside? The girls were still playing outside, and the queue of visitors, I could see through the window, still stretched for hundreds of yards from the entrance.

"Madame?" I said. She looked irritable and flustered, taking a few paces back.

"It's too hot outside," she said finally, plucking a handkerchief from her sleeve and swabbing at her brow. Then she looked at me defiantly, willing me to contradict her.

Hot or not, what was she doing nosing around my things? Had she leafed through my sketches? Did she poke her nose here, in my scribble book? I'm kicking myself. I simply can't understand why I would have left my journal just lying around, especially when Lewis has put the question mark in my mind about what is private and what isn't. Can she even read in English? Can she read *at all*? I have no idea. I won't do this again, leave my little book lying around. I'll take my old notebooks back to Father and Mother's place next time I go, and keep my current one tucked away somewhere safe or on my person at all times.

I got the courage to gather my things, and, lucky for me, she didn't stay or say anything more; she gathered her purse and waddled off toward the back door. Is she pregnant again? You'd think the papers would have said.

July 4, 1938

IVY AND FRED got married today in Toronto. Ivy has promised to phone me and tell me all about it. I'm so happy for them and more than a little bit sad for me. I'll be sorry when Fred leaves us for good, and the girls, the *girls* will be devastated.

I toyed with sending Fred and Ivy a Quint-stone as a gift. I know Ivy would laugh, but Fred might find that uncomfortable. I mentioned it to George, just as something to say, and he thought it was a very funny idea.

In the end I sent them a miniature of the girls in their bassinets as babies, based on sketches I did so long ago now. That's when Ivy knew them best.

July 5, 1938

Miss Emma Trimpany
Dafoe Hospital and Nursery
Callander, ON

Dear Emma,

First things first, it's true; the plane I'm working on *is* a fighter plane, called an FDB–a fighter dive bomber. Sounds dramatic, I know, but that's what makes it exciting. It's made entirely of metal and we've devised the riveting to be flush with the body so it's sleek as a fish. We have a Russian chap who's joined us, and it's his designs we're working off primarily, although I can say I'm the man in charge of the undercarriage. You'll also be interested to hear that the company has hired a woman to be our chief aeronautical engineer. Her name is Elsie MacGill and she's quite famous in my line of work. Some of the men are grumbling a bit about the idea of a woman at the controls, but I think she's really something.

Second of all: I think the work you are doing at the Dafoe Nursery *is* important, no question. There is so little hope and joy to spare, especially now. You have, in your care, five sweethearts who have brought the world so much happiness. If that's not important, I don't know what is.

I've been reading *Le Droit* in the hopes of improving my French. Yesterday the paper quoted a spokesperson for the Association of French Canadians of Ontario saying that, apart from Yvonne Leroux, not a single nurse has remained on staff at the Dafoe Nursery for more than 22 months (proof, he said, of the unhealthy environment in which the quintuplets are being reared). Based on this, I'd say this means your invisibility, at least in some quarters, remains intact! It is bold of me to say it, but your powers of invisibility have never worked especially well on me.

My feathered Howard and Bette send their best. They've been busy with a nest they built in a nook in the wall, but Howard still visits my sill to strut and coo-roo about his fine life.

Yours truly,
Lewis
11 Rue Saint Ida
Montreal, Quebec

July 15, 1938

A letter from Lewis that I can't get out of my mind. I'm flattered, I suppose, but also flustered. Perhaps I misunderstood the nature of this correspondence? I have no idea. I value his friendship highly, but I'm not quite sure where I stand or what he expects me to write in return.

July 28, 1938

Miss Julie Callahan is the girls' new teacher, replacing Norah—Miss Rousselle—who leaves us tomorrow. The girls absolutely adore Miss Callahan. She is very pretty with a lovely figure and dark, curly hair, rosy cheeks, and soft brown eyes. To see her with one of the babies on her lap, you'd think she was their big sister or mother. Clever, too, I gather, with a double degree of some sort from Dalhousie University. Miss Callahan told me her mother is Acadian-French, but she married an Irishman—hence her last name. There's no way the Dionnes could find fault with her French. She is as bilingual as I am, with not a trace of an accent in either tongue. She'll fit in so nicely here, I think. Everyone has warmed to her straightaway.

August 5, 1938 (*King Features Syndicate Inc.*)

DR. DAFOE'S COLUMN ON THE QUINTUPLETS AND THE CARE OF YOUR CHILDREN

By Allan Roy Dafoe, Personal Physician to the Dionne Quintuplets

We are always having fun with the stones around the nursery here in Callander, where the Quintuplets live. As I'm sure you all know by now, these stones are supposed to have some strange quality of fertility in them that brings children to any woman who carries one.

Every little while I get a letter from somewhere in the United States from some couple who visited us in the summer and took stones home with them. People who have been childless for years have written me that a baby was on the way shortly after they got the stones.

Well, I got one of these letters a couple of days ago that I thought rather amusing. A young couple came up here on their honeymoon a year ago.

He was a young engineer, from near New York City, and she was a particularly attractive young woman. I remember they came in to my office one afternoon and we sat and talked for quite a spell. Before he left, he showed me five little pebbles he had collected from the box out at the nursery. His wife blushed a bit as he showed them, but he thought it was a great joke. I hadn't heard anything more of them until recently when he wrote me a letter. First thing he told me was that his wife had just given birth to twins.

But that wasn't all. He explained that he had taken five stones away with him. When he got home, however, he didn't keep them all. Three young couples he knew wanted children, so he gave them each a stone, keeping two for himself.

"Boy, I'm glad I didn't keep

the whole five stones," his letter closed.

Always, when a motion picture company from Hollywood comes up here to make a picture, the actors and actresses have fun with our pebbles. They package them up and send them to fellow actors and actresses back home, who aren't anxious to have children. I've never heard whether any of these particular stones bore fruit or not.

When the children grow older and learn about this legend of the stones, they will never be at a loss for a wedding present to send to an acquaintance getting married. The only trouble is that at the rate the stones are being carried away now, there may not be any left by that time.

August 20, 1938

I'm back at the nursery after a wonderful day in Toronto with Ivy. She is so elegant and sophisticated now. It's hard to picture her as she was the summer we met—her face as flushed as a fire ant in that hot kitchen when we had the babies tucked in their crate by the stove, or peeling off her stockings when she got fed up with the heat in late August, before the Captain went to the hospital and Yvonne almost died. I loved the time we spent cocooned together at the nursery, but, her metamorphosis complete, Ivy has flown the length and breadth of the continent dazzling everyone she meets while I've stayed curled in my cozy shell. Today she was hell-bent on convincing me it was time to grow wings of my own.

"You could go anywhere! There are many, many households these days who can afford to have a nurse or a governess on staff, and they would leap at the chance to hire a nurse of the Dionne quintuplets."

Ivy forgets that almost no one remembers I've worked at the nursery as long as I have. I'm not in any of the newsreels or newspaper photos. I don't appear in any of the motion pictures; I've not once, to my knowledge, been mentioned in the papers.

"And I like it this way," I reminded her.

That sent her down her next favorite theme, which is my marriageability and eventual motherhood. Honestly, Ivy is worse than Mother.

"But you must be meeting so many nice young men who come by to meet the girls and Dr. Dafoe?"

I grimaced and shook my head. She said she'd heard from Fred that George has become quite the charmer at the Dafoe nursery, and that made me blush terribly. Then out of the blue she asked whether I was keeping in touch with "the shy man who delivered the stones."

Honestly, how on earth could she have known about Lewis? Had I mentioned him?

I used the opportunity to confess my plan of giving her a Quint-stone as a wedding gift, and she barely laughed at all.

"Oh, you should send one," she said earnestly. As if she actually believed in their magical powers! My surprise must have been etched in my face because she laughed then and shrugged. "You never know, Em, it can't hurt."

August 22, 1938

Miss Emma Trimpany
Dafoe Hospital and Nursery
Callander, ON

Dear Emma,

This is not the nicest thing you'll ever hear me say about the Ontario government (nor the worst), but my guess is they will never release the girls into the care of the parents, and they will never build that big house. Bottom line: the province has come to rely on the money it sees from visitors to the famous five. Quebec takes a very dim view of this, of course, and I can't help but agree they make a strong case that those girls should be leading a more normal life. But jealousy is also at play. Here's a French family that gives birth to the most popular Canadians in the world and that had to happen in *Ontario* instead of Quebec? Plus this isn't just a battle of French versus English, it's also Catholic versus Protestant, rich versus poor, the lowly peasant versus the eminent doctor. It would all make for a great piece of theater if there weren't five innocent girls at the heart of it.

As for our plane—at this point, no one will fly it. We are having trouble sorting out a problem with the upper gull wing. As it is currently designed, our pilots can't exactly see where they're headed, particularly on landing. So it's back to the drawing board for us.

Yours sincerely,
Lewis Cartwright
11 Rue Saint Ida
Montreal, Quebec

September 17, 1938 (*Toronto Star*)

CALLANDER PROTESTS REMOVAL OF QUINTS

Fear Loss of Trade if Babies Moved to Trout Lake: "Unwise, Unfair"

CALLANDER, Ontario— Protesting the proposed removal of the Dionne quintuplets from the Dafoe hospital at Callander to a new home on another site, a deputation of businessmen and councillors from that vicinity awaited on Hon. Gordon Conant, attorney general, yesterday afternoon.

Spokesmen for the deputation contended that it would be unwise and unfair to remove the famous sisters from the proximity of their birthplace.

"The quintuplets have flourished, physically and financially, at Callander," stated Kenneth Morrison, Callander businessman. "I estimate that upwards of $400,000 has been spent in and around the village because the Quints were there. All this will be a dead loss if the sisters are moved to a new home in Trout Lake, which we understand is contemplated."

Mr. Morrison stated removal of the Quints would be a terrible blow to Callander and district and that Mr. Dionne and the people of that district felt such action was unnecessary.

Oliva Dionne, father of the Quints, has petitioned council seeking action of protest against removing his daughters from the vicinity of their birthplace.

September 17, 1938

Nurse Corriveau took me aside today to tell me that she is keeping track of some of her run-ins with the Dionnes, and some of the personal threats and insinuations she says they've been making. She's a tense and twitchy woman, Louise Corriveau, but a sharp one. She says she's well aware of all the coming and going of staff we've suffered here, and she intends to keep notes of everything, in case she finds herself on the wrong side of the Dionnes, or Dr. Dafoe for that matter. She says I should be doing the same, keeping a record, that is. I mulled that for a while, then realized I've been doing just that. Not that I could ever show these words to a single soul.

September 20, 1938

AN UPSETTING COUPLE of moments in the nursery today. I'd managed, as usual, to worm out of accompanying the girls into the public playground. With Maman and Papa Dionne in there with them most days, plus Miss Callahan and Nurse Corriveau, it's easy for me to beg off.

Dr. Dafoe has suggested I work on a series of seasonal portraits of the girls with the aim of approaching a calendar company. I've done some nice pieces for the summer months with the girls in their swimming costumes, playing in the sandbox, and so on. Now I'm playing around with some autumn colors. I was absorbed in what I was doing and didn't even hear a creak or a footfall to hint that someone had entered the room. Indeed, I *felt* a presence, rather than heard it. My whole body stiffened and my hand jerked so that I daubed a thick swatch of blue paint onto Cécile's chin instead of her dress. When I turned, sure enough, M. Dionne was standing right behind me, radiating a chill that made my skin rise with goose bumps. What struck me in that instant was that he'd been about to touch my work, he was that close. Had I not turned when I did, his hand would have been on my things or, worse, on me. The last time a man had stood so close behind me it had been George, and that had flushed me with a warmth I felt all the way to my toes. This was more like ice water, sluicing down my spine.

I stood and walked quickly around my easel, so I was facing him. "M. Dionne," I murmured. "I was just packing up."

Of course I couldn't do anything with my painting, it was still wet, but I could gather up my tubes of paint and palette. My hands were trembling, but I carried my things over to the sink and took as little time as I could to get tidied up. It felt like his eyes were still boring into my back, but when I finally turned to look he hadn't moved and was still staring at the painting, his pointy chin tucked to his chest, his brow furrowed.

I didn't want to leave my work like that, unfinished and vulnerable, the glob of blue no doubt already dry on Cécile's chin. But I didn't want to have to speak with him either. I hurried from the room, and when I peeked back through the door a few minutes later, M. Dionne was gone.

October 5, 1938

THE ROYAL COUPLE is visiting Quintland! That's what the papers are saying. Dr. Dafoe came out to the nursery today and called a special meeting, swaggering like a turkey, to inform us that the King and Queen have confirmed they will visit our tiny corner of Canada. What's more, plans to build a new house are postponed until midsummer next year in order to focus attention on some much-needed repairs to the nursery now.

Visiting here! The King and Queen of England. I can't imagine what Ivy will say.

October 14, 1938

GEORGE IS ABSOLUTELY insufferable. He came into the nursery today, peering around as if in search of inspiration when the girls were gleefully playing dress-up. Annette had unearthed the crown that Yvonne wore when they were doing their "Song of Sixpence" photos earlier in the year.

"I am Queen of Canada," Annette was mustering in her most imperious French. "You"—she swept her arm majestically past her sisters—"are Kings of Canada. You must wait on me and bring me pies."

The crown seems smaller on Annette than it was on Yvonne, but, I realize, it would be small on Yvonne now too.

"Bow before Her Majesty," Yvonne squeaked at George, tugging at his wrist while Marie and Cécile tackled his shins and induced him to shuffle the length of the nursery, the girls "riding" his feet until he managed to shake them off and slip away. But later, when Nurse Corriveau was getting the girls washed up for supper and I was putting their royal finery back in the costume trunk, George popped his head into the room again, did a quick sweep, then turned to leave.

"Their Majesties are no longer at court," I called after him.

He smiled then and took a step back into the room, although I had the sense he had somewhere else he wanted to be.

"All this fuss," he said. "They'll be heartbroken."

"Why?" I asked, surprised.

George looked up at me sharply. "You don't think the royal tour is actually going to come all the way to Quintland, do you?"

I hesitated, and he gave a little laugh, which wasn't nice.

"Good God, Emma. The only reason the Royals are touring Canada now is to rally support for the coming war. Surely you know that?"

I hate it when George does this. I *hate* it.

"The girls are wards of the King," I managed. "The King and Queen are, in theory, their official guardians, their legal mother and father. It is their duty to visit them, isn't it?"

For a moment I thought George was going to laugh at me again—a terrible feeling. But his face softened a bit, the way it does when Marie or Cécile does something particularly sweet or funny, and he changed his tone.

"Emma, they already *have* a mother and father, much as we like to forget that. And think about it. Why now? With so much going on at home, why on earth would the King and Queen take the time to visit one of their most important Commonwealth allies?"

Before I could think of something to say, the girls rushed back in en route to the dining room in their pajamas. George stepped aside and smiled fondly at them as they barreled by.

Miss Callahan was following close behind, and George raised a hand as she passed.

"Miss Callahan, a document from the Department of Education has arrived for you. Dr. Dafoe asked that you review it and let him know your thoughts before he discusses it with the other guardians."

She paused, one eye on the little ones heading down the corridor, the other on George.

"Has he looked over it?" she asked.

George made a sound very close to a snort and shook his head.

"No, Miss Callahan. He's given it back to me unopened. I can bring it to your desk, if you like, or you can stop by tomorrow. I gather he's hoping you can provide him with a summary."

She laughed softly, as did George. It's been a standing joke between George and me, how very little Dr. Dafoe manages to accomplish in a day, between meeting important visitors, radio broadcasts, and speaking engagements. Clearly Miss Callahan is in on the joke too.

I wonder, why does Miss Callahan think the King and Queen are visiting Canada?

October 20, 1938

Miss Emma Trimpany
Dafoe Hospital and Nursery
Callander, ON

Dear Emma,

I must say I don't like the sound of your encounter with M. Dionne one bit. I can't help but dislike the man, based on everything you've told me, but at the same time I do feel some compassion for the position the Dionnes are in. Mme. Dionne has always struck me as broken in some way, and who wouldn't be? Living across the road from her own daughters—it's hard to imagine what that would be like. M. Dionne is harder to read. Does he love his girls, do you think? Truly love them?

The papers here are full to bursting with details of the Quints' upcoming tonsil operation. You'd think they were getting extra toes sewn onto their feet for all the interest the press is taking. Why do they even need these things out? Don't tonsils serve some kind of natural purpose? What *are* tonsils exactly?

The company bigwigs at Canadian Car and Foundry are haggling with the British government, which wants our firm to build them some planes: we are all on pins and needles, myself included. If this contract comes through, I won't have to worry about waking up from this dream, doing work I love. As much as I miss home, this is where I belong, doing this.

That said, I have a few days' leave over Christmas that I plan to spend in Callander and will be helping my father with the plowing and transfers to Quintland while I'm home. My brother and his wife will be in town with my little niece, Sheryl, who is about the same age as your Edith. Maybe we'll have the chance to visit? Some things, however, are easier to say in writing, so I'll just come right out and ask: I can't help but notice that you've mentioned George Sinclair in every letter. What should I take from this, Emma? Are you spoken for? Or are you merely friendly? I appreciate, in the year you've had, friends at the nursery are few and far between. And yet . . .

Yours curiously,
Lewis
11 Rue Saint Ida
Montreal, Quebec

P.S. Rock doves, unlike film stars and millionaires, are believed to pair for life.

October 27, 1938 (*Toronto Star*)

EDITORIAL: IN A CLASS BY THEMSELVES

Canada has her Niagara Falls, but she shares them with the United States; and Africa has Victoria Falls. Canada has the picturesque streets and conveyances of Old Quebec; New Orleans, too, has quite a strong French flavour. We have our Niagara Peninsula's peach trees; California has its orange groves. We are proud of the St. Lawrence; our cousins think highly of the Mississippi and Egypt is still watered by the Nile.

These attractions in Canada, though duplicated or approximated elsewhere, deserve all the praise they receive. But what is unique in this country, what we have that others have not, are the quintuplets. No wonder that, while there is no official word, it is practically certain that the King and Queen next summer will visit Callander. The possibility of the five little sisters themselves being taken somewhere to see Their Majesties is remote. Up to now,

Yvonne, Émilie, Annette, Marie, and Cécile have never been further than across the road from the house where they were born.

True, the day will come when the Dionne quintuplets will have to move about. If they are to be educated in a way befitting the responsibilities of world-fame, they will have to see the world. The problem of how to secure the privacy required in such travels will be baffling but it has not yet arisen. Someday these babies, as they grow into girlhood and young womanhood, will have to meet other friends of their own age, besides their brothers and sisters. They will meet young men. Yes, there will come a day when one of the quintuplets will be engaged. Imagine the furore then! And picture, if you can, the wedding day of the first of the Quints, unless, indeed, they wait for all to be even and hold one great quintuplet wedding!

Meanwhile, Their Majesties will have the pleasure of seeing

their five little wards, happy, childish, well trained, polite and considerate, playing their games, singing their songs, doing their dances, and saying their prayers. What occurred in the Dionne household in the early morning of May 28, 1934, under the incredulous eyes of Dr. Dafoe, made human history, which has become of cumulative interest to the whole world. When King George and Queen Elizabeth return to England, the first question their daughters are likely to ask is, "Tell us all about the Quints!" That is one part of the trip the absent princesses will be most sorry to miss.

October 28, 1938

All of the staff are going into North Bay to see the girls in *Five of a Kind* in the cinema there tonight. I've spent the past forty-five minutes trying to decide what to wear and another thirty minutes worrying about my hair. I've decided to wear a wide-brim hat and will leave it on until the theater lights go down.

Mr. Cartwright has been asked to ferry the rest of the staff, including the ladies from the kitchen. I saw Mr. Cartwright earlier today when I took some tea things back from George's office, and he was looking well. I asked after Lewis, and he said, "Very well, very well." Then he asked me if he'd be taking me in to see the picture later and I had to say I'd already accepted a ride with Mr. Sinclair. He seemed disappointed, I fear, but I assured him he'll be seeing plenty of me any day now, when the snow falls and I'll be calling on him to help me get home to see Edith.

I've decided on my green dress. It's not particularly new, but I think it looks smart with my navy hat.

October 28, 1938—almost midnight

THE GIRLS WERE so sweet in the motion picture; it is enough to shatter your heart into a million pieces. The cinema was packed and erupted with laughter and sighs and whoops each time the girls did something silly, especially performing some of their musical numbers and tumbling with their puppies. Jean Hersholt, Cesar Romero, and Claire Trevor were also very good, of course, but our babies stole the show.

I can't read George. I sat beside him in the theater and, when the lights went down, felt something like an electric current running between my knee and his, although he was a perfect gentleman and never so much as nudged me. Miss Callahan was on his other side, however, and I can't quite get a reading on her either. When he turns to speak with me, I feel like he's giving me every ounce of his attention. But then, I think that's just George, because he's as courteous and attentive with Nurse Corriveau and Miss Callahan as he is with me.

Oh, for heaven's sake, I sound like a silly schoolgirl. This isn't me. Truly.

Is it?

November 1, 1938

A LETTER FROM Lewis, asking me the most extraordinary thing, I don't quite know what to make of it, or what I should say in return. I can't possibly have mentioned George in every letter. Why on earth would I do that?

God, I miss Ivy. She would know exactly how to respond.

Meanwhile, all the girls can talk about is meeting the princesses. Of England, they mean. There's been so much talk about the King and Queen and whether they might come and visit us at Quintland. The girls have dug all of their prettiest dress-up clothes out of their trunks, even the gowns they can barely squeeze themselves into, and are playing "Princess" every day. We've tried to explain to them that the princesses won't be coming on the royal tour next year, but for whatever reason, they are adamant that it will be children who visit them, not the King and Queen. They are tired of grown-ups, Annette informed me. What does that tell us, I wonder. I don't want to think about it.

We're having a terrific storm today: driving rain and a howling wind lashing the nursery. Apart from Cécile, who is hooting with excitement and pressing her nose to the windows, exhilarated, the girls are a bit frightened by it and extra cuddly as a result.

November 9, 1938 (*Toronto Star*)

QUINTS IN "FINE SHAPE" AFTER OPERATION

Marie Leads Parade as All 5 Lose Tonsils On Dining Room Table

First Carried in at 9:10 and Last Carried Out at 12:15 O'clock

NO TRANSFUSIONS: None of Sisters Worried

The world's best-loved quintet is still intact.

Marie, Annette, Émilie, Cécile, and Yvonne—in that order— came safely today through the ordeal of having their tonsils and adenoids removed. The surgeries were performed onsite at the Dafoe Hospital and Nursery.

Early this afternoon the Dionne girls were all reported "in fine condition."

Marie's was the hardest operation of the five. The actual operating time was 13 minutes. Annette came next with actual operation time, 9 minutes. Then came Émilie, and it took 10 minutes of actual operating.

Both Yvonne and Cécile, who followed in turn, had their tonsils removed in 8 and a half minutes each.

The most precious fluid in the world—human blood— was brought here in shiny cans today against the possible need of a transfusion for one or all of the Dionne quintuplets.

The blood for transfusion, if needed, came from professional donors in Toronto in much the same way as the mother's milk was brought from Chicago and Toronto during the first few days of the Quints' existence four years ago last May.

At the same time, two human donors stood ready to supply germ-free blood of the same type from their own veins if surgeons felt a direct transfusion to be more desirable. These human donors are both parents, Oliva, the father, and Elzire, the mother.

Used with permission.

November 11, 1938

The girls are already up and about and eating coddled eggs and soft cereals with no trouble whatsoever. Last night they got vanilla ice cream, which they lapped up like kittens. Cécile wanted to know when they could get more tonsils taken out, so they can have more ice cream. I was foolish to worry so much, I suppose, but talking myself out of worrying has never been an option.

November 16, 1938

I AM TWENTY-TWO years old today. Old enough to know what I want, presumably.

November 20, 1938

Miss Emma Trimpany
Dafoe Hospital and Nursery
Callander, ON

My dear Emma,

How are you? How goes your painting and drawing? Any
gems you'd care to share? How are the little angels? I can tell
you, all of New York was riveted by the news of their tonsil
operation—I'm very glad that went well.

I'm enclosing a pamphlet that I hope you'll take a look at.
As you know, I think, I am one of the adjunct teachers at the
Art Students League of New York. The school has finally
launched the international scholarship program several of us
have been pushing for. There are five positions earmarked for
Canadian applicants, and I think you have an excellent chance
of being accepted. I'm happy to provide any feedback or suggestions you would need for your portfolio, and there are some
specific requirements for subject, medium, and techniques that
might take some time to put together. Your application would
need to be in by the end of May next year in order to be considered for entrance that year. I hope you'll seriously consider it. If
you'd prefer to discuss this by telephone, I'd be happy to arrange
a time to call you at the nursery.

I have little in the way of news—I'm teaching a fair bit, and
this has pushed my own work to the side for now, which I admit is getting me down. There is so much to drag one down,
I find. An old friend of mine was killed in the New England
hurricane you likely heard about, in September, and it's left me

feeling very low. Plus the events in Europe make it difficult to feel like painting, don't you find? A great number of people in the art world here in New York are Jewish, and we are all watching Mr. Hitler with our hearts in our throats. He's mad, I believe, yet no one seems willing to stop him.

I don't mean to end on a sour note. Please, my dear Emma, have a look at the enclosed and tell me if you'd consider it.

Warmest wishes,
Maud Tousey Fangel
145 East 72nd
New York, NY

December 7, 1938

I was planning to speak with Dr. Dafoe today about Mrs. Fangel's pamphlet. I scarcely slept, trying out what I might say or how I might phrase it in my head. It all comes down to the plans for this new house for all of the Dionnes and whether that's real or not. If there's a chance I'll be out of a job next fall—because there is no way M. Dionne would keep me on staff—well, it would make sense to plan ahead. On the other hand, I desperately don't want to go. Anywhere. Despite everything, I'm happy here and I feel like I'm still needed. Ivy would tell me I must absolutely apply, but then, Ivy took to New York like a duck to water. All of her thrilling stories! How on earth could someone like me get along in a place like that? I could ask George for his advice, but I worry it might sound like I'm trying to nudge him toward a different topic altogether, which I'm not. Truly. Odd as it sounds, I don't feel like asking Mother and Father. They are so bound up with little Edith they'd prefer to think of my life as settled on its course, their parental duties discharged. Not to mention they've come to depend on the income I send home. That leaves me with Dr. Dafoe. He might not be the most thoughtful, but at least he'd be objective.

I needn't have stayed up half the night worrying about it. Dr.

Dafoe has left again for New York, George told me when he arrived today. Meanwhile all of the doctor's correspondence, newspaper articles, lectures, and whatever else fall to poor George. He has dark shadows under his eyes these days and needs a haircut desperately, not to mention a secretary of his own. He's working late most nights, leaving to drive back to North Bay long after the rest of us have headed to bed, no doubt taking a stack of unread mail along with him. It's too much, I think. Too much for one man.

I've done a small pastel of George "taking tea" with the girls in the playroom, and I'm going to give it to him for Christmas. I hope he likes it.

December 20, 1938

I'M NOT SURE I can even set this down in print; my hands are shaking, my thoughts tumbling all over the place. But I can't sleep, can't switch off the light, can't cope with the dark, can't lie down. I've been pacing back and forth in my tiny room, waiting for my heart to slow down and my breath to go back to normal. I feel trapped, but also tiny and small. Erased and invisible. Oh, yes. Invisible as usual.

As if I could ever be anything else.

I'm kicking myself for not going home tonight when I had the chance. But imagine if I had? Oh God. I feel sick and foolish and angry and sad. Desperately sad.

Let me try to write this down.

Nurse Corriveau left for her Christmas holidays yesterday, and I was to go tonight. A relief nurse is coming from the Red Cross tomorrow to help Miss Callahan through the Christmas week until Nurse Corriveau returns. The problem is, all of the girls are down with a terrible bug, and I've got it too. My head has been throbbing like someone is beating it with a mallet, and there is a heaviness in my chest that makes me fearful of inhaling too deeply. If Dr. Dafoe were here, I'd have him listen with his stethoscope, but he's still away, of course. He is always away. Indeed, the doctor telephoned earlier in the evening, while George was still in the office, to say that he was extending his visit in New York until the New Year.

Mr. Cartwright came to the back steps at seven this evening to fetch me home with my bags, and Lewis was with him, which was a nice surprise. He looks well, Lewis, dressed sharply in a long gray topcoat with lovely, wide lapels, looking broader somehow—broad enough to match his height. And he looks younger too, if that's possible. As if time at a desk has helped to erase a year or two of worries.

Oh, Lewis. He's been so droll and candid in his letters with his talk of pigeons and planes. Perhaps we could have picked up from there if I hadn't been feeling so out of sorts and he looking less like a city man, so polished and poised. Instead it was as if we'd changed roles and it was I whose rough tongue was tripping all over itself, my eyes unsure of where to look. When I first came into the kitchen, Lewis smiled his broad smile, as open as I'd ever seen it, and it lingered on his lips until I said I wasn't going to go with them this evening. The thing is, I was feeling so poorly, and the girls were so sickly themselves I told them I'd better stay to help Miss Callahan through the night. I knew that the Cartwrights would be coming back in the morning to bring the relief nurse to the nursery, so it wouldn't be yet another special trip. I apologized profusely, and they were both very kind, saying not to worry, and of course I must get some rest and so on.

I left the kitchen, telling Marguerite that I wouldn't be need-
ing anything more. Then I stopped by the girls' room, and they
were all snuffling and snorting, but seemingly asleep. I poked
my head into the charting area to let Miss Callahan know that I
had decided to stay, if she needed me, but she wasn't there and I
didn't think to leave a note, I just climbed into my bed and was
out like a light, I'm sure, within a matter of minutes.

Sometime later I was woken by some thumps and muffled
voices. My heart started racing. I switched on the bedside lamp
and checked my clock: just after 11:00 P.M. My first instinct was
for the girls' safety, so I crept to their room as quick as I could.
The five of them were sleeping soundly, and I could still hear
murmuring and something being nudged across the floorboards
somewhere at the other end of the corridor, toward Dr. Dafoe's
office.

Perhaps I have a fever—it certainly feels that way now—but
my first thought was that Dr. Dafoe had come back and surely
I should tell him as soon as possible that the girls were ill. This
was irrational, I know, because we'd heard that very day that
he was hundreds of miles away, in New York City. But I simply
didn't think for a moment that it could be an intruder. There are
five full-time constables guarding the nursery around the clock:
it would be next to impossible for someone to break in. But
why wasn't I more scared? Why didn't I stop by Miss Callahan's
room to let her know that something was afoot and that I was
having a look, or that she should accompany me? I don't know
why. Or maybe I did, I just didn't realize it.

Only when I was right outside Dr. Dafoe's office did it regis-
ter with me that one of the voices was a woman's. Miss Callahan's. She has a lovely voice, a radio voice: a deep, slow, buttery
way of speaking, which I think is one reason the girls have come

to love her and do her bidding. Indeed, she's supplanted me as their number one choice of reader at story time.

I froze. She was in Dr. Dafoe's office with someone, that much was clear. With a man. It was none of my business, of course, how Miss Callahan was spending her evening when—I realized at that moment—she likely thought I was three miles away, in Callander, with my parents. But surely she shouldn't be in Dr. Dafoe's office unless she was with Dr. Dafoe himself? But with whom if not Dr. Dafoe? One of our guardsmen? *M. Dionne?*

I should have left well enough alone, I know that. I'm not usually so nosy. But the door was ajar and the room beyond, dimly lit. Bright enough, however, that if I stood well back I could peer in without anyone realizing I was outside in the corridor. So that's what I did.

It was Miss Callahan all right, laughing low and smooth, seated sideways on someone's lap. A man's lap, as if she were one of the girls asking for a bedtime story. She was seated sideways, laughing, on George's lap.

December 25, 1938

I HAVEN'T FELT like writing in my scribble book, and I can scarcely go back and read what I last wrote. Worse: what I've been writing for months. It's been a blessing to be home with Mother, Father, and busy little Edith—it's helped to take my mind off the nursery.

My cold has settled so soundly into my chest I worry it might be pneumonia. Mother made up a bed on the couch in the living room rather than keep Edith up all night with my coughing or risk her catching this. But Christmas was pleasant enough, with a fresh blanket of snow yesterday that made everything look clean and gleaming, just in time.

Mr. Cartwright and Lewis stopped in on Christmas Eve, early in the afternoon just as the snow started coming down. It was Lewis who brought me into Callander last week after that terrible night. Whether it is the pleasure of his work, or big city life, or the camaraderie of so many brainy men—and women— all toiling together at something they love, I don't know, but Lewis is subtly changed. Somehow, despite all these months of letters, I felt, seeing Lewis again, as if I knew him *less,* not more. Or rather, that there is a lot of Lewis still to get to know. He was as courteous as ever, no question, hastening to help me carry my bags and packages out to the truck. And his quirky eye for detail remains intact. As we drove the short distance from the nursery to Callander, I could do little more than shiver and snivel, deep in my own shame and self-pity—I'd scarcely slept the night before, after what I'd seen. But Lewis, undaunted, did his best to lighten the mood.

"The perils of Christmas punch," he said softly, pointing to a slumping company of snowmen in a farmer's yard, much the worse for wear after the mild weather last week. I managed a smile.

Finally, just as we were pulling up outside my old home, he said: "Is everything okay, miss?"

It wasn't, of course, but I had to laugh. "'Miss'?" I asked. "I thought we finally got past 'miss.'"

I think that made him blush, blush like the old Lewis, but he laughed as well. Then we sat quietly until I said I'd had a fitful sleep and was still feeling poorly. He nodded, and I worried for a moment that this would be that and I wouldn't find a way to say that I would like to see him another time, when I was feeling better. There was an awkward pause, then we both spoke at once.

"Would you and your father like to come around for tea?" I said. And he, in the same instant, said, "I've built a toboggan—do you think little Edith would want to test it out?"

That made us laugh a second time, and suddenly things seemed as companionable as they've come to feel in our letters. He agreed he and his father would stop by on the twenty-fourth, which they did. I thought Mother would have a dozen questions for me about asking a young man around for tea—she did fix me with a surprised look when I mentioned the invitation. But when they came by yesterday and Father and Mr. Cartwright commandeered all conversation, Mother seemed chiefly preoccupied with making Christmas as perfect as possible for baby Edith, and she did. It was.

December 27, 1938

LEWIS CAME TO call for Edith and me yesterday, bringing the toy sled he'd fashioned out of wood, rope, and airplane remnants in his Montreal factory. How he managed to bring this contraption home to Callander on the train I'll never know. Accompanying him on our sledding expedition was his brother's little girl, Sheryl. She must be a year or two older than Edith, but the two of them got along famously, treating Lewis as their own personal Clydesdale and bidding him mercilessly to go faster, *faster*. It's lucky he didn't furnish them with a driving whip.

The temperatures have dipped again, but the sky was blue and bright. For the first time this week the vise clamped around my lungs (and heart) felt like it was starting to ease its grip. And what a treat to be out in the winter sun, bundled snugly against the cold! For a time I stood stamping my boots at the bottom of the gentle slope while Lewis toiled up with the toboggan, again and again, the little girls taking turns climbing into his lap to careen back down. Soon enough, Lewis convinced me to try out his invention, hauling it up to a higher point on the hill and settling me into it while Edith and Sheryl clapped their hands and jabbered in encouragement. When I said I was ready, Lewis gave me a stout push, and I started whooshing down, winter nipping at my cheeks. I yelped as I gained speed, not out of fear—I swear—but something much simpler: exhilaration and joy. For those few fast and sparkling seconds I felt like a child again, bursting and glad. Lewis must have heard my shriek because he came bounding down the hill behind me, reaching me as the sled slowed to a stop. He was winded, his breath billowing in bright, white gusts as he dropped to his knees in the snow and put a hand on my shoulder, his eyes blinking with worry. Then he saw my beaming face.

"Again!" I cried, climbed to my feet, and staggered up through the deep drifts to join the girls.

I saw Lewis one more time this morning at the train station before he left to return to Montreal. We've agreed that I will speak to Dr. Dafoe if I feel in any way threatened, or pressured about the commissions I'm receiving for my work. And Lewis has said he will continue to write to me at the nursery for now, but that he won't write anything that might get me in trouble should his letters fall into the wrong hands. I wondered then—whose hands are the wrong ones, and whose are the right? I'm not sure I know. I also promised him that if I had any worries whatsoever,

I would post my letters in Callander myself or pass them directly to his father, who wouldn't dream of meddling with our correspondence, as much as he might be wondering about it.

My own parents are curious, that's clear. But Mother, for once, held her tongue. And what would I tell her if she asked about Lewis? I would have to say, He's a friend. A true friend. Perhaps the only friend I have left.

December 28, 1938

IVY AND FRED are in town for two nights to see her father and so that Fred can pack up his rooms in North Bay once and for all. I will miss his regular visits to the nursery now that they are stopping altogether, and I could tell from his face that he, too, will miss us, will miss the girls. I realize, next to me, Fred has probably seen the quintuplets more days of their lives than anyone else, more than Dr. Dafoe, more than their own parents and siblings. Isn't that strange? The girls will miss him desperately.

But if I'm not mistaken, Fred will not have too much of a wait before he has a child of his own. Ivy has a lovely bloom to her, different from her regular glow, and I noted her laying her hand on her stomach several times during our visit. She said nothing to me about her condition, so it may have been my imagination. Or it may be that we've simply drifted apart a little bit further, which makes me sad. It won't get any easier once the baby comes.

We had a very nice visit all the same. She had more gossip about the behind-the-scenes battle between the government and the Dionnes. On the one side are some nasty accusations as to how Dr. Dafoe and Mr. Munro have mishandled the girls' finances and, on the other, some vicious allegations against M. Dionne as well. I wish I'd heard some of these things before Lewis left for Montreal so I could get his opinion, although it's a good excuse to write to him, if nothing else. Mind you, even Ivy admits that much of these stories get exaggerated beyond recognition in the telling and retelling.

I did divulge to Ivy that Mrs. Fangel was encouraging me to apply for the art school scholarship in New York. Naturally, Ivy got very agitated on my behalf, swiftly assuming I'd decided against it and browbeating me with all of her usual arguments.

I had to wave my hands to get her to stop.

"I haven't ruled it out, I haven't," I hushed her, laughing. "I wrote to Mrs. Fangel before Christmas, asking for more details on what I might need for the portfolio."

Ivy was placated by this and asked a dozen more questions that I couldn't answer. The truth is, I wrote to Mrs. Fangel in a moment of despondency, my head thick with equal parts rheum and despair. I still can't picture myself leaving the nursery, but nor can I quite picture going back there next week, as if everything will be the same as it was.

1939

January 4, 1939 (*Toronto Star*)

"GREAT MISTAKE," SAYS DAFOE AS QUINT VISIT LEFT OFF ROYAL TOUR

Are King's Wards, He Reminds— Holds Ottawa Responsible

"I think it is a great mistake that the King and Queen are not coming to see the Dionne quintuplets," Dr. Allan Roy Dafoe told *The Star* from Callander today.

"The responsibility does not rest with their majesties, for they are bound to abide by the counsel of their advisers in Ottawa," he continued, "but it must be remembered that these children—probably the most important children in the world—are direct wards of the King, the pride of both races in Canada, and of the greatest interest throughout this continent.

"This part of the country is just as important as any other. . . . I am very sorry that their majesties are not coming to Callander."

Asked if it would be possible to take the quintuplets to Sudbury or some other point on the royal itinerary to meet the King and Queen, Dr. Dafoe replied: "It is out of the question. We have already refused an invitation to go to the World's Fair in New York. The same reasons apply in this instance, namely, the dangers of infection, excitement, and the bad effect of close contact with crowds. It simply cannot be done," he concluded.

The sisters have hitherto never travelled more than the one-eighth of a mile from the farm where they were born.

January 4, 1939

Dr. Dafoe was back today, finally, after Mr. Cartwright was able to clear the road.

The girls went wild when they saw his car pull up in the courtyard, then threw themselves at him when he came through the door, his boots puddling the floor. "Docteur, docteur," they hollered, saying it properly now, and bombarding him further with tales of *le père Noël, la Vierge Marie, le petit Jésus,* and *le bonhomme de neige*—all of whom they seem to credit with delivering their windfall of *cadeaux,* on Christmas Eve.

Dr. Dafoe himself was holding five big packages, beautifully wrapped in each of the girl's colors. They tore through the paper to find five identical Shirley Temple dolls with eyes that rolled and real curlers to curl their hair. The girls were ecstatic about the dolls, not paying any attention to the autographed photo that came in each box. Of course, they had no recollection of ever meeting someone named Shirley Temple, nor would they understand why she is famous, so they have no need for a signed photo. To them, these are simply five beautiful dolls, exactly the same, with hair that needs curling every morning. Just like them.

Dr. Dafoe made it clear that he's livid the royal itinerary does not include a visit to Quintland. After the girls opened their gifts, he stomped off with George to his office, anger steaming off him like an engine's plume in winter. We could hear him barking into the telephone so loudly his voice carried to the other end of the nursery. He and George were shut away the rest of the day—a relief, frankly. I don't know how to act around George now, or where to look, although he is as friendly with me as ever. It will only be worse when Miss Callahan returns from her break this weekend. All I can picture is his face that night as I spied on them through the open door, the corners of his lips curling upward, his eyes dancing like a fire. It is giving me a cramp in the pit of my stomach.

January 12, 1939

Miss Emma Trimpany
Dafoe Hospital and Nursery
Callander, ON

Dear Emma,

I'm so glad you wrote back and I'm thrilled that you're considering the scholarship. I've enclosed a document listing the types of work you would need to include, which you should review in detail. You will need at least 12 completed pieces, including a mix of drawing samples and color, with a range of different mediums represented.

You will also need some still lifes and landscapes: I think you told me you spent time last summer doing some nature sketches? I hope so. It's also essential that you include a self-portrait. Here, my guess is you may have some work to do. I can tell you, as hard as you may find it at first, you will quickly realize what an interesting and rewarding exercise this can be. Don't shy from the truth—that's what I always tell my students. The truth is *us,* at our best and our worst, and our self-portraiture should reflect that.

Perhaps you could send me a list of works you feel could be included today, and those that you'll have to complete before the deadline. Better yet, if you still have that handsome photographer making his daily visits, see if he can take some photographs of your completed work and send some prints my way.

Yours in anticipation,
Maud Tousey Fangel
145 East 72nd
New York, NY

January 18, 1939

Miss Emma Trimpany
Dafoe Hospital and Nursery
Callander, ON

Dear Emma,

Your news is distressing but I truly don't know how much or how little to make of Ivy's gossip. It is thirdhand, or more, as you say. It's all upsetting, but I also think you need to use your own eyes and your own wits and make your own decisions. Much of it seems pretty far-fetched.

Have you been pondering Mrs. Fangel's scholarship? If you can't get your mind around a move to America, what about applying closer to home? The Ontario College of Art in Toronto, perhaps. Or even the École des Beaux-Arts here in Montreal. Back when my father was trying to talk me out of aeronautics, he used to say, the simplest decisions lead to happiness. I tend to disagree. I have long believed that it is making the *harder* choices that makes one happy, and when I'm at my happiest, the hard things become easier. I've never been much good at gauging other people's happiness, but my sense is that it's your art, Emma Trimpany, that brings you joy. I would have to say, choose the harder path.

As for me, I'll be happy when the weather improves and we can test our planes. My poor pigeons, too, would be happy to see a sunny day again. It's been so many straight weeks of snow none of us can quite remember how the sky looked without it.

Yours sincerely,
Lewis
11 Rue Saint Ida
Montreal, Quebec

January 20, 1939

Mr. Munro visited today, shuttering himself with Dr. Dafoe for most of the morning, which of course made me wonder how much truth there may have been to Ivy's gossip.

After Dr. Dafoe departed, Mr. Munro summoned me to the office and spoke with me solemnly about my savings account and how the payments from the advertisers will be handled. He looks a bit like a sheepdog, Mr. Munro does. His bushy white eyebrows all but engulf his deep-set eyes, and he wears his thick, white mustache long and parted so that it droops low over his mouth. His whole face seems to bristle when he talks.

He took pains to explain to me that as long as one has a certain amount of money set aside, it will continue to grow, even if one doesn't add more. I wasn't particularly interested in my own savings. What I wanted to know is, Do the quintuplets have enough? We've all been hearing for years now that our girls can never go back to living like other children, they'll always need ways to protect their safety and their privacy. How much will that cost? And for how long? That's what I wanted to ask Mr. Munro.

January 22, 1938

MISS CALLAHAN IS back from her vacation, and I can't help but watch the way she and George carry on in front of the rest of us, plain as day. How did I miss this before? Right under my very nose. Sometimes when he doesn't know I'm watching them together, George lets down his guard and looks more like a slavering dog. As if Miss Callahan is the Easter ham, resting on the counter just out of reach. She is encouraging it, I realize. It's both fascinating and discouraging. Are all men like this, if they sense a willing woman? Would Lewis be like this? Was Fred? I'm sure I never saw Fred looking at Ivy this way, but perhaps I didn't know what I was looking for. George continues to be as jaunty and charming with me as ever, and it gives me the shivers. Not in a good way.

February 1, 1939

NURSE CORRIVEAU CAME and knocked at my door just now, bringing the notebook she's been using to "document" her interactions with the Dionnes. During the day she wears her wavy brown hair pinned low on the back of her head, her nursing cap on top, but tonight she had it loose, as if she'd just brushed it out. Strands suspended by static were drifting upward, making her look even more frazzled then she clearly already was. She's a private woman, Nurse Corriveau. I know very little about her and her life before she came to the nursery, and her flat expression and deep-set eyes typically give very little away. When she speaks it's in a high, quavering tone, and one gets the sense that she herself doesn't like the sound of it, because she doesn't mince words. The only time you see the ghost of a smile on her lips is when the girls do something silly. Miss Callahan is their current favorite in the nursery, but they clearly love Nurse Corriveau, too, although with more reserve.

I steered her into my tiny room and offered her the chair. She sat down reluctantly, as if she wasn't sure she'd be staying. She had her notebook on her lap and was patting it as you would a cat while the fingers of her other hand stroked distractedly at her mustache.

"I want to show you this," she blurted out, tapping the notebook. "I want another pair of eyes, if you will. In fact—" Her gaze darted around my room for several seconds before she continued. "In fact, I know you, too, keep a notebook. I wondered if you would consider copying a few things down, so we have a duplicate."

I could feel my eyebrows pop upward. I've started keeping my journal tucked in the crack between my bureau and the wall. I can't bear the thought of anyone reading this. But copy from her journal to mine?

She rushed on.

"I had another nasty set-to with Mme. Dionne today. I simply walked out on her while she was speaking, saying despicable things about me, about Miss Callahan, about Dr. Dafoe. I walked into the charting area and immediately started to set it down in my notebook."

Nurse Corriveau was watching my face, and I could see her lip trembling and saw that her eyes, while dry, were ringed in red.

"A minute later, or two minutes, the door flew open and it was M. Dionne. He stood over my desk and thrust out his hand, demanding I hand over my book." She blinked and shuddered. "Naturally, I refused, and I thought he, too, would start shouting at me. But he didn't. Instead he lowered his voice so that I could scarcely hear him, and started saying horrible things."

I frowned, but I could feel my heartbeat quicken as if it was me alone in the charting room, M. Dionne standing over me, snarling.

"What sorts of things?" I said slowly.

Miss Corriveau shook her head and opened her journal, leafing through it. It had a plain brown cover and coarse, thin pages, like the notebooks used by schoolchildren, which had the effect of making her thin voice, when she spoke, seem even less substantial.

"I've written it down, Nurse Trimpany. I've written it all down here." Her eyes looked at mine, flickering from side to side as if reluctant to settle on my birthmark.

"Would you please read it over and perhaps consider copying some of it into your own records? Many of these incidents have taken place when you were not in attendance, when you were working on your commissions or discussing them with Mr. Sinclair."

I blushed then. I hope in that dim light that she couldn't see it. I couldn't say whether I was blushing because of George or because I'd been discovered, that Miss Corriveau knew—and clearly accepted—that I'd successfully evaded the Dionnes by retreating to my canvases.

"Of course," I murmured. I saw her gaze casting around my room again. "My notebook is down in my drawer in the charting area," I lied. I felt bad, but also sheepish retrieving my journal from its hiding place in front of Miss Corriveau.

She looked alarmed. "Oh, I wouldn't do that, Miss Trimpany. I would keep it with you at all times."

I nodded, and she looked down at her lap, glancing over the pages, then closed the notebook and stood to go.

"Please hang on to it, review it tonight and tomorrow if you need more time," she said, handing me her book. "But keep it with you, please. I don't want the Dionnes to see what I've written."

At my door she paused, turning back, her face twisted. "I

think it would be best if we always had two staff members in attendance when the Dionnes are visiting, don't you think?"

Sample notes from Louise Corriveau's notebook

- July 5, 1938: Qs asking where Miss Rousselle has gone. Mme. Dionne tells Cécile and Annette that Miss Rousselle is dirty and not nice. Nice women speak French. Says they must always listen to Maman.

- September 3, 1938: Rain. Mme. Dionne in the playroom with the girls. Émilie asked Miss Callahan to read her another story, brings her an English picture book. Mme. Dionne enraged. Says Miss C. is the Devil, the Devil speaks English. English is dirty. Jesus speaks French.

- September 27, 1938: Children brought into bathroom for toilet routine and Émilie and Marie admitted telling "dirty stories"—Nurse Trimpany and Miss Callahan are dirty, Dr. Dafoe was dirty.

- November 8, 1938: M. and Mme. Dionne visit before supper. M. Dionne tells girls to kiss their mother goodbye. Marie and Émilie refuse, say Maman tells them bad stories. Mme. Dionne scolds Marie, says she is dirty, says she "plays with her posterior" (?). Tells Émilie she is a crazy girl. Émilie and Marie crying, Mme. Dionne crying. M. Dionne angry, takes Mme. D. from house.

- February 1, 1939: Mme. Dionne accuses Miss Callahan in playroom of turning the children against her. Children

upset. Miss C. and I walk out of playroom and she follows, yelling insults and threats in French. Girls are frightened. M. Dionne follows us and says despicable things.
Calls Miss C. "une putain." Calls me "une salope."

February 2, 1939

I STOPPED BY the office this morning to speak with Dr. Dafoe
about Nurse Corriveau's notebook, but George says he won't be
in today.

It is different now, trying to winkle information out of George.
I realize how much the getting of the information used to seem as
important as the information itself. Today again, George looked
sallow, as if he'd been up half the night, and indeed his clothes
seemed creased and slackened—unusually so for him.

"Are you all right?" I asked, in spite of everything.

"Dr. Dafoe has asked me to pull together a list of all the canceled, current, and pending endorsement contracts." He sighed
and dug the heel of his hand into an eye socket. "It's a lot."

February 10, 1939

I MAY AS well work on some of the things Mrs. Fangel has
suggested, if only for the practice of doing it, nothing more.
I tinkered with some "still life" charcoal sketches using some
of the girls' playthings—a doll, balls, a rocking horse. There's
something disconcerting about a pile of children's toys with no
rowdy, tumbling children nearby.

Later, I took my things up to my own room and spent an

hour looking in the mirror, my sketchbook on my knee, trying to figure out how I'd do a self-portrait. Each effort ended up in the wastebasket. It's as if I haven't learned anything about proportion or shading or balance whatsoever. By the time I'd given up, I'd missed supper.

I wandered down the hall to the girls' room, all of them sleeping soundly. I sat on the window seat where Ivy and I used to whisper about what the future might hold. I have no more of an idea now than I ever did. Ivy was so certain, even then, about the life she wanted, and now she's gone out and got it. Lewis too. Me, I'm still a note in the margins of someone else's story.

Annette stirred in her sleep, murmuring something. Yvonne flung an arm over her eyes, as if to block out the moonlight.

Maybe this is all I need. Listening to the girls sleep, all of us tucked away safe and sound, spared from the strife sweeping the rest of the world—surely this is more than enough to make us happy. But then why am I even obsessing over Mrs. Fangel's pamphlet and all her portfolio suggestions? Just to prove to myself I can? Why bother, if I have no intention of following through?

February 20, 1939

MISS CALLAHAN, NURSE Corriveau, and I have agreed that there will always be two of us with the girls when the Dionnes are visiting. It makes me realize how much I've been slipping out of my duties in recent months, probably longer, to avoid some of these tense visits.

I will absolutely hate this when the public play area opens again for the season. It was bad enough feeling like thousands of people a day were baffled by the sight of me and my birthmark in such close proximity to Canada's famous five. Now the idea of arbitrating any friction between the children, their parents, and the nursing staff while visitors gasp and wave with a smile fixed on my face—it's almost too much to imagine.

Today, thank goodness, was my turn to sit out, leaving the others to deal with the Dionnes. It is a beautiful, twinkling winter's day, cold but bright. The girls were eager to play in the snow, so I helped button them into their woolens and warm boots. The Dionnes arrived right after the girls went out, following them into the private yard without so much as a *bonjour*.

I retreated to my bedroom in the hopes of having a private hour to muddle along with a self-portrait. I'm trying to use two mirrors now, my image bouncing from one to the other so that I'm not looking directly into my own eyes but watching myself in profile, my good side. I prefer this to staring at myself directly, wondering who exactly I see.

I was engaged enough with the effort that I didn't notice M. Dionne at my door until he spoke. "The artist at work," he muttered softly and took a step into the room so he was right behind me, his heavy eyes in the mirror watching me. Maybe it was the effect of the glass, but he looked much larger than he is. Taller and straighter. I didn't turn around, but I could see his face perfectly in our reflection. He was giving me the strangest look, part fury and part something else. It rattled me, which must have shown in my face, because he gave a tight smile, or sneer, something between the two. I wanted to stand, but I had the sense that he was so close behind me and I was twisting so awkwardly to see him that I couldn't move from my seat without somehow making contact with him. It was awful.

I realized his eyes had dropped to the drawing on my lap. Rough pencil strokes, hardly recognizable as a portrait. "You'll be sure to include the corn syrup tins, won't you?" he said, his eyebrows coming together above his cold eyes. "Or is it chocolate bars you are drawing today?"

I was angry then, because of course what I draw or paint most days are his beautiful daughters. His beautiful daughters *as they are in that moment*. Does he ever even think of them as they *are*? Just themselves. Then he reached past me—no, *around* me, over my shoulder, and took the sketchbook from my lap. I dropped my pencil. The anger I'd felt earlier fled.

Then there was a noise—the creak I'd assumed I should have heard earlier—and the door swung wide. Had it been closed? Ajar? Had M. Dionne opened it, then closed it behind him? I shivered.

"Ah, M. Dionne, there you are."

It was George, polite and businesslike. "I saw you come indoors. The report from Mr. Wilson's office is here, if you still wish to review it?"

M. Dionne turned sideways and fixed George with a look not much different from the one he'd used to pin me. But he gave a curt nod, slid my sketchbook onto my bureau, turned on his heel, and walked out the door.

I watched George as he stood aside to permit M. Dionne to pass. I expected he might meet my gaze, or nod, or do something to show me he, too, knew his timing wasn't a coincidence. But he kept his eyes trained on M. Dionne and followed him out the door, never looking back.

February 25, 1939

WE ARE TO teach the girls to sing "God Save the King" for a special radio broadcast that will be aired in Canada and the

U.S. next month. Dr. Dafoe is very excited by the plan, telling everyone it is bound to increase public pressure on Their Majesties to come and visit the Dionne quintuplets in Callander.

"They couldn't possibly stay away," he told us, a wide smile on his face.

George says the doctor has another goal in mind: he's hoping it will prove to Hollywood that the girls can indeed sing in English and cement lucrative plans to feature them in a new motion picture.

"What do the Dionnes think about them singing in English?" I asked George. He grimaced and put a finger to his lips.

Clearly the Dionnes have not been told.

February 25, 1939

Miss Emma Trimpany
Dafoe Hospital and Nursery
Callander, ON

Dear Emma,

We've had a patch of ugly weather, but the forecast has cleared up and, according to the weatherman, we can expect clear skies, mild temperatures, and low wind for the next several days. We've received the green light to test my landing gear on the FDB!

I'm so excited I can scarcely sleep. By the time you get this, the flight will be over and I'll be writing to tell you how it went. This is what I've been working on for a year now, Emma. I feel like I'm already soaring!

Yours sincerely,
Lewis
11 Rue Saint Ida
Montreal, Quebec

March 1, 1939

Things have settled into something closer to normal between George and me. I think he's realized I know what's afoot and has ceased to pour on the charm the way he used to. For my part, I've decided I'd rather have George as a friend than not at all. I don't go out of my way to seek his company, nor have I become particularly close with Miss Callahan, although we get along fine. If I'm honest with myself, it is hard not to like her; she is witty and warm and undeniably pretty. She doesn't let the Dionnes get her down, no matter what Mme. Dionne might mutter about her. She is a good fit for George, I suppose. I wish them well, if they are indeed intent on a future together. I have no idea.

Dr. Dafoe has been coming in almost daily, meeting with men from the government, Judge Valin, as well as M. Dionne and his lawyer. George says M. Dionne has successfully persuaded the Ontario government to audit the financials for the Quintuplet Trust Fund. It is falling to George to organize all the documents he's been compiling for Dr. Dafoe. He's taken to working late in the night, sometimes sleeping on the couch in Dr. Dafoe's office rather than driving back to his rooms in North Bay. Does Dr. Dafoe know? I can't imagine he does.

Tonight after speaking with George, I went back to my room and took another stab at my self-portrait, using the facing mirrors. Whatever perspective or effect I was hoping to get from this, it's lost. I kept picturing M. Dionne appearing out of nowhere, his cold reproach reflected in the glass.

March 7, 1939 (*Toronto Star*)

DIONNE OPPOSES OFFER TO BRING QUINTS TO KING

TORONTO, Ontario—"I would prefer to have the King and Queen come to Callander," said Oliva Dionne, father of the quintuplets today. He had just received from the *Star,* he said, his first intimation that the Ontario government proposes that the five Dionne sisters be brought to Toronto by private train to be presented to Their Majesties here, May 22. "I have not heard a word about it," he added. "We are anxious that they should be presented to the King and Queen when they come to Canada, but I cannot see why the government cannot arrange to have Their Majesties visit the nursery here," said Dionne.

March 8, 1939

The girls are ready for their broadcast tomorrow, or as ready as they'll ever be. They have loved learning the words to "God Save the King" and spent hours this week singing along to Miss Callahan, who is accompanying them on the piano.

Today they were belting it out heartily, if not altogether tunefully, when Mme. Dionne appeared at the open door of the playroom. She'd already been over that morning, so none of us expected her to return. The expression on her face when she heard the girls singing an English song could have frozen Lake Nipissing solid.

Miss Callahan kept playing through for several more bars, but the girls stopped singing, clearly worried about their mother's reaction.

"Cécile, come here," Mme. Dionne said in French. Cécile threw me a look but went to her mother, who then beckoned for the others to join. They hesitated but went to sit with her on the window seat, saying nothing. I worried she'd start scolding them, but instead she began singing *"Au Clair de la Lune,"* a song the girls have loved since they were toddlers, and soon enough they were singing lustily along.

March 9, 1939

THE RECORDING CREW has come and gone—the whole exercise was a dismal failure. At the last minute the Dionnes came over to watch the broadcast, and the girls were clearly rattled. When the time came, the girls refused to sing. Yvonne, always the boldest, announced: "We can only sing in French."

Dr. Dafoe stepped up to the microphone, plainly flustered but tried to make light of things, saying, "Ah, our poor girls have stage fright! We will have to listen to them sing another day."

He gestured at Miss Callahan, and she whisked the girls out of the room, Mme. Dionne huffing in their wake.

I stayed to watch what Dr. Dafoe would do next. So did M. Dionne, I noticed, a ghost of a smile on his thin lips. The doctor didn't look angry so much as befuddled. A quick-thinking announcer took the opportunity to turn the broadcast into an interview, asking the doctor what the girls had been up to during the winter, what were their favorite games, their favorite foods, their favorite songs—in French and English. Dr. Dafoe warmed to this topic and quickly saw how to twist things to his advantage.

"Our greatest hope, of course, is that His Majesty and Her Majesty will come and see all this for themselves," he said. "I know their visit will be very busy, and Canada is a big country, that's for sure. But this is one thing I and the other guardians agree on absolutely, as do Mr. and Mrs. Dionne: Their Majesties must not miss this chance to see the Quints, and the Quints should not take the risk of traveling to see the King and Queen. M. Dionne and I spoke of this just the other day." Dr. Dafoe nodded at M. Dionne as he said this, his round head wobbling.

"We both strongly believe that the best option is for Their Majesties to take a detour through this beautiful part of the world. We would be delighted to host them here."

March 11, 1939

CHARCOAL, LOW LIGHT, my left side in shadow, my hand against my blotchy cheek. I was trying for pensive, but instead I look like I'm attempting to hide something, which I am. It's hopeless. I can close my eyes and draw any one of the girls as if she is standing in front of me—mischief, confusion, or tenderness written there plain as day. But me? My desires? My fears? I don't even know what they are, let alone how to put them on paper.

March 13, 1939 (*Toronto Star*)

DIONNE GIVES HIS BLESSING TO QUINTS' TORONTO VISIT

All 12 Children to Come

CALLANDER, Ontario—Oliva Dionne, father of the quintuplets, announced today he had accepted the invitation of the Ontario government to take his famous daughters to Toronto to be presented to the King and Queen, May 22.

Dionne said he had a "keen desire" to have the girls, who will be five years old May 28, meet Their Majesties and that he would take his entire family to Toronto if arrangements are made for their accommodation. The Dionnes have 12 children.

This would mean that Ernest, Rose, and Therese, now attending school in Quebec province, would return home to join the family for the trip. Daniel, Pauline, Oliva Jr., and Victoria [*sic*] are now at home with their parents, living in the Dionne farm home across the road from the Dafoe hospital which houses the quintuplets.

Annette, Yvonne, Cécile, Émilie, and Marie will be taken by special train to Toronto, 180 miles south of here, spending a single night en route, then back in their beds the very next night. The trip will be the first time the quintuplets have left their nursery grounds since being moved from their parents' home in September 1934, a little more than three months after their birth.

The father said Dr. A. R. Dafoe and Judge J. A. Valin and other members of the Quints' board of guardians have not yet been advised of his acceptance of the invitation.

Le Droit, the French language newspaper in Ottawa, published the text of Mr. Dionne's acceptance letter, addressed to Hon. Harry Nixon, Ontario provincial secretary, March 9, accepting the invitation.

April 1, 1939

Finally, a self-portrait, if I can call it that. I gave up on the mirrors and the angles, and gave up on drawing me the way I think I must look. Instead, I closed my eyes, pictured me at my happiest, and ended up with a line drawing of me and little Em, age two or three, curled in my arms. It lacks the detail I expect is required for a portfolio, but I don't care. I'm not sure it's even recognizable as a woman and child. It's certainly not recognizable as me. But the more I look at it, the more I'm pleased. In technical terms, it's not the best thing I've ever done, not by a long shot. But I love it. It's simple and sparse, with a softness somehow. I've captured something important to me.

April 2, 1939

SOMETIMES AT NIGHT I hear footsteps in the hall, the shy squeak of a hinge. I've not gotten up to investigate. I assume it is Miss Callahan slipping out to wherever it is George is sleeping in the nursery, or more likely George tiptoeing to her room. I am naïve, I know. I have only the most rudimentary idea of what it is that might be happening behind closed doors, all of it derived from my textbooks at nursing school and nothing more. I can't spend any more time thinking about this than I already have.

April 3, 1939

Miss Emma Trimpany
Dafoe Hospital and Nursery
Callander, ON

Dear Emma,

Our plane flies! It flies beautifully. It roared straight up into the sky as smooth as if we were diving into a lake, only in reverse (and much more noisy). Adye—that was the pilot—gave me the thumbs-up after working the lever to raise the wheelbase. He said later that the stick moved easily, with no need for force. He did a wide loop over the city, and I can tell you it was the most beautiful thing I think I've ever seen, Montreal laid out below like a feast, the cross on Mont Royal looking every bit like a candle on a cake baked to celebrate the day. I held my breath for a moment as the plane descended, worrying about my landing gear, but it settled into place smoothly as Adye released the lever and I knew we'd done something right. It took all of 15 months, but we've done something right.

I hope you were not angry or worried. I thought of telephoning you at the nursery the day of the flight, but I realize I'm not sure if that's permitted or what it might cost you to take a call from me, financially or otherwise.

Yours sincerely,
Lewis
11 Rue Saint Ida
Montreal, Quebec

April 16, 1939

Which is better," Annette asked me today, eyes wide, her face crumpled, "French or English?" I took her into my arms and hugged her tight. "They are completely the same," I said in French, then again in English for good measure. "They are both completely the same."

April 21, 1939

I ASKED GEORGE about the documents he had to compile for the government, and he told me he has submitted the records for every transaction since the girls were born. He says the trouble now is with the pending contracts. Apparently the offers from the radio people have been withdrawn because of the little prank the girls played last month when they refused to sing in English. The newsreel company, Pathé, has also given word that they will not be filming the girls' fifth birthday.

"Is that a lot of money?" I asked. George's eyes look so sunken these days, his lids heavy. Today I spotted a patch of skin along his jawline that he'd missed with his razor. I don't think he's left the nursery in days.

He grimaced at my question. "Yes, it is. It's a lot of money."

What I wanted to ask is whether there is sufficient money in the girls' trust fund that they will always be okay, no matter what. Whether they stay here until they're grown, or whether they will go back to live with their parents or move to a new home—will they always be okay?

Instead I asked him about the calendar company. I've been working on twelve paintings for the 1940 calendar commissioned by Brown & Bigelow. Last year's edition was a huge success, according to Dr. Dafoe. I felt sick asking the question, but I wanted to know for the girls' sake as much as for my own, so I managed to ask: "What about the calendar? Will the Brown & Bigelow calendar be renewed?"

George had gone back to the books and papers on his desk, pushing his hand through the hair that always swings forward, no matter how many times he swipes it back. He smiled ruefully at my question.

"The calendar contract is not in jeopardy, not yet at least." He glanced up at me. "A calendar can be both French and English," he added. "It doesn't need to speak either one fluently."

I made to leave, then turned back to ask, "Why 'not *yet*'?"

"They're growing up." He sighed. "Plus the coming war." He caught my eye. "It *is* coming, Emma. Sooner than you think. Canada is bound to have more on its mind soon than five little girls."

April 22, 1939

OFFICIAL WORD TODAY in the papers that Their Majesties will permit the quintuplets to be presented to them in one month's time, in Toronto. We'd already been counting on this, but still. To see it in print makes it real.

April 22, 1939 (*Toronto Star*)

NEW DIVE BOMBER IS CANADA'S CONTRIBUTION TO THE SKIES

Fighter does 300 miles an hour in tests over Montreal

MONTREAL, Quebec—A droning streak of fighting power has been cutting capers over Montreal. The FDB fighter and dive bomber, the first military airplane developed in Canada, has been put through rigorous tests and has exceeded 300 miles an hour at less than full throttle. Lewis Cartwright, a junior engineer of the Canadian Car and Foundry Co, working with Canada's first lady engineer, Miss Elsie MacGill, designed the plane with retractable landing gear to give added streamlining. Canadian Car and Foundry Co, under Miss MacGill, has also stepped up production of the Hawker single-seater fighter dubbed the "Hurricane" under a special order from the British Royal Air Force.

Used with permission.

May 1, 1939

More confusion in the bath with the girls today with much talk in French about this being dirty or that being dirty. I had so hoped we were finished with this when Nurse Noël was fired, but according to Nurse Corriveau, who continues to jot nervous notes in the book she keeps in a pocket she's stitched into the underside of her nurse's apron, the girls have started saying it again. She wanted to show me the record she took of an exchange when they were splashing in the play pool yesterday, while their mother sat at the edge, but I told her she must take it to Dr. Dafoe instead.

I can well imagine what Mme. Dionne must have said. She has forbidden the new photographer to take any pictures of the girls in their little pool, never mind the thousands of people who come and watch them playing here firsthand. Her view, the view that she's teaching them by example, is that five-year-old girls frolicking in their swimming costumes or having their bath are "dirty" in their own skins. It breaks my heart. I scolded Yvonne for saying silly things as she was climbing out of the bathtub this evening, then bundled her in my arms when I saw her eyes pool with confusion. "Not dirty, my sweet girl," I whispered to her. "You are perfect. Every bit of you. Perfect."

I'm copying Nurse Corriveau's idea and sewing a little pocket into the underside of my apron for my diary. Can't hurt.

May 1, 1939

Miss Emma Trimpany
Dafoe Hospital and Nursery
Callander, ON

Dear Emma,

The whole factory is to be turned over to Hurricane fighter planes, which means we'll have to ditch many of the designs we've been working on, no doubt my landing feet included! No one is especially cut up about it—we're all so excited by the new planes. Today I looked up at the sky and pictured them soaring, diving, and swooping, then quite suddenly tried to imagine someone squinting up at our planes out of fear, not wonder. It gave me pause.

Unfortunately I won't be visiting Callander anytime soon and I, too, would like the chance to see you. Here's a bold proposition, and I hope you'll at least consider it: would you pay me a visit in Montreal? You could travel with the quintuplets to Toronto for their audience with the Royals, then continue on by train to Montreal. Surely the other nurses and staff could manage the return journey to Quintland on their own?

I've taken the liberty of asking my boss, Miss MacGill, about suitable lodging for a young lady traveling on her own, and she has kindly offered to host you in her own home, which is rumored to be very grand, on the west side. So you see, my intents are honorable—and from your letters, I figure you could use a proper break.

I would be thrilled to show you around Vieux-Montréal and maybe even take you out to the hangar to see our planes. Plus, we'd get a chance to speak of some things that don't belong in a letter. I'm sure you'd be very comfortable staying with Miss MacGill—you'll like her, I know it.

Hopefully I haven't shocked you with this idea. Give it some thought and let me know what you want to do.

Yours sincerely,
Lewis Cartwright
11 Rue Saint Ida
Montreal, Quebec

May 5, 1939

Mr. Munro was at the nursery today to collect the last of the documents for the government audit. He asked me to step into Dr. Dafoe's office when George was taking his lunch. He pointed me to a chair at the table, then took a seat across from me, peering out from under his snowy mane.

"I'm bound to inform you that the record of payments made to you, Emma Trimpany, since you started receiving commissions from commercial entities for your portraits of the Dionne quintuplets has been turned over to M. Dionne's lawyer, at M. Dionne's insistence."

I stared at him, wondering if I was supposed to be alarmed. He raised a hand to stop whatever I'd been about to ask.

"There's nothing to worry about," he said. "These payments have all been scrupulously documented." He tucked his chin and glowered at the papers in front of him before continuing. "Thank heavens for George, that's what I say. If only all of this had been managed differently from the outset."

He pushed a piece of paper across the table toward me.

"I want to be perfectly sure you understand your personal account," he said. "This is the name of the institution where your account is currently held." He poked with his pen. "This is the account number. A number of payments have come through since we last met. This is the current total."

My eyes must have bulged out of my head. I managed to look up at Mr. Munro, but his face was blank. "Royalty deposits will continue to be made accordingly, but no one can withdraw funds without your signature, do you understand? Not M. Dionne, not Dr. Dafoe. This money is yours. You are the only one who can access these funds."

I managed to stammer out my question. "But what about the fund for the quintuplets? Are they getting a share of the revenues? Do they have enough—?"

Mr. Munro snorted. "Fear not, my dear Emma. The quintuplets are getting their fair share. As for whether it's 'enough'— that's the problem with money, isn't it? No matter how much of it you manage to acquire, you will always feel the need to acquire more. This will no doubt be true even for the famous Dionne quintuplets, who have never seen a shop, or a bank, and wouldn't have the first clue what to do if silver dollars started falling from the sky, which"—he snorted again—"in their case has more or less been happening since birth."

He paused here to scratch at his mustache, blinking his eyes closed as he did so.

"Open your eyes, Emma," he said, though his own remained shut. "There's no shortage of money flowing in and out of Quintland, but, as best as I can tell, it's brought more strife than it has stability."

Mr. Munro inserted a pinkie finger into his ear and started rooting for something deeply buried. His eyes reappeared again through the dense thicket of eyebrow. "On that note, we're all done with the audit at the nursery. George and I agree that everything tots up."

I hadn't spoken, but he sighed as if I'd asked something else he didn't want to answer.

"Now Dionne is also asking for Dr. Dafoe's private records," he continued. "That's not my concern, of course. I'm only involved in managing the money being paid the quintuplets. But—" He spread his hands wide and hunched his shoulders toward his ears.

"Surely Dr. Dafoe's records will reflect the same thing?" I said. I was thinking, perhaps this is what has George working late into the night, trying to reconcile Dr. Dafoe's accounts with those of the nursery as some sort of duplicate record.

But Mr. Munro shook his head. "No, my dear, not the same thing. Dionne is asking for payments made to Dr. Dafoe *directly*." He saw my face and gestured at the framed photos and advertisements on the walls around us, the corn syrup ad I'd painted among them. Every square foot showed the girls since their infancy, pictured with everything from dental cream to automobiles to cod-liver oil, Dr. Dafoe sitting in their midst with his creased brow, his downturned mouth. Indeed, I realized, following Mr. Munro's gaze, that a dozen of the advertisements, perhaps more, didn't even include the girls—they just featured Dr. Dafoe. *Advice for Mothers from the Doctor to the Famous Dionne Quintuplets.*

My face must have registered a slow dawning of comprehension, because Mr. Munro started nodding. "You see what I'm saying. Direct payments. M. Dionne's lawyer has requested a record of all payments made *directly* to Dr. Dafoe, quite apart from any paid into the quintuplet fund."

May 8, 1939

A LETTER FROM Lewis inviting me to visit him in Montreal, and to pay for my ticket from Toronto after I've gone with the girls to meet the King and Queen. I'm not sure what to make of this. I would *love* to see Montreal, but to visit a man, in a different city? To have him pay for my ticket? I'm not sure what is implied in such an invitation. What would it say about me if I said yes? I admit, after the last few months and all the drama here, it's very tempting. I would very much like to see Lewis Cartwright.

But I'm not sure what to think or how to respond.

May 9, 1939

I SPOKE WITH Ivy by telephone this afternoon using the private line in Dr. Dafoe's office. Ivy had news: she'd bumped into Nurse de Kiriline on Yonge Street! Apparently the Captain never returned to nursing and still lives up North, on Pimisi Bay, but was in the city to see her editor—she's become renowned for her nature writing. Ivy and the Captain ended up going for tea and talking about "the old days" at the nursery. All these years later, "Boss Number Two" confessed to Ivy the real reason for her abrupt departure: Dr. Dafoe had asked her to marry him! She had turned him down politely, but he persisted, she said, and in the end she had quit her post to escape his ardent advances. Ivy and I had a fit of giggles over this, because it's simply impossible to imagine fuddy-duddy Dafoe in hot pursuit, although we could well remember how highly he thought of her. Still, I was very glad to hear the Captain was doing so well and had made such an interesting life for herself.

The real reason for my call to Ivy, of course, had been to ask her advice regarding Lewis's offer to visit. What is meant by it, what might be his expectations or intentions, and what would it say about me if I went? Once we'd finished gossiping about Louise de Kiriline, I couldn't bring myself to speak of Lewis. Ivy says she will come and meet me for a fleeting visit at the government offices in Toronto, where the Royals are to meet the Dionnes, but she has also suggested I come back to their home afterward, taking a few days' leave for a proper visit. I hemmed and hawed but didn't say yes or no either way. I know she can't understand my indecision.

Instead I prattled on about my portfolio, which is all done now. She's kindly agreed to ask Fred to photograph each piece for me, so I can put the collection together as an album and send it to Mrs. Fangel, or anywhere else for that matter. That's how it's done, I gather. I've packaged up and posted the whole lot to Ivy and Fred this evening, so there should be enough time for Fred to take the photographs and have them processed before I arrive in Toronto. Then I need to decide what to do with them.

First things first, I need to write back to Lewis.

May 15, 1939

JUST ONE WEEK before the big trip to Toronto and everyone is excited and anxious by turns. Miss Callahan is as sprightly as ever, especially so, perhaps, since she learned that George has been given a berth on the train in order to accompany Dr. Dafoe.

Nurse Corriveau, on the other hand, is a nervous wreck. Twice now Dr. Dafoe has summoned us to a meeting in his office to explain in solemn tones the complicated precautions and arrangements being taken for the special train that will transport us all from Callander to Toronto. There are to be five cars in total. One will be a day coach for the police guards and reporters, the second a business car for the use of the guardians and the railroad officials. Next are two sleeping cars to accommodate the guards, reporters, Dr. Dafoe and George, Judge Valin and his assistant, and the Dionnes and their seven other children. Last but not least will be the nursery car, complete with a playroom, where the girls can frolic, attached to four separate bedrooms. For the first time ever, the girls will actually be separated to sleep, two per room, with the fifth sharing with one of the female staff while the other two staff share the fourth bedroom.

Nurse Corriveau is absolutely adamant that she wants to sleep in the nurses' carriage with me or Miss Callahan, rather than have the responsibility of sleeping with one of the girls on her own. I'm the opposite. All these years we've never been permitted to sleep the night in the same room as the quintuplets— I've already said I'd be delighted to take this berth.

May 17, 1939 (*UP/Spokane Daily Chronicle*)

ÉMILIE DIONNE SETTLES QUESTION OF CURTSY WITH A HEAD STAND

CALLANDER, Ontario— Émilie, mischievous member of the Dionne quintuplets, had the entire nursery staff in a diplomatic dither today through her insistence that a royal curtsy must take the form of a head stand.

Her sisters—Yvonne, Annette, Cécile, and Marie—are letter perfect in the gestures of homage they will pay to King George and Queen Elizabeth at their audience on May 22. At the practice sessions they made graceful curtsies in the best court manner, but Émilie stood on her head.

The trouble is, Nurses Corriveau and Callahan admitted ruefully today, that they made the mistake of laughing when Émilie first performed the stunt. They fear that Émilie, the marked individualist of the five girls, will perform her upside-down curtsy to get a royal laugh.

The quintuplets will be presented to Their Majesties in the music room of the Ontario legislature buildings with only the royal couple, two ladies-in-waiting, Papa and Maman Dionne, and the two nurses in attendance.

Used with permission.

May 22, 1939

After the excitement of the day, Émilie is out like a light. I can't hear her soft snores over the clank and bang of the wheels on the tracks, but I've twice leaned into her bunk to make sure her eyes are closed and her breathing even. I worried about switching on the light so I could scribble in my journal, but she's sound asleep. It's been such an astonishing day, I feel all thrumming and jangly—like the train itself. I can't lie down without writing everything here before I forget. This journey is the start of something extraordinary for our girls, but also an ending. I can feel it in my bones. For the first time, the gates of Quintland swung open for them. They saw the world beyond the fence line and the world saw them. Whatever happens, things will be different from this point on.

I got my wish, which was to share this sleeping room with Émilie. The other girls all made a big show of saying they didn't think it should be Em getting the chance to share with Nurse Trimpany, it should be *me*, or *me*, or *me*. In the end, they were too excited and then too tired to put up much of a fuss about who was sleeping where. It was all so novel, despite all the efforts we'd made to tone things down. They've eaten their supper from the same dishes they use at the nursery and are sleeping under the same quilts with the same dolls and toys as they do each night. They are not the slightest bit fooled, however. They are merely exhausted.

In every other way, we tried to make the day seem normal. The girls woke this morning at the nursery the same way they always do these days, within seconds of each other. It's as if their eyelids are joined by invisible threads, one set of eyes blinking another set awake. I myself had been up for hours, had barely slept the night, then had to busy myself with the regular routine of toilet and bath, clothes and breakfasts. Like any other day, we followed our schedule of indoor and outdoor, quiet and active play. There were more cars than ever before coming to and going from the nursery, and the visiting hours were busier than we've seen them even in the height of summer. Everyone knew that today was the day the girls would leave the nursery for the first time. Presumably the crowds turned out in such great numbers in the hopes of getting the chance of seeing them being driven to the station. The girls felt it, they must have, the charge in the air. They kept saying, "When will we go? When will we go?"

Only after supper did the maroon and gold Chevrolet pull past the private gates into the inner courtyard in a cloud of dust. The car is a gift from the Ontario government, specially fitted with seats for all five girls in the back and Dr. Dafoe in front. Six additional policemen arrived earlier today from Toronto, and they helped keep the crowds back when the government car pulled inside. As far as I could tell, the gawkers were pressed ten deep against the fence trying to catch a glimpse of the quintuplets.

Marie was watching at the playroom window and gave a shrill cry when she saw the gates open and the Chevrolet glide in. Without question this was the grandest, most beautiful car they've ever seen at their nursery, despite the many new cars their father and Dr. Dafoe have driven over the years, not to mention the comings and goings of film stars and politicians.

At 7:00 in the evening we shepherded the girls out to the car, and I felt my heart pounding in my chest at the idea of taking them out into the frenzied throngs beyond the gates. All these years, it's been bad enough for me coming and going with Lewis or his father behind the wheel, but with the girls themselves? How on earth would we get away?

This was all planned out, of course. The policemen used their vehicles to block the road to keep anyone from following us to the train station, then escorted us away from the nursery, a whole flank of patrol cars in front and behind. One man tried to ride alongside us on his horse, but he was stopped by an officer who was waiting roadside less than a mile from the nursery. The man and his horse ended up turning north, trotting into a field, and waving at the girls as he did. I was being driven with George, Miss Callahan, and Nurse Corriveau in a car immediately behind the girls, so we watched them squirm in their seats, their faces pressed against the back window, to wave back at the horse and rider until they disappeared from view. I thought they'd be more nervous, but they weren't. They were excited, through and through. Not a fearful bone in their bodies.

The evening was warm. As we drove along the road toward Callander, windows down, I could feel some bite in the air, but also the warmth rising from the road as the land gave up the heat it had been soaking up all day. Once we were on the open road I stretched my arm out the window, feeling the wind eddy over my hand, warm below, cooler on top. You could hear the crickets starting their evening tune-up and a chorus of frogs from the streams and bogs, which took me back to the night the girls were born—five years ago, almost to the day.

Before reaching town, the car turned off onto the wider road that leads toward North Bay instead of continuing toward the Callander train station. I exchanged a confused look with Miss Callahan and Nurse Corriveau, and we all looked instinctively to George, riding beside the driver.

He turned and flashed a smile.

"The Ontario government made a last-minute change," he explained. "They're anticipating thousands of well-wishers at the Callander station, so they are actually going to stop the Quintland Express at Trout Lake junction, between Callander and North Bay, and that's where we'll board."

The Quintland Express. That's what it's called, this train carrying us through the night to Toronto, the words *Quintland Express* written in gleaming letters on every carriage. The paintwork is crimson and gold, the colors of the royal visit—same as the car that brought the girls. The sun was sinking in the sky when we pulled up at the junction, but it was bright enough that the gilded paint on the train looked wet to the touch, positively gleaming against the paler gold of the hayfields beyond.

I'd never thought about how people might board a train without a station, but sure enough all of us from the nursery as well as the policemen and newspapermen, plus the whole Dionne family, were swiftly ushered on board via a special staircase, and the train started up again within a matter of minutes.

Moments later we were swooshing through Callander. I've never in my life seen a railway station so busy. Crowds of people were lining the tracks before and after the stop, and on the platform itself, a line of uniformed guards, arms outstretched, were straining to keep people from pressing too close to the tracks or, worse, falling onto them. The train slowed down as it went through the station, and the crowd went berserk. A brass band struck up as we rolled through playing "Old Comrades," and the girls, all five of them, looked like their eyes might pop from their heads.

They had scrambled to position themselves at the windows of the carriage the instant we boarded, and there they stayed, flattened against the glass. When we started to see the crowds along the tracks, they began waving of their own accord, smiling, their eyes dancing over the people and children waving wildly in return. I couldn't help but wonder what they were thinking about all these boys and girls, most of them in clothes drab and worn compared with their own, but clearly at greater liberty than our girls have ever known, wriggling away from their parents and sprinting beside the tracks.

I'm so proud of my babies. They didn't cry or flinch or lose their tongues. They looked entranced, not afraid. I don't think they could have known that so many different humans existed in the world—people not dressed in nurses' caps and doctors' coats, or the top hats and fur coats of our celebrity visitors. They couldn't know that people come in many different shapes and sizes, and with so little in their pockets and stomachs. More than the men and women, it was the children in the crowds that captured their attention, small girls and boys gesticulating frantically at the train and holding up signs and drawings they'd made themselves, wishing *bonjour* and *bon voyage* to the Dionne quintuplets.

The train gathered speed again outside of Callander, and, after watching the countryside flit by for thirty minutes, the girls were convinced to pull themselves away from the windows. In the half hour before bed, they joined their brothers and sisters in the compartment fitted out to replicate the quiet playroom at their nursery. Mme. Dionne, sitting in a low sofa against the windows, was beatific, close to tears with her whole family gathered around. Maman has the same soft eyes as her daughters, I realized. All the children do. I've never noticed that before. Something caught in my throat, seeing this, but the feeling fled the instant I glanced at M. Dionne. He had a different expression on his face, a wary jubilation.

Now all the girls are bundled into their own beds and sleeping as they haven't slept in days. Weeks, probably. The excitement of the day has done them in. I'm beat too. It is almost 3:00 A.M., and we are due to arrive in Toronto before dawn. I'm going to set aside my book now and do a quick check to make sure the others are sleeping soundly. Then I'll come back to my nest here with little Em and do my best to fall asleep.

May 23, 1939 (*Toronto Star*)

QUINTS FELT RIGHT AT HOME WITH KING AND QUEEN

CALLANDER, Ontario—Happy and not the least bit sleepy, the Dionne quintuplets arrived at Callander station late last night after their visit to Toronto to meet the King and Queen. The five little girls, chattering eagerly about the trip by special train, wanted to know right away when they would be going back to Toronto. But they were whisked away in automobiles to their beds in the Dafoe hospital, where they will talk for days about Their Majesties.

A story about the Dionne quintuplets, since they have met the King and Queen, is worth more in England than anything about Hitler or Mussolini, or an international crisis. So, G. Ward Price of the London Daily Mail filed 3,000 words to his newspaper last night, the longest cabled story of his career.

May 23, 1939

I jumped from the train.

It slowed to pass through the town of Barrie, and I jumped. I didn't know it was Barrie. I didn't know where we were. It was still dark. I wasn't thinking straight. I'm not thinking straight now. I picked my way along the tracks in the sooty darkness, shaking, trying not to think of the pain. When I think of the pain, even now, my stomach heaves. I've vomited twice already. There is sick on my uniform, but that's not the worst of it, not at all. I can't think of this properly. Of what happened. Of what I've done. Of what was done to me.

I jumped from the train.

I followed the tracks in the dark until I reached the lights on the edge of town. I chose a quiet street with telephone lines, a house with a yard, well kept, a woman's touch, no children's toys on the lawn. A door where I might knock and feel safe. I waited in the bushes beside the house until dawn, until the door opened and a man, neatly dressed, kissed his young wife and strode off down the street. Then I knocked on the door. The woman took one look at me and her face stretched wide with dismay, but she said nothing. She hustled me inside, gently, gently. She looked quickly to the right and to the left, then closed the door fast behind me.

I've called Ivy. Ivy is coming for me. Ivy is coming.

The woman told me the name of the town, Barrie. And she told me her name, although I can't remember what it was. She led me to a bathroom and she filled the bath and then she brought me these clothes. She said: Can I call the police? I shook my head so violently she laid her hand on my arm to settle me down and said she wouldn't. The hospital? I shook my head again. Then I thought of Ivy. The woman called the operator, and, after a long time, the call was put through and the woman handed me the phone. Ivy's voice.

I've called Ivy and she's coming. She's coming for me.

I bathed. The water was hot, but it didn't help, didn't make me warm. Didn't make me clean. The woman has told me to lie down, and I have, but I'm shaking, everywhere. I can't stop. I can't sleep. I'm shaking. I'm so cold.

I stood and went to my ripped and bloodied uniform, bundled in a bag on a chair in the corner. I wouldn't let the woman take it. My cap is gone and my shoes. Did I walk here in shoes? I can't recall. But my notebook was still in the pocket of my apron, so he doesn't have that. No one will find that. They won't find me. But they won't find my notebook either.

What will my babies do when they find me gone?

The woman has just brought me a cup of tea. She's dismayed to see me sitting up. She sat at the foot of the bed and asked me again if I wanted to speak, and I shook my head. I want to write this down, that's what I want to do. But I didn't say that. I hid my notebook. I haven't told her my name, not my real name. When she asked, quietly, as if she knew I might not want to tell her, I said "Emily." It was the only name still in my head. *Émilie.* Everything else in my head is shattered and throbbing. I need it out of my head.

Ivy will be here soon, the woman said. Ivy is coming.

IT WAS LATE, and Émilie was fast asleep, and I was writing about the day because I couldn't sleep and I didn't want to forget about how the girls and I were driven to the train in the warm dusk, about all the people who came out to see us off. So much joy. I wrote it all here, then I put down my pen and I must have slipped my notebook into my secret pocket, although I don't remember doing it. The train was clanking and groaning like a ship, but Émilie was sleeping like an angel. I bent close over her head, her sweet, sweet head, and I breathed her in. She didn't wake. I unlatched the door to our berth and peered into the dark corridor, the motion of the train swaying me from side to side. To Yvonne and Marie's berth first. Both were sleeping soundly, Marie's lips parted—the shape of a small heart. No one sleeps as beautifully as Marie. I stepped into the corridor again and slid open the door to the third room, Annette and Cécile, sleeping as if drugged. Little miracles, all of them.

I returned to my own berth with Émilie, tired now, rubbing my eyes, trying to find my way. It was darker in my little room than in the others, the curtains closed. I don't remember drawing the curtains. I slid the door closed behind me and stepped toward Émilie's bunk for one last good night.

I didn't see him in the room. Did I sense him? How could I not have sensed him there? I started to lean over Émilie, squinting to make out her sleeping form. That's when his hand clamped over my mouth and his other pinned my arms. I screamed, or I tried to scream, but no sound came. The screaming was in my head and in the train itself, but it wasn't in that little room. It felt like the rush and chug and squeal of metal on rails got louder then, although Émilie kept sleeping, and, in the middle of that terror, I felt some relief. That she was still sleeping. She hadn't heard my scream, none of them had. In that instant, I was more afraid that Émilie would wake and be scared or be hurt herself than I was of what was happening. Of what was happening to me. He pushed me to the floor of the train, his hands on my face and throat, the left side of my face, my ruined left cheek, grinding into the carpet. I couldn't breathe let alone make a sound. I thought then that he was trying to kill me, that he was trying to choke the breath from me there on the floor of the train. This was all.

But that wasn't his intention.

Pain. Pain like nothing I've ever thought possible, bigger than any scream. I tried to pull his hand from my throat, but it was as if moving through sand, too dense, too thick. No force in my grip. His jaw pressed against my temple, cursing, growling, things I couldn't make out. His breath dank and foul. His hand so heavy on my throat I thought my head might break away. The pain so great, I hoped it would.

If the girls should wake, I thought. If Émilie should wake and sit up in her berth. If she should see me, like this. See him. I couldn't bear it.

So I didn't kick. I didn't fight. I felt the train scream beneath me, felt his mouth wet and hot on my ear, the fear and iron bitter in my mouth. Then his head thrust abruptly against my skull so hard, the agony so great, I must have blacked out.

And then he was gone. I lay weeping, I don't know how long, then sat up and was sick in my own lap. It was as if I'd been cleaved in two. And there was blood, I realized. So much blood, hot and sticky and shameful. I was sitting in it, in my own blood and vomit and horror. My uniform, I thought. My whites.

Then I thought again of the girls waking, of Émilie or one of the other girls seeing me like that. Of the guards who would surely be patrolling these rooms. Of Miss Callahan popping in to check on me. Of the reporters, night owls all, eager for a story.

Of him, coming back.

It dawned on me like a deeper kind of darkness that there was no one I could go to in that moment, no one who would help me, or point fingers, or allow any kind of fuss to be made. Not today of all days, but not any other day either. I sat there shaking. This is what men do. This is what men like *this* man do to women like me. Worse: I was not the first and I wouldn't be the last. The catch: what had happened to me doesn't happen in the lives of the Dionne quintuplets. It can't and won't, and if it does, I realized suddenly, it is erased. Ivy's stories came careening back to me: all the gossip and tattle I'd elected to shrug off and ignore. Even this has been erased before.

I managed to pull myself to standing, trembling. So cold, so cold. I slid open my door and poked my head into the corridor. I looked right and left: once, twice. Then I took a deep breath and stepped through the door. Terrified of seeing him, terrified of seeing anyone. No safe place to go. The thudding beat of the train in my ears, the chug and clang of my heart.

I made my way to the rear of the carriage, wrenched open the heavy door, and stepped onto the rattling platform in the open air. A sob welled up, mute and deafening, louder than the train, shriller than anything outside in the night. The train was slowing down. I could see the lights of a town in the distance, too small to be Toronto, but big enough. Big enough to take me in. We slowed, we slowed, and I didn't stop to think. I jumped.

CANADIAN PACIFIC TELEGRAPHS

ALL MESSAGES ARE RECEIVED BY THIS COMPANY FOR THE TRANSMISSION, SUBJECT TO THE TERMS AND CONDITIONS PRINTED ON THEIR BLANK FORM NO. W, WHICH TERMS AND CONDITIONS HAVE BEEN AGREED TO BY THE SENDER OF THE FOLLOWING MESSAGE. THIS IS AN UNREPEATED MESSAGE, AND IS DELIVERED BY REQUEST OF THE SENDER UNDER THOSE CONDITIONS.

14 AX CN   37 D.H.

11 Rue Saint Ida
Montreal, P.Q.
May 24

Emma Trimpany

When you didnt arrive on yesterdays train I called Callander and Davis household. Received no answers. Very worried. Please reply.

Lewis Cartwright
2pm

June 1, 1939

Miss Emma Trimpany
Dafoe Hospital and Nursery
Callander, ON

Dear Emma,

I received one hell of a telephone call at the hangar today from Ivy, who was choosing her words carefully. She said you are safe and in sound mind, but that she couldn't tell me where you'd gone or why—nothing beyond the cryptic message she said you'd asked her to pass along. She was upset by it, I could tell.

How on earth do you expect me to forget about you?

None of this makes sense. Wouldn't it be better if we spoke together, you and me? I've tried all week to reach you at the nursery, but your Mr. Sinclair has refused to give me any information, merely parroting that you are no longer working there. I hope they at least have the courtesy to forward this letter.

Miss MacGill has given me some days off next week, and I'm coming up to Toronto to see Ivy and Fred, whether they like it or not. I'll go on to Callander afterward and speak with your parents, if that's what it takes.

Please, Emma. This is no way to end this. We haven't even made a proper start.

Please write.

Yours,
Lewis
11 Rue Saint Ida
Montreal, Quebec

August 27, 1939

21 Heath Street
Toronto, ON

Dear Emma,

I telephoned and spoke with Fred, who was very kind, but firm. You are well, he said, but he wouldn't give me your forwarding address—a promise they made to you, I gather, Fred and Ivy. He did tell me you are enrolled in art school, although he said he couldn't tell me where, and that pained him, I think. He's proud of you. They both are. And they have a little girl of their own now, he told me. How wonderful. I forgot to ask her name.

Oh, Emma. How did I hurt you?

All of my letters to the nursery and to Callander this summer have gone unanswered. Did you even get them? I'm sending this last to Fred and Ivy so it will be sure to reach you, somehow, someday, wherever it is you've gone.

This *will* be my last letter: I leave for England tomorrow to do my part in the coming war. I hope to bury myself in my work and put all thoughts of you aside, impossible as that seems in this moment. Work has been the only thing that's helped with my confusion—and my sadness—over your decision to vanish. We've done good work here with our planes, Emma. It has been some small consolation, to feel so needed.

I'd like to say: write to me. But my heart says you won't.

Here's another thing my heart says, Emma. I love you. I wish I'd found a way to tell you sooner. I love you, and I wish you well.

I'm enclosing the letters you sent me over these last 18 months. I can't take them to England with me, can't bear to, but I don't want to leave them behind when there's no telling when or if I'm coming back.

Yours always,
Lewis Cartwright
11 Rue Saint Ida
Montreal, Quebec

[ENCLOSURES: Letters from E.T. to L.C., February 1938 to May 1939]

February 18, 1938

11 Rue Saint Ida
Montreal, Quebec

Dear Lewis,

Of course I'll write, but only if you address me as Emma! I've known you three years, you realize. No more "Miss Trimpany," please.

I hope things are progressing with your airplane landing feet. I had never given a moment's thought to what a bird does with its feet when it flies. I will have to remember to watch for this if a single feathered creature is fool enough to return to this frigid corner of the earth.

This winter has been particularly frosty in the nursery: Miss Tremblay was fired earlier this month and Nurse Noël got her marching orders yesterday morning. Dr. Dafoe was strongly opposed to some of the religious teachings they had taken to drumming into the girls, calling them little sinners and making them feel shy in their own skins. I am not a great believer in God—my father is "lapsed" (as my mother puts it) and he planted the seed of doubt in my heart—but I do believe, if God exists and had the gumption to give the world these miraculous girls and let them live and thrive, then surely he is proud of every square inch of them, clothed or not. I firmly believe they need to be taught warmth and kindness, not shame and guilt. Still, I can't help but worry about how the Dionnes will react to the removal of staff they expressly wanted to keep. George Sinclair, Dr. Dafoe's secretary, has told me that M. and Mme. Dionne have asked to have exclusive say over the choice of nursery staff in the future. If that happens, I can't imagine I'll last much longer in my post. I've lasted longer than anyone else as it is.

Yours sincerely,
Emma
Dafoe Hospital and Nursery
Callander, ON

* * *

April 21, 1938

11 Rue Saint Ida
Montreal, Quebec

Dear Lewis,

These days, as you know, I don't even walk the short distance home to see my parents, let alone tramp to the top of a mountain. That sounded like quite the expedition. I hope your blisters healed quickly.

Here, as you've no doubt seen in the papers, we've weathered another dramatic departure: this time Dr. Blatz himself. I admit I was fed up by all the doctor's rules and schedules, and abhorred his so-called studies. But, as my mother likes to say, better the devil you know . . . If things keep up the way they've been going and the Dionnes get their way, I suppose the girls' next teacher could be Pope Pius XI. George tells me His Holiness has had so many run-ins with the German Reich, he may soon be looking for another job.

I don't know why I'm making light of things. Nerves, I suppose. I had a long telephone call with Ivy tonight and she told me some truly disturbing things. I started writing them in my journal, but the fact is, her story was so sensational, I don't feel like I can put it in a book that anyone might lay their hands on here. These days there is such a steady stream of strangers coming and going and staff who start and stop—it makes me think I should take more care. In any case, I'll set this down for you and perhaps you can let me know if you think it sounds like utter nonsense, or whether it is something I should worry about. I may also run this by George, who I trust. I suppose I could also ask Dr. Dafoe point-blank, but it's hard to imagine saying some of these things out loud.

You may have heard some of the scuttlebutt around Nurse Inès Nicolette. The rumors are mostly true: when she left the nursery a year and a half ago she was indeed pregnant. According to Ivy, who heard it from Fred, who himself heard it secondhand from a newspaperman at the *Star,* Nurse Nicolette insists that the father is M. Dionne. You may not know this, but she actually came back here with her little boy last fall, and there was quite a scene. Now, Fred's man at the *Star* says that Nurse Nicolette actually approached a Quebec newspaper to sell her story, but the Quintuplet Guardian committee was able to persuade her to keep quiet for the sake of the babies. Ivy says Fred's contact believes she was paid a large sum of hush money and she's now living out East, in Nova Scotia. I can't quite believe it. M. Dionne seems very devoted to his wife and family, and Nurse Nicolette was often a guest in their home.

Ivy had other gossip, too, relating to M. Dionne's demands that he be permitted to review all payments going in and out of the girls' trust fund. So far the other guardians have refused, but Ivy believes the departure of Dr. Blatz represents a real change in the tide. If power continues to ebb away from Dr. Dafoe, who knows what will happen?

I haven't told you, I don't think, but I have been hired as the official artist for the quintuplets, or that is how it was explained to me. I can't help but worry how M. Dionne would respond if he knew I was earning additional income through the commissions I receive for the paintings of his daughters. Ivy keeps telling me I need to leave the Dafoe nursery and lead my own life, not the lives of the Dionne quintuplets. I don't know what to think. For years I thought this might be my true calling, helping raise these girls to be healthy and strong, protecting them from harm. But this presumes that menace is something we could keep at a distance with all our walls and fences. Is it possible, Lewis, that all the things we've been doing to help these girls might somehow be doing more harm than good? On the other hand, how on earth did one of us, on the inside, come to be pregnant with M. Dionne's child or at least lay such a plausible claim to this that she could be paid to keep her peace?

Now I'm blathering. I sound certifiable. I don't know whether to destroy this letter or send it. But I'm not sure where to turn.

Yours sincerely,
Emma
Dafoe Hospital and Nursery
Callander, ON

* * *

June 11, 1938

11 Rue Saint Ida
Montreal, Quebec

Dear Lewis,

You are a true friend to listen to the ramblings of what must
sound like a mind deranged. It is just the constant uncertainty.
And no, I don't worry about the privacy of my mail. It has never
been tampered with, as best as I can tell, and I trust George implic-
itly. He is a good man and this work is taking its toll on him too.

As for my art, I'm not sure I'm a "true talent," but it is kind
of you to say. By way of thanks, I'm enclosing a little sketch I
made of the girls gathering daisies on the lawn. I hope it makes
you think of home.

It was their birthday last month: four years old! It seems like
just last week we feared they couldn't survive four hours. I love
them so much it feels sometimes like I've got more air in my
lungs than I could possibly need for breathing: I might burst.
The whole Dionne clan came over for lunch on their birthday,
and it was hard not to think of Ivy's stories. Émilie ran to me
when play got too rough, and the look on M. Dionne's face when
he saw her burying her head in my neck—I don't think I've seen
him look at me with such fury since that awful day in the courtroom when my silly doodle of a syrup tin seemed to sway the
jury in favor of Dr. Dafoe. This time Oliva Dionne glared at me
as if he could read everything I'd written to you in my last letter. Oh, Lewis—my whole life I've enjoyed a certain invisibility;

I'm unsettled to think this protection may be wearing off here.

Last thing: these planes of yours with the retractable feet—what is their purpose? I assumed you were designing planes for commercial air travel, but I woke up this morning and realized with a start that you are probably building military planes. Is that right? Dr. Dafoe is receiving more and more letters from desperate families in Europe who've been caught up in Herr Hitler's ambitions in some way. George and I argued about it yesterday: he insists the storm clouds are gathering and the armies whetting their swords while I "bury my head in the sand" at the Dafoe nursery. But I have to believe we're doing important work right here, keeping the girls safe from all the evils outside the fence and behind the glass, at least until they're old enough to understand how special they are.

So tell me: why does Canada need your planes?

Yours sincerely,
Emma
Dafoe Hospital and Nursery.
Callander, ON

* * *

July 22, 1938

11 Rue Saint Ida
Montreal, Quebec

Dear Lewis,

Thank you for saying you think our work here is important. I believe this in my heart of hearts, but how will history judge us?

I had an odd run-in with Maman Dionne, who I startled, poking around my sketchbooks and easel. She swiftly shuffled off again, looking sheepish. First I worried she might have leafed through my private journal, but the fact is I don't think she can read and scarcely speaks a word of English.

After she left I thought: what if she simply wanted to see a painting of her own children? Does she even have a true likeness in her home? No photographs are allowed of the Dionnes with the quintuplets—different agencies hold the rights to these photos. This means if the Dionnes wanted a photograph of the five girls, they'd have to clip it from the paper or buy it from their own souvenir stand—with most of the proceeds going to the Newspaper Enterprise Association. It's absurd, I know. I've never warmed to Mme. Dionne. She's not a warm woman herself—so strict and rough with the children and forever making the sign of the cross, surrounded by us sinners. But every now and then her stern veneer will fall away and you'll glimpse the haunted look she wears underneath, as if she's yearning for a different life.

Mind you, she may yet get her wish. All the papers now say the government is moving ahead with plans to build a large home on a nearby property where all the Dionne family can live, plus apartments for the nurses and staff. George says Dr. Dafoe has told the other guardians that such a house will be built over his dead body. I don't know who to believe. For years we've heard that our fragile girls simply couldn't survive crammed with a half dozen siblings into the ramshackle farmhouse across the road. The fact is, the girls are now as hale as can be; they're simply not accustomed to that style of life. I might feel differently if the Dionnes themselves were different: if Maman and Papa were kinder, sunnier, less pious folk, and their other children weren't so jumpy and fearful. If they seemed more loved.

And you, Lewis. You are building warplanes! So will Canada join this war? Who will fly these fighter planes of yours?

Best wishes,
Emma
Dafoe Hospital and Nursery
Callander, ON

* * *

September 28, 1938

11 Rue Saint Ida
Montreal, Quebec

Dear Lewis,

Politics is not my strong suit, but I must say: it's refreshing to hear you say something that's not 100 percent polite for a change. My news: I had a strange run-in with M. Dionne. He came into the room where I was painting and I didn't notice him until he was standing right behind me. You know, he's never actually spoken to me directly? Nor have I ever been alone in a room with him. I just leapt out of my seat and started busying around trying to clean up my things and left him planted in front of my painting. I didn't like doing that. It felt like I'd left one of the girls in some state of jeopardy, which of course is ridiculous.

But all of us feel such constant pressure to keep them safe.

In my nightmares, Yvonne finds a door left unlatched or Marie jimmies open a ground-floor window and the five of them blithely amble out into the bustle and roar of the crowds, where they are trampled, struck by a car, whisked away, held for ransom, or worse. One day, I know, our girls will be young women who will want to see the world and to come and go as they please, but how do we get from here to there, Lewis? When will it be deemed safe enough for the gates to swing open? It's hard to imagine the world letting them lead a normal life. Because where would that be? Would there be a place for me? Every entrepreneur within ten miles around is crowing like a rooster about the necessity of keeping the quintuplets in Callander, whether they move to this Big House or not. George on the other hand says the government will probably move them to Toronto or Ottawa, which are easier for tourists to access. I think George is pulling my leg, but I can't tell.

Have you sorted out your upper gull wing problem? Flying has always sounded rather romantic, but not being able to see the ground when you're trying to land strikes me as a good deal less alluring. And speaking of romance, I keep meaning to ask about your rock doves. Have they had their young? I read in the papers that the human Mr. Hughes has moved on from Bette Davis to a different bird altogether. I hope your Bette fares a bit better.

Sincerely,
Emma
Dafoe Hospital and Nursery
Callander, ON

* * *

November 13, 1938

11 Rue Saint Ida
Montreal, Quebec

Dear Lewis,

We are all recovered from the Great Tonsil Adventure—
everything went just fine.

Why can't Britain build her own planes? And how on earth
would you even get the planes over the sea to England? Where
would you put down for fuel?

You asked me whether M. Dionne loves his daughters. My
first thought is: of course he loves them. Even the coldest
hearts have melted at the sight of them trundling around in
the public playground or mugging for the cameras. And yet
my next thought is, How can he love them when he doesn't
even know them? How can anyone? We played a little trick
today that proves my point. As you know, each of the girls
has her own special color that she's supposed to wear, but
this morning I proposed that each swap outfits with one of
her sisters. At first they were anxious—a new look on their
sweet faces and I can't stand it—but after a few minutes they
realized what a great joke this would be and they were back
to being the clowns I know and love, each of them trying to
out-silly the other. Marie is a clever little mimic, and after
plucking a pink hat from the shelf did a deadly impression of
bossy Yvonne scolding her sisters. I burst out laughing, and
the others followed, even Yvonne, and I realized how long it's
been since we've all laughed like this together. Still giggling,

they raced into breakfast and took their seats in their regular places, then scuttled gleefully from one chair to another, each trying to remember who she was supposed to be and where she ought to sit. I could see Nurse Corriveau's nostrils working like a bellows, worried she might be the butt of the joke, while Miss Callahan carried on in her sunshiny way, unaware of anything amiss. Then Dr. Dafoe arrived, and they charged over to him announcing their borrowed names amid squeals of laughter, but he just called them his "funny little monkeys" and tottered off to his office. These are the quintuplets the world knows and loves—miraculous mirrors of one another, sweet as a consequence of being indistinguishable. What I've realized is that these are the girls Dr. Dafoe and the other guardians want the world to know and love, so that the advertisers keep knocking and the tourists come in droves. I know and love something different: five unique and headstrong little girls. One who loves bumblebees and bath time; one who loves thunderstorms but is scared of the dark; one for whom the only thing better than building sand castles is getting to knock them all down; one who loves to fingerpaint and knows how to tie her shoes; one who hates beets but is not the least bit squeamish about blood. Now who are the girls that M. Dionne loves? I can't say. You'll tell me he hasn't been given the chance to know them, that he was stripped of a father's natural right to learn how to love his own daughters, and that's certainly true. But there are also chances he's squandered. These last four years, he's wasted more time shouting over books and payments in Dr. Dafoe's office than he's ever spent with his girls.

I have two weeks' leave over Christmas, so there should be

plenty of time for a visit. And as to your bold question: no. Mr. Sinclair has become like a brother to me here, and I'm grateful for his friendship.

Yours truly,
Emma
Dafoe Hospital and Nursery
Callander, ON

* * *

January 2, 1939

11 Rue Saint Ida
Montreal, Quebec

Dear Lewis,

Thank you again for taking us tobogganing. It was exactly what I needed to shake off the winter blues, and Edith talked of little else for the rest of my visit. That's no mean task, upstaging Santa Claus.

I'm back at the nursery again tonight, and much to my gratification the girls swarmed me like a hive of honeybees and tried to plant as many sticky kisses on me as possible. Annette almost popped my shoulder out of its socket trying to climb me like a rope ladder.

After you left, Ivy and Fred came to town so Fred could pack up the rooms he's let ever since the girls were just a few months old. It feels like the end of an era, Fred moving away.

Ivy had more extraordinary, albeit thirdhand, gossip, about

Dr. Dafoe, the guardians, and the Dionnes. She told me that Mr. Munro, the man in charge of nursery finances, heard that a reporter at the *Star* got a tip that the police had investigated M. Dionne on a complaint of seduction and illicit connection, brought forward by the parents of a girl who was helping at the farmhouse when the babies were born. According to this anonymous source, which the reporter was never able to verify, police didn't press charges because of the intense media scrutiny the farmhouse was facing at the time.

Meanwhile, Mr. Munro himself has accused M. Dionne of hiring a private detective to prove that Dr. Dafoe and Mr. Munro are embezzling funds from the girls. I simply can't believe this. Mr. Munro—you must remember him: a lanky, older gentleman with a white, shaggy mustache and a head like a mop—seems to be absolutely scrupulous about everything, and is careful to keep me updated about the payments I receive for my drawings and paintings. But according to Ivy, Mr. Munro has been unable to provide certain documents and says that these went missing when his home was burgled, a break-and-enter, he claims, that was orchestrated by M. Dionne.

Good gracious. It must be a measure of my cloistered little life or my winter-addled mind that I'm stooping to all this tittle-tattle. I sound worse than Marguerite! Promise me you'll throw this letter on the fire when you're done.

Yours truly,
Emma
Dafoe Hospital and Nursery
Callander, ON

* * *

February 10, 1939

11 Rue Saint Ida
Montreal, Quebec

Dear Lewis,

Your letter caught me off guard: I hadn't even thought of applying to another art college or even to Mrs. Fangel's school in New York, for that matter. It's easier to imagine staying right where I am, continuing to care for the girls with the freedom to paint when and what I choose.

If only I knew what the future holds for the girls, and for me—whether my place is here with them indefinitely or whether the Dionnes will oust me the first chance they get. Ivy has always nettled me with questions about my "plans," and I have never had an answer. It's like bumping around in a dark room groping for a match. I can't picture the quintuplets "all grown up" and living a life outside the nursery any more than I can picture that for myself. And what an odd expression that is: picturing yourself. I've been dabbling with a self-portrait, just for the challenge, and the fruits of this labor have been laughably bad. What does that say about me, I wonder: that I am completely incapable of drawing a reasonable likeness of my own face? Someone I recognize as myself? Or worse, that I fundamentally don't know who I am or what I should be.

Mr. Munro was at the nursery last month and sat me down to explain how I'm being paid for my latest paintings. I hadn't realized I would be paid a commission each time the same picture was used. I have mixed feelings about all this. I know these advertisements bring in much-needed funds for the girls, but they also keep the girls front and center, don't they? In any case, it seems I have a little nest egg for my own shadowy future, whatever it holds.

Yours truly,
Emma
Dafoe Hospital and Nursery
Callander, ON

* * *

March 20, 1939

11 Rue Saint Ida
Montreal, Quebec

Dear Lewis,

I expect you've gone up in your plane and come back safe and sound or I would have read about it in the papers. Next time I'd much prefer you just told me after you've returned to earth in one piece.

As you've no doubt heard, the girls will now be traveling to Toronto to meet the King and Queen. They are excited beyond words, but what on earth will they make of the ragged world beyond the gates? The rest of us are ill at ease, partly because this abrupt change of plans seems to have come about through some crafty manipulation by M. Dionne against the wishes of Dr. Dafoe, who ended up looking a fool. The doctor has always insisted that it wouldn't be safe for the quintuplets to leave the premises, not even to cross the road to visit their brothers and sisters in the house where they were born. The lethal germs of the outside world would be too much for their delicate constitutions, not to mention the constant threat of kidnappers, blackmailers, and barren couples poised to snatch one of our precious five and keep her as their own. Fear and precaution have been the code we've lived by for nearly five years, so to watch Dr. Dafoe now waving them aside like a puff of pipe smoke just because he's been granted an audience with the Royals has been, well, a little unnerving. Everything seems on the verge of crumbling down. It's dawning on me that all these rules, walls, and fences may not have been for keeping danger out, but for locking us within. And who knows what we'll find when the doors swing open and we stumble from our cells, blinking in the light.

Write and tell me about the flight. Did everything go smoothly? How about your landing feet? I hope they tucked up and down exactly as you expected.

> Best wishes,
> Emma
> Dafoe Hospital and Nursery
> Callander, ON

* * *

April 18, 1939

11 Rue Saint Ida
Montreal, Quebec

Dear Lewis,

Your letter arrived today describing the FDB's maiden flight. I could feel your exhilaration coming off the page in gusts—a welcome distraction from the matter on everyone's mind here: the visit to Toronto to meet the King and Queen. The girls spend every waking moment peppering us with questions about how a train goes uphill, who pushes it, how fast, and so on. They simply can't believe they themselves will go somewhere by train just like the children in their picture books. And I was worried about your flight, I won't pretend otherwise. But even more than that, I was happy for you. Thrilled. And proud. You've worked so hard—I know how much you wanted this.

Will you pay a visit to Callander this summer? I would love to talk to you, really talk—not just about all this gossip from Ivy. I can't think of any other person who listens as well as you. Let me know if that's in the cards.

Yours truly,
Emma
Dafoe Hospital and Nursery
Callander, ON

* * *

May 9, 1939

11 Rue Saint Ida
Montreal, Quebec

Dear Lewis,

Your letter inviting me to visit arrived the day before yesterday and I have read it a dozen times, probably more. I've decided to take a page out of your book and speak plainly in a way I could never do if you were standing here in front of me. These letters have done that for us, haven't they? Allowed us to say what's on our minds.

The thing is, Lewis, I can't tell you what I "want to do," because I don't know what that is myself. For as long as I can remember all I wanted to do was to paint and draw, and to have the freedom to ogle the world without the world ogling me, recording everything in my scribble book. Then, in the queerest twist—because I've never paid much attention to children and never felt I was cut out for motherhood—I fell in love with five baby girls and for better or for worse became the closest thing to a mother they've ever had. My priorities shifted. Suddenly all that mattered to me was that they simply survive, that they grow healthy and strong, and that they love me the way I loved them.

And then, out of nowhere, art sauntered back into my life.

I wonder sometimes if I'd never met Mrs. Fangel or Dr. Dafoe hadn't insisted I show her my work—if I was merely a "nurse" here and nothing more: would I be just as happy? Would I have stayed so long? I'm not sure. Being paid for my art, being admired for it and knowing it's made a difference, however small, in the fortunes of the quintuplets has for some time been a source of real pride.

But Mr. Munro visited again the other day, showing me my current bank balance and explaining that M. Dionne has received copies of all payments made to me, which makes me squirm. Mark my words: I'll be hustled out the door quick as you please if M. Dionne decides that I've profited too much off his family. What's dawning on me now is that he won't be entirely wrong. I've worried for so long about whether the quintuplets would have enough money to keep them safe forever: safe from the prying crowds, from the poverty of their parents, and from dangers I can't even put a name to. Now it seems the only thing money has done here has been to poison people against one another, coloring their every thought, and leaving them hungering for more.

But things are changing here, we all feel it. If not later this month when we board that train for Toronto, then the next month, or the next: change is around the bend. The girls are growing up and Europe is rumbling toward war while Canada taps its feet and feigns disinterest. And you, Lewis. You are building Canada's planes.

But that doesn't address your question about a visit. I've spoken with Dr. Dafoe and received permission to take some time off after the royal visit, so getting leave is not the issue. In fact, Ivy has also invited me to stay several days with her in Toronto, so I'm feeling popular. I do need to see Ivy, not only to catch up but because Fred is photographing my portfolio—I've sent everything to them this evening. I could, however, spend the night of the 22nd with them, then take the train on to Montreal the next morning. I am not due back at the nursery until the night of the 28th.

So here's my question, Lewis. Are we simply good friends? Is that why we're writing back and forth? Over the past few months your letters have been the brightest moments in some otherwise gloomy days. You've made me smile while everyone around me seems to have forgotten how. When you went up in your plane I was worried, truly worried, about whether your invention would manage to bring you safely back to earth. But I've wondered, what grounds do I have to be concerned? Or rather, on what terms?

Let me be frank. I don't have the best instincts and I'm a

poor judge of people, men in particular. I tend to see meaning in the lightest words and gestures, but am blind to everything real, everything important, taking place right in front of my very eyes. I've made a fool of myself in the past with unfounded assumptions and hollow hopes, then regretted them dreadfully. I don't want to make the same mistake here.

Yours sincerely,
Emma
Dafoe Hospital and Nursery
Callander, ON

1954

Epilogue

August 9, 1954 (*The Canadian Press*)

TRAGIC, SOLEMN: QUINTS BID ADIEU TO ÉMILIE

5,000 Wait in Rain to Pay Respects

By C. M. Fellman

Callander, ONTARIO—It was like those famous old years all over again—but with solemn, tragic overtones. Crowds stretched in long lines in front of the Dionne home today, just as they did in the 1930s. They spilled out onto the grey asphalt parking grounds where cars stood row upon glistening row.

This August afternoon in 1954 was typical of a warm Sunday afternoon from 1934 to 1940 when the Dionne quintuplets were on display.

It took death to revive that old familiar scene.

Today there were no impish children on exhibition behind huge one-way-view windows in the public pavilion. Instead the long lines of men and women turned left to an imposing yellow brick Georgian mansion where the body of Émilie, fourth-born of the famous five, lay in state.

For two hours in the afternoon a stream of 5,000 persons flowed in and out of the quiet Dionne living room where the open casket was placed.

Outside the gate of the iron fence surrounding the Dionne property had been flung open to the public for the first time in 14 years. Not since the public viewing of the girls was discontinued in 1940 had a public visit been permitted by the publicity-shy Dionne family. The four grief-stricken quintuplet survivors—Yvonne, Annette, Cécile, and Marie—sat beside Émilie's body from the time of its arrival from Montreal at 10 p.m. Saturday until 2 a.m. today.

Among those who came to pay their final respects today were nuns and priests from schools where the quintuplets and their siblings had studied over the years, as well as many of the physicians, nurses, orderlies, teachers, guards, secretaries, and domestic staff who once worked at the Allan R. Dafoe Hospital and Nursery.

Used with permission.

November 2, 1954

303-555 West 57th
New York City, NY

Dear Emma Trimpany,

You likely won't remember me, but as a young girl I was great friends and pen pals with your little sister, Edith, who I came to know during the many holidays I spent with my grandparents in Callander. I don't recall whether I ever met you back then, but I knew from Edith's letters and Christmas cards that she had a big sister—an artist—who left for New York and never came back. My family and I were deeply sorry to hear of the accident that took your parents and Edith last year.

We are coming to terms with our own family tragedy now. As you may know, my Uncle Lewis drowned on the Humber River during Hurricane Hazel last month. I found your letter in a bundle of mail when I was helping my mother clean out his flat in Toronto and recognized your name and the New York address, as well as the Callander postmark. Perhaps you saw my uncle when he attended the Dionne girl's funeral in Callander a few months ago? Her death affected him profoundly, I think: he ended up spending several weeks in the area, which had been his boyhood home, and has made several trips back again over the last month. I don't know if you knew him before he went away to England. He was a wonderful man—funny, imaginative, and kind, with a lucky streak that kept him safe through the whole war, always landing with his backside in the butter, as my father used to say. But his luck ran out. It's been extremely hard to accept that he could have survived all those years zipping around the Jerries in his beloved planes only to be taken from us now. In any case, I'm returning your letter as I found it, unopened, and I hope I'm not surprising you with our sad news.

Yours sincerely,
Sheryl Cartwright
292 St. Paul Street
Burlington, ON

[ENCLOSURE: Letter from E.T. to L.C., October 1954]

October 10, 1954

239 75th Street
Toronto, ON

Dear Lewis,

Tonight the rain paused (no doubt to refill its buckets) and I walked our route down to the lake on my own, missing you, wondering what you were doing at that very moment in the honk and bustle of Toronto. I couldn't help but sense the curtains twitching in every window in Callander as I strolled the streets of my childhood. My reputation as the gin-swilling, paint-splattered, communist-leaning, Gotham-corrupted spinster has no doubt been enriched beyond measure, since I've been shacked up for weeks *with a man* in the old Trimpany home. And with the shell-shocked Cartwright son, no less! A wag already established in the county records as an unrepentant bachelor. My parents, bless them, must be turning in their graves.

At least we've given the busybodies something fresh to talk about, something other than Émilie's death. I've tried not to think about how this tragedy has thrust the other Dionne girls back into the spotlight again, just as they were starting to find normal lives for themselves. All those photographers and reporters milling around at Em's funeral, just as they used to do in front of the farmhouse and the nursery—it makes me cringe. Because normal isn't possible for them now, is it? And I had a hand in that, despite my best intentions: painting my pictures for all those adverts and calendars, helping to keep them in the public eye. Celebrity couldn't keep them safe and it didn't keep me safe either, it just made the shadows offstage that much darker. We did everything wrong, Lewis, we all did. Even those of us who thought we were doing some good. The worst part is, even now, knowing what I know, I can't tell you how on earth we could have done any better.

Seeing the four of them at the funeral after all these years, the weight of their grief—I don't think I could have made my way back out of the church if you hadn't at that moment laid your hand on my sleeve. I've told you this a dozen times over the past two months, but seeing you again, so changed yet so much the same, it was as if my lungs were being filled like bagpipes, like a stone was being rolled off my heart.

I digress. What I mean to say is that I couldn't care less what the wagging tongues of Callander might be saying about you and me and our middle-aged romance. The truck comes Tuesday to collect the few things that I'm keeping from the old home, and the buyers have agreed to take the rest. I've spent these last days scrubbing and scouring (I found your suit button, by the way—it had slipped into a crack in the floorboards, underneath the bed). Now I'm exhausted and ready to be gone. Colin Stuart, my old classmate from New York and now an instructor at the Municipal Art Centre, has taken care of all the arrangements for my accommodation in Ottawa, plus organized my train tickets. All I need to do is show up at the station here Wednesday, board the correct car, and he's done the rest. I speak to his art class at the centre on Thursday.

I'm looking forward to having a few days to prowl around

the National Museum and perhaps take my paints and easel somewhere along the Ottawa River. The colors should be spectacular now, as long as the weather holds. Here in Callander the maple trees are finally dropping their fiery hues, leaves drifting down like sparks. The weatherman on the radio keeps warning about a hurricane they've named Hazel, brewing in the Caribbean and expected to make its way up the Eastern Seaboard: promise me you'll keep away from your planes and stay on solid ground if it starts heading your way. I'm hoping it will peter out before Ottawa so I can do a little painting en plein air. The opening for my exhibit is Saturday—if you can get away for the night, please do come. Otherwise I'll see you on the 18th in Toronto. I still shrink like a violet at these public events, although they've gotten easier. I like to remind myself of something you told me many years ago, although you've likely forgotten. I was dithering about whether to apply for art school and you told me in no uncertain terms to "do the harder thing." It was very pithy, however you put it. Something like, it is in doing the hardest things that we find ourselves the happiest, and that when we're happy, the harder things come easy. I've lived by those words for a long time now.

And the thing is, I *am* happy, Lewis. I'm happier than I ever thought I could be. I was terrified at the idea of coming back here, to Callander, for Em's funeral, of running the risk of seeing, face-to-face, the man who haunted my nightmares for so long. But I couldn't *not* come, could I? I feel I owed that to Em, at the very least, and I owed that to the others too. No one has loved them like I have. My whole life long.

I shudder to think: what if I hadn't forced myself to come back for the funeral? What if you hadn't gotten leave to attend?

I'm a staunch atheist, but it's hard not to believe in some greater force, yanking on invisible levers to make our paths cross again, all these years later. What I realize now is that what happened to me back on that train didn't ruin my life, but it certainly sent me on a radically different course. Probably, I must admit, for the better. If it hadn't happened, I'm not sure I would have followed through with Mrs. Fangel and the Art Students League, and I likely wouldn't be the person I am today, a woman who could come back to this place, my head held high. Lewis, I can't help but wish we hadn't spent all these years apart, you and I, that I had summoned the courage to tell you everything earlier. But I wasn't ready for this back then. I'm ready now.

It was a perfect evening on the shore, crisp and clear and calm: it's a damn shame we didn't get to share it. Even your blue heron, swooping low over the lake, seemed sorry to see me sitting alone. The lake was still, and when the clouds parted it was as if the twilight had been burnished, the breeze stirring the water coral, bronze, and copper. I couldn't mix that color with my paints if I tried.

I sat on our log (as I've come to think of it), listening to the leaves whispering their secrets and smiling over a secret of my own. Our secret, really, although maybe it's too soon to say for sure. Let me say this, for now. I was lobbing pebbles into the water and watching the gilded ripples rolling away as if through molten metal when it struck me: the shores of Lake Nipissing are absolutely littered with stones. Did you notice that when we were here together? I didn't until tonight, although I admit my attention was occupied elsewhere. I always remember you telling me that you and your father had dredged up every last one of these enchanted pebbles from the lake and hauled them away to Quintland. There, of course, they disappeared into the pockets of barren women, tourists, and collectors to be whisked away to the four corners of the world. And yet here they are, returned as if by magic and free for the taking. Shall I bring you one as proof? Perhaps Lake Nipissing was holding on to a few good-luck stones on the off chance we'd come back. Maybe it's our turn to be lucky.

I can't wait to see you.

Love,
E.

Author's Note

When he died in 1943, Dr. Allan R. Dafoe had amassed a personal fortune of $182,466—roughly equivalent to the savings of each of the Dionne quintuplets at that time.

* * *

In 1955, when Marie, Annette, Cécile, and Yvonne turned 21, only $800,000 remained in their trust fund.

* * *

Marie Dionne died of an apparent blood clot in 1970.

* * *

By the mid-1990s, Annette, Yvonne, and Cécile, divorced or unmarried, were living together on a combined income of $746 per month.

* * *

In 1998, bowing to public pressure, the Ontario government paid the surviving Dionne quintuplets and Marie's children a one-time sum of $4 million. Cécile's share was reportedly stolen by her son.

* * *

By 2018, Yvonne had died and Annette was living independently, but Cécile had once again been living as a ward of the state, subsisting off a basic government pension.

* * *

Between 1934 and 1941, tourism revenue amassed by the Ontario government related to Quintland was estimated to be half a billion dollars.

Acknowledgments

I'm extremely grateful to the following publishers for granting me *gratis* permission to reprint excerpts from the real-life articles included in my book: the *Toronto Star, Globe and Mail,* the *Canadian Press, UPI* (previously *UP*), King Features Syndicate Inc., and Postmedia, on behalf of *North Bay Nugget, Montreal Gazette,* and the *Ottawa Citizen.* The *New York Times* editorial titled "The Quintuplet Problem" was licensed and reprinted with permission. In some cases, news articles and/or headlines were edited marginally to suit my story, most notably the mention of Lewis Cartwright in "New Dive Bomber Is Canada's Contribution to the Skies" and the addition of the list of mourners to the 1954 article by the *Canadian Press.* The *King* Features columns were widely syndicated; I found these undated clippings via the City of North Bay Dionne Quints digitization project funded by the Ontario Ministry of Citizenship, Culture, and Recreation. The original publication dates could not be ascertained by the publisher, which granted permission. I chose dates that fit my story. *La Voix* is a fictional newspaper that kindly stepped in at the last minute when permission could not be obtained to reprint a bona fide publication.

I'm indebted to my readers, especially Ray Wood, who awoke

in me an early appreciation for books and a later affection for birds. The Distillibus Writers (Joanne Carey, Jorie Soames, and Glenna Turnbull), Ashley and Francie (*La Jooje*) Howard, Tyler Dyck, Shelley Pacholok, Albert Berkshire, Anne Fleming, Adam Lewis Schroeder, and Tamas Dobozy all helped me with my first faltering chapters or endured multiple drafts. Other B.C. writers graciously shared their wisdom, reassurances, and community: John Lent, Nancy Holmes, Ashley Little, Alix Hawley, Michael V. Smith, Sean Johnston, and Erin McNair. Many thanks to Pat and Tony Dyck for the generous loan of their Tuwanek "Crab Shack," where so much of this project was written, rejected, and written again.

In Ontario, I'm especially grateful to Natasha Wiatr of the Callander Bay Heritage Museum, who pointed the way to Quintland and helped me track down various bits and pieces, including key articles from the *North Bay Nugget*. In North Bay itself, my thanks go to Ed Valenti of the Dionne Quints Heritage Board and Elaine Pepin of the City of North Bay for giving me a peek into the not-yet-reopened Dionne museum. Farther south, props go to Brenda Liddle for a bed, a trout, and the shad flies.

Annette, Cécile, Marie, Émilie, and Yvonne: few can imagine what you lived through and my own efforts, I'm sure, fall short. If nothing else, I hope my novel leads more people to learn of your story and to keep it in their hearts and minds.

This novel came to life thanks to my editor at William Morrow, Lucia Macro, and my agent, Stephanie Sinclair, who somehow managed to squeeze me into a year of other, more monumental firsts.

To other friends and family who believed in me before I did: you rock. Rene Unser: in my moments of deepest doubt, I applied your "Motivation Station" to my writing, if not my stride, which goes a long way to explaining why I'm running in the middle of the pack with a book in my hands.

The Quintland Sisters is dedicated to my mum, who will never get to read it, who loved me more than most people are lucky enough to be loved in a lifetime, and who raised me to always do the harder thing. It's also for Tyler, who reads everything, who suffers me at my worst, and makes me want to be my best.

Bibliography and Sources Consulted

This book is a work of fiction. Its principal aim was to spin a make-believe tale that might help keep the truth from being forgotten; the facts themselves are stranger than fiction. Objectivity absconded long ago with its own share of the windfall, and I've made no attempt to track it down. Instead, I relied heavily on other sources that have tried, to varying degrees, to be more objective:

- Barker, Lillian, *The Dionne Legend: Quintuplets in Captivity* (Doubleday, 1951).
- Berton, Pierre, *The Dionne Years: A Thirties Melodrama* (W. W. Norton, 1978).
- Blatz, William E., N. Chant, and M. W. Charles et al., *Collected Studies on the Dionne quintuplets* (University of Toronto Press, 1937).
- Brough, James, Annette Dionne, Cécile Dionne, Marie Dionne, and Yvonne Dionne, *We Were Five: The Dionne Quintuplets Story from Birth Through Girlhood to Womanhood* (Simon and Schuster, 1965).

- *The Dionne Quintuplets*, documentary, National Film Board of Canada, directed and produced by Donald Brittain, CBC Television (1978).
- Gifford, Jim, *Hurricane Hazel: Canada's Storm of the Century* (Dundurn Press, 2004).
- Legros, Donalda, and Marie-Jeanne Lebel, *Administering Angels of the Dionne Quintuplets* (Northern Publishing Co., 1936).
- *Million Dollar Babies*, TV miniseries, produced by CBC Television and CBS Television (1994).
- Nodelman, Perry, *Dear Canada: Not a Nickel to Spare; The Great Depression Diary of Sally Cohen, Toronto, Ontario, 1932* (Scholastic Canada, 2007).
- Soucy, Jean-Yves, Annette Dionne, Cécile Dionne, and Yvonne Dionne, *Family Secrets: The Dionne Quintuplets' Autobiography*. Translated by Kathe Roth (Berkley Books, 1997).
- Tesher, Ellie, *The Dionnes* (Doubleday Canada, 1999).

The "Act for the Protection of the Dionne Quintuplets" was redacted slightly for use in this novel. The full Act is available online.

More time than I care to admit was spent devouring the lavish news coverage of the Dionne quintuplets between 1934 and 1939 (and beyond). Almost every day for those first five years, the international press dished out Dionne details on everything from tonsils to turkeys, and the adoring public lapped it up. Decades later, so did I.

All newspaper articles are used with permission.

About the author
2 Meet Shelley Wood

About the book
3 Author Q&A
7 Reading Group Guide Questions

Insights,
Interviews
& More . . .

Meet Shelley Wood

About the author

Tyler Dyck

Shelley Wood is a writer, journalist, and editor. Her work has appeared in the *New Quarterly*, *Room*, the *Antigonish Review*, *Bath Flash Fiction*, and the *Globe and Mail*. She has won the Frank McCourt prize for creative nonfiction, *Free Fall Magazine*'s short prose contest, *Causeway Lit*'s creative nonfiction prize, and the Tethered by Letters *F(r)iction* award. Born and raised in Vancouver, she has lived in Montreal, Cape Town, and the Middle East, and now has a home, a man, and a dog in British Columbia, Canada. ⌇

Author Q&A

Q: What drew you to this story?

A: In my local library, I stumbled across a book called *100 Photos That Changed Canada,* which included a picture of five identical toddlers. I recognized most of the other topics in the book, but these girls? I'd never heard of them. The more I looked into it, the crazier it seemed that I had never known their story. I've since learned that there have been mega-fans over the years: people who have followed the Dionne quintuplets since birth, who've kept scrapbooks, collected and traded memorabilia, and, more recently, have Pinterest boards or Facebook groups. A half-dozen books have been written about them over the last fifty years, including several autobiographies coauthored by the quintuplets. At the time I started researching *The Quintland Sisters,* however, nothing had been published since the late 1990s. The two surviving quintuplets live private lives and very seldom speak with the press. Moreover, the generation that for decades had followed every tidbit of news about the quintuplets has largely passed away, and this story, I feared, was in danger of vanishing with them.

Q: Yet you chose to write a novel rather than a nonfiction account. Why?

A: Partly I chose fiction because others have already covered this topic more journalistically. In particular, Ellie ▶

3

Tesher's and Pierre Berton's books are probably the most rigorous and impartial, closely documenting the sad twists in the lives of the famous girls, including during the many decades after they left the nursery. Nonfiction lovers can still track those books down.

Novels, on the other hand, reach a different type of reader, so that was one of my chief motives. I also liked the idea of writing about a period that can't be pinned down by facts—even the newspaper accounts of the day swerved closer to propaganda than objective record. By writing about the first five years of their lives, I was able to zoom in on a period that the two surviving quintuplets would scarcely remember. Also, all of the other eyewitnesses to these early years have long since died. This allowed me to create a fictional character, Emma Trimpany, who could stand in for the reader— an insider, someone who could observe and grow alongside the babies themselves, someone who could wrestle with the issues, but, most of all, someone who would love these children *as children*, nothing more.

Q: *Do you feel there are heroes and villains in the story of the Dionne quintuplets? Or is this a situation of everyone doing what they think was best at the time?*

A: Among the fictional characters in my novel, as well as the real-life figures of the day, there were those who acted for the good of the Dionne quintuplets and others who may have acted with more nefarious intent. What's more, motives changed as the years went by. Without a doubt, the Dionne story represents yet another instance of the Canadian government electing to take children away from parents deemed unsuitable and later failing to take responsibility for the safety and well-being of those children.

My hope is that people reading my novel who already had an opinion as to who was "good" and who was "bad" might see things somewhat differently through the course of the story. For those who knew nothing about the Dionne babies before picking up this book, I will have done my job if they, like Emma herself, are left with more questions than answers and struggle to understand how things could have been done differently to give the children a normal, happy life.

Q: You visited the site of the former nursery and the Dionne property while writing this book. What does Quintland look like today?

A: It doesn't look like anything! I think this is truly surreal and helps emphasize my earlier point that the Dionne story is in danger of disappearing altogether. Driving the old road from Callander to Corbeil, I literally passed right by the original nursery, which is still standing, without batting an eye. There are no signs to mark the spot where cars once crammed into the makeshift parking lots and tourists lined up by the thousands. Set back some distance from the old nursery is a nondescript shed that was actually one of the turnstile entrances to the viewing corridor, which surrounded the public playground. A little ways further down the road, unmarked, is a building that now looks to be a private home but was once the Midwives' Pavilion and souvenir stand. The only way to figure this out is by comparing photographs from the 1930s and 1940s with these somewhat dilapidated structures still in use today. Hats off to Natasha Wiatr, the curator at the tiny Callander Bay Heritage Museum, who has taken the trouble to document what's still standing and has drawn a map to point curious visitors on their way.

One other important building can be spied on the Callander side of the old nursery: the "Big House," built to accommodate the entire Dionne family when the girls were nine years old. Now a retirement home, this formidable mansion gets a mention in the last few pages of my book. What's not detailed in the postscript but loomed large in my thoughts while writing was how the girls fared once the family was reunited. These years have been vehemently disputed. Public sympathies and those of the press during this period swung back to support the Dionne parents—the other Dionne children describe a happy upbringing. The quintuplets themselves, however, have since said they were sexually abused by their father and beaten by their mother, calling the Big House "the saddest home we have ever known."

The exploitation of the Dionne quintuplets in childhood and the extent to which they were "forgotten" as teens and adults is something I struggled with while writing this book. Early on, I planned to donate a portion of the proceeds from *The Quintland Sisters* to the Dionne museum. What I discovered when I visited is ▶

Author Q&A *(continued)*

that there are two separate collections in the region today: one located in Dr. Dafoe's old home, which is now the Callander Bay Heritage Museum; the other housed in the original Dionne farmhouse, relocated to North Bay. I wish the very best to both museums and to their efforts to keep this story alive, but I've elected to make my ongoing donation to the Canadian Centre for Child Protection.

Q: Identical quintuplets captured the imagination of people the world over, but do you think there were other factors at play that turned them into one of the world's first "reality" stars? What lessons can be learned from the Dionne quintuplets' story?

A: The oft-repeated number is that the chance of a woman giving birth to five identical babies, at the time the Dionne quintuplets were born, was 1 in 57 million. The fact that they all survived—particularly given the remote, rustic setting—truly was a miracle. This was smack in the middle of the Great Depression and during the tense lead-up to World War II, yet these charming and photogenic little girls in faraway Northern Ontario seemed to be living a fairy-tale life. Being able to read about them in the paper, see their pictures every day, listen to them on the radio, and even go and see them firsthand if you had the time and money must have transported people out of their sorrows and debts and given them something to root for.

I'm not sure what lessons were learned in terms of how the lives of children like these can be better protected from the spotlight. The Dionne quintuplets themselves wrote a public letter in 1997 to the parents of the McCaughey septuplets warning that "multiple births should not be confused with entertainment, nor should they be an opportunity to sell products." Since then, however, multiple reality TV shows have come and gone, featuring different families, and only time will tell how those children will weather the limelight.

The Quintland Sisters has another lesson, I think, about people serving on the margins of celebrity. What happens to Emma in the novel is entirely fictional, but it's not implausible: as modern-day events have made all too clear, the brighter the spotlight, the darker the shadows. Emma's story, I hope, gives voice to women hushed and swept aside when their complaints are at odds with the feel-good story in the public eye. ∼

Reading Group Guide Questions

1. Were you already familiar with the story of the Dionne quintuplets? If so, how did you first learn about the sisters? If not, what surprised you about their story?

2. Did your opinion of Dr. Dafoe, the Canadian government, or the Dionne parents change over the course of the novel? Who was in the right? Who was in the wrong?

3. "Normal" motherhood is absent in *The Quintland Sisters*. Both biological and substitute mothers in the book can't or don't "mother" according to conventional norms, and Emma herself says that she has no intention of becoming a mother. What do you think are the essential components of motherhood, and how were these present or absent in the lives of the quintuplets?

4. Emma insists she would be happy to stay at the Dafoe Nursery for as long as she possibly can, but what are her motives for staying? Are they purely altruistic, or are they selfish?

5. Emma tries to capture the true individuality of each Dionne girl in her art with her pencils and paintbrushes. But Emma's art also helps perpetuate a fairy-tale world. Discuss how Emma's progress as an artist serves as a metaphor for the deepening tensions at the heart of the story.

6. *The Quintland Sisters*, we learn at the outset, consists of archival "fonds." How do these documents both support and undermine the central "facts" of the Dionne story? What do we gain from seeing this world from Emma's vantage point? What do we lose?

7. Emma prides herself on noticing quirky details, yet her eyes are so focused on her young charges that she fails to fully see what's going on around her. At the same time, the people in power work hard to make sure the public sees only the official version of events and nothing more. What does ▶

Reading Group Guide Questions
(continued)

Emma's predicament share with modern-day celebrities and those who work in the margins of fame?

8. Imagine the Dionne sisters being born today under similar circumstances, but in the era of social media and twenty-four-hour news. Would they have fared better or worse? ∿